INTERRUPTED

Also by Patrice Lawence:

Orangeboy
Indigo Donut
Snap

ROSE, INTERRUPTED

PATRICE LAWRENCE

*Hodder
Children's
Books*

HODDER CHILDREN'S BOOKS

First published in Great Britain in 2019 by Hodder and Stoughton

1 3 5 7 9 10 8 6 4 2

A CIP catalogue record for this book is available from the British Library.

ISBN 978 1 444 94065 7

Typeset in Berkeley Oldstyle by Avon DataSet Ltd,
Bidford-on-Avon, Warwickshire

Printed and bound in Great Britain by Clays Ltd, Elcograf S.p.A

The paper and board used in this book are from well-managed forests
and other responsible sources.

MIX
Paper from
responsible sources
FSC® C104740
www.fsc.org

Hodder Children's Books
An imprint of Hachette Children's Group
Part of Hodder & Stoughton
Carmelite House
50 Victoria Embankment
London EC4Y 0DZ

An Hachette UK Company
www.hachette.co.uk

www.hachettechildrens.co.uk

To everyone who understands what it's like to be Rose or Rudder or their mum – I hope you can make the rules work for you

Rose's Ten Point Programme for Being a Perfect
Worldly Wise
Also Known As
The Complete, Absolute and Final Decommissioning
from God's Pilgrims (Woodford Sanctuary)
and All Other Sanctuaries Thereof

1. Worship idols. Actors, musicians and fictional
characters are all allowed.
2. Dress immodestly
3. Act immodestly
4. Find out how to vote.
5. Get worldly boyfriend/s
6. Beget immodesty with worldly boyfriend/s.
7. Send Christmas cards to Grandma Yellow, enormous
ones that play carols loudly when she opens them.
8. Visit the Natural History Museum and the Science
Museum every month until it feels normal.
9. Watch the prohibited films and read the prohibited
books (or read reviews if they're boring).
10. Make sure Rudder is completely, absolutely and finally
decommissioned too.

1

Rudder hated Central Library. It wasn't the rules pinned to the noticeboards or in plastic covers on the tables. Those were real rules, like the ones they'd had in the Pilgrims. Rules *should* be written down, so everyone knows what they are. It was the secret rules that hurt his head, the rules that seemed to be written in invisible ink everywhere he went.

He didn't even want to be here, but Pitt Academy's library was closed because two Year Nines had a fight in there at lunch time. Why did *he* have to be punished? *He* hadn't been fighting. And why had he given Rose his unbreakable vow that he wouldn't come home until six? Though, two hours in Central Library was better than walking in on her and Kye doing . . . stuff.

Rudder had almost walked straight back out of the library when he saw Bella. That seemed to be another secret rule: if he didn't want something to happen, it did. He hadn't wanted to see her, but there she was, sitting at a table over by the window. He quickly looked away. Rose said that Bella was just an attention-seeker and Rudder should ignore her. Rose didn't know how hard that was. Bella always managed to catch Rudder's eye and mouth wicked words at him. Today, she was staring into space, probably thinking up new jokes to play on him. If Rose and Kye got married, Bella would be like Rudder's sister. God's Pilgrims should see love in everyone, or else why else would they act to save souls? But when the End of Days came and the Clean Slate tallied the redeemed souls for ascension, Rudder wanted Kye's and Bella's to be right at the bottom of the list.

He spotted a space on a table near the checkout kiosk. Everyone else sitting there was from Merryvale's Academy. Was it against the secret rules for him to join them? If he mucked up again, Bella would be quick to let everyone know. She always was. She hadn't noticed him yet, so he took a deep breath, dodged round the Turkish bilingual shelves and sat down. A couple of the Merryvalers glanced up and then back at their work. This was a good thing to remember: in the library, no one cared where you sat. He breathed out again and pulled his folder of worksheets and pencil case from his bag. He laid them next to each other on the table. He needed his phone too. He found it and switched it on. Yes! Wi-Fi! Suddenly, it buzzed with a message notification. His heart banged. The real rules said he was in the quiet area. No one even looked at him. They were all busy scrolling through their own phones.

He slid the physics worksheets out of the folder. It was weird how being a Pilgrim made physics easier. It was just like the Bible. All he had to do was remember what the words and numbers meant, what order they came in and when to use them. He would never tell Rose that the Bible still felt more real than isotopes and neutrons. He wished he could talk to Dad about it. Maybe he could write him a letter.

Something soft hit the back of Rudder's head. Rudder touched the spot and looked around. There was a scrunched-up ball of paper on the floor by the table leg. He straightened up and caught Bella's eye from across the room. She didn't make a face at him or do the finger thing. She just kept staring at him. Rudder couldn't see a librarian. There was no special rule about throwing things, but he was sure it wasn't allowed. If Bella did it again, he hoped she'd be caught and thrown out.

The Merryvale boy opposite was staring too. What had Rudder done wrong this time? Then he remembered. Last week the Deputy Head had been yelling at the Year Eights in assembly for fighting with Merryvalers outside the chicken shop by the roundabout. The girl on the bench behind him had whispered to her friend that the beef had been going on for years. Now Rudder was sitting here with his Pitt Academy logo shining from his blazer like leprechaun gold. He must not look at the boy. Looking at people you didn't know was bad, even if you did it by accident. (That was a secret rule he'd learned early.) Rudder's eyes dropped to the table. Someone had drawn a tiny . . . male thing in red ink, bang in the middle of the table top.

The boy was leaning forward. Rudder sensed it. He could whack Rudder and the librarian would be too far away to do anything. Rudder's chest hurt. He'd forgotten to breathe.

The boy rapped the table near Rudder's fingers. 'What happened to your hands, man?'

'My . . . my hands?'

'Yeah.'

The girl next to the boy was looking too. Of course they were. He should have noticed where they were looking. He looked down too, even though he already knew the way the skin puckered on his palm and the lumpy scribble of scars on the back and how the nail on the little finger of his left hand might never grow back.

The girl said, 'Did they get burnt or something?'

'Yes.'

Rudder waited for more questions, but the boy just said 'respect' and went back to scrawling notes over his revision book. No, the burns happened because Rudder *hadn't* respected. It was his rightful punishment.

'Do not be surprised at the fiery ordeal that has come on you to test you, as though something strange were happening to you.' Peter 4:12.

Rudder made sure his mouth stayed closed as the words flickered behind his eyes. That had been another painful lesson. The Worldly Wise weren't impressed when you quoted scripture at them.

Rudder plugged his headphones into his phone and skimmed through his playlists. He'd start with the one Rose called *Rudder's Sound of Silence*. The first track was 'The Boxer'. Rudder's mouth moved silently, his feet tapping and

5

flexing their dance moves under the table. Gently, though, in case he kicked the girl opposite. He could probably do physics at home. He'd check history. *Summarise the social, political and economic factors that contributed towards the Representation of the People Act 1918.* Mrs Skermidge had told them to construct a detailed analysis of how, why and when some women gained the vote. He'd had to google voting. Pilgrim women didn't do it. Nor did Pilgrim men.

His stomach rumbled. How many times had he told Mum that his lunch account was in debt? Even the nice supervisor had made him take his baked potato and cheese back. He'd decided to use his last coins on two cans of Coke from the vending machine because all those bubbles must take up space. Now he could feel every drop pushing down and his stomach was so full of gas he could make his own universe, if universes were really made that way. He couldn't go to the toilet now or he'd lose his seat. He shifted in his chair and crossed his legs. It didn't help. If he yawned too hard, Coke would probably shoot out of his belly button and knock the Merryvale girl out. If he sneezed . . . He uncrossed his legs. He needed a toilet straight away, because now he wanted to sneeze badly. The library toilets were probably as nasty as the school ones. It was three minutes to five o'clock on the library clock. He could hold on for another half an hour. He could. He crossed his other leg over, but it just made his waistband dig in. No. He couldn't hold on. A loud laugh went up behind him as if everybody knew.

Two whole cans of Coke.

If he concentrated really hard, he might forget about it. He switched to another playlist. Audrey was singing 'Suddenly Seymour'. It didn't help.

'All right, then! I'm going!' A girl's voice.

It sounded like Bella. Rudder muted Audrey. Chairs were scraping and there was another voice, a deeper one. Rudder sneaked a look. Bella was hoisting her bag on to her shoulder. She was with a boy. An older boy. Rudder hadn't been expecting that. He was tall with a shaved head and looked about eighteen or nineteen. He was standing really close to her, like a boyfriend. Bella had a boyfriend? After all the horribleness she'd been giving Rudder about her brother being with Rose?

Bella flounced away from the boy, around the desks between the bilingual shelves. She was coming in Rudder's direction, heading for the exit. He bent over his worksheet, but he could still feel her rage steaming towards him. He let his eyes slip sideways and down as she passed by, black lace up shoes and clean, bright trainers right behind. The rage faded away. Now she was gone, he could relax, but his bladder was starting to hurt. It would be bad enough if he sneezed, but if he coughed . . . There'd be no coming back from that. He turned off his music, popped out his ear buds and stuffed his phone and worksheets into his bag. As soon as he stood up, a Pitt girl slid into his empty seat. After he'd used the toilet, he'd walk home slowly. That way he wouldn't be too early.

There was no queue for the toilet by the stairs, although the lock was turned to red. Rudder could try downstairs, but they might be busier. There were more people down there. Sometimes he imagined the queues were because it was a special type of toilet, one where you stood in the toilet bowl and flushed yourself away to the Ministry of Magic. Or maybe, if he could choose where to go, to Grandma Yellow's. He'd have to make sure Grandma was out, though. And he had to keep reminding himself that magic was evil.

Rudder squeezed his thighs together as he waited. What if he'd had three cans of Coke? He had to think of something else! Anything else! The Old Testament books in order. Genesis. Exodus. Leviticus. Numbers. If the door wasn't open by Judges, he was going to knock. Deuteronomy. Joshua. He strained to listen. He couldn't hear banging or yelling from inside, so they weren't stuck in there. Judges. He wouldn't knock just yet. Ruth. Samuel one. What if they'd fainted? Samuel two. Kings one.

'Are you waiting?'

The man standing at the top of the stairs looked even more desperate than Rudder.

'Yes,' Rudder said. 'Sorry.'

The man glared at him. 'Right.'

He stomped off. At last, though, the toilet door was opening! A boy came out. He was short, probably a couple of years older than Rose. His orangey-blonde hair was scraped back into a topknot. He smiled at Rudder.

'You all right, mate?'

Rudder nodded. Another secret rule. If you're not sure, nod. It must have been the right answer because the boy swaggered off towards the stairs.

Rudder went to open the door, but it was locked. How? HOW? Did one of the Merryvalers have an invisibility cloak? Or the one true ring? It felt like there were four Cokes inside him now. The drink molecules were expanding. He twisted one leg round the other. *Hurry up! HURRY UP!*

The door was opening again. Rudder moved forward, then jumped back. The boy coming out was the one who'd been in the library with Bella. His bald head and lined face made him look like an orc. He stood there, his eyes moving slowly up and down Rudder as if each blink was taking a picture of him. Rudder looked down at his shoes and at the black spot between them and the ice pole wrapper on the floor by the toilet door. Kings two. Chronicles one. Chronicles two. A blur of movement and a hand thumped against Rudder's shoulder, knocking him back. He just managed to stop himself tumbling over. No words, just the slap before the orc moved away.

Rudder frowned. Why were the two boys in there together? He couldn't think about that now. He lunged towards the door, twisted the handle and . . . it didn't budge. This couldn't be happening to him! Oh. Okay. He could feel movement behind the door, the lock was turning and the door was pushing against him. He let go and it swung open.

'Rudder?'

'Bella?'

She was different, all big eyes and whisper. She made a sobbing sound and wiped her eyes.

Bella was crying? Bella wouldn't ever cry, because she was the one who always did the upsetting. It looked like real crying though. She made the sobbing sound again.

He said, 'Are you . . . are you all right?'

She sort of shook her head and nodded at the same time. Her face was shiny, like she'd been splashing water over it. Splodges of make-up were smeared under her eyes and her fringe was wet and stuck to her forehead. Bella was in the toilet with two boys? Even for the worldly world, that wasn't normal, was it?

She tried to flick the damp hair off her forehead. 'You get my note, Rudder?'

Was she was trying to make him look stupid again? 'I don't know what you're talking about.'

'You've got to tell Rose. Don't let Kye do it.'

'Bella? You coming?'

The orc was standing at the top of the stairs. His lips were pressed together, eyes taking those slow pictures of Rudder again.

Bella's eyes narrowed and her face settled back into the smile that wasn't a smile. Rudder knew what was coming next. It was a nasty name for him.

'Don't tell Rose I told you. Please, please don't, Rudder.'

He looked from her mouth to her face. Yes, that was her nasty words expression, but she'd said . . .

She glanced at the orc then back at him, straightening herself up. Her make-up looked evil now, instead of sad. 'Now go and pee for God, holy boy!'

She turned away and ran past the orc and down the stairs. Rudder stared after her, even though his body was moving him through the open toilet door. The seat cover was down and all the toilet paper was strewn across the damp floor, dirty footprints stamped across it. Bella had been in this toilet with two older boys. Bella, who'd always made Rudder feel lower than a troll, had been in here *with two older boys!* She'd been crying, though. Or had she? He closed the door, locked it and did what he needed to. Peeing for God. Yeah, that was more like her. She was trying to get in his head. His hands were itching and he tried to run the cold water tap hard, but the flow wouldn't go beyond a dribble. He wiped his hands on his trousers and left.

He went down the stairs to the next floor. It felt like all his thoughts were bashing into each other. Bella was in the toilet with boys. Older boys. What were they doing? Rudder's cheeks were getting hot. Grandma Yellow used to lecture Rose about worldly girls and how they didn't wait for their husbands. Rudder used to think worldly girls were sprinting along the street, too fast for their husbands to catch up. Rose had put him right on that one. His cheeks were getting even hotter just thinking about it. Rose said that the Pilgrims

11

wanted to take all the fun out of life, but Bella hadn't looked like she was having fun.

He was on the first floor now. Bella had been on at Rudder from the moment he started at Pitt. Since Rose and Bella's brother got together, it had been even worse. But those had been proper tears, the sort of tears that were so big, they blocked up your throat. No one could fake that. Rudder knew. She'd given him a message for Rose. Rose mustn't let Kye do it. Whatever 'it' was, Rudder agreed. Maybe Bella's note said more. Note? He touched his head. *That* note.

Rudder span round and ran back up the stairs to the library, puffing into the study space. The ball of crumpled paper was still on the floor. The girl who'd taken his seat frowned down at him as he scooped it up from by her feet. He went back out on to the stairway and uncrumpled it. The writing was in pencil, light and faint. He squinted at it. It looked like three words. The first two, were they 'HOT DOGZ'? The third sort-of word was just a muddle of letters and numbers and didn't make sense. It was all merged into the paper, which made it even harder to read. It didn't mean anything.

This must be the wrong note, or else Bella was making fun of him again. It was all a big act. She was probably outside, sniggering at him. He shoved the note into his pocket and walked down the stairs. Only last month, she'd got her friend, Jamal, to hide Rudder's shoes in the changing room during PE. Rudder had been late to history because he'd been trying to find them. They'd been jammed under the lockers.

Rudder didn't care what Rose said. He was going to go catch his bus and go home. She'd just have to tell Kye to go. He stepped out on to the square outside the library. It was like the different benches were reserved for different schools. A group of Pitt Academy girls were grouped near the fountains, shrieking and laughing. On the bench opposite, a Merryvale's boy had slung his arm around a girl's shoulder, both studying his phone. Traffic lights beeped. Cars eased to a halt. Rudder checked down the road to see if his bus was coming. He looked back. There she was, Bella, across the road by the alleyway in a huddle with the blond boy and the orc. Any second now, she'd see Rudder. In school, she'd point at him and laugh. But the way she was stepping back from them, mouth moving like she was shouting . . . She glanced over the orc's shoulder, seemed to meet Rudder's eyes, then look away.

The lights turned green. A bus chugged past, then a cyclist, another cyclist, a van advertising Eskimo Ice. Bella had come out of the library toilet crying. The orc had stared at Rudder like he wanted rip out his soul. Rudder should just walk on.

Except – he was still a Pilgrim. Even if Rose said he wasn't, he was. He had to atone, amend and act to save souls. He couldn't just memorise the scriptures – he had to act on them. When one cheek is smiteth, he had to offer the other. He had to prove that Pilgrims were better than the Worldly Wise.

A woman with a buggy was waiting by the crossing. These lights always took ages. Rudder could see Bella between the gaps of speeding traffic. The orc and the blond boy were still with her. The lights flicked to amber and then red. Traffic trailed off either side of the lights. The woman with the buggy was halfway across the road. Why wouldn't his legs move? The traffic light timer said eight seconds left. Move! Rudder tipped himself forward and the rest of his body followed. Three seconds. One second. Red man, green light.

Rudder ran across. He looked up and down the street. They couldn't have disappeared that quickly. He moved closer to the alleyway and peered in. They were there, at the far end, their backs to him.

His heart was beating so hard his ears hurt. Now what? Pilgrims fought with prayer, but these boys looked like they'd need the biggest prayer circle in the world to help them. It was just Rudder, and he had to do something. Now. He peered around into the alleyway again. The orc was looking straight at him. He came towards Rudder, with the blond one behind him, both filling the air with bad words.

Bella dodged round them and shot past Rudder. 'Just go!'

The orc froze, his eyes on the road. He held up his hands like a shield. 'Bella! No!'

Bella was still running, looking back at Rudder, calling him. Rudder turned towards the road. He tried to yell but his tongue wouldn't move and his mouth stayed shut.

Smack the robot! Yellow alert!

It was the most powerful warning ever, the one he and Rose had always used when trouble was seconds away.

Smack the robot! Yellow alert!

A delivery cyclist had overtaken the bus, body raised off the saddle, feet hammering the pedals, too fast to stop for the red light.

SMACK THE ROBOT! YELLOW ALERT!

When the bike hit Bella, it felt like the whole world moved.

2

Rose checked her phone one more time, then slid it behind the toothbrush mug. Kye'd said he was on his way. He better be here soon or else he'd be walking up the stairs next to Rudder. She peeled off her jumper. According to Bicchi Blogger, woke girls went braless. Rose wasn't quite ready for that yet. Eighteen months ago, she'd been wearing tights so thick you could lay them down as carpet. Her skirts would have taken up two seats on the bus, if she'd ever been allowed out to go on a bus. Her long hair had been pulled tight off her face and just, well, abandoned, without even a smudge of edge control gel to calm down the front. Mum used to say Rose had her own halo, but never so Grandma Yellow heard. *'Favour is deceitful, and beauty is vain: but a woman that feareth the Lord, she shall be praised.'* Comparing a lowly human to an angel, that would have been blasphemy and at least another week spent in the atonement room.

Just thinking about it ramped up Rose's decommissioning gauge. She must be a good seventy-five per cent ex-Pilgrim by now. All those years with no braids, no bunches, no straighteners, nothing except the coconut oil that Mum had claimed she kept for cooking. Even bloody lip balm had been banned, so every winter Rose's mouth had turned to elephant skin until Mum had convinced Dad that Vaseline wasn't adornment; it was medicinal. Then Dad had to persuade the Actualizar Committee to agree – bloody Uncle Micah and bloody Uncle Joshua, with bloody Elder Enoch lording it over them, poring over every letter of their rule books to decide whether Rose could lick her lips without tasting blood.

Now her Bad Memories Box had been flung wide open and all those past Roses were swirling around the inside of her head. She touched her temples.

Decommissioning in progress.

Decommissioning in progress.

The light in the bathroom was rubbish. The one window was tiny and no amount of tugging was going to make it close properly. Or open properly. The fluorescent bulb over the mirror made her look like she'd just died, and it wasn't like she was pale to start off with. She flicked her bra strap down then back up on to her shoulder. She'd definitely keep it on for now. *For now?* She lifted her arm and squinted in the mirror at her armpit. Was that stubble or shadow under her arm? She ran her fingers across the skin. Stubble. She didn't have time to sort it out and it wasn't like Kye headed anywhere near her pits. She grabbed Mum's Sure deodorant and swiped the roller up and down. She didn't want to sweat over him.

She emptied her make-up bag on to the toilet lid. She better not go full fairy kei, because that freaked him out. So yes, lilac eye shadow and mascara, but no matching lenses or wig. She'd leave off the freckles too, but she'd definitely have to sort out her eyebrows soon. They looked like two cats having a fight. She'd distract him with her short pink skirt and the knee highs, but that would mean tights as well because, according to Bicchi Blogger, her eyebrows weren't the only hair she was supposed to get sorted. Bicchi suggested keeping a strip down the middle. Maybe Rose could dye it pink. Not today, though.

Was Kye busy doing all this too? When he'd taken off his t-shirt last week, his back had been very smooth, so maybe he did wax and moisturise. But it didn't matter. She wanted to do all this for him.

In those early days, when she'd been lurking on the Cast Outs site, an ex-Jehovah's Witness girl had asked about getting a boyfriend. Nearly everyone had advised her not to try too hard. They said it was a lot of hard work and not always worth it.

Kye was worth it. He was delicious. He was delicious in the way chocolate was delicious. He turned her into a cartoon. Homer Simpson licking his lips, or Scooby Doo nose-deep in Scooby snacks, or No-Face in 'Spirited Away' gorging on a feast. She didn't need to see Kye looking at her – she could taste his gaze. They didn't need to be kissing for her tongue to prickle. If only she could get keys cut for him so he could sneak in and surprise her. It would be like missing lunch and turning a corner to find a van full of free ice cream and no queue.

Just as well Rudder didn't know about last week. When Kye had kissed her neck, she'd licked his head. It was just the tip of her tongue running along a loop of curl, but still. She'd felt the tickle of him across her lips. Then his fingers had worked up beneath her shirt, pressing beneath the elastic of her crop top. Her heart had been like a . . . yes! Thank you, Avengers! . . . like a tesseract. It had been holding energy that she couldn't contain.

She touched her chest. It was like her heart was remembering. Kye had been unbuttoning her shirt and she hadn't tried to stop him. She'd even twisted round slightly to make it easier. And then he'd picked up his phone and turned the camera on her. *What are you doing?* The words had come out of her even though it was obvious what he was doing. Everybody did it, he'd said. She'd thrown a pillow at him and he'd dropped the phone and sworn. She'd made a dash for the bathroom, buttoned herself up and said 'goodbye'.

He'd texted afterwards to apologise. He'd even made a joke about it, saying that he was helping her with the decommissioning. He'd said that he'd go at the speed she wanted to and wait until she was ready. In the meantime, he'd said, she could always send him a boob flash. Maybe the joke was her? According to Cast Outs, he was right. Everyone did do it.

She slicked Pink Zinc across her lips. It was greasy but

it only cost 50p from a Chinese wholesale site, so she couldn't complain. Though did it have to be a choice between topping up her phone, some decent lipstick or helping out Rudder with his lunch account? Dad had to increase their allowance. It was ridiculous.

Her phone buzzed. Already? She glanced in the mirror. She'd Pink Zinced her front teeth. She tugged off a piece of toilet roll, wiped off the lipstick and dropped the tissue in the bin. She pulled her jumper back on, mussing up her hair. For God's sake! It was a pity Kye hated the wigs. Rose dug out a finger full of edge control and massaged it into the roots above her forehead, swishing the soft bristle brush over it. Why did it work for Bicchi and not her? Rose looked like she'd dunked her head in the kebab shop fryer downstairs. She dabbed her head with a towel and brushed some more. That was a bit better.

Her phone buzzed again. She ran into the bedroom, tore her skirt off the hanger and buttoned it on. Where were her knee highs? She should have planned this better. She pulled out her pink fishnets and struggled into them. Damn! She'd forgotten to light the incense! She fished for a stick of Summer Happiness from the crate by her bed, skidded into the kitchen, grabbed the matches and wasted two of them trying to light the stupid thing. Finally, a curl of smoke. She propped it up in a mug near the sink. Then back through the living room, holding the flat door open with a stool. She took the stairs down to the street two at a time and paused for a second. There'd never be a time when she wouldn't recognise Kye. Even with wood and reinforced glass between them, she knew it was him. His Kyeness seeped under the door and squeezed through the cracked putty. She closed her eyes. Her tongue tingled. He was looking at her right now.

She opened the door. They were nose to nose.

He grinned. 'What took you so long?'

She took his hand and led him up the stairs, kicking away the stool so the door swung shut. He pulled her towards him, twisting round so she was between him and the door. He kissed her again. No, she was she kissing him. No way was she going to open her mouth and just let herself be kissed. She didn't want passive immodesty. Decommissioning meant making the immodesty happen.

His hand slipped underneath her jumper pressing either side of her belly like he was trying to narrow her down. His thumbs stroked the edge of her bra. She swallowed. *Immodesty*. Actually, forget immodesty, *armpits*. His fingers were getting too close. She wriggled away from him, then reached around and hugged him in to her. For a second, he was stuck to her like spare clothes. She let her fingers burrow under the back of his jacket and—

Kye pulled away. 'Was that your phone?'

'I don't think so.' Hers was somewhere under her clothes on her bed.

He kept one arm round her and pulled his phone out of

21

his jacket pocket with the other, angling away from her and letting the cold air in between them as he studied his screen. The smell of doner kebab curled up from the shop below. The enormous cone of meat would be slowly rotating next to the grill.

His arm around her body tensed. His eyes were still on his phone. 'Shit!'

'What is it?'

'Don't sound like that.'

'I . . . ?' How had she sounded? It's not like she stressed out on him every time he looked at his phone instead of her. 'Sorry. I thought it was bad news.'

'It is. Bella's been in an accident.'

'Oh my God! Is she okay?' She'd made the 'okay' sound genuine, even if the little cow made Rudder's life a misery. Rose had to make sure her face matched her voice. 'What happened?'

He showed her the message. His thumb was over the sender. **Sis ran in the road. Hit by bike. Ambulance taking her to hospital**.

'Jesus! That's terrible! Is it bad?'

'She's been hit by a bike. What do you think?' Kye unhooked himself from her, still scrolling through his phone. 'I have to go.'

'Yeah. Of course.'

He dropped a kiss on to her forehead. 'Talk later.'

'Do you want me to come . . .'

He was already out of the door. She flicked it shut and ran over to the sofa, pushing her face against the window. She felt the vibration of the street door bang downstairs. There he was. Would he look up for her? God, she spent so much time watching out for him that if she ever had to pick him out in a police parade, she'd ask to do it from a high platform. She knew every detail of the top of his head. His dark brown hair, radiating from a spot on his crown like someone was trying to stir it. It wasn't quite central, so his hair fell longer on the right. It was those strands of hair that lifted in the breeze, his right hand automatically trying to flatten it. That's how she'd first seen the mole on the tip of his ear. He'd said that when he was little, people used to think it was dirt and try and wipe it off.

He was on his phone, hurrying to the bus stop. A 55 pulled up. When it glided off, he was gone. He hadn't looked up.

Rose peeled away from the sofa and went back to the bedroom. It was just as well she hadn't started scraping away at her armpits. God, if that was the first thing she thought right now, did that make her a really bad person? Her boyfriend's – *boyfriend's* – little sister had been knocked over by a bike and Rose was here thinking about pit stubble. She tapped her password into her phone. There was a message from Rudder.

Bella got run over! I'm scared!

Rose blinked. How the hell did Rudder know? He was supposed to be in the library!

Where are you, Ruds?

Why didn't you reply before?

Oh, God. She'd missed an earlier message from him. He'd be launching into stress mode. She called him.

'I'm sorry, Ruds. I just got your message. Are you okay?'

'No. I'm scared.'

He was outside somewhere. His voice kept blowing away.

'Why are you scared?'

'I saw it.'

'You saw Bella get knocked over? Fuck, Ruds. What happened?'

He sniffed. 'You don't need to use that word.'

She let a swear-shaped breath out through her nose. 'Ruds?'

Another sniff.

'Do you want me to come and find you?'

'I'm nearly home. My battery's—' The line cut off. Rose peered over to Rudder's side of their bedroom. His charger was plugged into the wall.

She lay back on her bed. Trust Rudder to witness something like that. He was always in the wrong place at the wrong time. It was like his head was still so full of scripture

24

there was no room for him to figure out how their new world worked.

She tapped on Kye's number.

How's Bella? Let me know if you need me xxxxxx

Six kisses were too much. She deleted three, added a heart and pressed send. She let the phone flop on to the bed and stared up at the ceiling. The brown patch around the light fitting seemed to be spreading. Mum said it was just water damage, but it looked like something worse.

If the Pilgrims saw where they were now, they'd say it was just punishment. Her, Mum and Rudder crammed into two and a half rooms, their hair and skin coated with the smell of chips and grilled lamb. The fact that she and Rudder had to share a room would make any righteous Pilgrim explode with outrage.

Mum had done her best when they moved in, flipping the mattresses and folding blankets over them before putting a sheet on top. She'd gone out and come back with a cheap clothes rail that they'd spent the afternoon trying to put together, installing it between the two skinny beds. They'd hung their clothes up straight away. The floor lamp came in from the main room so Rose could have her own light, because no matter how much they shifted things about, they couldn't find space for a bedside table. Most of Rose's best stuff was stashed in the drawers beneath her bed. Most of her secret stuff was in the cabinet in the corner. Mum had tried to hang a mirror on the back of the door, but the wood was flaking so she'd lent it against Rose's cabinet instead. Rudder had hooked a coat rack over the top of the door so it couldn't close properly. His Harry Potter robes hung there next to Rose's old Pitt blazer. Poor Ruds! How could Mum ever think it was a good idea for him to wear it?

She tried to sit up. It was like Kye had taken all her energy with him. What if Bella was hurt really badly and Kye felt guilty and dumped her? Some of the Cast Out girls said that worldy boys could be really unpredictable and made up the rules as they went along.

She checked her phone. Nothing back from him yet. Why should there be? His sister had been in an accident. Rose had to be patient.

She leaned over and fished out the new package from under her bed. Thank God *Ali Express* was cheap, but by the time the stuff arrived from China, she'd forgotten she'd ordered it. She dug her nail into the bubble wrap and peeled off the sticky tape. It was the Totoro tights.

In a few minutes' time, the flat would be filled with Rudder's panic. She mustn't roll her eyes at him, even in her imagination. He still needed to grow his tough worldy skin to cover the Pilgrim one.

She checked her phone again. Kye had seen her message. What if something really bad had happened to Bella? She clicked on his newsfeed. Would he put something on there?

No, he hadn't been on here for ages. She'd tried to get him to post a picture of them together, but he wouldn't. That had hurt a bit. He'd never been shy about it with other girls. She scrolled through his gallery. Was he ever going to delete that pic with the blonde girl at the musical festival? Or this one, with her and loads of others. Rose counted. There were eight of them, four girls and four boys, their arms round each other, with the boys at the end flipping peace signs. Eight. A nice neat number. Four pairs. Kye was smiling at the blonde girl, like he was every time she stopped on this bloody picture. Why did she do it? It always made her feel like she'd swallowed a chip of glass. The blonde girl wouldn't have minded when he got the camera out in his bedroom. She'd have thrown a special pose.

Rose made the blonde girl disappear, but the glass splinter poked itself in deeper, because she'd got to the picture of Kye with a black girl, darker than Rose, with natural hair twisted into bumps. She was tall and his eyes were level with her boobs. He looked happy. Did *she* let him take photos? Maybe she even suggested it.

Her phone rang. She almost jumped in the air. It was Mum.

'Can you get potatoes, Rose?'

'Potatoes?'

'For supper tonight.'

'I don't like potatoes.'

'Yes, you do. Nip to the Turkish grocer's and pick some

up, please. Not the big sack. The ones at the bottom are usually rotten. Just three big ones for baking. Are you still there, Rose?'

'Yes, Mum.'

'I need you to help, Rose.'

'Yes, Mum.'

'You've got time to put them in the oven so they bake properly. Prick them first, or they'll explode.'

'Yes, Mum.'

'Are those "I'll do it" yes-Mums or "I can't be bothered to listen" yes-Mums?'

'I'll do it!'

'Good. How was college?'

'Educational.'

She felt Mum smile on the other end. The glass splinter had almost disappeared. It was all just sharpness and ache.

'I think I'm pleased to hear that. I'll see you later. Probably around seven.'

'That will be eight, then, Mum.'

'It depends on the trains. You know that.'

Mum rang off. Rose's phone seemed to release itself from her hand and thump on to the bed. The flat door had opened. She'd missed the 'click' but felt the wave of hot, meaty air. Rudder was back. She kicked the bedroom door shut – or as shut as it would go. She needed a few seconds to pull back all the energy that Kye had taken with him.

3

Rudder stared at the closed bedroom door.

'Rose?'

She must be on the phone to Kye again. He was the only person she wanted to talk to these days. He knocked. 'Can I come in?'

'Just a minute.'

'I need to talk to you, but I can't with the door closed.' His words would get stuck in the wood or caught in the folds of his robes. Anyway, it wasn't all words. He'd show her Bella's note. He didn't have to say who it was from. He dipped his hand in his pocket. It was scrunched up like rubbish. His mouth was by the crack of the door and he let his voice sink to a whisper. 'Are you sure Kye's not there?'

The bedroom door swung open. 'Of course he's not. I told you.'

Even without those chunky shoes she wore, Rose could still almost rest her chin on Rudder's head. She hadn't done it for ages though, since Mum had told her it was demeaning. Rudder wished she would now and hug him like she used to do. And sometimes, he wished she'd look like she used to do. It was hard to remember this new Rose was Rose. She had three colours of make-up on each eye. She wasn't wearing her monstery purple contact lenses, but the light in the bedroom made her eyes look like they were full of fog.

She stepped out and her eyes cleared. 'Sorry, Ruds. Are you okay?'

He nodded, then shook his head. 'Bella was lying in the road. I thought she was dead.'

At last, she reached out and hugged him. She didn't look like Rose, but as he closed his eyes, he knew it could only be a Rose hug.

She let him go. 'You must have been terrified. Come and tell me what happened.'

She pulled him on to the sofa, crossed her legs and turned towards him. A corner of Bella's note was digging into his thumb. He took his hand out of his pocket.

Rose said, 'So?'

He just needed his words to settle down in his head so he could put them in the right order.

'I was in the library and so was Bella. I needed to go to the toilet and—'

'Too much information, Ruds! How come she got hit by a bicycle?'

She hadn't seen it coming. She'd been looking back at Rudder. He'd seen it, the cyclist, the glint of sun on their helmet, their feet on the pedals a blur and the skid, too late. Bella had screamed but it had sounded far away. The bus driver had jumped out and run over to her. The cyclist's cheek was streaked with blood and his helmet was on the ground beside him. Another cyclist wheeled the crooked bicycle to the kerb. So many people crowded round that all Rudder could see was Bella's foot. Her shoe had flopped off and her tights were ripped across the ankle.

Rudder had leaned back against the chicken shop window, pressing his palms flat against the glass. If he'd let go, he would have been the third person lying there. He should have let himself sink, so he could go in the ambulance too. He'd have held Bella's hand and told her he was sorry – he'd wanted to do something, but he hadn't known what. He'd have promised he'd make amends.

Rose tapped his knee. 'Ruds! Speak to me!'

'Some boys chased her,' he said.

Rose's eyebrows shot up. At least they were normal today, not pink or pale green. 'You saw her being chased?'

Rudder rubbed his face. Had he? No. Not exactly. The orc had been coming towards Rudder and Bella had pushed past them all. 'Not really chased her, but they'd been near her.'

'Near her? Rudder, you aren't making sense.'

His brain was throwing his words in the air and not catching them.

Don't let Kye— What was he supposed to say? She mustn't let Kye . . . do it? Was it *that*? He looked at Rose. She raised an eyebrow back at him.

He took the note out of his pocket and tried to flatten it. The pencil writing had faded into the creases.

'What's this, Rudder?'

'It's . . .' *Don't tell her I told you.* 'I can't tell you. But you mustn't let Kye do . . . do something.'

'Do what, Rudder?' She'd put on her tough face, the one she always used when he mentioned Kye. 'You seriously aren't making sense.'

He kept trying to smooth the wrinkles out of the note. The side of his hand was shiny with pencil.

'I was given this.' The words were stretching themselves into proper sentences now. 'And I was told that you shouldn't do *something* with Kye.'

'Can we leave the bit about doing something with Kye, Rudder? I'm not sure how it's connected to Bella getting knocked over.'

Every time he got his thoughts straight, Rose picked them up and shuffled them.

'I was waiting for the toilet, and—'

'Like I said, I don't need to hear that bit, neither. What happened outside the library?'

'Bella was with the two older boys. I think they were having an argument and she ran into the road.'

'Have you looked at this?' Rose held up the note. 'What's Hot Dogz? Where did you get it?'

'It was on the floor.'

She sat up straight. 'On the floor? God, Rudder.' She dropped the note on to the sofa, suddenly alert. 'I think I've got a message.'

She dived back into the bedroom and the note fluttered

on to the floor. She left the bedroom door open and Rudder could see her sprawled on her tummy, thumbs going full speed. There was only one person that made her act like that. It was like Kye had given her a love potion. Amortentia was the strongest and Kye must have made her drink a whole bath full of it.

Rudder leaned over and tried to rub more wrinkles out of the note. The pencil smeared even more. Rose swung off the bed and came towards the bedroom door, clutching her phone tight. She shut the door with her on the other side.

Rose?

Rudder turned, kneeled up on the sofa and jemmied open the window. A crowd of pigeons were squatting on the roof of the hostel opposite. If he could choose to be an animagus, he'd be a pigeon. He'd climb out on to the windowsill, push himself away from the wall and just as he was about to hit the ground, flap his wings and take off. He'd never be short of food and if he didn't fancy what was left on the pavement, he'd swoop down and grab the snack of his choice from the food vans by the market. No one would pick on him because he'd look like every other pigeon. He'd fly across London and visit the Queen. Even though Pilgrims didn't believe in queens, there'd still be quality snacks in her kitchen. After that, he'd make his way over to see Dad. He'd change back to his Rudder shape around the corner from Grandma Yellow's house. He'd walk up the path, knock on the door and tell Dad he was never leaving him again.

Rudder shut the window. Their bedroom door was open a crack. He could hear the murmur of Rose's voice.

He went over and pulled the door open wider. Rose looked up. 'Can I help you?'

'I just wanted to know about Bella.'

'Just one sec.' That was to Kye. Rudder had been right. She gave Rudder half the smile she'd been giving to the phone. 'She's fractured some bones and has concussion, but she'll be all right.'

She waved Rudder away. He closed the door and sat back down. Bella wasn't dead. She was going to be all right. Why did he still feel like he had the Devil's weight on him? Because it still didn't change the fact that he should have done something. He wondered if Rose was going to be much longer. He wanted his robes and his throw. He'd drape them over his head and his shoulders and across his face until only his eyes peeped out. He curled up on the sofa and let his hand flop over the side. The sofa must have been bright gold once, a long time before Rudder was born. Now the worn-down material was different shades of brown, the same as his hands. It was like camouflage. He scooped up the note, folded it into a small square and stuck it in his trouser pocket. When he was allowed back into their room, he'd put it in his book box. It was important. Bella had definitely wanted him to have it, even if it didn't make sense. He'd have to wait until he could ask her, after she came out of hospital.

If he could really transfigure into a pigeon, he'd fly to every hospital in London with the note in his beak until he found her. He'd start with the closest hospital. He knew that one well. His brain wouldn't let him remember too much about the first hospital they'd rushed him to as an emergency, but the one near here had the special burns clinic. Mum had complained that it was typical that they were moving closer to it now that he didn't have to go so much.

Rudder held his breath so he could listen. Rose was quiet, then she said 'What?' so loud Rudder jumped. The Devil's weight got heavier. Kye was probably telling Rose how useless Rudder had been. Rudder closed his eyes. It made the bang in his head louder and the Devil press down harder. He could almost feel the sharp edges of hooves as they carved grooves in his skin.

He opened his eyes and went into the bathroom. Rose had left her stuff everywhere. Mum was going to hate that. He swished water over his face and looked in the mirror. Rudder was a Pilgrim. He had to remember it. What did Pilgrims do when they were overcome with worldly burdens? They prayed and atoned.

'There are seven stages of atonement. Number one, recognition. Number two, embarkation. Number three, exploration. Number four, connection.' The glass Rudder mouthed the instruction along with him. 'Number five, immersion.'

Immersion. Embracing a programme of re-education through

prayer and mission. Making amends to those you have hurt.

Suddenly, Rudder felt a little lighter. Making amends. Of course! He didn't have to be a pigeon to find Bella. He'd go and say sorry and check what she wanted him to do. He dried his face and crept back to the bedroom door.

'Rose?' He drew back his fist to knock. She laughed, a whispery laugh he'd never heard before she met Kye. Rudder let his hand drop. He'd leave her a message. No, why should he bother? She'd probably still be on the phone when he got back. He shoved his travel card in his pocket and closed the flat door quietly behind him.

The bus stopped right outside the hospital. Half the people on the bus got off with him, heading towards the large automatic doors at the other side of the car park. The ambulance would have taken Bella to the children's emergency department. Rose said that's what had happened to him. The burns clinic was in the opposite direction. Mum always made them stick to the pedestrian pathway, but Rudder wasn't with Mum now. He zigzagged between the cars and followed an old man on a walking frame into the foyer.

He took a sharp right into the reception for children's A&E. A man was leaning against the desk while the receptionists checked the computer. About ten or eleven people waited behind him. Rudder joined the end of the queue, scanning the rows of seats. Was any of Bella's family in here? Two white women sat together with a toddler slumped across their laps. One of them stroked the little one's head. A young woman in a headscarf was comforting a boy a bit younger than Rudder. He was holding one of those cardboard cups they give you when they think you're going to be sick.

'I'm afraid we're not allowed to do that.'

A receptionist's voice had risen. The man was leaning right over the desk now. Rudder could hear the sharpness of his whisper, but not the words.

'Yes, we do understand.' The second receptionist was even louder. 'Unfortunately, we can't divulge confidential information without the carer's permission.'

A security guard was walking towards the desk. The man saw him, straightened up and walked off. He was crying. Rudder rubbed his hands together. They felt hot and tender. Under this light, the pale streaks of skin looked almost white.

'What are you doing here?'

The voice was behind Rudder. He turned around. It was the orc, taller than before, his eyes bigger, unblinking. Just behind the orc, a porter pushed a bed. Rudder could make out a person-shape under a blanket, a tube snaking out into a canister. They carried on down a corridor, stopping by what must be the lift. The security guard passed by on his way back to his desk.

The orc's finger jabbed into the soft spot between Rudder's ribs. 'Answer me.'

Rudder nodded. In the library, a nod had been right. It didn't look like it was now.

The orc's eye narrowed. 'That's not an answer.'

'I . . . I come here a lot.'

The finger pushed harder into Rudder's skin. 'First I see your ugly face in the library. Then you're busy minding our business on the street. And now, you're right here in front of me.' The orc's voice sunk to a whisper. 'Are you following me?'

Rudder shook his head.

'So it's just a coincidence, right?'

Rudder took a deep breath and held out his hands. 'I come here for treatment. There's a special clinic.'

He could feel the tips of his ears turning red, but the orc wouldn't know that was Rudder's lie alert.

The orc screwed up his face. 'What's wrong with your hands?'

'They got burnt.'

'Jesus!' The orc poked harder like he wanted to burst Rudder's heart. 'Get out of here.'

Rudder nodded again and turned around. He could feel the orc standing there, waiting and watching as the door slid open and Rudder ran out across the car park.

Rudder's list of food he never wants to eat again

1. Bananas that are squishy at the bottom
2. Cornflakes when the flap hasn't been put back properly
3. Pink meat in a tin
4. Tinned tomatoes heated up
5. Milk lumps

Rudder's list of food he wants to eat again

1. Biscuits with lumps of chocolate inside them
2. Butter beer, but not the one Rose tried to make
3. Tinned spaghetti and hot dogs
4. Beefburgers with a slice of flat cheese on top
5. Mum's special rice with cut up ham and peas

4

Rose let the plastic bag swing in her hand. She wanted to spin round like a tornado, let the bag go and watch how much damage three baking potatoes could inflict. Maybe one of them would bounce off the side of a bus and smash that moped driver in the mouth. He'd never want to yell crap like that at any girl again. Maybe one potato would go right up to heaven, so that if there really was a God, He'd write a message on it to prove it. That would make Rudder happy, at least. And the other one – that would be reserved for Rudder himself. Straight between the eyes. How dare he disappear like that and not tell her? She'd spent so long worrying about him that she'd been late getting the potatoes and Mum was in mood evil, because somehow it was also Rose's fault that the agency had mucked up Mum's last shift and someone else was busy cleaning the office when Mum got there. But since that little git Rudder came back, all he would do was sit on his bed and not talk to her.

Rose unlocked the street door, climbed the stairs and nudged open the door to the flat with her elbow, back-kicking it shut behind her. Rudder had ramped up the music in their room just to damn well annoy her. They weren't Pilgrims any more. He had the choice of any music in the whole wide worldly world and he chose Simon and Garfunkel, two sad old American blokes singing sad old songs. They probably weren't even alive any more. If they all wanted was to go and look for America, they should damn well take Rudder with them.

She thumped the bag down next to the sink.

'You're not just going to leave them there, are you, Rose?'

Mum was in the bathroom, the door open a crack. Steam curled out with the smell of lavender bubble bath, the posh one that Mum wouldn't share. She must have kept the door open just so she could yell at Rose, even though she knew Rudder stressed out if he glimpsed any part of Mum that wasn't her hands, feet or face. In a place this small, it was hard not to see the different parts of each other. It was like Mum had taken one step out of the Pilgrims and found her immodesty straight away. Rudder was probably blasting out Simon and Garfunkel to drown out Mum's sin.

'What do you want me to do with them?'

'For God's sake, Rose! You know how to make baked potatoes! Prick them like I told you and stick them in the microwave. We haven't got time to bake them properly now. Start them on twelve minutes and check after each additional minute. You got the cheese, didn't you?'

Shit!

'Rose?'

'I'll go back down. Though you could always send Rudder.'

'He's in one of his moods. I haven't got the energy.'

'Why does he get out of doing any chores?'

'Just do it, Rose! And don't worry about the cheese. I hate the cheap stuff. It tastes like Lego. We've got beans and sweetcorn, that's enough. Make sure you give the potatoes a good clean, though. God knows who touched them before us.'

The bathroom door clicked shut. Rose rinsed the potatoes and dried them with kitchen towel. Not too much, though, or Mum would explode about wasting stuff and then Rudder would go into an even bigger sulk because they were arguing and go to bed early. Then Mum would get all angry and pull out her sofa bed. Rose wouldn't even be able to escape to the bath because Mum had probably used all the hot water. She stabbed a fork into the potatoes, plonked them on a plate and into the microwave. She set the timer for twelve minutes. The microwave sounded like it was building up to a planet-sized explosion. Imagine, instead of beasts rising out of hell and angels descending to take the tally of reformed souls, the world ended because of a dodgy microwave in a damp, smelly kitchen. That would really muck the Pilgrims up.

She stared at the rotating potatoes. If the end *was* on its way, she intended to spend the last few minutes with Kye. He could take as many photos of her as he wanted. She fished for the cans of beans and sweetcorn in the cupboard. It had taken her so long to bribe Rudder to stay out this afternoon and then, typical – Kye couldn't stay. *Rose, you are an evil, sinful person!*

She had to remember to feel bad about Bella. She'd listened to Kye tell her how the bike had smashed into Bella's shoulder and dislocated it. Bella had fractured her ribs and an ankle and cracked her head when she'd hit the road. It could have been worse, though, much worse. Luckily, they hadn't detected any brain injuries. Rose must have made the right sympathetic noises because then . . . then he'd invited her to his place tomorrow. It would be just them, while his mum was at the hospital. In the flat. By themselves. No sulky little brother playing 'Bridge Over Troubled Water' so loud it made the bedroom door shake. She wouldn't pack her bags and move in with Kye just yet, but a few hours away from all this would be good.

The microwave pinged, a small sound after something that'd sounded like it was about to end mankind. She opened it and squeezed the nearest potato. It could take out Goliath. She turned the potatoes over and reset for another ten minutes. A thump came from the bathroom, followed by loud gurgling. The kids in the flat above were louder, though. They must be baby vampires, because the darker it got outside, the wilder they went upstairs. One day Rose would leave a wooden stake outside their flat and see what happened.

'Rose?' The bathroom door was open a sliver. 'Can you pass me some leggings?'

'Sure.'

Rose pushed open the bedroom door. Rudder was lying on his bed.

He sat up. 'You should knock.'

'It's my bedroom too.'

'I always knock for you.'

'You're scared of seeing me naked.'

'It's wrong.' The embarrassment was practically wafting off him. 'I don't want you to see me naked, neither.'

'I had no reason to believe you'd be naked at this time of day, Rudder. And don't forget, I used to change your nappy. You haven't got anything I haven't seen.'

'So what? You're not seeing it again.'

'I don't want to, Ruds, believe me. Can I turn your music down? It's really loud outside and Mum's in a foul mood.'

'That's not my fault.'

'It didn't help that you wandered off. Are you going to tell me where you went?'

'It's still none of your business.'

Did he do it deliberately – make her want to grab his shoulders and shake him? She took a deep breath.

'Okay, Rudder. Whatever. Mum needs some leggings. They're over your side. Can you get them?'

He didn't move.

'Rudder!'

He swung himself round so his legs hung over the side of his bed. His face reminded her of one of those small dogs that rich women carried in their bags. He pulled his throw over his feet.

He said, 'Why do you like Kye so much?'

Yes, he did do it deliberately. Would it be so damn bad of her to finally get why Bella picked on him?

She said, 'What's that got to do with anything?'

'You like him even though he makes you lie to Mum.'

'Just pass me Mum's leggings, Rudder.'

'He comes over when Mum's not here and you say I mustn't tell Mum.'

'In your own words, Rudder, it's none of your business.'

She knelt on his bed and tugged at the plastic lid on the crate next to the window.

'Wait!' He lunged over and grabbed his alarm clock before it tumbled off. The Platform 9 ¾ logo glowed at her. At this very moment, she'd joyfully pay for a taxi to take Rudder to King's Cross so he could walk through a wall and disappear forever.

She said, 'I saw it. It was going to land on your bed.'

He nursed the clock in both hands. 'I don't think you should be with Kye.'

'And I don't think you should have an opinion.' She rummaged in the crate. It was almost all black leggings. She pulled out a pair. 'You won't understand some things until you're older.'

'I understand it now. And I am older. I'm a man.'

The leggings dangled from Rose's fingers. 'In the Pilgrim world, yes. But in this world, you're still a boy.'

'I don't want to be in this world.'

'You haven't given it a chance.'

'Yes, I have! And I hate it!'

'Stop lying.'

'I'm not!'

She flopped the leggings over her arm. 'So why are your ears going red now?' He touched his ear. 'You know, if you were still a Pilgrim, you wouldn't have a box full of Harry Potters under your bed or your damn throw or your alarm clock, or any of it. You've got more reason to get out of the Pilgrims than any of us, proper get out, not pick and choose the bits you want. And you know what, Rudder? What with you and this stupid flat and trying to pass those damn exams, Kye is the only thing keeping me sane right now.'

'Rose! Leggings!'

'I'm going to take these to Mum or you'll definitely see her naked.'

She climbed off his bed. He'd gone sulky again. Just as well Pilgrims taught self-restraint. She needed every damn drop of it to stop herself swiping that damn alarm clock off Rudder's lap on to the floor. She banged the door shut. The hooks over the top made it bounce open again. Rudder slammed it back so it jammed nearly-closed.

'Why don't you two shut it a bit harder?' Mum was standing in the bathroom doorway in just her knickers and t-shirt. 'It's not like this flat isn't stuck together with spit.'

'Rudder can be an arse, sometimes.'

'Don't rile him.'

46

'I didn't.'

Mum took the leggings and pulled them on. She staggered and grabbed at the door frame.

Rose ran over to her. 'Mum?'

'I'm all right.' Mum's wet hair drew a damp patch down her t-shirt. 'I just lost my balance. My head's a bit woozy. Those devil children upstairs have been keeping me awake all this week.'

'I thought you had those earplugs now.'

'They'd have to be made from concrete to block that lot out. Can you get my things for me?'

Rose gathered the joggers and shirt from the bathroom floor and shoved them into the laundry basket. Mum let go of the door frame and stood still for a moment.

She said, 'I could have done without that mix-up tonight, but they're going to try and find me an extra shift.'

'You look knackered already.'

'Thanks for the compliment!'

'Sorry, I just thought you were going to faint.'

'No, I'm pretty sure my fainting days are well and truly over.' She picked her towel off the toilet seat and draped it over her hair. 'Though today has been more stressful than I needed.'

'Sorry about the potatoes.'

'Oh God, Rose, it's not you! You just got the butt of it.' Mum rubbed her hair. 'Your dad called.'

'Dad? Jesus!'

Mum raised her eyebrows. Rose giggled.

'Sorry,' Rose said. 'I don't know why I'm even laughing.'

'Probably because we'd have been more likely to get a phone call from Jesus than your dad.'

'Grandma hasn't . . . ?'

'Sadly, she's still going strong. Actually, Dad wants you to go round there tomorrow.'

Rose laughed again. Mum didn't join in. 'He what? Sorry? For real? After all this time? No!'

'Rose . . .'

'With Rudder, right?'

Mum nodded.

'Then double no. Rudder's already . . . He won't want to come home, Mum. You know that. And that's even if they let us in the house. You remember what happened when that counsellor tried to help us sort it all out. Grandma Yellow refused to let us through the door, remember?'

'I know Rose, but—'

'What if I'm busy? I've got plans that mean I don't spend Saturday with people that hate me.'

'He's taken a big step, Rose. He'd have had to jump through all sorts of hoops to get permission for you to come. I can't imagine that Lily-Beth is too impressed, neither.' Mum's eyes met hers. 'And maybe he'll give us more money.'

'Did he say that?'

'Not in so many words.' Mum threw her towel back into the bathroom. 'I have to be optimistic. We need a life buoy.

I can't tread water for much longer.' She flung her arm around Rose. 'Even this crappy place costs more than I can afford. I know it's a tough ask, but please go, Rose. Please.'

'And it has to be tomorrow?'

'Yes.'

The microwave timer went off again. Mum opened the door, stepping back quickly as the heat hit her. She found a knife on the washing up dryer and stuck it in a potato. 'Are these potatoes cursed, or something?'

She reset the timer. 'I know it doesn't seem it, but you're lucky, Rose. When my parents were kicked out, we weren't allowed to see anybody there ever again. Pilgrims in the street would cross over to avoid us. These were children I'd played with since I was a baby and now they were being told to look away from me. We stopped existing. We were like ghosts. No, worse, we were nothings.'

Rose put her arm round Mum's shoulders. Her t-shirt was still damp. 'They let you all back in again, though.'

'Yes, because we sacrificed my brother.'

Sacrificed? Mum had never put it like that before. 'I don't understand. You said he never wanted to go back?'

'He didn't. But he didn't want to lose everyone he'd ever known, neither. For them to let us back in, we had to believe . . .' She yanked open the microwave door. The motor carried on whining for a few seconds. 'We had to believe everything the Pilgrims said about him being in league with the Devil.' She laughed. 'Jeth could be a pain in the arse, but he was never quite the Devil's agent.'

'What did he do wrong?'

'My mother found a cassette tape under his pillow.'

'A cassette tape?' Rose nodded. 'Very sinful.'

Mum didn't smile. 'And where there's a tape, there's a tape player and the Devil's music, and maybe even dancing. Though I could have put them right on that one. He was listening to The Smiths.'

Who? No, now wasn't the time to ask. 'How did the Elders find out?'

'My devout mother told them. She thought prayers would sort it out. Instead, it was our family who were out. And the Excise Committee's all men of course, so it's not like she could go in person and defend her son. Though I've heard they've modernised now and us poor, inferior women are allowed in as witnesses. Not that they'd listen to us anyway. Jeth joined the army and you know what the Pilgrims think of that. He was sticking the boot in as far as it would go, in the deepest, most painful place.'

'It must have been really difficult for you.'

'For me, going back was worse than being out. Before we were excised, Dad was on the verge of being appointed an Elder. He went back to being a Brother. Not even an Uncle, just a mere low-rank Brother, a fetch-and-carry boy. Those were the terms. He had to sit at the back with Brothers half his age while his peers were way in front. Rose, if they'd ever made a film called *Pray Hard*, Dad would have been the hero. We were up at half four every bloody morning praying for atonement and the destruction of the Devil's agents in the most painful ways possible. Meanwhile, my Devil-seduced brother was serving in Iraq.'

'Uncle Jeth did all right in the army, though, didn't he?'

'He was just changing one set of rules for another. He did well enough until he was sent to war. When he came home, there was no family to greet him. He's never forgiven any of us for that.'

'Do you know where he is now?'

'Spain, Middlesbrough, Australia? Who knows? In the last year or so, it's like him and his girlfriend have fallen off the edge of the planet. I'm sure he'll get in touch when he's ready.'

Rose kissed Mum's damp cheek. 'I know this place isn't what you wanted for us, but it's a start. After everything else, it's amazing we've got this far.'

Mum gave a little laugh and picked up the cans of beans and sweetcorn, weighing one against each other. 'Is there any butter?'

Rose shook her head.

'Oh, well.' Mum opened the beans and then the sweetcorn. 'Let's be decadent and have both.'

5

Rudder draped his Marauder's Map throw round his shoulders. The fringes tickled his neck. If he could swirl round and catch himself in the mirror, Moony, Wormtail, Padfoot and Prongs would be emblazoned across his back. Though if he really could do magic, he'd learn a spell for sorting out the draft in here. Even when it was sunny, cold air gusted around the crumbling window frames. Rose used to say that it was the vampires upstairs trailing their cold undeadness when they went outside in search of blood. She hadn't mentioned it again after he'd had that nightmare, but he'd never forgotten.

Rose was in the main room with Mum watching TV. They'd tried to get him to join them, but why should he? They'd decided he was seeing Dad with Rose tomorrow without asking him. It wasn't right. Rudder should be the one making decisions. And Dad should have come to him direct, man to man.

Earlier, when he'd opened his bedroom door, Rudder had known something was up. Mum and Rose had been in the kitchen. There'd been that quiet. Rudder knew that quiet. It was the quiet before things were going to be said. Then Mum had said it.

'Your father wants to see you both tomorrow.'

Rose had been mixing corn into the middle of a baked potato. She must have known already, or she would have stopped and said something.

He'd looked from Mum to Rose. 'I thought we couldn't go to Grandma's house.'

'*I* can't,' Mum had said. 'Dad would have had to get special permission from the Actualizar Committee, but you're okay.'

'Me *and* Rose?'

Mum smiled. 'Yes. You're lucky.'

No. He wasn't. They didn't understand. If it wasn't for him, they'd still be there. *He'd* still be there. If Rose came, he wouldn't have a chance to ask them if he could come back. She'd be watching him.

He said, 'Doesn't Rose have other things to do?' He'd come so close to mentioning Kye's name. If he had, he'd have had to offer his other cheek to Rose for smiting and he wasn't in the mood.

She'd mashed more corn into her pulpy potato. 'I've had to change my plans.'

He said, 'If you don't want to go, maybe Mum can take me.'

'And sit outside by the road?' Mum shook her head. 'No, thank you. Anyway, I'm working, but you can get the bus to Liverpool Street and pick up the Central line to Chingford. A Pilgrim will pick you up from the station.'

'What if I don't want to go?' *With Rose*. She'd dropped her fork and glared at him as if she'd known what was in his mind.

'I don't want to go, neither,' she'd said. 'Last time they all just prayed and ignored us.'

Rudder remembered. He'd wanted to pray with them too, but he'd had to leave even though he felt like he was walking through a curtain of invisible needles on the way out.

'I need you to go, Rudder.' Mum had reached across for his hand. 'You'll be all right.'

He'd said, 'What if they want us to go back for good?'

Rose has stopped stirring her sweetcorn. 'You sound a little hopeful, Rudder?'

He'd shaken his head, but still caught the look that flicked between Mum and Rose.

Mum said, 'I know that going back seems the best option right now, but believe me, it's not as easy as you think, Rudder.'

Then Mum had started talking to Rose about a cheap shirt she'd seen in Primark. He'd finished his potato, then half of Rose's, and come back into the bedroom.

He'd have to find some way to get Dad by himself. If they'd let Mum's family back in before, they *had to* let Rudder back. He'd do anything to atone. He pulled the throw tighter around him and squinted out the bedroom window. The dirty blotches on the outside made it look like it was snowing, a dark snow full of doom. A lorry was trying to pull out of

Might's Cash and Carry opposite, but none of the traffic would stop and let it turn. Imagine having a spell that could freeze everything except you. He'd cast it now, just to give the driver a chance. Then he'd freeze Mum and Rose in front of the telly and go and see Dad alone.

There was a knock on the bedroom door and it opened. Rose came in and sat down on the end of his bed. She ran her finger across the flaky paint on the window frame.

'Anything interesting out there, Ruds?'

'No.'

'Spotted the Knight Bus yet?'

She was being extra-friendly. She was feeling guilty. He yanked the throw up over his head so the edge hung over his eyes. He pulled the corners together and turned to face her.

'No,' he said. 'I haven't.'

Her face was lit by streetlight. Her lips were lost in shadows. 'I know it's been a tough day, Ruds.'

'I thought Bella had died. I tried to tell you and you weren't interested.'

'You were trying to tell me about Kye, Rudder. That's different.'

'But Bella said—' No, he couldn't tell Rose what Bella said.

'What did she say, Ruds? Was it worse than anything else she's ever said about me? I'm really sad that she's been hurt. I never wanted that. But I do want her to stop bullying you and saying nasty things about me to Kye. By the way, I asked Kye about those two boys you mentioned.'

'Were they bullying her?'

'No. They're family friends and had come to walk her home from the library. She's been stressing out their mum by getting home late.'

'But she was in the toilet with them.'

Rose's eyes widened. 'What?'

'I tried to tell you, but you wouldn't listen.'

'I'm listening now.'

'I was waiting to go in, but the door was locked. First one boy came out, then another one and then Bella. She was crying.'

'Okay.' He thought she was going to say sorry for ignoring him, but instead she said, 'I'll talk to Kye about it. But first we have to think about going to Dad's tomorrow. It's really important.'

'I know that!' *Way more than she did!* He pressed his nose against the glass. It smelled of dust. 'What if . . .'

'What if what?'

He scrunched his forehead against the window. The pigeons on the roof opposite had flown away, but he imagined himself perched there, looking across at the flat.

He said, 'What if I want to stay with Dad?'

'I don't know what to say, Ruds. I don't have that problem. The world out here's tough, but no way do I want to be back in sanctuary.'

'That's all I think about.'

'I know. I don't want you to be so unhappy. I just wish

56

you'd give things a go. I see it like there's all these cracks in the worldy world and I just have to keep trying to force my way in. But you!' She laughed. 'It's like you've got some of that filler stuff that Mum bought for the mouse hole, and you're squirting it and squirting it . . .' She screwed up her face and pretended to squeeze out hole-filler. 'And when that tube's empty you're getting a second one and squirting in some more.'

He couldn't help laughing.

She said, 'I won't help you be a Pilgrim again, Ruds. If that's what you decide, it's up to you.'

'But then all the cracks will be filled up and you'll be one side of the wall and I'll be on the other.'

'Yup. That's how it works, Rudder. We both know that. Like I said, you have to decide if that's what you want.'

Why did Rose always make him feel guilty when he tried to talk to her about being a Pilgrim again?

He said, 'You don't have to come if you don't want to.'

'Did you have lunch today?'

'I wasn't hungry.'

'That's why you downed your potato in one and finished half of mine. I have to come to make sure we do the best we can tomorrow. Mum needs more money. Even I will be as sweet as honey if I have to. And we don't want Mum to look bad. They would love it if they thought she wasn't coping. Do you understand?'

'Yes.'

'Thank you. I know it's going to be really weird going back. I've got butterflies the size of dinosaurs bouncing through my stomach.'

Rudder had that every day before school.

He said, 'I wish Dad had tried harder to let me stay.'

Rose sighed. 'Maybe he did. Maybe the Actualizar Committee said "no". You know the Pilgrims hate the outside world, and thanks to us, the Woodford Pilgrims were on TV. Dad never stood a chance.'

Rudder frowned. 'It almost sounds like you're on his side. I thought you didn't care if you never saw him again.'

'That's not strictly true, Rudder. Me and Dad used to be close, but you know what it's like. As soon as Pilgrim girls hit twelve, we're handed over to the women. After that, I hardly saw Dad at all.'

She stood up and opened the door. In the main room, Mum had already pulled out her sofa bed and was lying on it watching telly.

Rose said, 'The tank should have filled up again. I'm going to have a bath.'

She closed the door softly after her. A few minutes later, the pipes started yelling at each other as the hot water tap was turned on. Rudder moved back to the window. Two buses passed each other, the one closest to Rudder squeezing past a parked taxi. The Knight Bus picked up witches and wizards who needed help. You just stuck out your wand arm and it appeared on the kerb to collect you.

But what if you didn't have a wand at the end of your wand arm? He shoved the window up and stretched out his arm. The buses passed on.

The Pilgrims' Seven Stages of Atonement

Also Known As
Rose's Seven Stages of Trying to be Purer and
Purer and Never Getting There

1. Recognition. Awareness of the immense burden of your soul. *Or, as Granny Yellow says, know you are evil and always have been.*

2. Embarkation. Understanding and confronting your story of temptation. *Otherwise known as being completely sure that everything that isn't Pilgrim is the word of the Devil. Then pray.*

3. Exploration. Meeting your sins one by one and naming them. *Which is why Pilgrim meetings are so so long.*

4. Connection. Drawing on the strength and knowledge of the Elders to reconnect you to the one Pilgrimage. *Ask the old men. They are always right. Even after what happened to Rudder's hands, they are still right. If you don't agree, YOU WILL BE EXCISED.*

5. Immersion. Embracing a programme of re-education through prayer and mission. Making amends to those you have hurt. *Getting up early for extra prayers, knocking on doors, handing out leaflets and saying sorry to everyone. Well, everyone, as long as they're not a Worldly Wise. Mum says Immersion takes much less time*

if you can donate to the Pilgrim Clean Slate Fund.

6. Subjugation. Willing acceptance of punishment leading to humility and forgiveness by God and sanctuary. More sorries. In front of everyone. Again and again and again with an Actualizar Committee thrown in if you're really lucky.

7. Assimilation. Return to the community. Burn your lipstick, chuck away your phone and try not to fall over your long skirt. Again.

6

Rose scanned the station car park. Rudder must be feeling as tight and anxious as she was because he refused to talk, let alone look at her. She was now invisible to her own brother as well as everyone else. When she wore fairy kei, people looked. When she was a Pilgrim, people looked. No one looked at her at all today. She'd managed to find a loose skirt that sat on her hips and hung somewhere close to her knees. Her leggings were silver with fuchsia butterflies, but they were still ruddy leggings. She'd stuck a pin in the top of her shirt to stop it gaping.

Mum had made Rudder change his Columba socks for plain brown ones. They couldn't afford the proper Harry Potter stuff, so Mum had decided that they'd invent their own Hogwarts house – and colours. So Columba House joined Gryffindor and all the others. A white and grey tie from a charity shop. Mum's old Pilgrim skirt for the inside of his robes. A dark grey scarf that Rose had found left on a wall. She could still see the little broken stitches where Mum had unpicked the name label.

Rose said, 'I think that's them.'

A red car pulled into the car park. The driver got out of the car. He was a tall white man who Rose hadn't seen before. He was wearing the shirt, buttoned-up waistcoat and over-shined shoes of devout Pilgrim men. There was no handkerchief in his waistcoat pocket, so he was still just a Brother. Maybe he was a backslider like her granddad, finally allowed to return. How many Pilgrims had made their excuses before this one agreed to pick up her and Rudder, hoping it would boost his atonement? Rose knew that there'd be a Bible in his glove compartment and maybe a spare one on the backseat for his children. There would definitely be no car radio or CD player. All Pilgrims had them removed as a matter of course.

Rose moved forward.

Rudder stayed still. 'Are you sure he's looking for us?'

'He couldn't be more Pilgrim if he had Pilgrim tattooed across his forehead.'

'Tattoos are forbidden, Rose.'

Rose sighed. It was going to be a long day.

'Ruds?'

'What?'

'Imagine we're on mission. Instead of saving souls, we're saving Mum.'

He shook his head. 'Mission doesn't work that way.'

Rose clenched her teeth together and walked off ahead of him. The driver dropped his eyes as Rose came towards him. What would he have done if she was wearing her usual clothes? Probably popped out his eyeballs and dropped them in his pocket until she'd passed on by.

He said, 'My name is Brother Eden. I have been tasked with taking you to Uncle Amos.'

He'd blinked hard when he'd said the word 'tasked'. He must have had the full briefing about them and how they'd brought the sinful world in to a Pilgrim sanctuary, with social workers and police tramping worldly dirt into Grandma Yellow's carpet. Then the journalists tracking down ex-Pilgrims to ramp up the story.

Brother Eden opened the back door of the car. Even if she was still a Pilgrim, Rose would never be allowed to sit next to him up front. Rudder would have, but he was tainted. She slid in first and yes, there was the Pilgrims' Bible between the backseat belt clasps. It looked new and untouched. Of course, there was no way Brother Eden would let the Worldly Wise like Rose and Rudder touch his home Bibles.

Rudder belted up and Brother Eden shut the car door. He folded himself into the driver's seat, turned on the engine and released the handbrake. The car jolted backwards and the Bible shot across the seat. Rose reached to grab it before it fell off. Rudder caught it first. She tried to smile at him, but he was looking out the window, the Bible now safe in his lap.

Brother Eden dropped them off outside Grandma Yellow's gate and drove away. Rose felt like she'd borrowed Rudder's Time-Turner. The street was the same, with the same bumper-to-bumper cars, the same hedges and recycling boxes and lampposts. The same pigeons were probably perched on the aerial on the roof opposite. The same street cleaner must chug by at six a.m., just as morning worship was almost done.

The house was the same too, detached from the Worldly Wise and shielded with thick net curtains. The front door was still blue and the gate was still slightly ajar for the Pilgrims coming to pray and give comfort. Mum always said that the best thing a Pilgrim woman could hope for was to be an Elder's widow, like Granny. You got to stay in the house, order around the aunties and build up a stack of their plastic tubs from the food they were always bringing round.

One thing *was* very different now. Rose and Rudder were part of the outside world. The gate should swing closed and lock itself as soon as Rose touched it. The blue door should stay shut.

It opened. It wasn't Dad. It was her – Grandma Yellow. Rose reached for Rudder's hand. For a second he seemed to offer it, then he pulled away. Grandma Yellow's lips were moving, the same verse she always used to ward away temptation. *'Many are the afflictions of the righteous: but the Lord delivereth him out of them all.'* Rose imagined the words dissolving into little puffs of holy air. Mum reckoned those would be the words chiselled on Grandma Yellow's headstone, if Pilgrims had headstones.

Rose took a breath, and another one. It stopped her speaking. *Affliction of the righteous?* What was righteous that made a little boy scream in pain, just for reading a book? What was righteous that built layers and layers of silence and pushed Mum and Rose and Rudder out, on to the other side of it? It was the same righteous that left them all huddled together in Room 27, Market House hostel, listening to the mice run up and down behind the skirting board and the man shouting in the room below. The same righteous that made Rudder cry all night in pain and spend all day begging to go back to the Pilgrims. Rose took another big breath. It felt like the holy air was fighting her back.

She made herself look at Grandma. The woman still looked too young. She might not celebrate birthdays, but thanks to Mum, Rose knew she was sixty-six. Her hair was still dark and her forehead was smooth. Mum said that between worship sessions and study groups, Grandma must feed off the blood of virgins to sustain her youth. At least in the Pilgrims Grandma would never go hungry.

Grandma wasn't wearing her yellow apron today, just one in the usual Pilgrim Aunty shade of grey. Rose could see the *Manual de Mujeres* – the holy handbook for Pilgrim women – bulging in the pocket. Grandma moved away from the door.

'You can come in.'

Rudder bowed his head and clutched his hands together in front of him. His little finger was twitching as if he'd trained it to seek out scripture. Rose stepped into the hallway next to him. There was the same grey rug, the same wooden shoe shelves and – yes – the smell! It was the cream Mum had used to scrub Grandma's cooker and the vinegar to shine up the taps. And the scented liners in the kitchen bin. Lily-Beth must be doing all that now. Rose didn't want to breathe any more, because every gasp of air made her want to cry. Why couldn't you just blink away smells? Funny, she actually knew the answer to that one. It's because the part of the brain that processes smells is close to the part that makes memories. Kye had looked it up after she'd covered herself with the Japanese Cherry Blossom tester in The Body Shop. He said he'd never be able to smell it again without thinking of her and she'd laughed so he'd Googled the thing about memories and showed her it was true. Kye. Rose's heart and stomach felt like they were playing tug of war. She should be with him now.

'God's blessings on you, Rose.' Grandma Yellow kissed the air a metre from Rose's face. 'And, you, Rudder.' She kissed *him* on the forehead, lips actually touching skin. 'You may have been steered away from the righteous life, but you will find your way back.'

Rudder gave her a little nod. His eyes were flicking backwards and forwards, as if he was trying not to look past Grandma and remember the garden beyond the back door. He rubbed his hands together. His memory must be churning up different smells to Rose's – the tang of a struck match, the stink of firelighters, scorched paper.

Grandma watched him. That's all. Just stood there watching him. Didn't she feel even a little bit guilty? Not by the looks of it. Rose turned her back on her and touched Rudder's shoulder.

'Shall we take our shoes off?'

He nodded again and slipped out of his trainers with the laces still done up. His brown socks looked dull against the light carpet. Rose pulled the bows on her Converse, tugged them off and lined them up below Rudder's shoes on the rack.

They followed Grandma Yellow into the sitting room. The cross-looking Noah was still emerging from his Ark over the fireplace, still pointing at his dove. When she was little, she'd always felt he was pointing at her. That hadn't changed, neither. Now it was like he was outraged that she'd dare to take even one step into a Pilgrim sanctuary. There was an extra Bible on the coffee table and a carefully arranged display of 'Pilgrims' Way' leaflets. There'd be boxes more of those upstairs. She saw Rudder looking at the wall of shelves either side of the door, groaning with books by Pilgrim authors. On the highest shelves were the *Libros Rojos*, the letters from the Founders. Rudder would have been old enough to handle them know. Rose had begged Mum to let her have a look at them, even though only men were supposed to touch them. Mum had double-checked that no one was around and stood on a chair and passed one down to Rose. They were all in the original Spanish with no pictures at all.

She'd asked, 'How do we know the rules are right if we can't understand them?'

'We have to trust the Elders, Rose. You know that.'

Mum had quickly slipped the book back in place and returned the chair to the kitchen. Had Granny ever found out? She probably checked the dust for prohibited fingerprints.

Rudder sat down on the sofa, knees pressed together, feet splayed. Grandma sat down next to him.

'You can sit there, Rose.'

Rose got the chair between the door and the window, the one usually reserved for the newest Sisters, married in from other sanctuaries.

Grandma turned towards Rudder, leaving Rose staring at her back.

'How is school, Rudder?' Grandma said.

She said 'school' like she'd got a pineapple stuck in her throat, skin, spikes and everything. She was probably imagining all the sinful assemblies, the PE in short skirts and vests, the condoms rolling on to giant plastic penises. Why should Rose bother saying that she'd missed all that? That actually she'd started proper school so late she'd missed learning anything that would help her have a life. That's why she had to struggle over maths and English GCSEs long after everybody else had passed theirs. At this rate, she'd still be trying to pass those damn exams when she was forty.

Grandma touched her heart. 'You were such a clever boy. Such a role model. I pray every day that you'll be saved.'

Not me, then? Rose bit her lip. That wasn't fair. Rose didn't want to be saved. Rudder was almost glowing, like he'd absorbed some of Granny's righteousness and was starting to make his own. If that was what Rudder wanted, Rose should let him have it. And maybe she would have, if she hadn't noticed him wearing his Time-Turner under his shirt. If she hadn't seen him straighten his Marauder's Map over his bed before they left.

She craned round Grandma's back and smiled at Rudder. 'We're doing okay, aren't we, Ruds?'

Rudder ignored her.

Grandma leaned in. 'We need young leaders, Rudder. As the world spins towards its destruction, we need more righteous Pilgrims to spread the word. Atone, Rudder, and pray.' She sat back. 'Rose?'

'Yes, Grandma?' Why did Rose automatically hush her voice? Even now?

'Are you and your brother still sharing a room?'

'Yes, Grandma.'

Grandma leaned forward and placed her hand on one of the Bibles on the coffee table. Her thumbs pressed into the hard cover as she muttered a prayer for them.

Rudder looked genuinely in pain. 'I'm sorry, Grandma.

I don't want to, but we've only got one bedroom.'

You shouldn't be the one saying sorry! Look how big this woman's house is. But Grandma was happy to sit there and let Rudder think everything was still his fault.

Rose said, 'I thought we were meeting Dad.'

'He'll be back soon.'

Grandma leaned towards Rudder again and started talking quietly so that Rose couldn't hear. A smile flickered across Rudder's lips. Rose wanted to go and plant herself right between them, or pull Rudder to his feet and take him out to the garden to remind him how this all started. She dug her nails into the cushion. Mum had made it clear last night. It was the extra money Grandma sent that helped them survive. Who cared if it was guilt money? Without it, they'd be on the street.

It was starting to rain outside. The woman in the house opposite killed the electricity on her power saw and untangled the lead from the branches. She'd only trimmed half the hedge. The hacked branches were heaped on the pavement. She grabbed a few armfuls and dropped them into a wheelbarrow.

A car drew up outside, taking a few attempts to nudge into a tight space. Finally, it stopped and the door opened. Grandma smiled, but Rudder's face changed.

He whispered, 'Dad?'

Did Dad look different now? Rose thought of when Rudder was little, and how he used to turn all his Lego men

71

into Pilgrims. He must have been inspired by Dad, with his short, dark hair and the slight shininess to his skin. Like the Lego men, Dad wore the same Pilgrim clothes every day and his expression never seemed to change. Even Dad's hands seemed curved, ready for a Bible or *Libro Rojo* to slip between his thumb and fingers. Only one of his hands was like that now. The other was trailing back, holding Lily-Beth's.

Rose had never seen Dad hold Mum's hand, ever. And the time Dad should have kept hold of Rudder's, he let go.

But Rose couldn't think about that now. Rudder must have seen what she just had. There was no way he could have missed it.

Lily-Beth was pregnant, so pregnant her stomach was bulging out from her coat. She was pregnant in a way that Dad had not bothered telling any of them before.

Grandma stood up. She looked from Rose to Rudder. 'The fruit of the womb is our Lord's reward for us.'

She glided out of the room and into the hallway. Rose heard the front door open. Rudder closed his eyes, the way he did when he was trying to catch the tears before they escaped.

She said, 'Ruds? Are you okay?'

'Did you know about the baby?'

'Of course not. I don't think even Mum knows, or she would have warned us.'

'Dad doesn't need me now.'

Rose shifted from the armchair to the sofa. 'Rudder, when

I knew Mum was having you, I didn't think you were replacing me. I wanted a brother or sister.'

'But that was different. We lived together.'

'Believe me, Ruds, for the first three years, I wished we didn't. You had croup and—'

He moved away from her across to the other side of the sofa.

Rose was clenching her teeth again.

'Okay, Rudder. This isn't the time for one of your dramatic moments. We always knew this was going to happen as soon as Dad got married again. We just have to get through it, for Mum's sake.'

Rudder answered with a sniff. Any second now, one of Rose's molars was going to pop through her cheek.

Grandma and Dad were talking in the hallway. Lily-Beth was probably standing a respectful couple of paces back, though with her stomach that big she couldn't get any closer or she'd knock Grandma over. Rose strained harder to listen. Dad was arguing that a pregnant woman shouldn't have to take off her shoes. Fraud! He'd never stood up for Mum like that! Lily-Beth was siding with Grandma. She'd learned quickly. A good Pilgrim wife always obeyed her husband – unless her husband's mother was Grandma Yellow.

The door opened wider. Dad didn't even have the decency to look sorry. 'Rose. Rudder. Thank you for coming.'

Rudder was giving him his angry owl stare. Dad tested a

smile. Rudder carried on staring.

Dad cocked his head sideways. 'Aren't you coming over to say hello, Rudder?'

You could have visited us and said hello any time, Dad.

Rudder stood up slowly, eyes on his feet, and shuffled over to Dad's hug. Rose saw Lily-Beth come behind Dad, her smile struggling to stay fixed. Dad held Rudder's shoulders, bent forward and kissed his forehead, right on top of his mother's kiss. It was like Rudder only had one spot that wasn't tainted.

'Say hello to Lily-Beth.' Dad stroked Lily-Beth's stomach. 'And your new little brother.'

Brother? Rudder stepped back. Rose heard the click of his heels against the door frame.

'We are blessed,' Grandma said.

Lily-Beth nodded and looked up as if she expected Jesus himself to drop through the ceiling to bless her in person. Dad nudged Rudder forward and he almost bounced off Lily-Beth's belly. Lily-Beth sort of patted Rudder's head then moved back behind Dad.

'Ruds?' It hurt Rose to look at him.

He still wouldn't meet her eye, but her voice seemed to guide him back to the sofa. He sat down. Dad turned towards Rose, but his glance skidded away from her. She wasn't wearing Pilgrim, but she was doing her best not to embarrass him. He obviously didn't care.

'Lily-Beth, come with me.' Grandma's voice from the

hallway. 'I've made cake. Rose and Rudder, I'll bring yours in.'

'One moment.' Dad followed Lily-Beth out.

Rudder was studying his hands. 'It's my fault Mum and Dad split up in the first place.'

Rose reached for his hand, but he pulled it away. 'It's not your fault, Rudder. None of this was ever your fault.'

'I shouldn't have read the books. I knew they were prohibited and I still read them. I let the Devil into my heart.'

'Reading books doesn't make you the Devil's agent, Rudder.'

'I should have prayed harder.'

'That wouldn't have made a difference.'

Poor Ruds. He'd been too busy winning scripture competitions to realise what Mum was doing. Why did he think Mum let them join a library in the first place? She had certainly never gone to the Actualizar Committee to get that passed!

Rose said, 'Haven't you ever wondered why Mum didn't report our prohibited toys?'

'I thought that maybe she'd checked with Dad and he didn't mind.'

Or maybe you enjoyed playing with them and you didn't want to ask questions, Ruds.

She had to go easy on him. 'I think she didn't want us to be too separate. She believed we needed to know about the worldly world. Just in case.'

His eyes finally met hers. 'In case of what?'

'In case something happened.'

Rudder didn't look away. Grandma's righteousness had definitely got to him. It was radiating from his eyes. 'Something did happen. We left, and now Dad's having another baby.'

'This is for you.'

Grandma pushed the door open. She was holding a tray. She laid it on the coffee table between the Bibles. There were two glasses of juice and two slices of cake with zigzag white icing. Rose could smell it. Lemon. The only cake Rose hated. It tasted like someone had poured washing-up liquid over it.

Rudder's fingers seemed to be having an argument, reaching towards the cake, then stopping. Like him, she'd struggled to eat her toast this morning and now her stomach was empty. Suddenly, he broke off a lump of cake and took a big bite.

Grandma sighed. 'No blessings?'

Rudder dropped his cake, bowed his head and his mouth moved. Grandma turned her steely eyes on Rose. Rose returned her gaze in full.

'Mother?' came a voice from the kitchen.

Lily-Beth called Grandma 'Mother'? Mum used to call her . . . Rose frowned. Had their Mum ever called her anything other than 'your grandmother'?

Lily-Beth poked her head around the door. Her face was

sweaty and a few stray hairs were pasted to her forehead. 'Amos says are you taking sugar in your tea?'

'Tell Amos I'm coming.' Grandma Yellow threw a quick smile to Rudder. 'And you tell your sister to bring the tray to the kitchen when you're done.'

Grandma backed out, clicking the door shut behind her. Rudder stared at the closed door. There was a smear of icing across his upper lip. Rose felt a shiver of anger. How could Dad invite Rudder here and just leave him? But then, how could Rudder still want to walk through that door after them? It was like he kept standing up just so someone could knock him down again.

She said, 'You realise we're not allowed to eat with them any more.'

'That's not true.' Rudder nibbled at a flake of icing. 'Maybe they have stuff to do.'

Stuff? 'If they had so much stuff to do, they shouldn't have invited us. They're making a point. We don't belong.'

He was owl-glaring her now. 'You don't belong. You don't want to. I do.'

'Jesus, Rudder!'

He lurched forward, like he was going to touch one of Grandma's Bibles. He stopped himself in time. 'Please don't blaspheme in here, Rose.'

She took a deep breath. She had to control this. If Grandma Yellow walked in and saw them rucking, there was no way they would be getting more money.

'Sorry, Ruds. You have to remember that I was here before it was this strict. You know I used to go to a worldly primary school until those . . . those Founders prohibited us from eating in the same room as the Worldly Wise. My school couldn't guarantee a separate supervised space for me outside the canteen, so I was taken out. I didn't want to go. I loved it there, but who cared what I wanted? I was home-schooled for a while, then the Pilgrim Free School started up.'

Rudder wiped his mouth. 'I liked our Pilgrim School.'

'It's the only school you've known, Ruds.'

'No, it's not! You don't know what school's like for me now. I don't want to be there. But who cares what I want?'

The door opened again. Dad pushed it shut, leaning against it. There was a moment's silence. Rudder looked like he was going to say something, but his eyes dropped from Dad to his not-Columba socks. Dad didn't seem to have many words, neither.

It would have to be Rose. 'Dad?'

At least he managed to look at her. 'Yes, Rose?'

'When's the baby due?'

'At the end of June.'

'In three months' time?' Why was she surprised? Lily-Beth looked ready to have it on Grandma's carpet. But still. 'You've known for ages. Why didn't you tell us before?'

Dad licked his top lip. 'In the past, Lily-Beth incurred God's wrath. We wanted to be sure that this time she had been forgiven and blessed.'

God's wrath? Rose frowned. Isn't that what they said when Auntie Eunice was pregnant and rushed to the worldly hospital? She'd incurred God's wrath. That's why she came back without a baby and no one was allowed to mention it.

'Sorry, Dad. Do you mean that you and Lily-Beth . . . that this isn't the first time she's been pregnant?'

'Yes, Rose.'

'With . . . with you?'

He didn't reply, but the air in the room felt thinner.

Rose said, 'You've only been married for six months. Mum says it was virtually the same day your divorce came through.'

'Don't play stupid, Rose. You know the marriage bond with your mother was broken when she left.'

'She was excised, Dad. Thrown out. She didn't have a choice.'

'Yes, she did, Rose. Your mother made choices long before Rudder's— before the accident.'

The *accident*? What was the accident bit of it? She glanced at Rudder. He'd slid his hands between his bum and the sofa seat, like he was trying to hide the evidence. Was it only Rose who really remembered what happened that night?

She said, 'I was there too, Dad. It wasn't an accident.'

'Yes, it was.' Rudder's eyes were on Dad. 'It was my fault.'

Dad? Are you going to put him right? Make him understand it wasn't his fault! Dad stayed silent. If that's how he wanted it, Rose would make him talk.

'You committed adultery, Dad.'

Rudder gasped. Dad drew himself upright. 'Do not use that tone in this house.'

'"*Whosoever shall put away his wife, except it be for fornication, and shall marry another, committeth adultery.*" Isn't that what it says, Dad? "*And whoso marrieth her which is put away doth commit adultery.*"'

'Do not taint the scriptures!'

'You cheated on Mum. We'd hardly been in the hostel any time before she got the letter asking her for a divorce. You probably couldn't wait for Mum to go.'

'God is our authority!' Dad's voice exploded out of him. 'He is our ultimate judge! He judged your mother sinful!'

Dad was using his height like a proper preacher, making his words fall down heavy. He knew that Rose, sitting there on the sofa, would have to look up at him. Everything she wanted to say dropped back down her throat.

'Your mother's family were always weak to temptation. I can see that weakness in you, Rose, the cracks where sin blossoms and grows.'

The worldly cracks. The ones Rose was trying to squeeze her way through. Dad's face had changed. There was still righteousness, he wouldn't be a Pilgrim without it, but he was showing Passion. You were supposed to keep your most powerful emotions for worship. Dad bit his lip and

80

slowly his face smoothed out.

He said, 'You're nearly eighteen, Rose.'

A few seconds ago, she would have answered him back. 'I thought Pilgrims didn't have birthdays.' Or, 'Yes, Dad. Have you found me a husband yet?' But now she couldn't talk, only look. The Passion was gone, but there was something in the slow blink of his eyes, the way he was clasping his hands behind his back and rubbing his thumbs together. The precise red triangle of handkerchief in his jacket pocket flashing her a warning.

She swallowed hard. 'Yes, Dad. I'm nearly eighteen. Why?'

Rudder shifted next to her. His hands were on his lap, clasped like Dad's. He was leaning forward as if he was waiting to be summoned.

She said, 'So what are your plans for my eighteenth?'

Rudder nudged her back. 'Stop it, Rose.'

Didn't he realise this was about him too? Dad drew himself up, inflating with Testament.

'You've chosen the worldly path, Rose. You are—'

'A Devil's agent.' Rudder's whisper from behind her. She turned round to glare at him, but it was like he'd been hypnotised.

'After . . . after . . . Lily-Beth incurred God's wrath, my mother and I sought God's counsel and forgiveness. We consulted the scriptures and instructions and Elder Enoch became our intermediary with the Founders. The answer was clear. We cannot, must not, in God's eyes, uphold your

81

sinful life, Rose.'

Rose stood up. He couldn't mean . . . 'You're taking away our money? I don't understand!'

'Your sinful life cannot—'

'Dad! You can't blame me if . . . if the first pregnancy didn't work out! You can believe it's God's fault, if you want, but it's not mine!'

The Passion was fighting its way back through Dad. He turned away from her towards Rudder.

'The agreement is to support your sister, Rudder, until her eighteenth birthday. I will fulfil that promise.'

'Just three months more and then you're stopping? And after that? Mum still has to pay rent and food for both of us. Ruds doesn't even bring home letters about school trips because he knows we can't afford it.'

Rudder stood up too. It was like they were all going to start dancing. 'I don't want to go anyway.'

Oh, come on, Ruds! 'But you want to eat, though. Dad, Rudder missed lunch yesterday because Mum couldn't top up his lunch account.'

Dad's expression didn't change. 'She can claim support from your government.'

'It's not that easy! She's trying, but it takes ages. She's got all these jobs, but it's still not enough. Sometimes she gets food from . . . from worldly churches. Worldly churches feed your son! Is that what you want?'

'I don't want to eat that food, Dad.'

Dad brushed past Rose and placed a gentle hand on each of Rudder's cheeks. 'I believe you, Rudder.'

He kissed Rudder's forehead again. There must be a dent from so many kisses. Dad pulled his wallet out of his jacket pocket, took out a twenty-pound note and placed it on the coffee table. Then he left. Just like that. No more words, not even 'goodbye'. He just opened the door, went down the hallway and into the kitchen to eat cake with the non-sinners.

She said, 'The best thing we did was leave all this.'

'No, it wasn't!'

She grabbed Rudder's hand and held it up. 'Really, Ruds? Really? Do you think stuff like this happens to the Worldly Wise if they read a book?'

He yanked his hand away. 'You were disrespectful to Dad. You didn't have to be.'

'Bloody hell, Rudder! Didn't you hear what Dad said?' If she came out with what was in her head right now, it would make all the *Libros Rojos* scorch and crisp. She lowered her voice. The last thing she needed was Dad and Grandma Yellow running in to take Rudder's side. 'He's stopping my support. In three months' time, we'll be getting half the money, Ruds. How's Mum going to cope now?'

'You should have thought about that before you were rude to him. They'll probably never let me come back because of you. You!' He poked her in the stomach. The little demon – yes, actual bloody demon – poked her.

83

She made her fingers lock into each other, tried to breathe out her anger, or there wouldn't be enough angels left in heaven to judge her if she did what she wanted to do to Rudder right now.

'Think hard,' she said, quietly, 'about all the things that happened to you here. Think really hard about that last evening, Rudder. And you know where we're standing, don't you?' She pointed up. 'Right under the room where Mum was shut away, again and again. You haven't forgotten how Mum was always in atonement, right? It's like they brought in new rules especially for Mum to break.' All of them, hidden away in sheathes of declarations that arrived every Thursday. Rose used to be allowed to watch Dad unwrap them, punch holes in their margins, hook them through the metal clasps of the *Libros Rojos* and snap them shut. Grandma Yellow made her stop when she'd turned twelve.

She watched Rudder's face working through his emotions. It was like there were mini-conveyor belts under his skin, all going in different directions. He glanced up at the *Libros Rojos* and the shelf of Bibles below it. He'd memorised the first line in every book of the Old Testament by the time he was nine. It was a pity that Pilgrims cut short the New Testament. Romans, both Corinthians and James, plus Revelation, wasn't much of a challenge for him to remember. The Pilgrim Elders had thought he was specially blessed, though.

He said, 'I want to be here because it's safe.'

He opened the door and left her there. She heard his light tap on the kitchen door, and it opening. She shut the sitting room door, sat down on the sofa arm and rubbed her face with her palms. It didn't get rid of the tightness, but if she'd had her fairy kei face on, she'd have smeared her eyebrows down to her mouth. Yeah, then she would have burst into the kitchen and scared the heaven out of all four of them. *Look at me! I really am the Devil! A pink sparkly one!*

Bloody Rudder! The little traitor. How could he think this place was safe? He'd almost lost the use of his hands here. What did he want to do, martyr himself? She imagined him slowly starving himself to death rather than touching food that a worldly had touched before him. Damn him! Seriously, damn him right down to the bottom of the hell that he thought was real.

She had to get out of here, now. Dad was right about the way sin blossomed and grew. Hers was now the size of one of those giant trees that look like their roots must drill down to the earth's core. She could feel it stretching through her, down to the tips of her fingers, making her long to tear every one of those books from Grandma's shelves.

Grandma's wall clock said 11.45. There was another place her sin could take her – back to the station and on the bus to Kye. There was still time. She'd probably be early. She stood up and closed the sitting room door quietly behind her.

She reached for the front door latch and heard a sniff.

Rudder was standing at the other end of the hallway, between the prayer room and the kitchen. Both doors were closed. He was holding a plate with another slice of cake, using both hands like it was too heavy.

They'd opened the door, passed him more food and shut him out again. Dad may have kissed him, but Rudder was still a worldly. He was prohibited from eating with them. He was prohibited from praying with them.

He must have heard her come out, but he wouldn't look up. *Still want to come back, Ruds?*

If she could work out the way to the station, she could be with Kye in an hour. He'd probably still be in bed. He'd open his door, smelling of sleep, maybe just his joggers on, no top. He'd smile at her and he'd take her hand and she'd follow him in. She'd reach round and hug him to her, burying her face in the mussed-up softness of his hair.

Rudder sniffed again. He was crying, but still holding on to the plate. She went over to him, took it from him and put it on the floor. She wiped his eyes with the back of her hands. She could hear them in the kitchen, Dad leading a canta and the women singing the chorus. It was one Rose didn't recognise.

He said, 'They won't let me in.'

'I know.'

Rose imagined releasing Kye, walking away as he called after her.

'Come on.' She led Rudder back to the sitting room and

86

picked up Dad's twenty-pound note. 'I saw they were showing Kiki's Delivery Service in a cinema near the station.' She nudged him. 'It's got a talking cat.'

And witches. But for now, she'd keep that to herself.

7

Rose lay back on her bed and watched a spot of weak light scribbling lines across the ceiling. Rudder and that bloody torch pen. He must be casting spells again. Why couldn't he cast one to calm Mum down? She'd had to go to her late shift after hearing Dad's news and be nice to drunk people who'd muddled up their pizza orders. Before going to bed, Rose had pulled out the sofa bed and tidied the sheets ready for when she got back. Rudder had placed Mum's slippers together neatly and folded her leggings and t-shirt on her pillow.

Rose rattled the clothes rail. 'Do you really have to do that now?'

The light disappeared. She imagined it as a bubble beneath his duvet, running up and down the pages of his book.

A flicker of light between the clothes. 'I'm reading.'

'I know. What?'

His hand appeared between her Sailor Moon skirt and his school trousers, holding a 'Pilgrims' Way' leaflet.

'You can't be serious, Rudder!'

His hand disappeared. She really needed more strength than she had right now to deal with him. She checked her phone. No data for another three days. Great. She rolled over and held her phone towards the window. Damn. Café Hacked had added a password to get into their Wi-Fi. She could still send texts though, but Kye hadn't answered her last ones. There'd been nothing since half four. What the hell had he been doing for the last six hours?

She sat up and looked through the window. Three lorries were queueing to get in the cash and carry. Another lorry was already parked, its cargo being unloaded on to pallets. Soon it would drive off, light and empty. Why the hell wasn't it that easy with the Pilgrims? Every time you thought you were free, more guilt got loaded on.

She lay down again. She wasn't sleepy, but what else was she going to do? Telly was crap tonight and Pilgrim hell would freeze over before they could afford Netflix. She closed her eyes.

BANG.

The windows shook. Rose's eyes snapped open. Her heartbeats were racing to overtake each other, her breath tangling in her ribs.

'It's a lorry.' Rudder had pushed up the window and was leaning out. 'It's gone into a bollard.'

Rose placed her hand on the middle of her chest, rubbing gently. Massage was supposed to make you relax, slow things down. No one had told her heart that.

'Man,' Rudder said. 'They're really yelling at each other now!'

'The driver and the bollard?'

89

Rudder laughed. 'No, the driver and the guy who's in charge.'

Yes, Rose could hear the voices, short loud bursts, like barking dogs.

She said, 'Go to sleep, Rudder. You know you can never get up in the morning.'

He groaned, but she heard him thump back on to the bed. 'Rose?'

'Yes?'

'Is Mum back soon?'

'No. She sent a text. She said the agency lied about how many offices she's supposed to clean. It's taking her longer than she thought.'

'I thought she was at the pizza place?'

'She was. She finished at ten and then had to go back and sort out the rest of the offices.'

'Do you think she'll be really late?'

'Probably after midnight, she said.'

'Can I go and watch a DVD?'

'No, Rudder! Go to sleep!'

'I'm not tired.'

There was a slight whisper as he shifted in his bed, drawing up his knees and turning himself into a comma.

She closed her eyes again.

Bang.

And another one. It was in her head this time, but it still made her heart start up again.

Bang.

Rose turned over and buried her face in her pillow, pulling the ends over her ears. It just made the sound louder inside her memories.

Bang.

The small bookshelf on Grandma Yellow's landing toppled over. The thud, thud, thud of books slamming against the walls and ceiling like they'd been fired from machine guns. Rose cowering under her duvet as the footsteps moved downstairs, books smashing against the other side of her bedroom door.

Bang.

Spines split, covers bent, pages splayed, though she hadn't seen any of that because, at first, everything was dark. When the banging stopped, the shriek had almost cut her in two.

'Demons!'

Silence. Then Grandma had opened Rose's door. She hadn't been alone. She was the leader, rallying her army. Aunty Deborah. Aunty Esther. Aunty Elizabeth. All in a row at the end of Rose's bed, blocking the light from the hallway, casting their deep shadows over her.

'Demons!' Grandma's voice was low and angry now. 'Which agent of the Devil brought demons into our home?'

'Demons!' The Aunties echoed her. 'God, bring us your mercy! Your mercy!'

Grandma Yellow had crouched down, her face too

close. 'Look me in the eye, Rose.'

Rose had eased the duvet from her face. Grandma was holding a book by the corner of its cover, its pages flapping open. Rose couldn't see the words, but she didn't need to. She'd read it to Rudder so many times, she could recite it as well as the Dawn Invocations.

Grandma thumped the book. 'Did you bring this devilry into my house?'

No! It was Rudder! He'd said he'd hidden it! He'd promised. And where was Dad? He had authority. He could make them close the door and go away.

'Grandma . . . ?'

'Get up, girl.'

They'd watched as her wobbly body half fell out of bed and she'd scrabbled for socks and a jumper to hide her nightdress, their voices rising in prayer, filling her room. Any moment soon, Dad would come. He'd say it was a mistake, not for Rose's sake, but for Rudder's. He wouldn't let anyone hurt Rudder.

Grandma led the group out, Rose next, the other Aunties behind her like they were stopping her from running away. She'd kept her eyes focused ahead, on the stab of Grandma's shoulders against her blouse, as her feet slid on the injured books on the landing. They marched Rose down the stairs and through the kitchen to the gathering in the back garden. Elders, Uncles, Aunties, some of them had brought their children to drink in the lesson. Mikhail had been next to

Elder Enoch. She'd tried to meet his eyes, but he'd looked away. Of course. Mikhail was an Elder's son. He could never acknowledge her again. Elder Enoch had handed Rose a Bible. She'd taken it, like God himself had forced her to accept it.

That's when she'd seen Rudder. He'd been zipped into a thick jacket, pyjamas tucked into his welly boots. The Bible in his hand looked too big for him. Dad was next to him, hands clasped behind his back, head bowed. Even Rose could see that Rudder was shivering. Why couldn't Dad see it too? Rudder's eyes widened when he saw her. Could he hear her words without her saying them? She touched her mouth. *Don't say anything, Ruds. I can take the blame. It's easier.*

Dad had lifted his head as Rose arrived and then looked away. No! He couldn't have agreed to this, could he? They must have waited until Mum wasn't there, because she definitely would have fought their corner, holding on to Rose and Rudder so tight that no one could have torn them apart.

A small mound of sticks had been carefully laid out on a paving stone in the bare flowerbed. Rose had started shivering too. The night breeze had been chilly, but that wasn't it. It was seeing Dad, still as a statue, letting these old women pull his daughter from her bed, letting his son stand, shaking, next to him. He could have put his arm round Rudder and pulled him close. Dad could have stopped this.

He could have, but he didn't.

Grandma dropped the book on to the pile of sticks. There

was a flash of light from the bathroom in a neighbour's house – someone was throwing a party. There was rough, bass-heavy music, words half-spoken, half-sung. Grandma started a canta, Aunties, Uncles and Elders following, lifting their voices to drown out the celebrations. Elder Enoch crouched down, lit a match and dropped it. The crinkle of newspapers, the stink of firelighters, the fire flaring. The plastic cover melted and shrunk away, leaving the bare bones of the book. Cardboard, paper, ink, silvery stags and dragons. The book was full of magic. It shouldn't have burned at all.

Rudder had cried, huge sobs that shook his body inside his jacket. Dad just stood there, his mouth moving in prayer. For a moment, he'd taken hold of Rudder's hand. Then, he'd let go.

Rose opened her eyes. She must have fallen asleep. Their bedroom door was open and a wedge of light from the main room fell across the carpet. Rose waved. Mum waved back. The door closed.

Rose's List of Potential Idols to Worship That Would Upset Grandma Yellow More Than Words Can Say

Idols to worship	Notes
Emo	Not much different from old clothes
K-Pop	Some K-Pop stars are actual idols. Need a better internet connection and memory to remember everyone. Some groups have more members than the Pilgrim prayer circles.
Gamer	Millions of games with millions of players around the world. Lots of cult games to play that people spend all day worshipping. That bit's too much like being a Pilgrim.
Duran Duran	Mum says this was a thing when she was a teenager on the outside. Looked at one of Duran Duran's videos. I'm not riding an elephant or a boat.

Harry Potter	Claimed and earned by Rudder
Football team	WHICH ONE??
Druid	Worth it because it would really upset Grandma Yellow. I don't know how to do it, though. I haven't seen many brown Druids, but I haven't looked very hard.
Samuel Shenton, Flat Earther	Might as well stay a Pilgrim
?	
?	

8

A stretched-out Sunday. A nothing-to-do Sunday. That's what Rose had always wanted, waking up early, just so she could go back to sleep again. Falling out of bed around midday. Lying on the sofa with her breakfast tray on her stomach. *What'd be on the tray, Rose?* Toast and jam, or chocolate spread and banana, or a little stack of cute pancakes with pink icing and sugar flowers. The telly would be on, showing extreme makeover shows. People, houses and gardens all transformed from shabby to wonderful. After breakfast, Rose would do her nails, hands and feet a different colour, lilac, pink, silver, mint green.

But this was a real-life Sunday. Rudder snoring. The loud hum of the boiler as Mum ran a bath. Men yelling outside the hostel. The vampire family upstairs dropping blocks of concrete on to the floor – because that must be what they were doing to thump so loudly. And bloody, bloody Kye, who still hadn't replied.

Rose pushed aside the clothes on the rail and peeked at Rudder. He was on his back, head crooked against his usual wall of pillows like he didn't trust lying down. He'd spread his throw out on top of his duvet, and his arm was flung out over Wormtail and Prongs. A corner of the throw was flopped to the side of his chin like he'd been sucking it. At least the lorry crash hadn't made him have nightmares last night.

It was impossible to imagine Rudder marauding and solemnly swearing to get up to no good. He just didn't know how to. It hadn't stopped him adding his own footprints and name in permanent marker to the map though. And at least he was still underneath it, rather than awake and bugging her. His 'Pilgrims' Way' leaflet had slipped on to the floor next to *Prisoner of Azkaban*. They were side by side. That summed up Rudder. Why couldn't he just let go of his past life? He would hurt a lot less.

She let the clothes drop back into place and reached into her cabinet for her notebook. She was being too tough on him. Wasn't she still caught between the two worlds herself? Or else, why was she still waking up so early on a Sunday, ready for the minibus rounds to collect the Aunties and Uncles for Sunday prayer circle? They were miles away, so why could she still hear the cries of joy as the men found the Spirit, or the women singing cantas up to Heaven, or the children giggling and reciting their scripture?

And why the hell did this ever make her feel good? It wasn't good.

Rose opened the notebook and scanned her decommissioning programme. How was she doing so far? *Worship idols*. Huddled against Mum in Room 27 at the hostel, with the smell of smoke coating her skin, it had been easy to make that number one. Idols were the most prohibited thing and she'd imagined there'd be hundreds to choose from. She could never have imagined that her idol would be Kye.

She dropped the notebook on to the duvet. Kye. Was he an idol or a demon? Idols didn't entice you in, they were just objects of desire. Demons took over your mind and possessed your soul. Grandma Yellow would never understand how the constant vigilance, the barrier of prayers against everyday evil, the constant warnings, made the thought of them more exciting.

Rose checked her phone again. Where was he? She could call him, but what if he was at the hospital? Actually, that wouldn't be so bad. She could be genuinely sympathetic. She could say that she understood what it's like sitting in the waiting room, with that horrible feeling in your stomach, then walking into the ward, eyes straight ahead so you didn't feel like an intruder in all those other stories. She'd never talked to him about all that before.

She didn't want to talk to him on the phone. She wanted to see him. Not at the hospital. She couldn't just turn up on the ward, even if she knew the right one. What would she do? Slide herself between Kye and his mum and make polite conversation while Bella side-eyed her from the bed? But what if he wasn't at the hospital – what if he was still in bed, like she'd imagined yesterday? What if he tumbled out from under the covers, wiping sleep out of his eyes and saw her there on the doorstep? He'd smile. Not the 'you're-talking-Pilgrim again' smile, but the quick wide smile that had lit up his face when she'd let him unbutton her shirt. The smile that had disappeared so quickly when she'd knocked the camera from his hand.

She'd liked that smile. She knew how she could make it come back. But could she do it? Just turn up on his doorstep? One of the girls on Cast Outs kept going on about being conditioned to believe men were the ultimate authority. *They stride down the path and we follow them.*

Rose was decommissioning. She had to make her own path.

The boiler fired again and the pipes ticked. Mum was topping up her bath. Rose checked on Rudder. He was still asleep.

If, just if, she did go to Kye's, what would she wear? She unhooked a hanger from the rail. All her clothes were so tired. She needed inspiration. She pulled out her phone and googled. Buffer. Buffer. Buffer. No connection. Of course, the bloody café had a new Wi-Fi password. She flung the phone on her bed. She didn't need help. Kye was always clear about the stuff he liked.

She spread out two skirts on her bed. What about the pastel rainbow tutu? No. Kye said it reminded him of Angelina Ballerina. He'd had to show Rose a picture for her to get it – Angelina was a dancing mouse. Rose hadn't expected that. She'd go for the stripy blue and yellow knee-

100

length skirt with the pink t-shirt and lilac jacket. She looked best with her hair pulled back, even if her roots were coming through. She'd have to have a go at it with the straighteners to get it through the bun ring, but the socket was over on Rudder's side. She'd keep her make-up calm except for the dark pink lipstick, the really shiny one. Not proper fairy kei, but Kye liked it.

So, yes. She was going to do it. She was going to get the bus, climb the stairs to Kye's flat and knock on his door. He'd open it and see her and— Unless, what if he didn't answer because he was with the blonde girl, or the black girl with the boobs, or even someone else?

Her stomach was prickling. He could be. Or he might be sitting there too busy sulking about yesterday to tell her how much he wanted to see her. She laid the clothes out on her bed. She'd wear tights and shorts under her skirt as she'd probably go up to the top deck. Phones in Japan had to make a sound when they took a photo to stop perverts snapshotting up girls' skirts. They should do that here.

She checked the time on her phone. Twelve minutes past eight. It was still so early.

She opened the bedroom door and closed it quietly behind her. She almost jumped in the air.

'Mum?'

Mum was on the sofa sipping a mug of tea. The *Sunday Mirror* was spread out in front of her. 'Good morning, Rose.'

'I thought you were in the bath.'

'It must be the lot upstairs freshening up after a night draining jugulars.' Mum showed Rose her arm. 'Me, I'm as clean as I can get. Pit me against any Devil's agent and they'd just slide off my pure and spotless form.' Mum shifted her feet so Rose could sit down. Her toenails were sparkling with Rose's Mermaid Shimmy nail varnish. 'Yesterday was a stupid idea. I should have thought it through more before sending you to your father's. But I just hoped . . .'

Rose could feel the hard ridges of Mum's feet through her leggings. 'You were right to try. You weren't to know about the baby.'

'I can count months, Rose. I should have seen it coming. I know how it works. As soon as they were married, it was their duty to increase the numbers of good Pilgrim stock. I'm surprised it took them so long.'

Rose bit her lip. Mum bent over and flipped a newspaper page. It landed on the horoscopes. Mum had circled the one with the woman holding scales. 'Mum?'

'Yes?'

'Are you happier now?'

'You had sixteen years of them, Rose. I had thirty. In spite of everything, I feel born again. Every day. But I can't help wishing there was an instruction manual for worldly life.'

'Written on a scroll by quill for Rudder.'

'Yes.' Mum laughed. 'Definitely.'

'He really wants to go back.'

Mum sighed. 'I know.'

'What if they decide to let him in again?'

'I wish he'd understand that it won't solve all his problems.' She flicked over another page. 'When my family were allowed back in, I filled my head so full of teachings there was no room for anything else. When you were born, and then Rudder, it was like being torn in half. I still tried to make myself believe. I could shout as loud as anyone about the evil Worldly Wise, but somehow I still ended up going against your grandmother and sending you to a worldly school.'

'Poor Miss Wormwood.'

'Yes. She was only doing what she thought was right.'

Miss Wormwood, the only teacher Rose really remembered. She must have been the same age as Mum and it had been a shock seeing her in those skirts that stopped at her knees. Her hair had been twisted into thin dreadlocks that she coiled onto the top of her head. Each day she'd have a different colour butterfly clip to hold them in place. Rose used to try and remember which colour went with which day. Grandma Yellow had met her once, when Grandma'd had to collect Rose from school. Rose had heard Grandma shouting later. Dad should be ashamed. He'd let Satan talk him into exposing Rose to his sinful agent who blatantly flaunted the style of drug-taking idol-worshippers.

The last thing Miss Wormwood had done before Rose was whisked off to join the Pilgrims' Free School was to persuade Mum to let Rose join the library. That had been the best part of the week, racing up the library steps and into the open reception, looking around to check she and Mum hadn't been seen, weaving through the bookcases to the children's section. Then checking out the Harry Potters, one at a time, with Mum shifting them into her shopping trolley as quickly as possible.

'I showed you a glimpse of outside,' Mum said. 'I of all people should have realised what it was doing to you. It's so hard going against everybody you know, everything you've ever thought. Though this –' she waved her hand around the room – 'this isn't what I had in mind when we left.'

Rose bobbed forward and kissed Mum's cheek. 'It's much better than the hostel, and anyway, it won't always be like this this.'

'I'm worried it's going to get worse.'

'I can get a job. We'll be okay.'

'Yes. I'm sure we will. I shouldn't be pessimistic.' Mum tore a corner off her newspaper. Rose saw a scribbled word on it. 'Here's the café password. There's a muffin in the kitchen. I had to buy it out of guilt. Save half for Rudder, will you?'

'Thank you. And Mum?'

'Rose?'

'I'll be going out later.'

Mum had flipped back to the horoscope and was running her finger along the small print. 'Where?'

To make a beautiful demon smile. 'To the library to do some homework.'

'Pleased to hear it.' Mum tapped her newspaper. 'And, according to my stars, better luck is on its way.'

Kye must really be a demon to make Rose lie so easily.

9

Rudder opened his eyes. His shoulder was hurting. He lifted his body and felt underneath. He'd been lying on his alarm clock. He dug it out and stood it on the windowsill. It was nearly 10 a.m. The fringe of his throw was wet against his cheek. He must have been sucking it in his sleep again. What would happen if he ate a whole throw? He'd be like that man on TV who had to finish giant burgers and mega-hot chilli chicken. His stomach would get bigger and bigger and when he got towards the end, he'd have to pull the throw apart and swallow it one thread at a time with some milkshake to mix up the flavours. When it was all eaten, it would come together again in his stomach and make him feel warm inside.

He sat up and peered through the clothes. Rose's bed was mussed up, but she wasn't in it. He wrapped the throw round his shoulders and went into the main room. No Rose and no Mum, neither. Mum must be at work and Rose . . . he wasn't even going to think about that. She was so full of sin that it must have burst out of her and carried her away on a wave of it. All that sin had splashed on him too, or else Dad wouldn't have . . . he wouldn't have let them shut the kitchen door again.

It wasn't just Rose's fault. Rudder had forgotten that prayers didn't work if you said them in secret. They had to be shouted out loud. '*This is the day which the Lord hath made; we will rejoice and be glad in it.*' Rudder could rejoice properly now, while no one was here. He closed his eyes, but the words wouldn't come. Of course they wouldn't. He'd clothed himself in worldly magic. Rudder let the throw drop to the floor and nudged it away with his foot. He closed his eyes again. Still nothing. He knew the prayers were there, but it was like they were hiding behind a thick, black brain curtain. He was like Kiki in the film yesterday. She'd lost her witching powers because she wasn't happy, but they'd come back to her at the end. His prayers would return. They *would*.

Though he had to stop thinking about witches.

And avoid all worldly temptations.

He went back into the bedroom and sat on the bed. All his old friends would be gathered in the hall by the canal, studying their Bibles and singing their praises. He'd have been with the other boys, right at the front, mouthing the words, knowing them without looking at the thin, cream pages. He'd felt it, every time, his body filling with so much light and air he had to grip the back of the chair in front in case he took off and soared around the room. Today his body was full of stones. All he had to do was let his head empty so the prayer could come in. He'd done it so many times. He crossed his legs. His knees started to hurt. He moved on to the floor and kneeled, squeezing his eyes shut.

Yes! It was happening! The feeling! Inside his head was so light he could float away. The prayers were coming! The Spirit!

His eyes snapped open. Rudder had to breathe, but his breath was climbing steps across his lungs. Instead of prayer, his head was full of whirring pedals, a thud, a quiet scream.

Bella was in hospital and he still hadn't made amends.

He stood up again. His Columba robes were there, hanging from the back of the door. His breathing seemed to come easier as he looked at them. '*Blessed is the man that endureth temptation for when he is tried, he shall receive the crown of life, which the Lord hath promised to them that love him.*' And that's what the robes were doing, tempting him. Rudder knew it. He must resist. He reached out and touched them. He would unhook the robes and burn them, right here, right now. There'd be no more temptation. No, he couldn't do that in the flat. He wouldn't receive the crown of life if he burned down his bedroom. But he could drop the robes in the kebab shop's wheelie bin. He'd poke them into one of those big oily tins so they'd be spoiled for good.

He took the robes off the hook. He buried his nose into the fabric and sniffed hard. It felt like magic was stealing through him. '*Blessed is the man that endureth temptation.*' Rudder would be blessed, just after this one last time. He slipped his arms into the sleeves, went back into the main room and turned the television on. Two old guys were cooking and talking. He switched over. This was better, an

American comedy, one he liked. There was a character that didn't always get stuff the way other people did so his friends laughed at him, but he was the cleverest and he didn't care. He also had his special spot on the sofa. Rudder wished he had the same – a special spot that Rose and Kye would never dare go near.

He went and unplugged his phone from the charger. Mum had left him a note underneath it. She'd got the call from the catering agency. If she didn't say 'yes', she'd go to the bottom of their list. Then there was loads about the mess Rose had left in the bathroom. Rudder stuck his head round the bathroom door. Rose's make-up tubes and brushes were piled up by the sink and a clump of hair was stuck in the plug hole. Mum had also left half a muffin in the kitchen. Rudder closed the bathroom door quickly, found the muffin and settled on the sofa, hoisting up his feet so he was in a Columba cocoon.

Rose said he must never tell Mum how much he missed Dad on Sundays. They didn't like Rudder remembering the good times, like when he and Dad had sneaked off between prayer circles to collect all the big autumn leaves from the park by the cemetery. They'd taken a bag of them home and the next day they'd brushed them with paint and made prints. Dad was the one who'd read Rudder his first Bible stories, making all the sounds as Noah and Shem led the animals on to the Ark. Dad always put his hand on Rudder's shoulder as they walked to the Men of God section of the hall. Dad would do all that with his new son instead.

The American comedy show was over. A happy woman was telling everyone why she liked her mop and showing how clean her floor was. Rudder rolled off the sofa and back to the TV. He changed the channel. This was better! He hammered up the volume. It was a show about musicals. They were talking about *West Side Story*. He turned the volume up even higher and touched his heart. It was already doing the la, la, la, la America beat. Were they going to show it? Were they? They were! He stood up, stretching out his spine and his chest. Anita was in her purple dress, spinning and swishing her skirts, then it was over to Bernardo and his friends in their smart suits and thin ties.

Rudder ran over and slid the latch on the door, then took up his position in the middle of the room, arms held high, robes spread wide. Ole! He spun left. He spun back around again. He let his robes drop to the floor. His arms were Anita's arms, swaying like a Whomping Willow branch, then thrust out to ward away danger. He swooped, he jumped, he sang, because he knew. He understood. Things didn't always turn out how you expected. Sometimes you left everything familiar behind, like Anita had done, and you believed what everybody said – that the world was better somewhere else. Then it wasn't better. Rudder spun and spun and spun. Then he dropped on to the sofa, his breath popping out in short puffs, his face slick with sweat.

The programme moved on. It was *The Sound of Music*

next. Rudder needed to add 'America' to his playlist. He picked up his phone. He had a message. The only messages he usually had were from Mum and Rose. The caller's number was withheld. Maybe Dad? No, Dad would never, ever have a mobile phone. And this wasn't a word message, it was a picture. He tapped on it. A girl was sitting on a bed. He couldn't see her face, but he could see . . . he could see . . . Her legs were crossed, she was wearing underwear, but just on her bottom half. Her shirt was open and she was leaning forward so her immodesty filled her screen. There was writing across it. It said: *'Next time it's Rose.'*

God shoved him in the back. He fell forward on to his knees, clamping his hands together.

Blessed is the man that endureth temptation. Blessed is the man that endureth temptation. Blessed is the man that endureth temptation.

Rudder hadn't endured. Rudder had been tempted. He'd looked. He deserved to be punished. The more he sinned, the more punishment he should have. He squinted at the picture again. It wasn't Rose, but this was a warning. She was going to be punished too.

10

Sunday buses were busy. Rose had instantly picked out the churchgoers – women in wigs and smart coats, or long dresses in bright purples, oranges and greens with matching head wraps. If they had any idea where Rose was heading, they'd drag her along with them to pray for her.

Her finger was poised, with two stops to go. Should she send the text? Should she tell him that this time she wouldn't knock his phone away. She'd look him in the eye, unclip her bra and smile.

She rubbed her ears. If she rested them on the window, they'd burn right through the glass. The Pilgrim in her was refusing to let go. That's why she had to do this.

Point number 6 on the decommissioning list – *Beget immodesty with worldly boyfriend/s*.

Pilgrim girls who showed as much as a calf after they turned twelve had to bear witness to God's intervention. It meant sitting on the floor in the middle of a prayer circle while everyone prayed their hardest for God to save you from your worldly desires. It had happened to the Sister from Croydon. Rose had been shocked that the Sister hadn't looked even vaguely remorseful, let alone subjugated. Now Rose understood. When she slipped into her lilac camisole or baby-blue lace short skirt, she felt the threads of worldliness pressing against her skin. It had felt so heavy at first, but now it was like air.

Beget immodesty. Kye said top half pictures were normal. Everybody did it. According to Cast Outs, everybody didn't. Or they did. Or they shouldn't. Or it was their own decision as long as they knew the risks. She was obviously going to. She'd even had a go at shaving her legs. Mum's razors were pretty blunt and now Rose's legs looked like cactuses emerging from a desert, but it was better than before.

She was nearly there. The text was ready to go.

I'm on my way over.

No, that sounded too firm. She added a **xxx** to make it less harsh.

Was that better?

She could see her stop ahead. *His* stop. His block of flats was there on the other side of the road, sandwiched between the Chinese supermarket and a shoe shop. This was it. She pressed the bell button and made her way downstairs. She waited to cross the road with a couple holding several wrapped bunches of roses. Maybe one day she'd go to the flower market with Kye and that would be her grinning and clutching her flowers closer to her. She checked the panel of buzzers by the outside door. Kye's name plate was blank. Apparently his mum liked to be low-key. She took a deep breath. Decision time.

She heard a noise from behind the door. A woman came out holding a tiny, black dog in one hand. Rose had seen squirrels bigger than that. The woman smiled and held the door open.

'Are you going in?'

Rose nodded.

The woman carried on smiling. 'Nice jacket.'

Rose smiled back. 'Thank you.'

She went through and the door clicked shut behind her. She checked her phone. Her message was still waiting.

I'm on my way xxx

Send.

She climbed the stairs slowly, one flight and then the second one. Kye had been to hers more than she'd come here. Much more. It didn't seem to bother him, texting her from the street outside her door, his hand on her back as he followed her upstairs, closing the door behind them in her flat. If she was begetting immodesty, she had to mean it. She walked quickly.

This was it. Kye's door. She lifted the letterbox flap and let it fall. It stuck half way. She slapped it down and it hit the door hard. She jumped back. She was a Pilgrim. She should know how to knock on a door properly. Footsteps thudded down the hallway and the door swung open.

Kye stared at her. 'What the hell are you doing here?'

Those weren't the words he'd said in her head.

'I . . . I thought you might want to see me. I thought it would be a surprise.'

He scratched his head. 'I am surprised.'

'I couldn't help it. I wanted to see you.'

'Right.'

'After I couldn't make it yesterday.'

'Now's not a good time, Rose.'

She frowned. Was that laughter from inside? 'Have you got a girl in there?'

'Of course not!'

She tried to step around him. 'I don't believe you.'

'Rose, you just need to go.' He grabbed her wrist, his fingernails piercing through her sleeve into her skin.

'That hurts!' She tried to tug her arm away, but he was holding her too tight. 'Let go!'

'Mate! You got any snacks? Hey! Who's this?'

Kye's grip loosened. She shoved his hand away. The boy in the back of the hallway raised his eyebrows and smiled. His head was shaped like a squashed ball, shaved so close you could see the nicks on his scalp. His forehead was creased as if he had too much skin and it was trying to overlap itself. He looked like an old baby. That should be funny. But it wasn't. His eyes were like dents in the ball, thumbs pushed in just before the ball collapsed. He blinked slowly, like his eyes were snapping a picture of her.

Rose let her eyes drop, but she could tell he was still watching her.

His feet came right up to behind Kye. Kye had let him keep his trainers on. He'd always been pretty clear with Rose that she had to take her shoes off inside.

'Didn't you hear me, Kye? I said, who's this?'

'Rose.' Kye pulled her arm, guiding her towards the door. She let herself be guided. 'She didn't know I was busy.'

Suddenly, the old baby was in front of them, shunting the door shut.

'Hey! Don't leave so quickly, Rose. I'm sure we can persuade Kye to make some time for you.'

He put one arm around her and the other across Kye's shoulders. Rose wanted to shrug him off, but he was already propelling them into the sitting room where another boy was kicking back on the sofa. He looked mixed race though lighter than Rudder, with bleached curly hair, dark roots coming through. He'd kept his shoes on too, but his feet were up on the sofa, soles brushing against a cushion. He looked at her, taking her in from her ankles up. It had been a good thing to wear the shorts. It felt like extra protection.

He said, 'Are you the cult girl Kye's been on about?'

Cult girl? Rose felt a bubble of fury rising. Was that the way Kye talked about her? She turned to him.

'Kye?' He looked away. 'Okay. You were right. I should have let you know I was on my way. We can catch up later.'

116

The old baby dropped into an armchair. 'Don't go! We've got a film on. Have a look.'

Kye swore and the baby laughed. He leaned forward, tapped a laptop on the coffee table next to him and turned the screen round for Rose to see. A woman was sitting on a wooden chair. Her legs were apart, her head turned towards the camera, her arms behind her as if they'd been tied up. She was naked.

Rose felt zapped, blasted with dirt and heat, from her forehead to her chest. She wanted to scratch at her skin and peel it off. Kye lurched forward and stabbed at the laptop. The image froze on the woman's face then disappeared.

The old baby laughed. 'Not your cup of tea, Kye?'

Kye snapped the laptop cover down. 'Bastards.'

The boys just grinned back at him.

The old baby stroked the laptop cover. 'Your cult girl's a bit innocent, isn't she, Kye? I thought you were gonna sort that out.'

Kye nudged Rose's shoulder. She had to stop herself flinching. His body next to hers felt hot and tight.

He said, 'I'll see Rose to the door.'

The blond one stood up. 'She's welcome to stay.'

Old baby nodded. 'Fancy some breakfast with us, Rose?'

Rose looked away. Kye's flat had floor boards instead of carpet. They were stained a rich brown but dust was trapped between the edges. Rose wouldn't stop looking at the floor, not while those boys were looking at her. Kye was moving her now, crossing the floorboards, out the sitting room, back to the hallway.

Kye said, 'I'm sorry.'

'You're sorry? Is that it? You let your friends come here and look at stuff like that on a Sunday?' On a Sunday? Like a different day made it right? 'That woman . . .' She was open, like a house standing with its door so wide that anyone could come in and take everything they wanted.

He said, 'Forget it, Rose.'

'She was tied to a chair!' It exploded out of her. 'How the hell am I supposed to forget it?'

'It's not real.' His voice was light. 'There's worse stuff out there.'

'Worse stuff? You been checking that out too?'

'No!' He tapped the side of his head with his fingers. 'I don't mean that. It's just . . . it's just, just common. I can't really explain. I'm used to it. You're just not yet. And we weren't watching it. They put it on to wind me up.'

'Nice friends you've got, Kye.'

'They're not my friends. The one with the shaved head is my brother.'

'You've got a brother?'

Kye's arms dropped to his side. 'Briley's my half-brother, on my dad's side. You see how he is. No one says 'no' to him.' Kye came to her again and wrapped his arms around her. 'If they weren't here, of course I'd want you to stay. I wish you'd told me you were coming.'

'I did.' Her voice was tiny.

He took his phone out of his pocket and checked it. 'Ah. That was a bit late.'

'Sorry.'

'Me too.' He eased her closer, his hands beneath her jacket. His thumb was rubbing a groove in her shirt, massaging the heat and dirt deeper into her pores. She pulled away and placed a hand on the latch.

He put his hand on hers. 'Next time, let me know earlier. I'll make sure there won't be any nasties waiting for you.'

'Nasties? Is that what you call it?'

He laughed. 'It's a joke, Rose.'

She squeezed the latch. His hand pushed down harder.

She said, 'I'll be going then, Kye.'

He took his hand away and rubbed his eyes. 'Sorry, Rose. I'm a bit crap today. Everything's a bit rough right now. I really do want to see you.' He leaned in to her. 'I need you. I really am sorry about the film. I wish I could explain just how sorry I am. Please don't dump me.'

'Dump you?'

'Why would you want to be with someone who's got an idiot brother like Briley?' He took her hand. 'If you give me another chance, I'll plan our perfect Sunday together.'

The razors, the hair that was still blocking up the plug hole, the breath that couldn't make it past her throat. Demon Kye, sucking out her soul and squeezing it into nothing. He stepped back. Was he doing it so she could have a better

119

look at him? His long legs seemed wasted on a boy, his slim fingers should belong to a musician. He'd laughed when she'd asked him if he played an instrument. He'd said he had gamers' fingers, that it was evolution. She'd told him that only a few months before, she'd actually had to look up evolution. He'd laughed and hugged her closer.

'We'll meet up this week, Rose. I'll make sure of that.'

The sitting room door opened. They both looked round. No one came out, but there were sounds, a woman's voice, a chair scraping back.

'Kye! You're missing the bit where he unties her!'

Kye slammed the door shut again. 'Sorry, Rose. We'll chat later, right?'

She nodded. He opened the front door and she was back outside again. She ran down the stairs and burst out on to the street. Her shoes weren't good for running, but she could walk quickly, quickly down the hill until she was tired and needed to catch a bus.

Rudder's Top Villains

10. Stormtroopers. Because they're like robots but with people in them. No one can see who they are so they follow orders even if they're wrong.

9. Charles Darwin. Because he made mum cry when she took us to the museum. Rose said it was good tears, but mum didn't look happy.

8. The witch in Narnia. She lied to Edmund.

7. Bellatrix Lestrange. Women shouldn't be evil.

6. King Herod. He killed all the baby boys.

5. The other King Herod. It was his fault Jesus was killed.

4. The Jets. Even Tony, because of what they did to Anita. She was only helping Maria and trying to stop Tony being killed.

3. Kye. He wants Rose to be sinful.

2. The orc. His eyes are like Satan's and he hates everyone, including me.

1. Eve

11

Rudder's eyelids were pinned to his forehead. The lorries turning into the depot opposite sounded like they had rocks in their wheels. The bass booming in the cars at the red traffic light were giants' steps, stamping on the spot before running down the road. The voices at the bus stop and in and out of the take away – even the homeless man with his dog who begged for money under Sainsbury's cashpoint – sounded so close he could be hiding in the clothes rail. When Rudder rested his ear on his pillow, he could hear the thud of blood in his veins like it had been thickened with sin and was struggling to push its way through. There were words in his heartbeat.

'And the ten horns which thou sawest upon the beast, these shall hate the whore, and shall make her desolate and naked, and shall eat her flesh, and burn her with fire.'

The girl in the picture was naked, but it was Rudder who'd succumbed to worldly temptations, Rudder who was desolate and should be burned with fire – again. He'd been given a warning once before and had ignored it. He deserved the flames. The sweat and burn of them blanketed him every time he closed his eyes. He blinked. Skin melted like plastic.

'Ruds? I'm not sure if you're asleep, but you just made a really weird sound.'

A massive cough was caught in his throat. Everything was too tight to let it out.

'Rudder? You okay over there?'

Just one word. Force it through. 'No.'

He probably said it in his head because she didn't reply. The TV went silent in the main room followed by a clang and thud as Mum pulled out the sofa bed. The lid of the wooden trunk banged against the wall as she reclaimed her bedclothes. She'd be plugging in her headphones now. When he went to the toilet at night, he saw the lead trailing off the sofa on to the floor. It looked like Mum was trying to charge herself up.

'Rose?' This one came out loud.

'Yes.'

'I need to atone.'

'Sorry, Ruds. I'm really not in the mood.'

'I had a message. I don't know what to do.'

'Sorry. Nor do I.'

Cold air puffed around the crack in the sash window. The curtain fluttered. If he dared look out, he'd see the glass ice over and a hooded figure with hell-pit eyes opening its mouth to suck out his soul. No, he wouldn't. Dementors weren't real. They were part of the evil magic that was turning him worldly. He sat up, scrunching together the corners of his throw under his chin.

'Rose, Satan's trying to claim me.'

The clothes rail was shoved along so hard it banged the door. He expected Mum to come rushing in, but she didn't. Rose was sitting up in her bed. Her light was off; she was Rose by streetlamp.

'Jesus, Rudder! And don't you bloody tell me not to blaspheme!'

'I . . . I . . .'

'It's like you want to keep on hurting. You've made that choice, even when Dad and Lily-Beth slammed the door in your face. If you want to believe God's told you it's sinful to read Harry Potter, carry on, Ruds! If you want to have a big guilty drama every time you sing along to a song you like, go ahead! I've got stuff I need to work out. I haven't got room for your stuff too.'

He braced himself for the crash as the clothes rail was shunted back in place, but she just sat there. Her shoulders were moving, like she was crying. Rose never cried. He couldn't stare too hard in case she shouted again. A police car screamed past outside. When did he get to know the difference between a police car and an ambulance and a fire engine? It was definitely a police car, though. And there was another one.

Rose's shoulders stopped moving and he heard her sniff.

He said, 'Why are you crying?'

'I'm not.' Rose's nose was tipped with orange light. 'Go to sleep, Rudder. And don't worry about Satan. He has his pick

124

of way worse people than you.'

She eased the clothes rail back and Rudder heard her thump back down on to her bed. He slipped down under the duvet and closed his eyes. The immodest girl was still in his head. It was like the smell of her skin was caught in his pillow case. The lorries rumbled. The car stereos stamped. More sirens, an ambulance this time. And now it was starting to rain, hammering against the window. His thoughts were shouting louder than all of it.

Immersion. Embracing a programme of re-education through prayer and mission. Making amends to those you have hurt.

12

Rose turned off the shower just as the water started running cold. It was good to have the flat to herself, even if she had to leave in twenty minutes. She could have done with the extra time in bed. Last night, she'd dreamed about that woman in the film. Rose was trapped in a room with her. The woman was still naked on the chair and Rose was frantically trying to undo the binds tying the woman's hands. Every time Rose freed a knot, the strands curled back tighter.

She wiped the steam off the mirror and studied her face. Her skin was looking pretty clear but it was a pity she'd passed the attack of the random acne on to Rudder. He probably thought it was evil bubbling out his pores.

Kye hadn't replied to her last message. On Mondays, he had double geography first thing, then a gap until politics after lunch. The bench was their place. That's where she'd be waiting.

It was in that short break between second and third lessons that they'd first seen each other. Rose was on the bench by herself because nobody else would talk to her. If Pitt Academy had been tough, City Guild college was worse. Mina and Tammy, who sat behind her in maths, befriended her at first. When they found out about the Pilgrims, that's all they'd wanted to talk about. Were there any famous Pilgrims? Did girls get married at thirteen? They'd quickly lost interest when she wouldn't feed them details. She couldn't even make something up. It all still hurt too much. No one else had spoken to her. Everyone had been all huddled in their little groups, the Turkish boys together, the African girls together, the Asian girls in headscarves all together. The white girls and the Caribbean girls had mixed it up a bit, but they didn't want Rose in the mix. Kye said it wasn't personal. Most of them already knew each other from schools and mosques and other places. Later, he said it was because she didn't look like anyone else. Her fairy kei clothes were making a statement that no one knew how to answer. Kye said he'd been intrigued. She'd noticed him looking at her, then smiling, then he came over and sat down next to her on that bench. He'd offered her his chips and she'd taken one.

She rubbed the concealer stick over her eyebrows, layering it on, like Mum icing Rudder's birthday cake. Then foundation, powder, contour. Back to the eyebrows – pale pink, to match her hair. Pale blue eye shadow, lilac mascara instead of the glitter lashes. Sparkle lipstick. And clothes? The canary yellow prom dress with the frilly petticoat and stripy knee highs. She checked the mirror and smoothed down the skirt. Yes. She was ready.

As soon as maths finished, Rose checked her phone. Still nothing. Maybe he was going to surprise her instead. She

127

grabbed her bag and raced down to the square. A few kids were queuing at the hot-dog van parked up on the side, but most were heading to the chicken shop or McDonald's. She sat down on the bench and tapped out another text.

I'm waiting.

She was in a sun spot, heat blasting the side of her face, searing her foundation solid. The wood was cold under her thighs. She hoped it wouldn't leave mucky stains on her skirt.

She stood up again. She checked her phone. Nothing, nothing, nothing. What if he'd gone to her maths room to surprise her? No, he'd never done that before. He probably didn't even know where her maths room was. There could have been an emergency with Bella and Rose was filling his phone with messages demanding to know where he was, and he was—

Her phone buzzed. Yes! It was him!

Busy

That was it? Just 'busy'? Just one bloody word after all that longing. Busy. Busy doing what? Busy watching naked women tied to a chair? Busy with someone else? Rose could scream so loud it would flatten the square. She could thump this bench and make it shatter into a hundred pieces. Instead, she would just sit here by herself, with her insides feeling like they'd been sucked down a plug hole. She looked around. Everyone was in their groups, chatting and laughing and eating their hot dogs and tipping back their heads drinking Coke.

Was she going to stay here? The only one on her own? No, she damn well wasn't.

*

Rudder's eyes were on his feet: left, right, left, right, along the science wing until he was outside Ms Leppard's door. He knew what he had to do. He must have had a revelation dream last night, even if he couldn't remember it. This morning, he was filled with purpose. He'd been tempted in the past. He hadn't endureth, but God was going to keep on testing Rudder because he knew Rudder could win. The greater the temptation, the bigger the victory.

He dodged a prefect and two teachers holding mugs and laughing. Even though Ms Leppard had written him that note to say he could come in early, he still hated the way his hands trembled when he had to take it out and show it. No one looked at his note. They all looked at his hands.

He peered through the small square of glass in the door. Rudder's problem had been that he'd jumped to stage five of atonement too quickly. He wasn't ready for Immersion yet, for making amends to those he had hurt. He felt okay with stages one and two. He was already aware of the immense burden of his soul, and he'd been busy understanding and confronting the story of his temptation for a while, but what about number three, exploration? Had he met his sins and named them one by one? Mum used to be taken to the Elders to do that. Rudder had to find a different way. Like the Elders, Ms Leppard was a teacher, even if she was a woman.

Ms Leppard was in her room spraying water mist over the cactuses on the windowsills. She was his last hope. If he was prohibited from a Pilgrim intervention, he had to find the worldly alternative. He would confess his sin and open himself up to God's wrath.

He'd nearly told Mum everything this morning. He'd looked at the picture again to make extra sure she wasn't Rose. The picture girl was definitely darker than Rose and there was a tear shape, like a scar or a birth mark on the inside of her left wrist. She was wearing dark blue bracelets. Rose had lots of jewellery, but he'd never seen her wearing anything like that.

He'd come out of the bedroom and sat on the sofa with his phone on the low table in front of him, sentences trying to make themselves in his head.

I was sent a picture, Mum. It's of a girl.

Who?

I don't know, but she's not wearing anything.

He'd pass the phone to Mum and duck his head so he didn't have to see Mum's face.

Who sent you this, Rudder?

A Devil's agent.

130

Then Mum would look closer. *Rose? What the hell has this got to do with Rose?*

I don't know.

Instead, before he'd got the chance to say anything, Mum had held up a box of oats and said, 'Would you like some porridge?'

Then he'd said, 'Have we got any golden syrup?' Those weren't the words he'd meant to say, but it was too late.

Mum tapped the syrup tin. 'Courtesy of the food bank. You look like you need the sugar boost. Bad night or Monday morning blues?'

He watched her pour oats into the saucepan, add a pinch of salt, a splash of milk and water. She lit the cooker and started stirring.

He said, 'I couldn't sleep.'

He picked up his phone. It was already chunkier than everyone else's, but this morning it looked extra-chunky. That's because it was a vessel of evil. He didn't even have many contacts or games or anything else to block the evil out, so it must be seeping through the electronics and turning everything Satan-coloured. It even felt damp in his hand.

Mum said, 'I hope Rose isn't keeping you awake snoring.'

'Rose snores?' And then he'd let the conversation veer off, too fast for him to catch it up and turn it back the right way.

'She did when she was little,' Mum said. 'Even when she was awake, she sounded like Darth Vader. Though of course, no one else had any idea who Darth Vader was.' Mum had turned off the cooker and placed a plate over the saucepan to wait for the porridge to set. 'I thought Rose had asthma. Your grandmother wanted me to go to the Pilgrims' doctor, but I sneaked out and took Rose to a specialist in Ilford. It turned out she had polyps, like little grapes, in her nostril. She was given some spray and it stopped bothering her. Your grandmother wasn't best pleased.'

'Is that why you were in the atonement room?'

'You remember that? You were very young.' Mum poured the porridge into a bowl. 'Come and add your syrup.'

'You tried to read me a story through the bedroom door.'

Had she known how long he'd sat on the other side trying to be brave enough to give a little knock? Or how many times Grandma Yellow had seen him there and carried him away again?

He sloshed on the syrup, wiped the drip from the tin and sucked his finger. He could tell Mum about the picture now. She'd told him a secret about Rose and now he could spill the secret in his phone. Then Mum had changed the subject. She'd been looking out the window at the neighbour's grimy wall.

'We'll probably have to move out of London,' she said. 'No matter how many hours I work, I'm never going to afford anything more than this. Not even this.'

'Would we go back to Woodford?'

'You know that's not an option, Rudder. I was thinking

132

more the seaside. Or somewhere with fields and woods. How does that sound?'

Rudder had sat down. His bowl had hidden the phone. He'd wanted to tell her that wherever he went, he would be tested unless he atoned, but Mum had rushed off to get ready for work.

Ms Leppard was rearranging the pots. Rudder wanted to press his hot face against the cold glass, but if Ms Leppard turned around she might be frightened. He leaned against the door instead. Maybe she was too busy and he should leave it to another day. Then the door was pulled away from him and he stumbled into the classroom.

'I thought I saw you there, Rudder. Come in.'

Ms Leppard smiled. It was the special smile she saved for Rudder. She smiled at everyone but there was something held back, just for him.

She said, 'How are you this morning, Rudder?'

Heavy with sin. 'Fine, thank you, miss.'

'I'm glad you came in early. We still haven't finished talking about your GCSE options.'

'I . . . I wanted to talk to you about something else, miss.'

'Of course.' Another special Rudder smile. 'I'll just have to wait for another time to persuade you to take French. I do wish you'd give it a go. It's a Latinate language, Rudder, inspired by the words of the common Romans. Just the everyday people like you and me. I bet when those poor soldiers were marching through Gaul, they had no idea that they would influence the way a whole nation says "I love you".' She twisted round a tall, spiky plant so the other side faced the sun. 'That's the thing, Rudder. You may be going about your daily business and never know the impact that you have on our world.'

'Yes, miss.'

She said, 'Sorry, Rudder, you wanted to talk about something. Fire away.'

'I . . . it's my phone.'

She frowned. 'Have you lost it? I don't think—'

The door burst open. Cain stormed in, glaring at Rudder like he wanted to start a fight.

Ms Leppard smiled at Cain as well. It was different from a Rudder smile. This one looked more tired. 'Can you just give me a few minutes, Cain?'

'I came in specially. You said you wanted to see me.'

Ms Leppard slapped her forehead. 'Of course I did. Step outside and I'll be with you in a minute.'

'Yes, miss.' The door slammed behind him.

Ms Leppard said, 'I'm sorry about your phone. Let me know if you don't find it.' She was walking towards the door, expecting him to follow. Just before she opened it, she turned around.

'Have you ever tried drama?'

'Miss?'

'Plays. Acting, Lighting, that sort of thing.'

'My sister says I'm a drama king.'

She laughed then stopped suddenly. 'I'm sorry to hear that. Speaking as an older sister, I know we aren't always the most sympathetic of people, but you might find it's your thing.'

The thing was in Rudder's bag. It was a sin that he had to name.

Ms Leppard was pushing down the door handle. 'Would your mum mind if you stayed behind school tomorrow? I know it's short notice, but if you get the form signed and bring it back tomorrow morning, it's fine.'

She was asking Rudder to hang out with her after school? 'Mum won't mind.'

'Excellent. I run the Year Seven and Eight drama group. It's not just for actors. Nobody's forced into doing anything they don't want to, but everybody seems to enjoy themselves.'

Oh. It wasn't just Ms Leppard. Rudder wouldn't enjoy himself. He knew it. She let go of the handle. Behind her, Cain's angry face was pushed against the glass.

He said, 'Thank you for asking, but I don't think I better.'

'Are there still religious reasons why you can't come? I understand if there are.'

He shook his head. 'I'm decommissioning.'

She smiled. 'What a lovely way of putting it. I do worry about you, though, Rudder. I know it's been tough for you, having to leave everything you know and finding your way in this mad world. But the drama group are a friendly bunch. Maybe you'll make friends and find some allies to help you make sense of things.'

'It's all right, miss.'

'And the best thing? We order in pizza.'

Pizza.

She shone her Rudder-smile so bright, he couldn't help smiling back. The bell rang. The door opened and Cain hurtled back in, followed by the rest of the tutor group. Rudder dumped his bag down by his seat. He'd endured the temptation to bring *Order of the Phoenix*. He knew it by heart anyway. It was the one where Harry was having visions. Things were happening in his head that were put there by someone evil. Harry made a terrible sacrifice, but in the end he won.

13

Rose hadn't realised that streets could sweat. Maybe it was the tourists leaking perspiration and frappés over the pavement, or puddles from the hanging flower baskets above the pubs. Maybe it was the sun blasting the strip of road between the alleyways and shop doorways, sucking out the last drops of last night's rain. Rose flicked down her sunglasses. The world turned orange-pink.

She should have left off the knee boots. They were squeezing hard and a bubble of sweat was rolling down her calves. She dabbed her forehead. A smear of concealer coated her hand. It didn't matter. Where she was heading, she was probably going to be sweating even more. That's if she could find it.

There were ten points to the decommissioning programme. Kye was just part of it. So what if she'd wanted to climb into his skin to be closer to him? This world was more than him, even if the chip of hurt in her stomach felt like the damn Shard. It was more than the tiny, stinking flat and the college she still got lost in and the boy who was too 'busy' to see her. If she was going to win the battle between Pilgrim Rose and Worldly Rose – and she bloody well was going to win – she needed to remember the good things.

Let decommissioning resume! Proper decommissioning.

Now she had to find Neon Paradise. It was definitely just off one of these streets. She'd almost laughed out loud when Kye had brought her here. He'd promised to break her Pilgrim prohibition on dancing, leading her down the stairs to the lights and noise and scattering of people shoving money into the machines. The dance games were in the corner, treadmills in front of a screen flashing up videos and arrows. She'd watched a man dressed in shorts and a vest, his feet stomping rapid patterns, fingers gripping the rail behind. The queue had been too long for them to have a go, but they'd returned the following week. She'd been awarded a C at the easiest setting. She'd promised Kye next time there'd be a proper battle.

She didn't need him to help her. She could go down those steps and put money in the machine on her own. She wiped away the sweat from her hairline.

'Rose?'

Was she thinking of Kye so hard she could hear him calling her name? She flicked out her earbuds.

'Rose!'

No, it was definitely outside her head.

'Rose! Rose, it's me!'

A fat drop of rain landed on her nose. Seriously? How could it rain? Just two minutes ago her make-up was melting.

'Rose!'

The voice was louder, coming towards her. It was him!

Jesus, it couldn't be. No, not Jesus. She mustn't blaspheme. She mustn't. Her chest throbbed. Her feet had stuck themselves to the pavement. It was. It was Mikhail. He was striding towards her in his polite trousers, his fat tie swinging, his pale grey shirt dark with sweat around the empty sleeve holes of his waistcoat.

She smiled. His face lit up. Damn. She shouldn't have done that. Her Pilgrim ready-to-please button still popped up too quickly.

'Rose! I thought it was you. I wasn't sure if you'd heard me.'

Mikhail's hair was trimmed close to his head. His body was shaped like a man's. Did he know that? Did Pilgrim boys lock themselves in their bathroom and study themselves in front of the mirror? She imagined him turning from side to side, checking the curve of his chest and probing his arms for muscle. Maybe he did push ups against his chest of drawers and had dumb-bells stacked in racks next to his bed before trapping himself in his old man's shirt and waistcoat and picking up his Bible.

He was staring at her intently. Another raindrop landed on the pavement.

He bit his lip. 'You do remember me, don't you?'

'It hasn't been that long, Mikhail.'

His face brightened even more. He wiped a raindrop out of his eye. The rain was blending in with the sweat on his shirt.

He said, 'The Lord is sending us a rainstorm.'

He touched her arm, his fingers on her bare skin, then ducked between scaffolding poles outside a closed-down dress shop. She followed him under. The boards above their heads were full of gaps. The rain would seep through, showering them with dirt. How long had it been since she was this close to Mikhail? More than eight years since Aunty Elizabeth pulled their hands apart when she'd seen them together. Nearly two years since he'd stood in Grandma Yellow's garden watching his father set fire to Rudder's book.

Now here he was, with a proper man's body, tall and broad, his face shiny with belief.

He said, 'It's good to see you. I wondered . . .'

'Wondered what?'

'How you were getting on. I pray for you.'

Of course he did. He'd been bathing in Pilgrim rules from birth. His family went three generations back. His grandmother, Aunty Zillah, was the only woman with the Founders' authority to consult the *Libros Rojos*. Mum said this had absolutely nothing to do with Aunty Zillah's late husband leaving her a six-bedroom house in a prime location that the Pilgrims would love to add to their property portfolio.

More rain, but still in slow motion, like the heat was making it evaporate before it reached the ground.

She said, 'Outside isn't like what they say. It's not frightening or evil.'

He frowned. 'I know what outside's like, Rose. I'm not stupid.'

'I didn't mean . . .'

'Yes, you did. You think I don't know anything. You think that God makes me blind.'

'No . . .'

'God sees everything, Rose. He's sees the way girls like you . . . he sees what the Devil does to you.'

One night in Room 27, when Rudder was finally asleep, Mum had said that Pilgrim men were no different from worldly men. Their eyes betrayed them. Mikhail's did now, travelling slowly past her naked calves and thighs to the hem of her skirt and her vest. Her arms ached to hug herself. She lifted her chin and stared at him. He looked right back. It was as if the spattering of rain had washed away his shine. His eyes were sharp and angry.

He said, 'You don't have to be this way, Rose. You could return to us. With God's grace, I can persuade my father to authorise your atonement.'

Her head buzzed with anger. He thought she wanted subjugation? Assimilation? She was going to hold it in, not give him the pleasure of knowing that he'd got to her. 'You don't have to be this way, Mikhail.' She smiled. 'You could leave and have a real life.'

Another glance from him, this time the elevator glance, plummeting down, then up. 'I have everything I need, Rose. I have my friends, my family, God's love. And you?

What do you have?'

She bobbed forward and kissed him on the cheek. She caught the sharpness of his sweat and the dull notes of the deodorant he'd used to armour himself against the heat.

'I have me, Mikhail. The real me.' She stepped out from under the scaffolding and folded herself into the crowd.

The rain had stopped. A straggly cloud was stretched thin across the sky and the sun was high and hot again. Rose kept her head down until she was close to the street corner then risked a peek. Two older men were pulling a plastic sheet off the piles of 'Pilgrims' Way' leaflets on the stand. She didn't recognise them, or the girl with them. She couldn't be much older than Rose, her hair scrunched into a low pony tail, a pale green apron covering her long grey skirt. Mikhail appeared by her side. She turned to him and even from here, Rose could feel the heat of her smile.

Rose ducked down an alleyway, away from the main road. Rain water had puddled by the wheelie bins. The extractors hummed and guffed the smell of frying through the narrow lane. She leaned against the wall, letting the wetness saturate her back. It was always going to happen. The Mikhail who used to share her secrets was always going to transform into this.

Rose breathed in. She could feel the cooking oil settle on her tongue and slide down the back of her throat. A polystyrene box sat in a puddle by the bin wheels. It shivered like something inside it was alive. She pushed away from the wall. The alley led on to another main road. She pulled out her phone and waited. Yes! Free Wi-Fi from a coffee shop on the other side of the alley. She checked her map. The arcade was two blocks away. It would take her seven minutes to get there. Seven minutes until her head was full of the ringing and thuds of the machine. Seven minutes until she could dance away Mikhail.

But now her head was pounding. How the hell had Mikhail done that? He'd only been with her a few minutes and suddenly Pilgrim Rose was clawing her way out. The thought of walking down the steps to the arcade made her stomach leap. Even if she made it into the basement, she'd just stand there like an idiot with the machines blaring and flashing around her.

She walked down to the end of the alley. The bright weather had brought the tourists out. At least she wasn't a tourist any more. Not quite. She wasn't short stay, in a hostel or on a street corner handing out leaflets before running back to the relief of Sanctuary. It was time to go right back to where she'd first felt the pull of the outside world.

That Christmas had been their first Christmas. The first of two, so far. Mum had taken them to Trafalgar Square. It had been cold and drizzly with security guards in hi-vis jackets stationed by the lion statues to stop people climbing up to take selfies. A group of drunk men in smart suits had walked past them shouting and laughing. Mum had pulled Rose and Rudder closer to her. The chilly air had swilled round Rose's ankles. The donated trousers were slightly too short for her, the fabric rubbing together as she walked. Trousers had felt so different from skirts.

Mum had taken them right up close to the Christmas tree. The trees in the shops they'd passed had been bright with different coloured lights and shiny baubles and tiny presents. The tree in Trafalgar Square was tall and thin and all the lights were white. Rose had imagined climbing the branches to the top, poking her head through the clouds and seeing Heaven. Then she'd cramped up with guilt. Only Pilgrim Elders were guaranteed ascension to Heaven.

Mum had crossed the square to the model nativity scene inside a glass and wood box. Rudder hadn't known what it was. Rose shouldn't have neither. Long before Rose was born, the Founder banned children's books with pictures of Jesus, angels and male saints to kill the temptation to idol worship. Ms Wormwood seemed to forget to send Rose out when the class was rehearsing for the Christmas assembly. Rose would sit at the back of the hall with her knees drawn up to her chin, peering through her fingers at her classmates on the stage.

Rudder had poked the glass and quickly pulled away.

'Those are the three wise men,' Rose had explained. They were all holding gifts. One of them was pointing up to the damp sky, though Rose had wondered why he wasn't pointing at Jesus. A shepherd was lying on his side like he was getting ready to roll out of the stable and on to Rose's feet. That had made her want to giggle.

'Idols!' Rudder had gasped.

'No,' Mum had said. 'They are wooden models. Nothing more.'

Mum had insisted on taking Rudder to the toilet in the art gallery spanning one side of the square. The toilet in the hostel was like a poo bomb had exploded in there. Mum had said she'd rather dig a hole in the ground like the missionary Pilgrims in rainforest Venezuela than let her children use it.

Rose had followed them out of the dark and damp and been transfixed by the colours on the walls, hot reds and blues that twisted her heart. She'd moved closer to look at the paintings. Baby Jesus and Mother Mary, different faces, different frames, but always those colours. Her heart had been squeezed smaller and smaller until she'd thought her blood had stopped pumping. Women couldn't receive the Spirit, Rose knew that. But this . . . this was better. She'd let the colour seep into her dull clothes. She would never wear boring, modest grey again.

Trafalgar Square was much busier today. A pavement artist was chalking the world's flags on the ground, inviting passers-by to chuck coins on to their countries. Just along from him, Yoda from *Star Wars* was grasping a long pole and seemed to be sitting on air. People were leaning over the gallery balcony, staring down on the square, almost as if they were waiting for Rose's arrival. Of course, they weren't. They were chatting and taking pictures, families, friends, tour groups. A few of them stared at her as she walked past them. She made herself smile back.

First stop inside the gallery – her favourite Jesus. She should have brought Mikhail with her to annoy him. Jesus was blessing some bread in an inn. He had a round, young face that reminded her of Rudder. How could this Jesus be wrong? Why couldn't Jesus look like a normal person? Though, according to the Pilgrims, any painting of him was a sin. Imagine what they'd make of the other pictures in here. Two years later, she still felt her cheeks flush as red as they did that first time. Here, in the same room as Jesus and the saints, were the women, clothes hanging off their bodies like the artists had reached in and pulled the cloth away.

Rose closed her eyes. Just beneath the noise of the other visitors, Rose could almost hear the women whispering to each other from their frames. Talking pictures. Rudder would love that! She glanced up at the Virgin in the bright blue hoodie, eyes raised to heaven, doing some serious praying, but after the lights went out, she'd be sharing rude jokes with Saint Gregory the Great. Meanwhile, Judith and Salome would lean out of their canvasses swapping tips on beheading. No surprise that Rose had only learned their stories after she'd left the Pilgrims. The Elders didn't want women to know they were strong enough to lop off a man's head. Every Pilgrim girl knew the story of Susannah, though, bathing immodestly and shamelessly tempting the Elders. There were two Susannahs in this room. The Elders in both the paintings looked like the villains.

Rose still had to brace herself to look at *the* picture. That evening, waiting for Mum and Rudder, she'd ended up standing right here. She'd had to look away quickly to check that no one in the gallery was staring at her and shaking their head. She'd read the label on the wall – *The Rape of Europa*. Seeing that word written down had made her heart jolt. Rape happened in dark, secret places when immodest women like Susannah inflamed righteous men's senses. But in worldly society, there were pictures painted of it for everyone to see.

She hadn't understood it. Why was there a baby with wings and an arrow there too? And a bull wearing a crown of flowers? Why was that girl's top pulled down so her immodesty was exposed? Why wasn't she full of shame? Then it had struck her. Europa was a harlot and a temptress. This was what she'd wanted. A few weeks later, when Rose had found the Cast Outs forum, she'd asked if she was right. She'd got a whole load of answers telling her why she was wrong. There was only one she really remembered. Their forum name was Lucifer's Love. She said rape was like having the core torn out of you.

A grey-haired man with a young woman squeezed themselves in front of Rose. They looked at the painting for a few seconds then moved on.

Rose's phone vibrated. It was like the bull had flicked out a hoof and caught her ribs. It was Kye.

Just had some bad news about Bella.

Bad news? How bad? Bad enough to stop him being 'busy', obviously. Bad enough to make him text more than one damn word to her.

It better be really ba . . . Her thumbs hovered above the 'b' and 'a'. No, something *could* be really bad. She deleted it all and started again.

What's happened?

It's complicated. Please come round. I want to see you.

He wanted to see her? He could have seen her an hour ago on the damn bench! Why should she go running to him? It was *his* brother who'd looked at her like she was Susannah or Europa. It was him who'd been 'busy'. She'd been waiting for him all alone in the middle of the square for everyone to see. She glanced at Europa. Her eyes were raised as the bull-Zeus flew away with her. How did that story end? Rose had never wanted to find out.

I know I've been a dick. Please come. I need you.

Kye needed her. Again. Her heart unwound, inflated. This time, he could carry on her needing her.

Rose please talk to me.

She was only heading to the foyer because she'd had enough. She would have to be ninety-nine per cent decommissioned before she could hang out with the boobs mixed with holiness for any longer. Outside, Yoda was still perched on his miracle chair. *May the force be with you.* She was walking to the bus stop because this was the one she had to go to anyway.

Please tell me you're coming

When she was on the bus, she'd reply.

Kye's flat smelt of burnt toast. The waft hit Rose as soon as he opened the door. Kye kept one hand on the handle, still open wide enough for her to back out.

He said, 'Sorry. The toaster's crap and the bread gets stuck.'

He leaned forward like he was going to kiss her. She stepped back.

'Of course,' he said. 'Sorry. It's just I miss you so much when I don't see you. I didn't know if you'd come or not.' He touched her cheek. 'Please stay.'

She shouldn't have let him touch her. 'I can't for long.'

'I understand. Thank you.'

He closed the door behind her. She followed him into the

149

sitting room. She could see the curve of his spine beneath his thin t-shirt. He sat down on the sofa, right where the blond boy's trainers had been. There was only a mug on the coffee table now, but how was she supposed to forget the woman tied to the chair?

Kye must have noticed her hesitate. He said, 'Briley won't be back.'

'Ever?'

He glanced away. 'I can't promise, but I'm doing my best.' He gave her a little smile and placed his hand on his heart. 'Believe me?'

She had to stop herself covering his hand with hers. 'I think so.'

She sat down, close to him, but not touching.

He said, 'I thought . . . I thought you might want to know about Bella.'

'I do.' He looked serious, but not upset. It couldn't be that bad. 'What's happened?'

'She's probably going to be discharged day after tomorrow.'

'That's good, isn't?'

His fingers were resting a nail away from hers. She didn't move them closer. Neither did he.

He said, 'Bella's not coming back.'

She stared at him. 'What do you mean? Is she going into care, or something?'

'She's going to live with my aunty for a while.'

150

'Your aunty?'

Their fingers curled together. Was that him or her? She'd just let her hand stay there for a minute or two then wriggle free. She had to make him work for this.

He said, 'Aunty Rini, Dad's sister. Dad's been moaning about Bella doing crap at school, so he's sending her to school with our cousins.'

'How does your mum feel about that?'

'She's pretty upset. When she and Dad split up, there was a big fight about who we'd live with. Mum had been seeing this other bloke while she was still married, so Dad thought he should have us because the break-up was Mum's fault.'

Kye shifted closer, so his thigh rubbed against hers.

He said, 'You know what it's like when families break up.'

She turned to him. This was a different Kye, open, older than the one before. His thumb was tracing shapes in her palm. It felt like stars and swirls.

She said, 'It feels like you're being pulled in half. Dad was never going to leave the Pilgrims and he really wanted both of us to stay, especially Rudder. Rudder was always Grandma's favourite. She was always boasting about how well he knew his scripture, even though Pilgrims weren't supposed to boast.'

Kye shook his head. 'That's why I'll never join a religion. They're all hypocritical.'

That wasn't what she was trying to say. For a second, she wanted to pull away from him. He was right, though. The

151

Pilgrims were as bad as any of them. Her decommissioning level must be sinking. She'd defended them way too quickly.

He said, 'Sorry. I didn't mean to be rude.'

'That's okay. You're right.'

He squeezed her hand, his thumb pressing into the centre of her palm. 'Your lot were more of a cult than a religion, weren't they?'

'Cult?' She did pull away that time.

He looked surprised. 'Sorry, I was just going by the way you described it. I didn't mean to offend you.'

His hands dropped on to his lap and she shifted away from him. The silence stretched between them. His t-shirt had become free from his jeans, revealing a narrow finger of skin.

He said, 'It's just the way you were cut off from everybody and weren't allowed to think things through for yourself. You've even got mysterious leaders in America.'

'Spain.'

'Okay, Spain. But I looked them up. They were originally from America and they moved, didn't they? Have you seen their houses? They're massive.'

'No. I've never been invited.'

He made a face. 'You don't have to go there. Just Google . . .' He laughed. 'Of course. You're weren't allowed technology, were you?' He picked up his phone. 'I can show you.'

She shook her head. 'I've been out for nearly two years,

Kye. I could have looked it up, but why should I? It doesn't help, especially as Mum was saying stuff like that about their houses, even when we still lived there.'

'Your mum sounds great. She doesn't follow the crowd. That's what I like about you.'

They looked at each other. He took her hand and placed it on his heart. How had he known she'd wanted him to do that? She wasn't sure if she could feel his blood moving or her own.

He said, 'I really thought I'd lost you.'

'You haven't.'

They moved towards each other at the same time. His tongue flicked hers. That still felt strange. He let go of her hand and wrapped both arms around her.

He said, 'Thank you for coming, Rose. I missed you so much.' He suddenly let go of her. 'Let's go out. I don't trust myself alone with you.'

Was it too immodest to grab his hand and pull him back to her? Yes, probably. She took his hand.

She said, 'I don't mind staying.'

'Are you sure? I still hate myself so much for what I let Briley do yesterday. I wanted to see you so much today, but I felt so stupid, I didn't even go into college.'

Instead, he'd just let her sit there by herself. She should tell him how much he'd hurt her, but Rose knew guilt. Kye was full of it. He didn't need her to give him extra.

She said, 'I'm happy to stay, Kye. I want to.'

He nodded. 'Okay. I've got Netflix if there's anything you fancy.'

Like what? Didn't he get that she'd never seen Netflix in her life? How the hell would she know what to fancy?

'Or we could go into my room,' he said. 'I mean, just to talk. That's if you trust me.'

'I trust you.' *Did she? Could she?* Something had definitely shifted. This was the first time she'd felt equal.

She rested one hand on his thigh and squeezed the other between the sofa and his back. *Super-immodest! Yes!* As he moved, she could feel his ribs and the spaces in between. He glanced at the coffee table. She hadn't noticed his phone next to the remote control. They looked at each other.

He shook his head. 'I don't want to push you into anything. And anyway, my brother's made this place feel dirty. If you want, though, I could always come over to your place tomorrow.'

His phone buzzed. He reached for it, turned away from her and checked the message. He sighed and dropped his phone on the sofa.

'It's Mum. She's on her way back from Dad's. She's seriously stressed.'

Rose said, 'I better go, then. She won't want me around.'

He kissed her for so long they both had to take a breath halfway through. They pulled away, grinning.

Kye picked up his phone and stood up. 'I'll see you tomorrow. It's a date.'

Rose's Ten Point Plan for Being a Perfect Worldly Wise
Also Known As
Being a Bit More Decommissioned
Also Known As
The Story So Far

1. Worshipping idols needs money for merch and a decent internet connection for everything else. Though thank you, Bicchi Blogger, for the post on fairy kei. Idols plus recycling — perfect for a penniless ex-Pilgrim. Also, thank you, charity shop, for discounting the faded My Little Pony duvet that turned into my first skirt experiment.

2. I have dressed immodestly. I have shown more than my ankle. I have not followed Evil Eve's advice to fart on any pervs that are a step too close to me going up escalators or stairs. Not yet.

3. Act immodestly? I am forced to share a room with my little brother. If I leave a tampon box open I am acting immodestly.

4. Voting — how? Seriously, how? Apparently, we do not exist on the voting register because the people whose flat we live in don't want anyone to know they rent it to us. So, yes, we do not really live here, even though my hair smells like it should be inside a pitta bread and drowned in chilli sauce.

5. Ah. A worldly boyfriend. There's a scale of worldliness. If it's from one to ten, I plunged in at twenty-two.

6. Begetting immodesty with boyfriend. Yes. I did that. See above.

7. No Christmas cards to Grandma yet. I'll give her one next year and it's going to be BIG.

8. I've been to the Natural History and Science Museums twice. That's all it needed.

9. I tried to watch the prohibited films, but there are way too many of them. It covers nearly every film. I did turn on the telly to see a musical Jesus Christ. Mum wasn't impressed by the fact they made Judas black.

10. Rudder — not that I want to go all Biblical, but he's like the baby in the tug of war in the judgement of Solomon. Rudder's got Worldy-Wise grabbing his feet and Pilgrims pulling his shoulders and it's like neither of them plan to let him go.

14

Rose needed milk. Milk and sugar. Milk and sugar and chocolate. Did Kye take sugar? She couldn't remember. Had she made him tea before? She thought hard. No, but then she hadn't made anyone tea for a while except Mum and Rudder. Hang on – she'd offered Kye tea once, but he'd said that they didn't have long. It was usually just half an hour or so before Rudder came home and Kye always had plans that didn't include tea.

But today was different. Kye was different. It was like that moment when Pilgrim boys crossed the sanctuary and become Brothers. Their shoulders widen and their backs stiffen within a few steps.

At this rate, though, Rose would have to leave the shop without anything. The couple at the counter were having a full-on argument. The man looked about the same age as Dad, but he was wearing low-rise jeans and a white sweatshirt. Even if Dad was excised forever, she could never imagine him wearing anything like that. The woman was about the same age. Suddenly, she dropped her basket on the floor. Her rings clinked as she waved her hands around.

So far, it felt like everything today was against her. Every single one of Mum's razors was blunt so Rose had taken off most of her armpit skin along with the fuzz. It hadn't helped that they were down to a single nub of grey, scummy soap that clogged the blades. Then she'd wondered, did Kye expect all her hair off down below? It wasn't like there was going to be any full fornication happening. Kye was happy to wait for that and so was she because Poxy Roxy on Cast Outs said it hurt like hell and she'd got more than fifty likes for that. Fallen Angel said that there were alternatives to full fornication. Rose had had to lock herself in the bathroom to read that thread. At the end, HairyTic had posted a link to her guide on personal grooming. It had started by saying that women should do whatever they were comfortable with. How could Rose know what she was comfortable with if she hadn't done it before? Neither hair stuff *nor* fornication.

But that wasn't her main problem. The real reason today was against her was – Rudder. Bloody Rudder. He had refused point blank to let her and Kye be alone together. He was like that professor in *Harry Potter and the Half-Blood Prince* who'd turned himself into an armchair. One day she'd come home and find his feet had turned into tiny wheels and his head a giant cushion. It had been nearly two years. Why couldn't he have friends by now?

She'd texted Kye earlier.

Can't get rid of Rudder. Can I come to yours?

He'd replied straight away.

Mum's home. That's worse. Bribe him with chocolate.

Good idea. She'd said, 'I'm just popping out, Ruds.'

'Where?'

'To the shops. Kye's still coming around.'

Rudder had glowered at her. 'You know I don't want him here.'

'Well, I do.'

'This is my home too. You can't always have everything your way. What if I tell Mum?'

Was this the best moment to remember Jael banging her peg through General Sisera's head? 'That's up to you. You know that. But maybe if you made some friends, you wouldn't have to hang around here all the time.'

'I do have friends.'

'Real ones, Ruds.'

The argument ahead of her in the queue seemed to be on pause. Then the woman kicked the basket and stormed out the shop. Everybody made way for her as she left. One small thing was in Rose's favour – Dairy Milk was on offer. She bought a big bar along with a small carton of milk and a little pack of sugar. She paid and tucked them into her bag as she left the shop. The arguing couple were just ahead of her on the street, the woman still shouting. She stopped suddenly, mid-word, and staggered back slightly. The man took her hand and stroked it.

Rose took out her phone.

Miss u xx

The reply bounced straight back again.

**Miss u2. im on my way. meet me at the cupcake place
near college. we'll buy enough cake to keep Rudder
happy for eternity.**

He missed her. It was there on her phone. She grinned.
He felt the pull of her in the same way she was drawn to him.
They *had* walked those few steps to the other side of the
sanctuary. But they weren't Pilgrims. They could do it
together.

*

Rudder rinsed the last crumbs of toast off his plate and
stacked it on the drier. Why did Rose balance her wet bowls
in that stupid way against the glasses? It didn't take long to
stack them neatly. It was like she was doing everything she
could to stress him out. And then, on top of that, she was
bringing Kye here. He should tell Mum. He should.

Rudder dried his hands and went into the main room.
He opened the window over the sofa. Rose knew nothing
about his life. Nothing at all. She didn't care about Rudder
any more. All she was interested in was her stupid
decommissioning. And Kye. She didn't even know that
Rudder had friends. Real ones! He couldn't see Rose but he
still wanted to yell, *You don't know anything about me! I went to*

everybody knew Rudder was there and part of it. He'd said how brave Rudder was for sharing the stuff about his hands and he was so pleased Rudder had come along.

Rudder closed the window to stop the kebab smell trickling in. The traffic sounds were duller but the frame still rattled with the buses and lorries. Rudder could hear a lorry now, its robot voice announcing that it was turning left. It was beeping too, its own language with other lorries.

He drew the curtains together and tucked them behind the sofa. He had that feeling in his legs, like they wanted to break away from his body and leap and twirl without him. His arms too. He sat on his hands. If Rose hadn't been so mean to him, he'd have been all right, but the more un-Rose she was, the harder it was to endureth. It was like being under an invisibility cloak that had turned evil. It stuck to him even when he tried to get out from it. It made everything look dark and his breathing hurt.

Music made it better. Was it really a sin? There was lots of dancing with tambourines in the Bible. Maybe Rudder should get a tambourine and that would make it all right. Pilgrims sang cantas because it brought them closer to God. Uncle Enoch had preached that music not dedicated to God stole your soul – *a wicked doer giveth heed to false lips* – but Uncle Enoch had never heard Simon and Garfunkel. Just the first few notes of 'The Boxer' and Rudder's soul was soaring like the Spirit. Uncle Enoch would say that was blasphemy, but that wasn't how it felt. No more evil invisibility cloak.

162

No more immodest girl. No more un-Rose Rose. Rudder would play 'The Boxer', then 'Bridge Over Troubled Water'. Then, if he had time, 'Scarborough Fair'. He'd bang his own tambourine and the world would glow around him.

Rudder went into the bedroom and unhooked his robes from the back of the door. The silvery-grey lining flashed bright as the sun hit it. He glanced upwards. God could see everybody all the time. Rudder didn't need to make things even worse for himself.

'They're not really magic,' he whispered. 'Mum made them for me.'

She'd spent ages sewing them together in the hostel. It was only fair to use them. One sleeve and then the other, lifting his arms so the robes swayed. He could almost feel the crackle as the evil invisibility cloak lifted. He swished back into the main room, switched on the speakers and turned them up until they hummed. Then he pushed 'play' and closed his eyes.

He let his head drop back and turned slowly one way and then back again. Right arm thrown out then clapped to his heart. Left arm following. Hands offered out, a gift. Another turn. His sock slipped on something smooth. He opened one eye. Stupid Rose and her stupid plastic packets. He nudged it under the sofa with his toe and closed his eye again. He didn't want to lose the music spell right when it was building because Rudder was the boxer. He'd left his home. He'd left his family. Rudder had been lonesome too. They were singing just for him because he understood. The chorus didn't need words. It just needed Rudder, his fists hammering out the syllables, spinning, again and again. The strings, whispering, rising, calling out their pain. The shy tap of the drums underneath and Rudder at the centre, his head dizzy with it as the melody wrapped around him, his voice meshing in harmony—

'What. The. Fuck?'

Rudder opened both eyes. His spin carried on, making him stumble. Kye was by the door, doubled over in laughter.

'You carry on, mate,' Kye said, and led Rose into the bedroom.

Rose looked back once, mouth open like she wanted to say something, then Kye pulled her in after him.

*

Kye stood with his back against the door.

'Doesn't this thing close properly?'

Rose shook her head. 'I'm just going to nip back in to Rudder. We've got the cupcakes and . . .'

Kye turned his back on her and opened the door again. Rudder's music was still on but there was no sign of him. He was probably hiding in the bathroom. Her face burned with his hurt. Kye unhooked the coat rack from the door and dropped it on the floor. He slammed the door shut. It closed properly.

He came and sat down next to her on her bed. 'That's better. Proper privacy.'

164

She said, 'Poor Rudder. I should—'

He touched her lips, pressing his finger against them so hard she could feel her teeth nip her skin. He let his finger drop and leaned forward to kiss her. She should go to Rudder. But Kye was here and now . . . *He's delicious.* Remember? Only last week, the thought of him sneaking into the flat to surprise her had sounded as perfect as a van full of free ice cream when you're hungry. So why was it that now, it felt like the ice cream had melted in the sun and the wasps were starting to land?

He said, 'Every minute with you is different, Rose. I've had girlfriends before. You know that. But something about you is really special.'

Kye's hands were on her, stroking the back of her neck and her cheek. He eased her jumper off. It was okay, though. She was still wearing her shirt. He kissed her nose.

He said, 'It's sexier to get some shots when you're still dressed.'

Her ears burned hotter. Had Rudder heard that? 'Bridge Over Troubled Water' was reaching its crescendo. He was probably still in the bathroom. She should definitely go to him.

She said, 'Kye, I'm not sure . . .'

He held his camera up and took a photo. 'It's okay. You don't have to go any further. This is enough to make me think of you.'

'Thanks, Kye.'

He unbuttoned the top button of her shirt. 'But I do think it's sad you keep your wonderful body hidden.' Another button slid free. 'Remember when you showed me your decommissioning list? You're amazing. Look how far you've come.'

Another button and he was holding up his camera. 'If you lean forward . . .'

'Kye! Stop!'

He lowered his camera and met her eyes. 'You said you missed me.'

She nodded. 'I do.'

'I thought you were happy for me to come round. I mean, yesterday, it was like you wanted this too.'

'I did. But I'm not sure . . .' She smoothed down the crumpled shirt he'd yanked from her skirt. 'It just feels a bit weird now.'

He shrugged. 'Okay.'

He stood up and slipped his phone into his trouser pocket. She waited for him to sit down again.

'I need to get back to Mum.' His hand was on the door handle. 'She's really upset.'

'I know, but—' She pushed her lips together. She wasn't going to beg him. The tears prickling behind her eyes had to stay there. 'I'm sorry about Bella. It's so tough for your mum.'

He blinked a few times, his eyes flicking round her. 'Yeah, it's been really tough on all of us. Mum blames herself. She thinks she's been a crap mother and that it's all her fault. From what you said, your mum feels like that too.'

'Yes.' She stood up too. 'She does.'

He stroked her back. 'That's why it's good that we've got each other. I didn't mean to pressure you, Rose. I just really wanted to have a picture of you. Something I can sneak a look at when I'm at home listening to Mum crying or arguing with Dad on the phone.'

Somehow, they were back by the bed, Rudder's bed, but she wouldn't tell Kye that now. Somehow she was letting him unbutton her shirt and unclip her bra and smiling as he gave her instructions about the best way to pose. Somehow, she was two Roses. One was smiling and pouting and leaning low then thrusting her shoulders out. The other was hovering above, watching herself. The two Roses came back together when he put his phone away. He mouthed 'thank you' and opened the bedroom door, flicking it shut behind him. She felt the wall tremble as the door to the flat shut. She could count the seconds until the street door banged. She could look out and see him. Maybe he'd look up, but Rose number two made her button her shirt up, tuck it back into her skirt and pull her jumper on. Rose two would also make her go into the main room and talk to Rudder, but not yet.

Mum's Top Ten Bible Women, as told to me, Rose, in Room 27, Market House Hostel

1. Deborah, because she rallied Barak and an army of 10,000 men against General Sisera and the Israelites
2. Jael, who banged a tent peg through General Sisera's head. Mum originally said, 'Jael pinned him to the ground.' She didn't mention that she'd done it through his head.
3. Shiphrah, a disobedient midwife
4. Puah, the other disobedient midwife who refused Pharaoh's orders to kill all newborn Hebrew boys. Mum said the Bible would be a different book without them and probably a lot shorter.
5. Hagar, a slave who bore Ishmael. Mum was upset that Hagar was one of the most popular Pilgrim baptism names. Hagar was supposed to be a shining example of obedience, subjugation and punishment, though Mum reckoned Hagar didn't have much choice. Her owner gave her away to her own husband for sex, and then she and the baby that came along were banished into the desert. Hagar gave back attitude and started a dynasty.
6. Miriam, Moses' older sister. Older sister to a boy know-it-all
7. Rhoda, because it means Rose. She was a lowly serving girl who'd been too excited to open the door to St Peter,

who'd miraculously escaped from prison and certain execution. Mum reckoned that Rhoda knew perfectly well that it was St Peter but had decided that the men should damn well open the door for themselves.

8. Mary Magdalene. Funny how she never got a mention in the *Libros Rojos*. She was the first one Mum told me about when they left. Mary witnessed Jesus's crucifixion and resurrection. Rudder probably still didn't believe that.

9. The Queen of Sheba. For some reason, I'd always imagined she'd have a snake round her shoulders. I never told Mum that, though. Mum liked her because she was supposed to be black.

10. Eve. Because.

15

Three days of messages, all stacked up, unanswered.

Message 1: **Missing u xx**

Message 2: **U ok? Missing u xx**

Message 3: **Taking Rudder to dentist. Talk later?**

Message 4: **Can't get thru. Call me back**

Message 5: **Getting worried. Are u ok? Is it Bella? Or your mum?**

Message 6: (draft) **Please tell me what I've done wrong**

Did Rose need him to tell her? Every second of that moment in her bedroom kept slipping back to her. He was unbuttoning her shirt as she was squeezing toothpaste on to her toothbrush. He was leaning forward to kiss her nose as she was staring at the squiggles the maths teacher called differentials. For the last three nights, whether she was wearing her earbuds or not, his voice rang in her head – *I miss you, you're special* – drawing out every atom of hurt and making them clank together. That's why she was shaking. All that hurt was vibrating inside her.

She'd thought about writing him a letter. She'd tell him how much he was hurting her. He'd known how hard it was for her to do what he'd asked, but he'd said he needed her. He'd said he understood. She didn't want much. She just wanted to know that he cared. She'd drop it through his letterbox late at night – except, maybe his mum would see it first. Or even worse, his brother would pick it up. She pulled her cardigan tighter, covering the small triangle of skin at the top of her shirt.

She glanced up at the main college building. She could go back in, climb the stairs and wait outside Kye's maths room, lean against the wall, try to look like she didn't care. The door would open and they would all come out, chatting and laughing. Maybe some of them would glance over at her. Maybe some of the laughter would be about her, because why else would he do this? Why would he stroke her neck and kiss her and untuck her shirt, then . . . Then run away and never talk to her again.

Really, Rose? You're going to confront him in front of his class? Why was she bothering even to think about it? She hardly had enough energy to think, let alone to be angry any more. She just had enough energy to stand up and walk away from this bench and pretend that she hadn't seen him pretending not to see her when they passed each other in the corridor yesterday.

*

Rudder watched Rose fill the saucepan with water. She'd only said three words since she'd got home from college and they were all swear words. She must have added 'blaspheme a lot' to her decommissioning plan.

He said, 'I thought you'd be seeing Kye.'

She slammed the saucepan on to the cooker. 'I thought you'd be at school.'

'Teacher training.' He flinched as she yanked open the drawer. She was lucky the handle didn't come off. It always did when Rudder pulled it too hard. 'Why don't you boil the kettle instead?'

Rose struck a match and lit the burner. 'Feel free to cook your own lunch.'

'Mum said you should.'

'That's what I'm doing. I don't need your commentary.'

Rudder picked up the kettle, manoeuvred around Rose and filled it with water. 'I'm going to see if this is quicker.'

Rose turned away from him and opened the cupboard. 'What type of pasta do you want?'

'What is there?'

She opened the door wider. He squinted at the packets. 'What are penne?'

'Tubes.'

'What are you having?'

'I'm not hungry.' She stood there with her hand on the cupboard door. Her pink nail varnish made her fingertips look raw.

He said, 'Why are you angry with me?'

'I'm not.'

'You're yelling.'

She spun round. 'Stop being so damn sensitive! Everything isn't always about you!'

The kettle clicked off. Rose pushed past him and went into their bedroom. Rudder just about held back his own blasphemy. It was so easy in the worldly world. The bad words floated to the top of your head, ready to pop out when you were cross. He hadn't said them though. He'd resisted the temptation. He'd endurethed. He opened the cupboard and took out the pasta shaped like butterflies. He poured some into the boiling water, his hands tingling from the steam. It was like his skin growled every time it was near something hot.

He pulled the wooden spoon out of the drying rack and gave the pasta a stir, quicker and quicker, making the butterflies spin in a whirlpool. Did God see this? How good Rudder was? Even when his sister was yelling for no reason, Rudder was being kind and thoughtful and cooking them both lunch. He heard the bedroom door open, but he didn't lift his head. If she caught him looking, she'd just start shouting again.

Her voice was quiet. 'Did you know, Ruds, in Japan, butterflies are a symbol of the living and the dead?'

He shook his head and carried on stirring. He didn't know and he didn't understand why he should know.

She said, 'I'm sorry I shouted at you. It's been a tough few days.'

He looked up. Her eyes were red and her make-up was smeared down her cheeks. He stopped stirring and the steam started burning through his scars. He jerked his hand away and the spoon banged against the pan. Rose took his hand and held it under the cold-water tap.

She said, 'Better?'

His hand was. Everything else was still wrong.

She said, 'We'll get through this, Ruds.'

She hugged him. He held his wet hand out so it didn't drip down her back. After thirteen, Pilgrim boys and girls weren't allowed to hug each other, even if they were related. Maybe not all things Pilgrims said were completely right.

There was a thud against the door. She let him go. They looked at each other.

He said, 'What's that?'

'I don't know. Maybe one of the kids upstairs kicked the door on their way down.'

She didn't look like she believed that. There was another thud, and another one. Rudder could almost see the shape of it through the wood.

He said, 'Should we open it?'

'No! Mum said we should never open the door to strangers.'

'We don't know they're strangers.'

More banging. The door frame rattled. Rose was holding his wet hand, squeezing a little too tight. It hurt, but he didn't want her to let go.

The noise stopped. His eyes met Rose's. Her smile looked like her mouth didn't want it.

She said, 'That's better.'

Another bang. It made Rudder's skin ripple. Then a man's voice, slow and muffled by the wood.

'I have a key. Either you open the door or I let myself in.'

Rudder tried to swallow but his throat had closed up. He had to breathe or he'd faint.

He said, 'Rose?'

She was biting her lip, not moving. There was stuff they could do. He should make them do it. Dive in to the bedroom and push the beds against the door and call the police. He couldn't move, though. He was *immobulused*.

The banging stopped. There was a scraping sound and the door flew open. Rose jumped back and flung an arm around Rudder. He could feel her heart beating through her shoulder. A man and a woman were standing in the main room. The man's t-shirt had a big skull on it, its empty eyes staring out from the man's chest.

Rose gripped Rudder even tighter, as if she was trying to stop herself from falling down.

She said, 'What do you want?'

The woman's eyes flicked round the flat. She was older than Mum, but if Mum had a sister, maybe that's how she'd look. She had the same pale brown skin and her nose was like Mum's too. She even had the same shadows under her eyes. Her hair was tucked up under a cap with a silver chain above the peak. She was thinner than Mum though, much thinner, even though most of Mum's clothes didn't fit any more.

The woman said, 'Where's your mother?'

Rudder opened his mouth, felt his tongue move. The ripple from the banging had caught in his skin. None of him would stay still. 'Work.'

The woman's eyes settled on him. He stared down at the floor. She was wearing heavy boots, special door-kicking boots. She would have used them if they'd locked themselves in the bedroom. They could never have escaped.

'When's she getting back?'

Rudder's mouth and tongue were doing the wrong things. They couldn't make words. The man slammed the flat door shut. The thud made the air shift sideways. He moved past the woman and opened the bedroom door. The backs of his trainers were scuffed, as if the woman had tested her boots on him first. Threads hung from the bottom of his jeans, catching on the insides of his trainers.

The woman said, 'You speak English, don't you?'

Rudder felt Rose nod.

The woman stepped forward. 'So when is she back?'

Rose's body tensed. 'Mum's doing a double shift. She'll be back late.'

The man came out of the bedroom. The trouser threads were mixed with a brown fringe. He was wearing the Marauder's Map like a cloak. Rudder opened his mouth but the man's face made him close it again. He tried to swallow again. It still hurt.

Rose said, 'That's my brother's. Put it back.'

The woman rested her back against the front door. 'Did she leave the money?'

The man twirled. The fringe flared out. 'Your brother has excellent taste, honey. My daughter's a big Harry Potter fan. She'd love something like this.'

The woman was saying something else and Rose was answering. The words sounded cross and frightened and Rudder tried to hold on to them, but it was hard when the man had Rudder's throw. It was upside down, Hogwarts' towers jabbing the floor every time he moved. The man smiled at Rudder. His mouth had too many teeth. He pulled the throw tighter round his shoulders and twirled quicker so it flapped against the back of his legs.

Rose held her free hand out to the man.

'Can my brother have it back, please?'

The man held the throw wide like wings and smiled again, lips bared back over his gums. The woman pushed herself away from the door and came towards Rose. Rose shrank back pulling Rudder with her.

'Your mum's had a bad time. But we've all had bad times, haven't we?'

The man nodded. The fringes swayed.

'She made an agreement,' the woman said. 'I let her live here, she pays me money. It's a common arrangement and not too hard to remember. I need that money by next week. Every single penny of it.'

She looked from Rose to Rudder, coming towards them,

the man behind her. Rose gripped Rudder's hand tighter, pressing the scars into his bones.

The woman tapped her ears. 'You two need to talk up. You know the message you're passing on, right?'

'Yes,' Rose said. She sounded like all her voice wanted to hide away.

The woman nodded. 'Good. Your mum knows where to reach me. And I know how to reach her.'

Rudder felt the throw drop round his shoulders. It was heavier than before.

The man showed his teeth again. 'I definitely have to get one of those for my daughter. Maybe next time, eh?'

The scuffed trainers and the kicking-door boots moved away. They paused and the flat door opened and closed. A few minutes later the street door banged shut.

Rose's hand went loose in his, but he couldn't let her go. He moved with her, over to the window as she looked out. He wanted to stop her. They might look up and see them, then come back.

Rose said, 'It's okay. They've gone.'

But they hadn't. The man's fingerprints were pressed into the threads of Rudder's throw. There was a muddy smudge from the woman's boots on the carpet by the door.

'Shit!' Rose ran into the kitchen. He followed her in. The water from the pasta had boiled over on to the stove. Rose turned off the cooker and came back into the main room. She sat down and he sat next to her. She tried to pull the throw over both of them, but he shrugged it off. She let it slip from their knees on to the floor and put both arms around him.

He said, 'I want Mum.'

'Me too, but she's not allowed to have her phone with her on shift. If she comes home, she'll lose money and that will make things worse.'

'I still want her.' He'd tried to hold it in, a sob as big as a shout. Now it had to come out. 'You have to get Mum!'

Rose slid off the sofa and crouched in front of him. 'Mum needs to earn money.'

'I want her. What if they come back? They will, won't they?'

Rose tipped forwards on her toes and rested her arms on his knees. It felt like he was taking all her weight. The throw looked a flat dead animal next to her.

'Please, Rose,' he said. 'Please call Mum.'

*

Rudder was asleep at last. Rose'd had to help Mum half carry him off the sofa and tuck him up. Rose picked up his throw, folded it into a square and laid it next to his elbow. His legs kicked in the air and he gasped. His hands flailed out then settled back on the bed, one above his head, the other half clenched by his side. This is when she needed real magic so she could she go into his brain and pull out the bad memories queuing up to turn into nightmares. She'd curl them into silver wisps, open the window and watch them float away.

She whispered his name, but he was deep into sleep.

Rose pushed back the clothes rail and stared out the window. It was past one o'clock in the morning and there were so many cars. Where was everybody going? Two men were sitting on the wall next to the hostel, smoking and sharing chips from a cardboard box. A lorry turned into the cash and carry. Two girls that looked around Rose's age were arm-in-arm, skipping down the road shouting and singing. A bus passed them and they screamed, chasing it to the bus stop. The driver waited for them before pulling off.

Rose was nowhere near sleepy. It felt like her brain was having a deep stretch before it went on a long run. Her body was full of its restlessness. She opened the bedroom door, catching it just before it creaked. Mum was flat out on the sofa, her arm dangling by her side. She hadn't even pulled open the bed. Her head was pressed up against one arm, her feet jammed against the other as if she was wedging herself in. Rose crouched down and kissed Mum's forehead. It was damp with sweat.

Rose went over to the kitchen and filled the kettle from the hot tap. Grandma Yellow had always insisted Rose used cold water even though it took longer, but Grandma Yellow's cold-water pipes didn't sound like there were elephants stampeding through them. Rose fished the chamomile teabags from the cupboard by the window. According to the back of the box, they were best before three months ago, but how could they go off? They were dried plants. She picked one out, sniffed it and dropped it in her mug. She topped up with hot water and sniffed again. It smelled like their sink. She rested the mug on the counter. It needed sugar, buckets of it, to be drinkable, but then she'd never sleep.

Mum turned on to her side. Somehow she managed to do it without falling off the sofa. She worked almost every day until late at night and she still didn't have a proper bed. Was it wrong to want more? Not much more, but somewhere they could open the window without smelling lamb fat, where they didn't have hyped-up kids thundering over their head and lorries beeping and reversing at all hours across the road.

Even if Rose did pass her English and maths, even if she did get a job, what difference would it make? If she added her money to Mum's, it wasn't going to buy her her own room again. And what job was Rose good for anyway? If she'd stayed a Pilgrim, she could have helped in a school or learned to make clothes. Out here, she was nothing. Maybe the Pilgrims were right. They'd got what they deserved, Rose especially.

That stupid decommissioning programme. *Worship idols.* That'd worked well, didn't it? *Dress immodestly.* So every pervy idiot in the world yells crap at you. *Beget immodesty with worldly boyfriend.* She wiped her eyes on the damp tea towel by the kettle. She tried a sip of tea. It didn't taste of anything, but she could still smell the familiar scent. *All girls did it.* Rose had done *it.* She was all girls now. She felt like fingers were grasping her skull, tighter and tighter until the tips were close to touching each other. Maybe demons were real.

She slung the tea into the sink and crept back past Mum into the bedroom. Rudder was sprawled but quiet. She slipped a jumper on over her t-shirt and her jogging trousers over her leggings. She rummaged under her duvet for her socks and pulled out an old beanie from the box under her bed. Her trainers were next to Rudder's school shoes. She unhooked her coat and shoved her keys and travelcard in a pocket.

She let herself out, gently bumping the door closed. Down eight, nine, ten stairs and out on to the street. Delicious Kebabs was closed, though sometimes the owner and his friends stayed late watching Turkish TV and laughing. Tonight, the shutter was drawn down. The beggar by the cash point was gone but he'd left his cardboard spread out for whoever was taking the morning shift. There was rain in the air; it would probably turn to mush. One of the hostel guys was still on the wall, his cigarette long dead. He was bent over staring at his feet as if he was testing to see how low he could go until he tipped on to the pavement. A car sped by, a sprinkle of orange ashes floating down from a back passenger's window.

Rose started walking. Buses passed her, people pressed against the glass. She walked past the 24-hour store. It was so close but she still hadn't been in there yet. Mum always said that the Turkish shop next to Sainsbury's was cheaper. A human filled out a blanket on the ground outside. They were turned to the wall like Mum on the sofa. The guy behind the till was checking his phone. Rose carried on up the hill, following the dark arches of the railway line and the gleam of the hospital in the far distance. The road curved past a museum and a supermarket car park shielded with hoardings. Rose knew there'd be people at work in there now, stacking the shelves. Mum had been one of them. She'd liked it but had never been able to catch up on her sleep and the doctor had advised her to stop. Then on past the skeleton of the market, past the library and the sleeping tube station. Three older Muslim guys in long tunics and caps were coming towards her. She imagined them meeting their friends and family, taking their place in the mosque and feeling the warmth of their faith surround them. They'd know everyone beside them, in front of them, behind them. As they passed her, they'd never think that Rose had once known that feeling too.

Rose carried on towards the towers and cranes with their pin pricks of red light. The city blocked the sky. It was too early for the sun to come up, but the blaze from the towers made its own dawn. A petrol station. An art gallery. A taxi stopped across the road, the passenger jumping out and dashing through the traffic to the cash point. He didn't glance at Rose. She was part of the night.

Her legs ached and she felt a nub of hunger. She ducked

into a shop, blinking at the bright light. The owner watched as she pulled money out of her pocket, picked up a Snickers bar and some mints, smiling at her as she counted out the coins for him. She tore open the wrapping and took a big bite out of the chocolate. The toffee-coated peanuts were hard to swallow. She went back into the shop and bought two cans of Coke. She opened one and stuck the other in her bag.

Walking, walking, one foot after another. Cardboard chicken boxes, chewing gum, a mess of lettuce and tomato from a dropped takeaway. And people. Girls in tight dresses and heels laughing with their boyfriends. Road workers in hi-vis and hard hats, their bodies sunk in a trough of pipes and wires.

The landscape was changing. Rose stopped by a sign. She could turn left towards the river and Tower Bridge or carry on through to the city. A rubbish truck crawled past followed by more men in hi-vis hurling bags into the crusher. A bin man paused beside her.

'You all right, love?'

She nodded. She was, because the more she walked, the more her idea made sense. Her fingertips were tingling from the cold can. She took another sip. Yes, there was a way out of all this.

A church was stranded in a muddle of roads. Further along, the Gherkin was reflecting back London's grey light, while neon lifts were shooting up and down a high tower.

Rose's feet wanted to stop, but she was going to carry on, one foot after another. She reached Leadenhall Market. Mum had brought her and Rudder here soon after they'd left the Pilgrims. His hands had still been in bandages, but he'd closed his eyes and smiled. The men in suits were really wizards, he'd said, and the women were witches. Ollivanders was behind The Pen Shop. You just had to know which bricks to press.

She was at the crossroads by the Bank of England. She let her fingers drag across its wall. *'Cast but a glance at riches, and they are gone, for they will surely sprout wings and fly off to the sky like an eagle.'* Proverbs 23:4–5. She laughed to herself. Grandma Yellow would be shocked that Rose remembered so much.

Rose had to keep walking, pounding her idea into possibility. She was on the main drag now but knew where she was going. Another church – so many of them caught between the shops and offices. She hurried past the shopping centre and cut through the square. It was funny how you could miss it, just a few metres away and drowned out by the shops. Then, suddenly, you were too close and it was too big to see in one go.

Mum had never been inside St Paul's Cathedral. Rudder, neither. Rose had. It was a class trip before she'd moved school and Mum had agreed with Ms Wormwood that it would be educational for Rose to participate. Ms Wormwood hadn't known that only Pilgrim men could sign the permission forms, or if she had, she was keeping it quiet. Rose had looked up into the giant dome and wanted to cry. If the Spirit was so big it could fit in here, it must be so squashed up in Grandma Yellow's prayer room. Rose had laid down on the cold floor and looked up at the paintings on the ceiling until someone in charge had complained that she was a fire hazard. She'd wanted to explain that girls weren't supposed to feel the way she did, only men could be lifted by the Spirit and only then in Pilgrim sanctuaries. This was wrong. This was worldly, but lying there, she'd felt arms lift her and float with her to the centre of the dome.

The gates to St Paul's churchyard were locked and the windows dark. Rose was not alone, though. A group of foreign students were sitting on the steps, passing round bottles of beers. Another couple were kissing by the arch. Rose walked to the top of the stairs and sat down, leaning against the great wooden door. She stretched out her legs. They didn't want to unbend. A bottle clanked on to the steps. The boy by the arch pulled the girl away, arms around each other.

The clock chimed. Quarter to three. She rested her head against the wood and closed her eyes. For the first time since leaving the Pilgrims, she prayed.

I want to do the right thing. Please help me . . .

She pressed her ear to the cathedral door. There was a whisper in her ear, as if the Spirit had answered her.

186

<u>Eight Stages of Soul, translated from Libro Rojo No. 1,</u>
<u>written down by Rudder Santos</u>

Fellow Pilgrim travellers. Do not forget our mission to atone for ourselves and others, to bring righteous souls with us to the glorious, bright world when Clean Slate makes a tally of the reformed.

1. The Soul of the Pilgrim Elder. Low trace of sin and automatic Prime Ascension at the End of Days.

2. The Soul of the Pilgrim Uncle. Low trace of sin and automatic Prime Ascension if preceded by vigorous immersive atonement and sustained mission.

3. The Soul of the Pilgrim Brother. A burden of sin quickly responsive to prayer and vigorous immersive atonement and sustained mission. Leaders as the Clean Slate tallies and automatic Second Ascension.

4. The Soul of the Pilgrim Woman. A burden of sin. Second Ascension predicated on response to prayer, vigorous immersive atonement, sustained mission and Elder authority.

5. The Soul of the Enlightened Worldly Traveller (male). Burdened by worldly concerns and temptations but uplifted by conversion, revelation, prayer and a programme of atonement. Reformed souls will be tallied.

6. *The Soul of the Worldly Man.* Weighted and concealed by worldly concerns, temptations and vanities.

7. *The Soul of the Worldly Woman.* Seduced by worldly concerns, temptations and vanities. Left to wander the world post Second Ascension.

8. *Excised Pilgrim.* A soul taunted by its proximity to Ascension then cast aside. Consumed by the fiery beasts of hell

Dear Rudder,

Right, I am so impressed that you remembered all this. By heart. And that you wrote it all down. I hope you did it because you needed to get it out your head. Now you have written it down, BURN IT, LITTLE BROTHER, BURN IT!

Do you really believe that all those Elders are pure souls? 'Low traces of sin'? Mum told you how that Founder was found drunk in a strip bar in Madrid. And number 4, Ruds. Are you happy with that? Women are always going to be lower than you just because they're women?

And I tell you what, I'd rather be consumed by the fiery beasts of hell than knock on people's doors to preach Pilgrim at them.

So BURN IT, little brother, burn it.
Your beautiful sister (consumed by Worldly concerns)
Rose xxxxx

16

Rudder was drowning. The water was thicker than mud and so heavy he couldn't open his eyes. It pressed against his face, pushing up through his nose and oozing down his throat. He tried to draw breath. His lungs were heavy and his tongue was coated with stringy weeds. He forced his eyes open. Through the thickening murk, he was staring into a skull's eye sockets.

He sat bolt upright. His hand was clutching at the sludge. He loosened his fingers and felt it drop away. He rubbed the stickiness away from his eyes and opened them. He was in bed and the throw was crumpled beside him. He reached across for his alarm clock. It was morning, nearly eleven. He must have been dreaming that dream for a long time.

'Rose?' His voice was a croak.

She was silent. He peered through the clothes on the rail. Rose's bed was empty and made up. Made up? Rose only ever made her bed just before she got into it. Something else was different. He could see Rose's bed without moving the clothes rail. There were gaps. His school blazer was there and his winter jacket, his good trousers and his three pale blue Pitt Academy shirts. Where was Rose's stuff? Her stupid skirts and her pink dress and her little jacket with the cupcake buttons? He pushed aside his shirts for a better look. Her sparkly shoes were gone too. He'd even helped her glue on the glitter and she'd told him that made them extra special. It was like they'd been suckered through the floorboards and into the fryer below.

The door opened. Mum was holding a mug and some toast and chocolate spread.

She said, 'I thought I heard you.'

'Where's Rose?'

Mum sat down on Rose's bed, though with the duvet pulled up like that, it wasn't Rose's bed any more. It looked like the ones on hospital wards. Mum pushed the clothes rail out through the open door. The room felt bigger, lighter, emptier. He and Mum sat on the beds facing each other.

Mum said, 'Rose has gone away.'

'Away?' His heart knocked. 'I knew this would happen!' He should have stayed awake. As soon as he closed his eyes, they must have come for her. The man with the skull on his chest could have easily picked her up and taken her away.

Mum said, 'We thought you were asleep.'

We thought? Mum let it happen?

'You sent Rose away? They'll hurt her! Get the money, Mum! Get it quickly!'

Mum frowned. 'Money?' Her eyes widened. She put her toast and mug down on Rose's storage box. She came and sat next to him. 'Oh, Rudder, this is nothing to do with those bastards yesterday.' She said the swear word so hard that spit came out. 'Well, it does have something to do with them, I suppose, but Rose isn't with them. God, no.'

Mum reached back for the plate and offered it to him. 'Please, Rudder, take some.' The toast had been cut in triangles and the chocolate spread was thick right to the edges. He took a piece and bit a corner. The spread coated his lips and worked its way between his teeth. He dropped the toast back on to the plate.

'Has Rose gone off with Kye?'

'Kye? That was an option I hadn't even considered. I didn't know they were that close.' She blew out her cheeks. 'I've got a feeling that there's lots of things I don't know . . .'

Rudder looked away.

'Well,' Mum said. 'It's a little too late to think about that now.' She picked up her tea and took a sip. 'The thing is Rudder, Rose and I had a long talk early this morning and, well . . . We knew this was going to be hard for you, but we thought it was for the best.'

What was for the best? Rudder dug his teeth into his lip, so hard it was going to scar.

'She's gone back to live with your father.'

Mum put her hand on his, as if that would make it better. He snatched his hand away. 'I wanted to go back! She knew that.'

'Rudder, it wasn't an easy—'

'She tricked me! She was pretending to be worldly! She

192

pretended she hated it, when all the time she was planning to go back instead of me.'

'Rudder, that's not true! She didn't feel that she had a choice.'

'There was a choice! They could have chosen me!'

His mouth clamped shut. Mum looked . . . did she look frightened? Then, it struck him.

'It's coming, isn't it? Rose knew and didn't tell me!'

'What's coming, Rudder?'

'The End of Days! Rose has gone back to atone.'

'Rudder!' Mum tried to draw him close again, but he wriggled away. Mum must have known too.

'That's what's happening! They know for sure, don't they?'

'Listen to me, Rudder!' Mum was shouting. 'Stop this nonsense!'

He and Mum glared at each other. How could Mum let Rose be in Sanctuary when it happened and not him? Why was he being punished the most? How could his sins be bigger than Rose's?

Mum said, 'Look, if you want to, send Rose a message. I've let her smuggle in her phone. She's promised to be careful.'

Phone. His stomach dipped. That was it. His biggest sin was on his phone. Maybe it was a sin even bigger than Rose's, because he knew better . . .

'Listen to me.' Mum took his hands. 'You know how much Rose cares about you. She wants you to live a normal life and have a chance to be yourself.'

'The Pilgrims were normal to me.' That's why he should have known straight away. Of course he was being punished. Of course his sin was bigger.

Mum lifted his hands up. It was hard to see his scars in the dirty light, but they both knew they were there.

She said, 'In the normal world, you don't get this for reading a book.'

'It was an accident, Mum!' And he shouldn't have read the book. Mum always shouted when he tried to remind her of that. Why did she and Rose think the worldly world was better? You were still punished if you did prohibited things. It was the same in the Pilgrims. Rudder had known the rules and broken them so God had sent fire. When sin had manifested on his phone, he should have cast it away. He hadn't. He'd looked at the picture. More than once.

Mum dropped his hands again. 'Those people who came yesterday aren't coming back, Rudder. But it's such a struggle. No matter how many hours I work, I can't afford to keep us going.' Mum spread out her hands. 'This is hardly better than the hostel, but even shabby little holes like this are in demand. There's a very long list of young people happy to pay top dollar just to say they live in Hackney.'

'It doesn't matter. We're not going to be here long.' The End of Days was near. When the Clean Slate happened, it didn't matter if you were in a cave or a palace, your soul

194

would be plucked out and judged.

'I don't know how long we're going to be here, Rudder! I'm no dream tenant. Single mum, two kids, no proper job, it was hard enough to get this.' She sighed. 'Are you listening to me, Rudder?'

He nodded. It was easier if he didn't have to speak. Mum had made him empty out his End of Days rucksack when they'd first moved here, because he needed the bag for school. He had to find all the things to go in it. Obviously, he wouldn't ascend with the Elders, but once the Clean Slate tallied the reformed and righteous souls, if he worked hard enough, he could ascend then.

He faded back in to Mum.

'. . . Rose's idea. She made a deal with your father. She'd go back to the Pilgrims if he paid all the remaining allowance for her upfront in one big lump sum. I was surprised he agreed. Guilt probably. Rudder, you must understand how much that'll help us. I can pay all that back rent and get those bullies off our case and even have some left over. Then hopefully, our benefits will kick in.'

He shook his head. 'It doesn't matter.'

'Of course it bloody matters, Rudder. Do you think I wanted Rose to go?' Mum stood up. 'I know this is a shock for you. I'll leave you to mull it over.'

Mum pushed past the clothes rail. He heard the pipes clunk as she turned on the kitchen taps.

Rose was gone. He'd sometimes wished for that. Not

quite prayed, but as close as he could without being blasphemous. All the room was his now. He could change beds. Rose's always looked more comfortable. Or he could take turns, one for weekends and holidays and one for school time. Or Mondays, Wednesday and Fridays he could sleep in Rose's. Or he could push them together and have one big bed, though his duvet probably wouldn't stretch across both of them.

And no Kye! NO KYE!

But it didn't matter. It was still all going to end soon. Rudder stood up and went and closed the door. The coat hooks were still on the floor from where Kye had dumped them, though Rose had folded up his robes and left them on the end of his bed. They'd slipped back on to the floor while he was sleeping. He rested his back against the door. How could Mum think this was right? Didn't she understand what was about to hit them? But that didn't have to stop Rudder being prepared. Rose had her plan. He would have one too. Rudder's recommissioning (and atonement) programme.

First, he had to rid himself of temptation. He eased out his book box from under his bed, pulled out his *Philosopher's Stone* and placed it on Rose's bed. Then, out came *Chamber of Secrets*. Then all of the others, one by one, stacked up in a wonky pile on the tidy duvet. He added the Platform 9¾ alarm clock, picked up his Columba robes and draped them on top. Then over that, his throw. Then he changed them round. The throw just made him think about the man with the skull on his chest twirling around so much he made the fringe flap. He spread the robes out so they covered all of it.

When Mum left for work, he'd gather together all the prohibited DVDs and the sinful CDs and bring them in here too. Even *West Side Story* with Anita and her jokes and smiles and her high kicks. Though, in the end, she . . . she wasn't laughing any more.

That just left his phone. It was charging in the main room. He bobbed past the clothes rail.

'So you're going to text Rose, then?' Rudder jumped. Mum was standing by the bathroom door watching him. He tugged his phone out the socket and ran back into his bedroom and closed the door.

No, he certainly wasn't going to text Rose. As far as he was concerned, he no longer had a sister. He was going to take his phone and rid himself of temptation. All his music and that picture. He just had to press delete. It would be gone for good. When Mum left, he'd cook the phone in the microwave for a few seconds. That should take care of it. If Mum asked where his phone was, he could show it to her, but it wouldn't be working.

Except –

He had message notifications. They were from the group chat. His new friends. He tapped into the messages, just to see. There were sixty-eight of them. Sixty-eight messages! He set the phone down on top of the books. Friends can lead you into temptation. He didn't need worldly friends, especially not right now when the end was coming. '*Whoever walks with the wise becomes wise, but the companion of fools will suffer harm.*' Only Pilgrims were wise. Everyone knew that.

Except –

The Pilgrims had left Rudder to fend for himself. And now they'd taken Rose too and left Rudder to the Worldly Wise. If he wanted to ascend, he had to atone – he had to save their souls and his own. And how could he save them if he didn't know anything about them? Rudder picked his phone up again and scrolled to the first message. Sash was stressed out because she wanted to go to church but her mum had fallen out with the pastor and stopped going. Rudder's mouth fell open. Things like this happened to other people too? Rudder scrolled down. Dom said he was making a rainbow cake for his mum's birthday. He'd added a picture of a bowl with cake mix next to loads of different coloured bottles. Mo posted a crying laughing emoji, and asked if it was because his mum was a lesbian. Rudder clapped his hand to his mouth. How could Mo say that? But then Dom had sent the same emoji back. '*You know it bruv.*' Dom's mum was . . . ? She was a . . . ? And Dom's dad didn't mind? The tips of Rudder's ears were burning with the thought of it.

Idil was also talking about her mum, who had gone back to Somalia for a funeral, and Idil really missed her. Dom posted a heart and crying emojis and below that Flossy added a GIF of a chocolate bar being opened. That last message was over an hour ago. Was it too late for Rudder to say something? Then Flossy was complaining that she was supposed to meet a boy tonight. Her dad didn't want her to. She wasn't really sure if she really wanted to meet the boy, but it was better than staying at home with her parents watching *Strictly*. Rudder frowned. He loved watching *Strictly*, especially in Room 27 when he and Mum and Rose used to snuggle up in the bed passing around Minstrels and Haribo. Was that wrong? It was just as well that he hadn't told anyone about that. Idil invited Flossy round to her house. Imagine having friends come around to hang out. Would Mum let him bring anyone here? Even if she was okay with it, maybe it wasn't a good idea. They probably lived in posh houses that didn't smell of kebab.

Flossy couldn't go anyway. She was grounded because she'd spent more than a hundred quid at Comicon. *A hundred quid?* Rudder's heart almost popped out. How can anyone have that much money? It wasn't just Rudder that thought that – Dom wanted to know too. But apparently it was money from Flossy's nan who'd died a few months ago. Her nan's death was making her dad grumpy. More hearts and hugging GIFs. It was weird though. When Pilgrims died, everything went to the Founders, who shared it out to whoever needed it the most.

Everyone was telling each other their problems and helping each other. It could have been nice to have friends. But he wasn't here for that now. There was no time, when the End of Days was coming. He had to learn, he had to atone.

Rudder glanced at the next message, sat up straighter on his bed and read it again. Ric was grounded because his mum had found some porn on his phone. It wasn't bad porn, Ric said, but she'd still gone mental. Rudder's heart pounded.. There was sinful stuff on Ric's phone too? What did he do with it? If it wasn't bad porn, did that make it good? Wasn't all of it sinful? Ric's dad had been called and even Ric's gran. *His gran!* Imagine Dad and Grandma Yellow being called because Mum had checked Rudder's phone. Rudder's ears were burning so hot they felt like they would fall off and lie smoking on the floor. Idil posted a poo emoji and left the conversation. Flossy replied that all porn was bad because it exploited women. Dom didn't agree because there was special lesbian porn and lesbians didn't mind.

There was WHAT??

Even Mo was surprised. '**Ur mum told u bout that?**'

'**No, bruv! Everyone knows it.**'

Everyone? Rudder didn't. And he didn't want to. Rose had sort of told him about – things – but he'd pulled his throw over his head and wouldn't look at her until she'd stopped talking. But if everyone knew, Rudder should too. And however hard it was, what he was learning was good. It would help him know what to do with the photo. It would help him atone.

He touched his forehead. There was a small painful bump. He could almost see Rose sitting next to him, laughing. *No, Rudder. You do not have plague boils. The world isn't starting to end*. The sky outside was getting dark, though. It was just a cloud over the sun. Not thunder. Not hail. Not the worst thunderstorm ever, but the End of Days could easily start this way – rain and lightning before the deluge of fire. He had to finish making his plan and put it into place as soon as possible.

Ric was saying that the stuff on his phone was real people doing it, not paid ones. They weren't being exploited because they wanted to film themselves so other people could see. The phone felt even damper and heavier than it had been before. Rudder dropped it on his bed. People couldn't . . . they didn't . . . why would they do that? It was definitely getting darker outside, and wasn't that a spatter of rain on the window? He wiped his hands on Rose's duvet and retrieved his phone. He had to understand this.

Flossy had written a long reply to Ric. Rudder read the first two lines and looked away. He needed to study this properly, without being disturbed. He opened the bedroom door, quietly, to see where Mum was. She was standing by the fridge scrolling through her phone. Did she know about this stuff? He closed the door again and went back to Flossy. Her sister's friend was at university. Her boyfriend had filmed them . . . *together*. She hadn't minded at the time, but then after she split up with him, he posted it on to something called a revenge site. No one could see her face, but Flossy said the slimeball made sure everyone knew it was her. She couldn't stop crying and had to leave the university. Her dad still wouldn't talk to her.

Rudder sat back. Dad would go mad if he knew Rose had been alone with Kye. What if she'd done anything like that . . . The last time Kye was here, they'd been in the bedroom. It wasn't for long, but when Kye came out he was slipping his phone in his pocket. Rose had stayed in the bedroom. When Rudder tried to go in, she'd yelled at him.

Rudder moved off the bed and sat with his back against the bedroom door. That was definitely rain outside. A pigeon was perching on the windowsill, pressing its fat flank against the glass, like it was trying to listen in. Imagine if Dad or Grandma Yellow somehow found the picture on his phone and even worse, saw the message about Rose underneath. That's why he was going to delete it. But wasn't that the easy thing to do? Would that be enough to atone? He'd already looked at it, more than once. He'd been tested and he'd failed. Should he tell someone about it? Should he name his sin? He took a deep breath and opened the message with the picture.

'Rudder?' Mum banged on the door. The phone jumped out of his hand on to the floor. It felt like his heart was about to land beside it. He flipped it over with his toe and kicked it under the bed. He stood up and opened the door.

Mum held out her own phone. 'Your father.'

'Dad?'

She passed Rudder the phone, closing the door behind her.

'Rudder?'

'Dad.'

Silence.

Dad said, 'Are you still there, Rudder?'

'Yes, I am still here, Dad. That's because you chose Rose to be with you.'

'Rudder, your sister finally understands that she needs to atone and seek forgiveness. We are a forgiving community.'

'I want to atone, too! But you won't give me a chance! It's nearly here, isn't it?' Rudder touched his forehead. Yes, the bump was getting bigger and it felt like there was a second one coming up next to it. 'The End of Days is nearly here.'

'Of course it is, Rudder.'

So he was right! Rudder pushed back a sob. The rain was coming in hard now. It was only midday, but it looked like night. 'Please don't leave me on earth alone, Dad. I know you're not an Elder yet, but you'll go first, won't you? You don't need to wait for the Clean Slate.'

Dad sighed, 'I've forfeited my place in the First Ascension. It's your mother who has been excised, not you. I knew you'd be upset, but I want you to know that you will return to us. At the moment, it's difficult. The matter with your hands means that . . . *intruders* . . . may have to come into your grandmother's house to make notes about you. We can't go through that again. But God works in mysterious ways, Rudder. Be patient. I have to go now.'

The line went dead.

Rudder stared at the phone. Maybe someone had interrupted him and he had hung up quickly. Dad wasn't supposed to use the phone and Rudder shouldn't encourage him to sin. He went into the main room to give Mum back her phone.

Mum swung her legs off the sofa so he could sit down. 'I'm sorry you're upset, Rudder. Rose just wanted to protect you. She hoped you'd understand.'

'Mum?'

'Yes?'

'Do you think that the End of Days is coming?'

'No, but I have ordered us some pizza.' She smiled and put her arm round him. 'Rudder, I know I teased Rose about her decommissioning plan, but in some ways, she's got it right. She's recognised the ways that Pilgrims scare the hell out of each other. We don't want you swallowed up in it again until you've had some distance and can make your own decisions. Imagine, no more Harry Potter. No more *Strictly Come Dancing*. Can you live without those?'

Yes, I'd rather live without those than my soul.

Mum turned over the TV. 'Look, it's that weird comedy you like about the scientist guys. I don't have to be at work until two. We can watch a couple of episodes together, if you like.'

Well, perhaps one episode wouldn't hurt.

But come tomorrow, he would do what he had to do. He would name his sin.

17

The atonement room had moved, though Rose wouldn't put it past Grandma Yellow to have moved it especially for Rose. It was now on the second floor next to the toilet in what used to be called the box room. It was still stacked with boxes of 'Pilgrims' Way' leaflets and empty *Rojos Libros* folders. They'd dug out a camp bed and a duvet and laid a Bible on her pillow, but there was nowhere for Rose to put the few things she'd brought with her. Dad had been strict. Nothing from the evil world outside should pollute Grandma's house. Rose had imagined the phone she'd jammed into her bra turning itself on and calling out to Grandma Yellow. It was just as well Mum had lent her a baggy jumper to wear over her jeans for her journey there.

Rose had wanted this. She had to remember that. Forty-eight hours ago, she'd virtually begged Mum for it.

Mum had been furious when Rose returned from her walk. Mum couldn't shout properly, because she hadn't wanted to wake up Rudder, but her face had said it all. She'd been waiting by that window for nearly an hour, she'd shout-whispered, trying to decide whether she should call the police. She told Rose she'd seen her get off the bus opposite, and that's when she'd dashed downstairs, grabbed Rose's arm and dragged her up into the main room.

'Where the hell were you?'

'I needed to think.'

'You needed to *think*?' Mum had her real face on, the one that didn't try and smooth out the worry. 'What sort of thinking makes you wander the streets of London in the dark?' Mum collapsed on to the sofa. 'Oh God, Rose. You aren't, are you?'

'Aren't what?'

'I . . .' Mum had wiped her eyes. It had seemed to make the shadows darker. 'I know I'm not around as much as I should be. I'll try and drop a few shifts so we'll have time to talk about things.'

She'd wondered if Rudder had snitched about Kye coming round, but Mum had carried on.

'I wasn't much older than you are now when I had you.'

Rose had sat down next to her. 'No, Mum. I'm not pregnant, if that's what you're asking. I haven't . . .'

Not now. There are so many other ways I can mess up, Mum.

'So what's on your mind?'

'I want to go back, Mum.'

'Back where?'

'To the Pilgrims.'

'Are you mad, Rose? No!'

'Rudder's having nightmares again.' Mum's face dropped. Rose took Mum's hand. 'When those people came yesterday –' Rose took a deep breath – 'when they came, you should have seen his face. It was like he was by the fire again, watching his book burning.'

Mum clasped Rose's hand. 'I wasn't there then, either. I'm so sorry.'

So am I, Mum. For more than you know.

'It's not your fault, Mum. It's just . . . I went for a walk to help me think and I had an idea. We need money and, well, what if we ask Dad to pay all the allowance he was going to pay up until I was eighteen in one go? Why string it out? And in exchange, I'll go back. They'll have saved another soul.'

'Your soul is worth more than that, Rose. I cannot let you go back into that world. I know how they treat backsliders.'

'Mum, Rudder's right. Out here is tough too. At least I know what to expect there.'

Mum had clutched Rose's shoulder. 'No, you don't know what to expect! I was the damn barrier between you two and the rest of them! If you go back, how can all the crap we've been through be worth it?'

Mum had started crying. That hadn't been the plan at all.

'Your grandmother said that you were born worldly,' Mum had said, sniffing. 'It was supposed to be an insult, but for me, it meant that if I took that great leap out, you would survive. Your grandmother, though, she saw it as a challenge. You would be a Pilgrim, no matter what.' Mum had grabbed some toilet roll from the bathroom and wiped her face. 'It seems that she was right. Saving your soul, Rose? That's the

207

least of it.' Mum shook her head. 'You'll be their greatest victory.'

The toilet paper was disintegrating in Mum's hands. Rose tore off some kitchen roll and gently wiped Mum's face.

'We have survived, Mum, but what's going to happen next? Those people are going to be back knocking our door down, aren't they? Can you pay them? If we can't stay here, where are we going to go next? Let Grandma think it's a victory, Mum. Just for a little while.'

Mum rested her forehead against Rose's. She felt damp and sticky against Rose's cold outdoor skin.

'I can't let you be that girl,' Mum said, 'the one so full of worldly sin that everything you do is wrong. You'll be a Pilgrim, yes, but the lowest of the low.'

'No, Mum. I won't be that girl, because I know you're here and Rudder's here, and I promise I'll come back.'

They'd been extra quiet packing her stuff. Rose didn't think she could face the look of betrayal in Rudder's eyes if he'd woken up. Dad had picked her up a couple of hours later, parking in the side street next to the hostel until she was ready. She'd checked on Rudder, then carefully lodged her phone in her bra next to the twenty-pound note Mum had made her take. Mum said she'd heard of returners having their possessions searched in front of a committee to check they weren't bringing sin in with them.

Dad had stayed silent, starting and stopping, hitting rush hour. Rose had watched his profile, willing him to speak. As they waited in a long queue behind some temporary traffic lights, she'd finally said, 'Thank you for helping us. I know you'd prefer it was Rudder.'

'Both of you are my children.'

Grandma had been waiting by the door and brought Rose straight up to the box room. Rose had seen one of the coffee-table Bibles poking out of the pocket of Grandma's apron.

Grandma had said, 'Kneel, please.'

Rose had opened her mouth, then caught the glint in Grandma's eyes. If Rose was going to survive this, she'd have to choose her battles. She'd knelt. Grandma had started reciting a prayer of atonement. Rose had glanced up and seen Grandma's words weren't directed down at her – her grandmother's hand had been reaching up, guiding her prayer to God. The Pilgrims had missed a trick by banning women from preaching. Grandma would have been a wonder.

Then Lily-Beth had brought Rose a glass of water, a cheese sandwich and a bag of her pre-pregnancy clothes. Rose had emptied the bag on to the camp bed. These must have been Lily-Beth's door-knocking outfits, nothing too bright in case they scared potential converts, clothes that meant you could merge into the background if you had to. Rose held up a skirt. It was pale grey with a thin darker check, a wide waistband and a hem that would brush Rose's feet. It was just as well that Mum had stopped Rose bringing her silver leggings. She couldn't have resisted wearing them underneath this.

Rose laid the skirt down. She was a Pilgrim girl again. She had to peel off her worldliness and let the old rules wrap themselves around her, tight, no spaces to think of anything else. She opened her Bible. *'In the beginning, God created the heaven and the earth. And the earth was without form, and void; and darkness was upon the face of the deep.'* Yes, there was darkness inside her. She clamped her teeth together. She would not give that boy any more tears.

The box room door opened again. Now Rose knew why Rudder complained when she didn't knock.

'Are we to pray again, Grandma Yellow?'

Grandma blinked. She reminded Rose of the plastic dolls in the Pilgrims' nursery. Their eyelids clicked up and down when you moved them. 'Your father has spoken to your mother and brother.'

'Poor Rudder. How is he?'

'As you'd expect.'

'And Mum?'

Grandma closed the door behind her as she left the room.

Rose let her smile drop. Yes, poor Rudder. He must hate her. She should talk to him, but not now, with Grandma Yellow bursting in all the time. Rose would wait until after-supper prayers. Hopefully, Mum had done her best to explain why Rose had gone. Well, as much as Mum knew about it. Maybe Rudder would be so angry, he finally would tell Mum about Kye. That would make Mum worry even more. *Please, Rudder, keep your mouth shut. Kye's over. Mum doesn't need to know.*

Rose lay down on the bed. She placed the Bible on her chest, feeling its weight pressing heavy on her. Below her spine, the camp bed sagged in the middle, like it was all too much to bear. Her old room was just above. It must be a guest room now. Had Grandma Yellow kept it the same? Had she ever worked out where the invisibility spot was? The hidden triangle of floor between the wall, the door and the wardrobe, where Rose and Rudder shared their worldly possessions. It was there that Rudder had pulled the robot out of his school bag. It was orange with big black wheels and a face that was all sad eyes. WALL was written across its body with a white E in a red circle. Rose had supposed that was the name of the company that made it. The robot was scratched and it looked like the previous owner had tried to bite off one of its pincer hands. Rudder had dumped it on the carpet.

Rose had jumped up and slammed the door shut. 'It's prohibited!'

Rudder had hugged the toy to him. 'Why?'

'It's a bad force!'

He'd set the robot down on the floor and switched it on. 'It's not a bad force, Rose. It's got batteries.'

The robot had trundled away over the carpet. Rose had found herself laughing as Rudder had dashed across the room, picked the toy up and sent it back to her. Suddenly, the robot had stopped moving, its arms chopping and its head jerking sideways.

Rudder had giggled. 'It looks like Brother Martin!'

'No, Rudder!' But it did. When the Spirit took Brother Martin, he'd rise from his bench like there was a string hooked into the top of his head. When he was finally standing, the string was cut and his body would sag and his head waggle until his body went stiff as the Spirit reclaimed him and made him move. Brother Martin had big, dark eyes too, like the robot.

Rudder stared ahead, stood up slowly and started waving his arms. In a robot voice he said, 'I am Brother Martin! I am Brother Martin!'

Rose hadn't been able to stop laughing and they'd missed the door opening. A voice roared into the room as Grandma blazed in the doorway, a bright yellow kitchen apron covering her dark skirt.

'What in the name of the Lord is happening here?'

Rudder had kept giggling like his on-switch was stuck. Rose had knocked the robot sideways, so it crashed over, its wheels still spinning. She'd smacked it hard on its scratched side, once and again until it twitched and stopped moving. Now she knew she'd probably dislodged one of its batteries. Then she'd – oh, God, how had she done it? – she'd looked Grandma Yellow right in the eye and said: 'They are trying to corrupt my brother, Grandma. He was tricked into bringing a demon into our house.' She'd hit the dead plastic lump again. 'By the grace of God, we are safe.'

Grandma's mouth had set into a narrow line as she glanced over to Rose's bedside table for the reassurance of the Bible.

'I will not have—'

'Shall I deal with this?'

It was Mum. She'd been wearing an apron too, pale blue and covered with poppies. She gently drew Grandma Yellow away from the door.

'Rose?'

'Yes, Mum?'

'You know what to do.'

Rose had nodded.

Mum had held her hand out to Rudder. 'Come with me to your room to pray.'

Mum had closed the door behind them. Rose had listened to the footsteps recede then pulled out the chair from under her desk and set it by the wardrobe. She'd climbed up and pulled the handle of the dark green suitcase that was stored on top of it until it was overhanging the edge of the wardrobe. She'd opened the clasps, climbed off the chair, picked up the robot and opened the suitcase wide enough to slip the robot in. She imagined it nestling among the other forbidden items – the copy of Roald Dahl's *The Witches*, the Christmas card from a girl in her primary school, the He-Man action figure she'd found stuck in the front garden holly bush. Rose had snapped the case shut and pushed it as far back as she could. She'd climbed down and replaced the chair.

And then she'd started laughing again, infected by Rudder's giggles. Her bright yellow grandmother had stood there in the doorway watching Rose wallop a toy robot. It had stuck, Rose and Rudder's own joke, a silly warning that Rudder wouldn't forget.

Smack the robot! Yellow alert!

She'd whispered it in his ear when she'd left this morning without waking him up.

The green suitcase was gone. Grandma had found it and Mum was in the atonement room for three weeks. Rudder would sit by the door, trying to talk to her until Grandma or another Aunty carried him away. No one was sitting outside the room today. Rose could hear the bustle of the house, people walking up and down the stairs, the light ring of the doorbell as Pilgrims came by for late morning prayers. Outside, a plane was coming in low, probably heading towards City Airport. And a few miles away, Rudder would be hating her with every cell in his body.

*

Rudder kept his eyes on the pavement. That was the easiest way. It meant he didn't end up looking at someone who looked at him back. Everyone seemed so cross. There were a lot of souls weighed down by earthly sins. He had to work out how to start saving them. It had been different when he went out with Dad to bring souls to God. He and Dad and the other Uncles prayed before they left and Rudder could feel the lightness in his soul before he set off on mission. Now he was walking back from his worldly school by himself looking at chewing gum marks, his feet so heavy they might as well be stuck to the pavement.

'Rudder!'

Don't turn round. That was the one rule he'd learned early, thanks to Bella.

'Rudder! You deaf, man, or what?' Then a giggle.

He knew that voice. It was . . . Quick footsteps getting louder and he was slapped in the back. It was Dominic, from drama group. He was with Rash. And they were holding hands. Rudder hadn't realised they were boyfriend and girlfriend. It was so easy for them. The first time Rudder had to sit next to a girl in assembly, he had to concentrate so hard on not feeling sinful that he hadn't heard the boys behind him unbuckle his bag and turn it upside down. A teacher had spotted him trying to retrieve his stuff from the hall floor and had run over to help him. That had just made everybody look at him more.

He glanced over at Rash. She had a beautiful face, like Rue from *The Hunger Games* film but with hair like Rose's when Mum used to comb it out ready for plaiting. It made Rudder want to smile. He wasn't lusting or coveting, though.

Dominic said, 'You wanna walk with us?'

'Yes, please.'

Rash laughed. 'You are *so* polite.'

It was strange walking with other people. Rudder was closest to the road, next to Dominic, but whenever anyone walked towards them he dropped behind to let them pass. Soon Dominic and Rash were ahead with a fringe of people between them. All Rudder could see was the back of Dominic's trainers, the cloud of Rash's hair and a flash of her bright orange rucksack. He slowed down. They probably just wanted to be together anyway. Just for a while, though, it had been good.

'Rudder!'

He looked up. They were waiting for him. For him!

Rash grinned. 'Get a move on, Ruds.'

Ruds. Only Rose had ever called him that. As he drew close, Rash looped her arm through his. For a second, his blazer sleeve brushed her chest as she had turned to say something to Dominic. Had she noticed? Should he say sorry?

'All right, Ruds?' She'd turned back to him, still smiling from a joke with Dominic.

He nodded. When he worked out how to save souls, Rash's would definitely be on the top of his list – after Mum, but he wouldn't mention that right now. The three of them went forward together. Rudder couldn't move back to let people pass because the arm loop was too tight. People had to go round him. He didn't mind.

Rash said, 'Rudder's an odd name. Is it your real name?'

'It's my birth name and my baptism name.'

Dominic peered round Rash. 'You get different names when you get baptised?'

Rash unhooked her arm from Rudder to gently bash Dominic on the chest. Dominic grabbed at his heart and gave a dramatic shriek and stagger that made people look around. Rudder felt himself blush.

Rash rolled her eyes. 'Drama queen!' She relooped with Rudder. 'My gran's got different names. She had twelve brothers and sisters and the priest named them after saints. So she was called Olympia because she was born on St Olympia's feast day. The only problem was that she had an older sister with the same birthday so they both got the same names. Everybody called her Veronica instead.'

Dominic said, 'So there's a Saint Rudder, right?'

'Ignore the idiot!' Rash said.

She squeezed Rudder's arm tighter. It rubbed against her chest again. He kept his eyes on the ground. He would have to do a whole month of atonement, at least, just for this.

'So does Rudder mean something?' Dominic asked.

'Pilgrims usually have traditional names.'

'Like what?'

Rudder thought about the other Little Brothers who'd been in his class at school. 'Zechariah or Nahum or Uriel, after our Founder.'

Rash said, 'I can't see you as a Nahum. So why Rudder?'

'It was Mum's idea. She told our grandmother she was calling me Rudder to remind me to steer close to God and my sister, Rose, was named after the Rose of Sharon, from the Song of Solomon.' *Solomon verse 2, chapter 5*. 'But actually we're named after calypso singers. She's after Calypso Rose and I'm after a singer called David Rudder. Mum only told us that recently. Calypso singing isn't allowed in the Pilgrims.'

'You don't sound very happy about your name,' Dominic said.

No. His name was a lie. He would definitely ask to be rebaptised, if he could.

'I like your mum,' Rash said.

Rudder frowned. 'Have you met her?'

Rash laughed. 'I don't have to. I like the sound of her.'

Dominic said, 'She should meet mine. They'd get on.'

Mum didn't have any friends. That would be good, even if Dominic's mum, even if she was . . . *Romans, chapter one, verse twenty-six . . . 'Vile affections . . .'* The passage came back to him unbidden. He blinked hard, blanking out the verse that seemed to float in front of him.

Rash said, 'Can you quote the Bible?'

Rudder nodded. 'You start to learn our Bible as soon as you can talk. We'd have competitions for children. A Pilgrim leader would read out the quote and you had to say where it was from. And then it was the other way round.'

Rash said, 'Were you any good at it?'

'Pretty good.' He'd won the trophy twice. All the Elders had clapped and told him how blessed he was, and the Little Pilgrims had wanted to know how they could be like him.

'This is our bus stop,' Rash said.

Already! No! It was too soon. He was going to ask about the photo, but Rash withdrew her arm and he was left with an empty space. He let his arm drop to his side.

Dominic said, 'I'm still impressed that you can quote the Bible. I'll have to introduce you to my grandma. She'll love you. She's a Bible freak.'

A Bible freak?

Rash slapped Dominic's back. It made a hollow thud.

'What's that for?' he shouted.

Dominic looked really cross and for a second, Rudder wanted to pull Rash away from him. She made a face and rubbed the hit spot on Dominic's back.

'Sorry, hun. I didn't mean to whack you so hard, but you were rude. He isn't a freak. I hate it when people say they follow a religion and don't know nothing about their holy books.' She smiled at Rudder. 'I think you're really cool.'

He smiled back. She'd definitely be at the top of his soul list.

18

Rose was skidding along the vines and trellises of the wallpaper and bouncing off the upper curve of the wardrobe. The skateboard dropped from her feet and she was clinging from the curtains, feeling the tight weft of the cotton scrape down her palms until she released them and landed back on the deck. One flick of the nose and the skateboard spun, so did Rose, executing a perfect cartwheel and landing on a squat on the bed, skateboard in hand.

She opened her eyes. Her Bible was still open on the pillow next to her. God knew what time it was. What was that verse? *'But, beloved, do not forget this one thing, that with the Lord one day is as a thousand years, and a thousand years as one day.'* One hour here felt like a thousand years to Rose.

She swung out of bed and tried the bedroom door. It opened. Why did she expect it to be locked? Atonement was voluntary and Pilgrims could leave the room any time. The Pilgrims had made such a deal about that when the newspaper started running those stories after Rudder's accident. No one was locked in. No one did anything against their will – as if it was that easy. As she headed towards the bathroom, she could hear the murmur of voices from the prayer circle downstairs. She used the toilet,

220

washed her hands and checked her face in the cabinet mirror. So, this was the real Rose, scraped bare and dull-skinned. It was the face she'd had for all those years before she'd joined the Worldly Wise. Would Kye have still wanted her like this? He probably hadn't noticed she was gone. She rested her forehead against the glass. Her body was like one of those dogs that sit on a grave howling long after their owner had died.

She opened the cabinet. Cocoa butter? The biggest tub you can get, as well. How come that was allowed and Mum had to virtually beg for Vaseline? She untwisted the lid. It was well-used. She smeared some over her face and closed the cabinet door again.

The pull of him was so hard it made her stomach hurt. But him? He was probably just flashing that photo around to his brother and his brother's nasty little mate. Maybe that was it. It was some kind of game. *Well done, Kye. You've won.* It felt like her insides were being scraped out one teaspoonful at a time.

She opened the door.

'Rose?'

Grandma Yellow was standing in the hallway. Instantly, Rose felt her skin pull tight under the sheen of cocoa butter.

'I was just returning to atonement, Grandma.'

Rose waited for her to move, but she didn't.

'You have a visitor, Rose.'

'A visitor?'

'Rudder?'

Grandma turned and billowed down the stairs. She was moving too slowly for Rose to run. Rudder had come to see her? Why hadn't Mum kept him at home? That's what they'd agreed. God, knowing him, he'd probably run away.

She burst into the sitting room. Her smile froze.

Grandma bobbed her head. 'A righteous Brother and a trusted one.'

Mikhail was standing in the middle of the room holding out his hands to Grandma Yellow. Grandma clasped them.

'The Lord be with you, Brother Mikhail.'

He bowed his head. 'And also with you, Aunty.'

For a moment, Rose could almost feel the shape and sound of the prayer pass between them, missing her out.

'I'll leave you to consult.'

Grandma left the door open, but still, she *left them*. A boy and a girl together, though Mikhail was very much a man now.

Mikhail smiled. 'Welcome home.'

'Thank you, Brother Mikhail.'

'I haven't come to sneer, Sister Rose. I want your happiness, whatever you choose. But I can't say I'm sorry to see you.' Another smile. 'Shall I sit down?'

'I think you may be more at home here than me.'

'Hopefully not for long, Sister Rose. If you open up to God, this will become your home again.' He settled down on the arm chair, pinching the fold of trouser fabric over his knees and hoisting it up.

Rose sat on the sofa. Hang on! Did she really wait for him to sit down first? Was it so easy to slide back into it all? Rudder'd better not get his hopes up for when she came back. She crossed her ankles, then uncrossed them. Out in the hallway, the front door opened and voices filtered through. The prayer group must be leaving.

She said, 'I thought I was in isolation until the completion of the atonement period.'

'A Pilgrim woman requires the support of a man for full atonement. You alone do not have sufficient reach to God to recompense for your sins.' He lowered his voice. 'I do have your spiritual welfare at heart, Rose.'

'You do?'

He frowned. 'Of course I do. Rose, I've worried about you. I've prayed for you. As a Pilgrim Brother, it is my duty to help you fight temptation.'

He looked so serious. She had to remember how real it was for him. She crossed her legs again.

She said, 'Thank you, *Brother* Mikhail.'

His mouth twitched. 'This is why I must enquire . . .' He leaned forward. 'Why did you really come back?'

Why? Because . . . because . . . Mum was out all hours, slumped like a dead woman on the sofa every night and she still didn't have enough money to pay the rent. Because of Rudder crying in his sleep over dreams he didn't want to remember in the morning. Because their flat was slicked

223

with oil from the shop below and feet thundered across the ceiling at strange times of the day and a man and a woman had hammered at the door and wanted to take even this away from them. And also . . . because of Kye, who had wanted her, and then he hadn't. All of it was as heavy and compact as a cannon ball stuck below her ribs.

It must be tiredness and *him* and missing Rudder all mixed together, because now Rose was crying. Mikhail shifted over to the edge of his seat, reached forward and held her hands. She was crying big proper sobs, so many fat tears they should dissolve everything. She would dissolve herself too.

'Brother Mikhail?'

Grandma Yellow was looking from one to the other. Next to her was Aunty Hagar, glaring at her son. Rose tried to pull her hands away, but Mikhail held her, cradling her fingertips between his thumbs and fingers. He lowered their hands allowing her fingers to drop on to her lap. He sat back.

'I think Sister Rose is close to atonement, Aunty. She feels deep sorrow and regret.'

Grandma Yellow and Aunty Hagar turned to stare at her. Grandma Yellow did not look convinced. Rose imagined her sniffing the air in case Rose had rubbed onions in her eyes. She wiped her cheeks with her sleeve.

Mikhail stood up. 'I would like to propose that Sister Rose accompanies me on mission tomorrow.'

What? Mikhail wanted her to stand on a street corner

handing out leaflets? Or even worse, knock on strangers' doors? She'd known she might have to, but already? She'd never been picked for any of that, even though Rudder had been on mission a few times.

Mikhail was looking down on her. 'I understand that there are still so many parts of your past life you may need to atone for. I'm willing to be your guide and sponsor. I believe you will learn more about the importance of our Pilgrim mission if you actually come on mission. Isn't that correct, Aunty?'

Grandma Yellow muttered something. Aunty Hagar was squinting a side eye that almost made Rose laugh. Was Mikhail winding them up deliberately? He couldn't have turned eighteen that long ago, but now they had to defer to him. She stood up and lowered her head at Mikhail.

'Thank you, Brother. I would be honoured to accompany you.'

'Saturday morning at nine thirty. The Lord be with you.'

'And also with you.' Aunty Hagar and Grandma Yellow muttered their response. Rose smiled to herself. God would need good ears to hear that.

*

Mum had left a note for Rudder stuck on the TV. The agency needed urgent cover for a care home in Walthamstow. It was only until ten and not that far away, so she shouldn't be back too late. She was sorry. She'd wanted to be there for his first evening without Rose, but he knew how it was. She said he should call her if he needed anything, but he shouldn't worry. The rent had been paid and those people wouldn't be back. Rudder had still pushed the armchair against the door, then heaved Mum's clothes trunk across and wedged it in front. He'd reached behind the armchair and tried the door. It wouldn't open. Good.

At last, Rudder felt his body relax a little. He went into the bedroom and dropped his blazer and rucksack on his bed and took off his shoes and socks. He pulled out the box of CDs from under his bed. All of them had to go. He was definitely going to do it, take them to the charity shop on Saturday. But for those that tempted him the most, he had to do something special.

Back in the main room, he flipped open the CD player. Rose reckoned it was on its last legs, but it was good enough for now. He clicked the CD in place, and when the tray slid back in, he fast-forwarded to track eleven, 'Neville's Waltz'. Rudder couldn't be a pigeon animagus. That would need sinful magic. But he could want to be Neville. That couldn't be wrong. Rudder understood Neville. Neville had always been on the edges, the one people smiled at behind their hands, but Rudder had always known that Neville was brave and a hero. Rudder stood in the middle of the room, arms poised. One, two, three. One, two, three. The notes from the violins almost brushed his skin as they swept past him. One, two, three. One, two, three, until his head was spinning.

He took the CD out of the player and took it into

the kitchen. He'd researched this. He had to be careful. He picked up a mug from the side of the sink and placed it in the microwave. He rested the disc against it, closed the door and set the timer for five seconds. Start. Rudder stepped back. The mug turned once and the CD sparked. He wouldn't take it out yet in case he breathed in poison, but when it was cool, he'd put it back in the case to remind himself of his sins.

He went into the bathroom and started running a bath. The bathroom was bigger without Rose's stuff. All her bottles and palettes and lipsticks were packed in a cardboard box behind the sofa, but bits of her were still here, like the pale pink ring from her hair dye bottle on the smudgy cream tiles and the little knot of hair in the overflow. She wouldn't be able to spend ages in the bathroom at Grandma Yellow's house.

Rudder climbed into the bath, closed his eyes and tipped his head back so just his ears were poking out. His body felt like it was floating, the bubbles streaking his skin. Rose wasn't the only one who could atone. He was doing it anyway, but now he had to be quicker. He ran through his Seven Stages in his head.

1. Recognition. Yes, he was aware of how heavy his soul was. It felt like there was another Rudder made of bricks hiding just under his skin.
2. Embarkation. He'd done nothing but think about his

temptations. That's why the biggest ones were in a pile on Rose's – the other – bed, and cooling down in the microwave.

3. Exploration. Um . . . lustful thoughts. Dancing. Music. Not tearing up Rose's decommissioning plan so that she didn't debase herself. Idolatry, especially touching the wooden box with the idols in it in Trafalgar Square. Eating birthday cake. Laughing at the talking cat in Kiki's Delivery Service. Reading the prohibited book and making Mum get excised, though she probably wanted to get excised anyway. And that picture. But all he had done was name them in his head.

4. Connection. It was hard drawing on the strength and knowledge of the Elders if he wasn't in Sanctuary. Mum wouldn't listen. Maybe he'd go back to Ms Leppard.

5. Immersion. He was re-educating himself already. He'd read his Bible every day. He was already working on the best way to save souls.

6. Subjugation. He'd always been willing to accept his punishments, but it wasn't just that, was it? He had to make amends.

7. Assimilation . . . Yes. If you were Rose. Dad had promised, though. Rudder would return and he and Dad would walk across to their section of the prayer circle together.

Rudder sighed. The water moved against his chest. *Make amends.* Who had he hurt? He closed his eyes. The sparkle of sun on a bicycle wheel rim. The thump of a girl as she's hit, and falls. Bella. He'd hurt Bella. He'd have to make amends to her. Who else? He opened his eyes. Even though the water was getting cold, he could still feel his ears and face burning. Yes, there was someone else.

He slid the plug chain between his toes and lifted the plug out. He stood up and reached for the towel catching his reflection in the steamy cabinet mirror. He looked like a worldly boy now. He definitely had to act to atone for his sins, starting with the biggest.

He dried himself down, creamed his skin and went into his room for his trackies.

He pulled his phone out of the charger and tapped on the pizza Rash had chosen as the drama group icon.

Dom
Where y'all?

Rash
right next 2u, idiot!

Dom
Everyone else! Has there been an apocalypse? Rudder, you lurking?

Rudder shook his head. *No! I'm here.* He took a deep breath.

Rudder

Hi

Dom

It was good to talk earlier. I think you're a man with many secrets

Rash

at least man can keep secrets. U think everyone needs 2kno ur business

Dom

Did I tell you my dad's gay?

Rudder's phone slipped out his hand and bounced off his knee. Dominic's dad was . . . So, how did . . . How come there'd never been a sermon about this? He scrabbled for his phone. Rash had sent a gif of a yawning baby. If it didn't bother Rash, it shouldn't bother Rudder. But still.

Dom

If i'm so boring, you tell me a secret

Rash

man, I need 2get my bus

Dom

You still there Ruds?

Rudder

Yes

Dom

Does your church believe in the rapture?

Did they? Rudder had never heard that. Maybe it was because the Pilgrims weren't a church. He started typing but Dominic had carried on.

Dom

You know, like when the world ends & all the good people go to heaven

Ah. He meant Ascension and Clean Slate. Of course, Rudder believed in it. Rose used to complain that all that stuff was burnt into their bones before they were born so they didn't have a choice not to believe it.

Rudder

Yes, we do

Dom

You mean you still do?

Rudder

Sort of

Dom

A gif of a cyclist swerving to miss a badger

A badger? Huh? Rudder frowned. Why – oh! Rudder had swerved round the point! The badger didn't matter.

Rash

damn bus driver wasn't going 2stop for me. Some big Rasta guy was hammering on the door until man had to open it. Cussing, man

Dom

Are gay people allowed in your church? Like if my mum wanted to be a pilgrim, she could, right?

Rudder felt his cheeks burning.

Rash

leave him alone. U know the answer to that. It must be weird tho Ruds. Yr in the outside world with all this stuff u never knew about. What's been the hardest?

Everything! How people said Sunday instead of Our Lord's Day. Sitting next to that girl in assembly. The days starting and ending without saying prayers.

Rudder

Lots of it. Rose has just gone back and I think I want to go back too.

Dominic and Rash must have replied at the same time, but Dominic's came up first.

Dom

No way, Rudder. Think of all the things you can do now. You'd hate it if you had to go back

Rash

I had 2move primary school Year 3. I hated my new school & I didn't even stop hating it when I left for secondary. I still hate it now

Dom

Haters gotta hate

Rash

Shush, man! What's stopping u Ruds?

He couldn't put the words together. There were too many things. Even Rash might not understand atonement and Dominic definitely wouldn't.

Rudder

I have to show that I'm good enough to be a Pilgrim again and I have to understand the things I've done wrong and make things better for the people I've hurt.

Rash

I can't imagine u hurting anyone

Dom

Or doing bad things

Rudder

I have. Something really bad

Rash

I seriously don't believe that

233

Dom

Because Rashida knows everything

Rash

Yep. U got it. What u done, Ruds?

Rudder

I got sent something.

Rash

Someone sent u something. Why does that make U the bad one? What was it?

These were Rudder's friends. Was this why God had stopped him deleting the picture? If you couldn't connect to the Elders, you had to still draw your strength and knowledge from people who knew more than you. People who could help you name your sins and tell you what to do.

He found the picture. It flickered, like the girl was saying 'goodbye' and he pressed send.

One second. Two seconds.

Dom

Shit, Rudder. I thought you meant a horse's head or something

Rash

Why would someone send him a horse's head?

Ric

Man, u seriously don't kno what ur supposed to do with it?
Gotta send this over to my bro

Rash

Don't you dare, Ritchie!

Ric

TOO LATE!

Rash

IDIOT! Sorry someone's sent it to u, Rudder. There's loads
of this stuff going round. But what's the writing at the bottom.
Do they mean ur sister, Rose?

He'd forgotten that was on there. Now everybody had
seen it. And Ritchie's brother had too. Typing . . . typing . . .
More messages filling up his screen.

Idil

What the hell? I thought we were talking drama here!! I don't
need to see this!

Boo

u know what they say bout church boys. They the worst

Rash

give it a break, Boo. Everyone seen them dick pics u took on
holiday last year

Boo

that was my brother, I told u. Least I'm not pretending to be no holy man. My bruva needs 2c this

No! NO!

Rash

U still there, Ruds?

Idil, Boo, Ric . . . Their brothers . . .

Rash

Rudder, hun, I don't know if ur still there, but u just sent round a booby pic to everyone. I kno u didn't mean to, but I don't think that girl meant that 2happen neither. U haven't done nothing bad, but if that girl gets recognised, some bad things r heading her way. Ruds? Rudder? U still there?

19

Rudder's phone was gathering force beneath his bed. The mattress, the sheets, the duvet, his throw – even all of them together weren't enough to keep him safe. The messages about the photo had just come and come and come. When he'd realised they weren't going to stop, he shoved the phone under his bed. By now, there'd be hundreds.

The light outside wasn't proper morning light but the streetlight was off, so it definitely wasn't still night. The lorries were calling to each other as they moved around the cash and carry carpark. A bus braked outside. Another bus driver slammed brakes on late. A car hooted. Rudder knelt on the bed and stared out. Two old guys and a woman were sitting on the wall outside the hostel drinking beer. They were bundled up like they were expecting snow. Rudder had sort of got used to the shouting from the hostel. He didn't need to jam the pillow over his head any more. When the noise used to make him cry, Rose had told him that the people in the hostel were squibs – non-magical members of magical families. It's hard for them, she'd said. The wizarding world thinks they're second class and even their families reject them. But really, Rudder, they're there to keep watch, to keep the Dementors at bay.

Rose shouldn't have lied to him. Only prayer and vigilance keep demons away from your soul.

Why did Rose keep sneaking into his thoughts when he didn't want her there? He sunk back on to the bed. Because now he had another sin to name, more people he had to make amends to. It wasn't just the picture of the girl he'd shared. Rose's name had been on there too. His hand dropped to the side of the bed and his fingers curled round his phone. He could throw it out of the window or go and drop it down the toilet. Or he could go back to his original idea and microwave it, though the kitchen did smell funny for a while after he'd cooked the CD.

Rudder turned the phone on. There were ten unread messages on the group chat. Just ten.

'Rudder?' Mum pushed open the door. She was already dressed. 'I've got to rush. I'll see you about six. I've left breakfast out and don't forget to double lock the door.'

He nodded.

'If you need me, text me. The care home owners make us leave our phones in our lockers just in case someone takes a dodgy picture, or something. I'll check it at break time.'

She blew him a kiss and rushed out. Rudder let the phone drop to the floor and slid back under the covers. He had to go to school. He had to walk into the classroom and maybe everybody would know what he did. Unless . . . unless he got in early again. He could still talk to Ms Leppard. She wasn't an Elder, of course. And she was a woman. But in

238

this world, she was the closest he had got.

The bus stopped at every stop until it was so full that every time Rudder moved, he brushed against a stranger. He waited for them to turn around and denounce him, but no one did. The orange minutes ticked by on the bus's digital display. He probably wouldn't even get to school for normal time now.

He ran from the bus stop, tucking in with the last group of students allowed in before they were officially late. He fast-walked down to his registration room, tried to open the door quietly, but everyone still turned around to look at him. Everyone except Ms Leppard. She had her back to them, checking through some slides on her laptop. Rudder saw a stone head then a map followed by a brown jug. She looked up, then back at the computer. She'd forgotten to smile at him.

He sat down, dumping his bag by his feet under the table. When he surfaced again, Zabia, Henry, Joelle, Mercy, Una, all of them, were staring at him. He looked up at Ms Leppard. She was looking at him too. The room was quiet. No shouting, no jokes, no burst of songs from anyone's phone. The *Libros Rojos* said the Clean Slate tally would be like this, everything paused so that the chosen souls could wriggle free from their human cargo and ascend. Noise bubbled up around him again. Everyone went back to what they usually did, except Ms Leppard, who was sitting behind her desk, scribbling on a piece of paper. The buzzer went for end of registration and the class started jostling their way out. Rudder bent down to pick up his bag. He felt a hand slap the back of his head. It was Joelle.

'Nice one, holy boy.'

What was nice? Joelle wasn't.

'Joelle! Go to your class!' Ms Leppard had come out from behind her desk. 'Rudder, I need to speak to you.'

I need to speak to you, miss! But everyone was leaving too slowly.

'Told you, miss!' Abi was by the door. 'Them churches are full of pervs.'

Ms Leppard went over and closed the door. *Pilgrims don't have churches. They're against worldly scriptures.* The words whispered at Rudder.

Ms Leppard came towards him. She seemed to be blinking too much. 'We've been asked to go and see Miss Loston. Do you know who she is?'

'The head of maths, Miss. But I don't need help with maths. I wanted to talk to you.'

'Oh, Rudder.' Her eyelids were still doing double blinks. 'I'm sorry, but we don't have time now. Miss Loston's also the safe-guarding officer. Do you know what that means?'

He shook his head, but that made Grandma's words pop up. Safe-guarding. Social workers. Worldly invaders.

Ms Leppard touched his shoulder. 'I know you didn't mean to do it.' She sighed. 'I honestly believe there was no malice. I wish you could have talked to me about the things you didn't understand, but the school takes these things really seriously.'

He was blinking too much too. If there was a second Rudder made of bricks just beneath his skin, it was crumbling.

'Perhaps it's my fault for encouraging you to join the drama group,' Ms Leppard continued. 'You seemed to need friends and I knew they were a nice lot. Was it one of the members that suggested you share the image?'

Share it? She knew he'd done that? Had he made Ms Leppard share his sin by looking at it too? The last brick turned to dust and he slumped on to the table.

'Rudder?' Ms Leppard looked like she was going to cry. 'We have to go now, but I'll be there to support you, okay?'

His sin felt like oil, sliding between his clothes and skin, between his toes and deep into his pores. If he tipped his head, it would leak out of his ear. Drip, drip, drip, a dark puddle spreading across the desk. His legs let him stand up and take steps. His shoulders let his bag rest on them. The phone was sunk into the depths of his bag, between his science books. *Thy nakedness shall be uncovered, yea, thy shame shall be seen: I will take vengeance.* It was the girl's nakedness, but Rudder's shame. He was receiving punishment. He must accept it and feel the humility to atone.

The morning lessons had started so the corridors were

241

empty. They headed through the school and back towards reception. The receptionist looked up at him as they walked past. She didn't smile. *She knew.* The staff corridor was between the visitor toilets and the small hall. Some Year Sevens were having a PE lesson there, setting up benches and mats for circuit-training. Some of the girls were wearing shorts, their legs bare between the cuff of their shorts and their socks. He quickly looked away. Ms Leppard hadn't noticed him staring, but if she had, could he explain how crooked everything was in his head? The girls in their PE shorts and the naked girl caught in his phone and Mum with the bathroom door open and Rose in her short skirts – all of it was immodest. But some of it was still okay. He tried to understand but always got it wrong.

He said, 'I'm sorry, miss.' His voice was creeping out of him.

'I know you are, Rudder.'

They stopped outside a closed door. The sign outside said, 'Mr A Abdi – Deputy Head.'

Deputy head? 'I thought we were going to see Miss Loston.'

'We are, Rudder. She's here too.'

There were chairs outside, but if Rudder sat down, his soul was so heavy he'd have to stay there.

'Just a moment, Rudder.' Ms Leppard went in without him. She was out a few minutes later. 'Okay. Ready?' She ushered him in.

Everyone was sitting round a small table. Miss Loston, Mr

Abdi, some empty chairs and . . . Dad? Dad! Dad knew. Had they made Dad look at the picture? Nobody had told Rudder that Dad would be here. Even Mum would have been better. But Dad! Why couldn't Rudder breathe? His sin had filled up every gap that air could come through.

Dad, I wanted to atone.

Dad, I wanted to understand my sins.

Dad, I need your help.

Miss Loston said, 'Would you like to sit down, Rudder?'

The chair she pointed to was next to Dad. Everyone else had tea cups and glasses of water in front of them. Dad had a notepad, a pencil and his fingers were resting on a Bible. He hadn't looked up, even when Rudder came in.

'Or there's a free chair here.' Ms Leppard pulled out the one next to her. Rudder went and sat down there. It wouldn't be fair to taint Dad with his sin.

Mr Abdi said, 'Thank you for coming, especially Mr Santos. I know this was very short notice for you and not the best time.'

Dad gave a small nod. He still didn't look over.

'Shall we begin?' Mr Abdi said. 'We've already introduced ourselves and Rudder, I believe you know everyone here. We're holding this meeting to discuss the distribution of inappropriate pictures.'

Ms Leppard leaned forward. Dad's body disappeared. All Rudder could see was Dad's hands on the table. 'It was one picture,' she said, quietly. 'Just one. And Rudder wouldn't understand. He doesn't know any better.'

Dad's fingers opened his notebook and picked up his pencil. Ms Leppard stopped talking, though she'd sounded like she had more to say.

Mr Abdi said, 'No culture or religion condones the circulation of explicit pictures, Ms Leppard. The image of this young woman went to how many people, Miss Loston?'

'Nine, sir.'

'Nine chances to screengrab it and send it on,' Mr Abdi said. 'Which is indeed what has happened. An inappropriate picture of a minor has now gone out to wide circulation.' He focused on Rudder. 'Do you understand the severity of what you've done?'

Ms Leppard said, 'We don't know she's underage.'

Mr Abdi frowned at her. 'And we don't know that she's not. I think we should proceed with caution, Ms Leppard.'

'And I think we should ask Rudder what happened.' Ms Leppard took a sip of water.

Dad's pencil hovered above the notepad. His other hand still rested on the Bible. Ms Leppard sat back. Dad was staring at the table.

Miss Loston said, 'Would you like to tell us what happened, then, Rudder?'

He'd pressed 'send', because Rash had looped her arm round his and talked about secrets. He'd had a secret and wanted his friends to help.

Mr Abdi cut in. 'How did you get the photo?'

'It was sent to me, sir.'

'Who sent it?'

'I don't know.'

'So, to be clear,' Miss Loston said, 'someone you don't know had your number and sent you this picture. Is that right, Rudder?'

Miss Loston sounded like she believed Rudder should be telling a different version of the story.

'I don't think anyone I know could have sent it.'

Miss Loston leaned forward. 'Why's that?'

'Because I don't know many people any more, or I didn't, before drama group.'

Ms Leppard took another sip of water. Rudder looked down at his lap. His hands were spread out on his knees. Last time he'd been round a table like this, they'd still been bandaged, itchy and sore beneath the dressing. Mum and Rose had been on one side and a social worker on the other. There'd been a woman from the police and another one who was in charge of the meeting and someone from the hospital. There'd been a chair set out for Dad, but it had stayed empty.

Dad was here now. Why didn't he say something?

'Rudder?' Ms Leppard touched his arm. 'Is there anyone at all you can think of that would send you a picture like that? One of the drama group, maybe?'

He shook his head. The only people who'd known his number were Mum and Rose and Dad, even though Dad would never call it. Though—

He said, 'Last year, I signed up for a chat group on the internet.'

Mr Abdi said, 'What kind of chat group, Rudder?'

Rudder glanced at Dad. 'I'm really sorry.' The words made his throat sore. 'A Harry Potter one.'

The room was silent.

Rudder said, 'I put my real phone number on my profile until Rose made me take it off.'

'Yes,' Ms Leppard said. 'A scammer could easily have harvested your details from there.'

'My son is the victim.' The side of Dad's mouth moved. Rudder could see his lips, his throat, his hand still on the Bible. 'Outside of our community, my son has no protection from the influence of Satan's agents. Rudder would not initiate such an act himself.'

More silence.

Mr Abdi turned to Dad. 'I understand your concern for your son. We know that he has only recently left your community and that may make him vulnerable to exploitation. This is why we need to understand what happened.'

For the first time Dad looked at Rudder. 'Who made you commit this sinful act, Rudder?'

The Bible must have shrunk. Dad's whole hand covered it, like it was being absorbed into Dad's body. God's own words were flowing through Dad's blood.

'No one made me do it, Dad.'

'Satan came to you directly and you complied.'

Ms Leppard said, 'I'm not quite sure if—'

'Rudder? Are you telling me that you committed this sinful act with full knowledge and awareness?'

Rudder bit his lips. The sharp pain stopped his tears. 'Yes, Dad, but I only wanted . . .' Ms Leppard filled Rudder's water glass and nudged it towards him. Rudder went to pick it up but he didn't think his hand was strong enough. 'I only meant to send it to two people.'

'But your intention was to share it,' Mr Abdi said.

'Yes, sir.'

Rudder heard Ms Leppard's chair shift.

Mr Abdi looked towards Dad. 'Sadly, these pictures aren't unusual. Sometimes, young people don't fully understand the implication of what they do. Sometimes, though, they are persuaded or manipulated into doing things they'd rather not. We don't know the girl's situation, which is why we want to find out as much as possible.'

Rudder's cheeks burned. He hadn't thought about that. Maybe the girl hadn't wanted to have the picture taken. What if that was the warning . . . *Rose?*

Miss Loston said, 'It will help if we know the age of the girl and if the picture was taken with consent. Are you sure you don't know who she is?'

'Yes, miss.'

Ms Leppard bent her head so it was closer to him. 'The picture mentions Rose. You have a sister—'

Dad's hands slammed against the table. Everyone jumped back.

Mr Abdi said, 'Mr Santos, can I ask you—'

'Rudder! Has your sister debased herself?'

'No, Dad! It's not Rose! It's not Rose, Dad. Someone's written on it that Rose will be next.'

'Thank you, Rudder.' Miss Loston frowned at Ms Leppard. 'I think that answers the question. We just need to explore all possibilities.'

Dad's lips moved and his face relaxed. He was praying, but maybe only Rudder knew that. Mr Abdi took a gulp of tea and clinked his cup back on to the saucer. 'Rudder, I understand that . . . that certain things are new to you.' He glanced at Dad. 'However, I feel that you should be aware that sending pictures like this to other people is wrong. We don't know the girl's identity or age so as a precaution we are reporting it to the police.'

The police?

Ms Leppard said, 'I don't think involving the police at this stage would be helpful.'

The police?

Dad was gripping his Bible between both hands, his mouth open wider to let the silent prayers come out.

The police, who'd put Pilgrims in prison because they didn't want to fight in wars.

The police, who'd tried to get Rudder to say bad things about his family and had led the worldly invasion into their Sanctuary.

Rudder said, 'Dad?'

Dad opened his eyes. 'I'm thanking God for Rose's timely return to Sanctuary.'

The police. Were they going to put Rudder in prison? Everyone knew how the imprisoned Pilgrims were put in cells with old soldiers who were allowed to hit them without anyone in the prison stopping them.

But if prison was his means of atonement, Rudder would have to accept it. Pilgrims could still save souls there. The Cumbrian Pilgrims held monthly prayer circles in their local prison.

'We have always been very clear that this school has to take a firm stance against cyber bullying,' Mr Abdi went on. 'Even if the picture was taken consensually and the girl is over eighteen, we can be sure that she would not have consented to it being sent on to a group of strangers. The fact that it was done without malice doesn't change that fact, nor the considerable harm it could cause her. We have no choice but to exclude.'

Ms Leppard sighed. 'I really don't think—'

'We can't make an exception, Ms Leppard. Rudder, you are excluded for ten days.'

Mr Abdi was looking at Dad. 'Do you have any questions, Mr Santos?'

Dad didn't reply.

Mr Abdi turned to Rudder. 'Would you like to ask anything?'

He nodded. 'Please, what am I excluded from?'

Ms Leppard sighed again. 'From school, Rudder. I'll be in touch to make sure you stay up-to-date with your work. Mr Santos, our appeal procedures are online, if you would like to challenge the decision.' She was doing that blinking thing again. 'Of course, you can also pick up a printed copy from reception, if that's more . . . more appropriate.'

Mr Abdi stood up, holding out his hand to Dad. Dad didn't take it.

Dad was looking towards Rudder. His look made Rudder want to cry.

Dad walked ahead. His shoes were polished to a shine. When the light hit them, they looked white. His Bible was still in his hand, swinging by his side. Rudder imagined God's words being scattered in the cracks of the pavement, waiting to take root and grow.

Rudder said, 'I'm sorry, Dad.'

'Please hurry up, Rudder. I had to cancel my appointments this morning.'

'Where are we going?'

'Home.'

Home? He was taking Rudder home! At last! Rudder should never have questioned God's plan for him. God knew Rudder's heart was with the Pilgrims. He'd forgive Rudder his temptations. Rudder would pray harder than before. He'd ask Mum to send over his Harry Potter books and DVDs and Simon and Garfunkel and *West Side Story* and even the Time-Turner pendant that Rose gave him in the hostel and the Marauder's Map throw and his robes. He'd set the fire himself and burn them.

That's if he was allowed to talk to Mum. He'd check with Dad later. Maybe the only way the worldly authorities would let him go back for good was if Mum agreed. That meant he'd be allowed to talk to her.

Dad turned the corner. Rudder trotted after him. Dad's car was there, at the far end of the street by a post box.

Dad stopped suddenly and turned around. 'Satan and all his temptations are all around us, Rudder.'

'I know, Dad. I'm sorry.'

'Do you still read your Bible?'

'I try.'

Dad rubbed a hand though his hair. It made the grey parts stick out at the front. 'And those other books, Rudder? Do you still read them?'

'I won't any more, Dad. I want to read the Bible.'

Dad carried on walking. Even the back of Dad's head looked angry.

'Dad, please! I want to read the Bible!'

Dad reached the car and unlocked the passenger side. He opened the door and stood watching as Rudder slid in and pulled on his seat belt. The seat had been pushed right back. It must be so Lily-Beth had room for her tummy. Dad's new baby would grow up as a Pilgrim. It would know how to resist Satan's call. Dad would never be called to hear about sinful pictures when the new baby grew up, because it would have God's protection in a Pilgrim school. Rudder rubbed his hands. They were tingling just below the skin, as if the sin had worked its way through the scars. Dad settled into the driver's side, stowed his Bible in the glove compartment, buckled up his belt and started the engine. He checked the mirror and pulled out.

Rudder said, 'I didn't know you were going to be there.'

'The school couldn't reach your mother and they have my home number as an emergency. God willed it that I was home and found the message soon after they called.'

Message? Was it still on Grandma's answerphone?

Dad said, 'If my mother had heard the message and understood its meaning . . .' He glanced at Rudder. 'You are not lost to her, Rudder. You will never be lost to her, but I believed it was best that I deleted the message. It would have upset her greatly.'

Rudder nodded. 'Thank you.'

Dad drove on, his mouth moving in prayer. Rudder stared out the window. What would Rose say when she saw Rudder walk through the door? She'd probably be angry at first, but happy to return to the worldly world. That's why she'd kept all those immodest clothes. Mum preferred her anyway. Rudder had always been the odd one out when they were together.

Dad stopped at the junction opposite the bus station.

This wasn't the way to Grandma Yellow's.

'I thought you were taking me home.'

'Correct.'

'This is the wrong way.'

'This is your street.'

'But I want— I don't want . . .'

Dad looked at him. The itching beneath Rudder's skin was worse. Rudder slid his hands under his thighs, pressing the backs against the seat. His trousers felt slightly damp. Drip, drip, drip, sin.

'You don't want what, Rudder?'

'I want to come back with you, Dad. It's hard. I don't understand things out here. No one likes me. They think I'm stupid. I'm always doing the wrong thing. Please take me back with you.'

Dad looked away. 'I can't, Rudder. Not yet.'

'It's the new baby, isn't it? You don't want me any more.'

'No, Rudder.' Dad's voice softened and he touched Rudder's cheek. 'The accident, that evening, it almost destroyed our community. Many still blame me for all those social workers and the newspapers with their vile lies.'

Mum had tried to hide the newspapers in Room 27, but Rudder had seen them. *Boy falls into fire in secret cult ritual.*

'After you left,' Dad said, 'people would drive past our houses and shout wicked words. They'd call our children names in the street. Some of our families moved away and joined the Sanctuary in Cumbria. My mother and I

253

want you to come back, Rudder. But not yet.'

'When?'

'You heard what the Worldly Wise in your school said. The police will be involved. We cannot accept the authority of the police. We cannot bring more disgrace to our community.'

'But Dad . . .'

Dad nosed into a gap in the traffic and accelerated through the lights. They'd be outside the flat in a few minutes. Rudder wanted to grab Dad's hands on the steering wheel, make him turn a different way.

'Dad? Please take me with you.'

'I'm sorry, Rudder.' Dad pulled into the street by the side of the hostel. 'Do you need help crossing the road?'

'Can you come in with me?'

'You know I can't do that.' He took his wallet out of his pocket and peeled a twenty-pound note from inside. 'But please give this to your mother.'

'I'm scared, Dad.'

'Pray, Rudder. I will pray for you too.' He opened the glove compartment and pulled out his Bible. He handed it to Rudder. 'Arm yourself against Satan and you may yet return to us.'

Rudder opened the car door and stepped on to the street. He reached back to shut the door but Dad had pulled it closed already. The engine started. He tried to jam the Bible into his blazer pocket, but worldly clothes weren't like Pilgrim clothes, with pockets for Bibles and handbooks. He pushed the button on the traffic lights and waited. Looking back, he saw that Dad was gone.

The traffic stopped and Rudder crossed the road. A woman was sitting outside the shop today. Her knees were covered with a sleeping bag and she was wearing a bright green hat with earflaps. What was it the scriptures said? '*He that hath pity upon the poor lendeth unto the Lord, and that which he hath given will he pay him again.*' This was another test for Rudder. He was being vigilant.

God made Dad give him the money so he could pass it on to someone who needed it more.

He checked his blazer pocket. The money wasn't there. It wasn't in his trouser pockets, neither.

'Looking for this?'

Rudder knew that voice. A hand offered him a twenty-pound note.

'Take it then,' Kye said.

Rudder snatched the money. 'What do you want?'

'I want to give you your money back.' Kye nodded back across the road. 'I was sitting on the wall by the dosshouse and I saw you drop it.'

'Rose isn't here.'

'I know. She's in English all morning.'

'She's not. She's gone back to the Pilgrims.'

Kye blinked. 'She's gone back? I hope it wasn't something I—' He gave a little laugh. 'Back to the Pilgrims. Right. I didn't see that coming.'

Rudder tried to step round him, but Kye was right in front of the door.

'It wasn't Rose I was waiting for, though. It was you.'

Rudder stepped back. 'Why do you want me? All you ever do is make fun of me.'

'I know. I'm sorry.'

'And Bella. She used to make fun of me too.'

'I know, Rudder. We were both out of order.'

'So why do you want me?'

Kye raised his eyebrows. 'Do you need me to tell you? You've just been kicked out of school. I thought I could help.'

Kye knew? He wasn't in the drama group! He wasn't even at the same school. Rudder put a hand out to steady himself.

Kye said, 'Are you all right?'

Rudder lifted his head just enough to study Kye's face. There was no trace of that smile that made Rudder feel tiny. He shook his head.

'I didn't mean to scare you. Someone at your school told me what happened to you. I'm sorry. Look, I really need to talk to you. I think there are ways that we can put this right.'

Kye had come to him to put things right? To Rudder? Kye, whose devilment tangled up Rose on the sofa. Kye, whose own sister warned Rudder against him. The last time Rudder had seen him, Kye had sworn at Rudder and laughed.

Rudder scowled at him. 'Pilgrims have words for people like you. A double-minded man, unstable in all his ways.'

Kye grinned and shook his head.

Rudder had to find his keys and get inside. As he shrugged his bag off his shoulder, the strap slipped through his fingers, knocking Dad's Bible out of his hands. Kye lunged forward and caught it. He held it out.

'See? I saved you twenty quid and a holy book.'

Rudder looked from the Bible up at Kye. 'I need to go in.'

Kye said, 'Can I come in with you?'

'No!' Rudder shook his head so hard it hurt. 'No! You can't.'

'We have to talk about what happened, Rudder.' Kye put a hand on Rudder's shoulder. 'You sent a private picture of a girl round to loads of people. That could make things tough for her. You want to make it better, don't you?'

He gave Rudder's shoulder a nudge. Rudder stumbled backwards, banging against the door behind him.

'Have a think about it, Rudder.'

Kye turned and walked away.

20

Rose watched Grandma Yellow turn on the tap to fill the kettle. Grandma's anger was so strong it sparked. She must be in danger of electrocuting herself. Although, it would be ungodly to even consider something like that.

There was a new scripture on the blackboard hanging next to the kettle. Chalk should be soft and powdery, easy to wipe away. Grandma must have used a chisel to score the words in.

'And when thou art spoiled, what wilt thou do? Though thou clothest thyself with crimson, though thou deckest thee with ornaments of gold, though thou rentest thy face with painting, in vain shalt thou make thyself fair; thy lovers will despise thee, they will seek thy life.' Jeremiah 4:30.

No matter what Grandma wrote next, she wanted to make sure Rose remembered what was underneath. *'Thy lovers will despise thee, they will seek thy life'.* Rose didn't need scripture to remind her. She had Kye's silence and the quick look he'd given her in the canteen before looking away.

Grandma dried her glass on a towel and stormed out the kitchen. Rose wanted to yell after her. *'I didn't ask Mikhail to reprogramme my atonement. I'd rather be upstairs too.'*

Rose opened the fridge and cleared a space on the top shelf. An Aunty who refused to make eye contact with Rose had called round earlier with a tray of chicken bake. It still sat on the table. A puddle of oil had seeped over the foil and was starting to solidify. Rose stuck her finger in it and tasted it. It was all right – better than microwaved baked potatoes, anyway. Now Mum only had Rudder, the free stuff she picked up should go further, though she hardly had time to cook it. Rose slid the chicken in next to a tub of green salad and closed the fridge. Rudder would love the chicken, but he'd never touch that lettuce.

'Clothest thyself with crimson.' That bloody scripture was going to be following Rose round the kitchen. She should give Grandma her most innocent look and ask for a different verse. How about Matthew 19, verse 9, Grandma? *'Whosoever shall put away his wife, except it be for fornication, and shall marry another, committeth adultery.'* Rose should chalk it on the wall opposite Dad and Lily-Beth's bedroom.

Rose went over to the sink and turned on the cold water. She let the water gush over the inside of her wrists, the cool soaking through her body. That was better. She turned off the tap. The water dripped down her arm and under her sleeve. She had chosen to be here. She could do this.

She heard the front door open. Was that Dad back? God— *gosh*, she meant – must remember 'gosh' – Rose was supposed to check on Lily-Beth and offer her some ginger tea or

259

something. Rose dried her hands and went into the hallway. Dad was sitting on the stairs unlacing his shoes. Earlier, he'd left so quickly, Rose hadn't noticed he was in his formal wear – jacket, waistcoat, shirt, shiny shoes. He slotted the shoes back into their space on the shelf. She waited for him to spring up and run upstairs to check Lily-Beth, but he stayed there, arms on his knees, his head bowed.

'Are you okay, Dad?'

He was praying. She should wait. It reminded her of Mikhail, not big man Mikhail, but Mikhail when he was still boy-shaped and they used to play 'Lot's Wife'. One of them would stand facing the corner and had to turn around suddenly and catch the other person creeping up on them before they had a chance to freeze. Mikhail had been good. He'd always seemed to freeze instantly and not move again until she'd turned back.

Dad was completely still.

'What's happened, Dad?'

He looked up at her then back at his feet.

She said, 'Where did you go? Is there anything I can do to help?'

She should put an arm around him, but it had been such a long time. Now she was too old to touch him. His foot twitched. He stretched out his fingers and flexed his shoulders. She could see the breath flowing back through him.

He said, 'I believe your brother may be lost to us.'

'My brother? You mean Rudder? Dad? What's happened?'

Dad stood up. 'Satan's agents are everywhere. Your brother's soul is burdened with sin.'

'What do you mean, burdened with sin? He's less worldly than me, you know that. He doesn't understand the outside world. He makes mistakes.'

'I truly believed he was still a Pilgrim, learning to recognise temptation and challenge it, even in the sinful world outside.' He glanced at her. 'Even with poor influences. We guided him for ten years, Rose. We helped him journey alongside our Lord. He knew God's words better than many older than him. Has he lost it all so quickly?'

Dad spent the next hour in the prayer room. Rose could hear the soft sound of his prayers and then silence. Each time the words stopped, she waited by the door for him, but he didn't come out. Were all those prayers for Rudder? What the hell had he done?

Lily-Beth stumbled downstairs. It was weird seeing her without her headscarf. She'd tried to pull her hair into a thick braid and the front had fluffed up. Her face was pale and her eyes circled by shadows.

Lily-Beth stuck the kettle under the tap. She kept her back to Rose.

Rose said, 'Would you like me to help you? I can make the tea and bring it to you.'

Lily-Beth put the kettle on to boil. She plucked a teabag from the jar under the cupboard. Okay. That's how it was.

Rose sat down at the kitchen table and studied the cover of the 'Pilgrims' Way' leaflet that Grandma Yellow had left there. A mother, a father, their daughter and son were standing by the gates of heaven. The woman and daughter had blonde hair almost down to their bottoms, covered to the neck with headscarves. The father and son had short buzz cuts, long slightly flared trousers and jackets. That's what Grandma Yellow must have hoped for with their family. Mum, Dad, Rose and Rudder, just like that, though a bit browner, the brightest lights in the Pilgrim community. In the picture, the gates of heaven had opened a crack so the family could glimpse the blaze of glory within. The shadow of an invisible gatekeeper stretched out in front of them.

The kettle clicked off. Lily-Beth didn't move. She was leaning over the sink, shoulders hunched. Rose went over to her. She was breathing heavily, holding her stomach. Her throat was moving like it was jammed on swallowing.

'Are you okay?'

'Leave me alone!' Lily-Beth gasped out the words. Part of Rose wanted to laugh. Lily-Beth looked so pale Rose was surprised there was blood left in her tongue to make any sounds at all. She should just have a thin flap of skin stuck to the bottom of her mouth. She straightened up. 'Why are you here, Rose? You are not a believer. We all know that. Why have you brought your sin to taint our household and . . .' Her hand rested on her stomach. Rose imagined the baby arching underneath, its forehead pressing against Lily-Beth's hand. 'We all know you're not going to stay. Why don't you go now? Why?' Lily-Beth was crying. 'I can't even bring myself to eat with you.'

Lily-Beth ripped off a piece of kitchen towel and rubbed her eyes.

Matthew 19, Verse 9! Matthew 19, Verse 9! You and dad got together before he and Mum were divorced! Rose tried to press it back down and keep her voice even. 'When you married Dad, you knew he had us.'

'No, he did not! You were gone! You're supposed to stay away. An excision means never coming back without full central assent. It should take years, but here you are!'

'You know children can't be excised.'

'And you know that Pilgrim womanhood starts at thirteen. You? Can you really call yourself a child? Why am I expected to eat with you, to talk with you, pray with you? Do you really surrender to God when you pray, Rose? Or do you close your eyes and dream of worldly things? You and your sinful brother!'

'Go back to bed, Lily-Beth.' Dad was standing by the kitchen door. His look of tenderness towards Lily-Beth made Rose's stomach hurt. 'I'll bring your tea.'

Lily-Beth rubbed her eyes again and dropped the kitchen roll in the bin. As she passed Dad, he touched her cheek. She carried on walking.

Rose said, 'Didn't you hear what she said?'

Dad unhooked two mugs from the stand. 'Leave Lily-Beth

be. She's purer than all of us. Her soul hurts from the sin she sees in the world.'

'No, Dad. She hates us. Me and Rudder, she hates us.'

He flicked the kettle on. It turned off almost immediately. 'Pilgrims don't hate within the family. We offer love.'

'Did that sound like love to you?'

'She's upset and angry. She wants to be out on mission with kindred souls.'

'Clean Pilgrim souls. Not heavy sinful ones like mine and Rudder's, right?'

Dad poured boiling water into the mugs.

'What did Rudder do, Dad? Please tell me.'

'Prepare yourself, Rose. Brother Mikhail and Sister Gayle will be here for you soon.'

Dad walked out, a mug in each hand. Rose heard the heaviness of his tread on the stairs and the bedroom door open and close above. She waited a few seconds and followed him up, ducking into the box room. She shut the door and waited. Dad passed by outside and back down the stairs. She opened her wardrobe and retrieved her DMs, unravelling the knee highs she'd crammed into them. She pulled out her phone from the toe of her left boot. She tried to turn the phone on. It was dead. Damn. She pulled her charger out of the other boot. Rose paused. A car slowed down outside then carried on by. Grandma Yellow wasn't back yet. Rose plugged in the charger. She just needed to speak to Rudder. That was it. She'd ignore absolutely anything that looked like it had come from Kye. She wouldn't just ignore it, she'd delete it straight away.

The phone flicked on and she tapped in her password. Up popped three notifications from Kye. Her stomach blipped. Why were bodies so stupid? She'd just text Rudder, then turn the phone off. No, she'd delete Kye's messages and then turn her phone off.

But Kye could be apologising. He could have found out she'd gone back and be feeling guilty. Why else would he text her now? Or maybe there'd been an update on Bella and he wanted her to know.

The messages were from yesterday. The first one was three words long.

You silly bitch.

Silly bitch? Kye who'd pulled her towards him, who'd told her how much she meant to him, who'd smiled and stroked her back when she'd told him how hard it was to leave everything she'd known and start everything again.

There was more.

You want revenge? Don't forget, I can play that game too. I don't know how you got it, but read the words beneath, Rose. Everyone you shared it with is going to see that too.

265

Shared what? What the hell was he on about? Why did he call her a bitch? How could he switch to hate so quickly?

There was a third message, a file to download. Rose couldn't do it without Wi-Fi. Right now, though, she needed to be smaller, so tiny that nobody could see her to hurt her. She curled up on the floor with the phone beside her, pressing her face to the carpet. *Silly bitch.* Every time he'd looked at her, it was all pretend because in his head, that's all she was.

'Rose!' Dad's voice was calling up from the bottom of the stairs. 'Brother Mikhail has arrived to take you on mission.'

Rose had to do it. She could not let them know that the worldly world could break you. She had to make herself big again. She had to rinse her face and pick up her Bible. She flipped her phone over. *Silly bitch.* It hurt. It hurt so much. Now she couldn't even pretend that he'd ever cared about her.

You want revenge?

Revenge for what? Him hurting her so much? Yeah, she'd happily take revenge for that. But what was the game she was supposed to be playing? It was his rules. It always had been. *Read the words beneath.* She straightened out and sat up. She'd come back here to try and free herself from him. It wasn't working. She tucked her phone into her bra. She needed to hook into some Wi-Fi and make herself see what Kye thought she'd shared.

21

Soho Square was half sunlight, half shade. Had Mikhail deliberately brought Rose back to this particular area for mission? When she'd come downstairs, he'd been talking to Dad. Then, he'd sat in the front of the car on the way over, talking to the Brother on transport duties. Somehow, Mikhail could never make eye contact to tell her where they were going. Being back in Soho was probably meant to help her name her sins, by seeing versions of her worldly self parade up and down the streets. Pity he hadn't realised. It was perfect. Rose knew all the free Wi-Fi places. She just had to wait for the right moment.

That could be hard. Rose recognised Sister Gayle from the last time she was here, and she didn't seem at all convinced by Rose's transformation. She was wearing the same ankle length grey skirt with black suede boots and a jumper too thick for today's sun. A blue scarf was looped round her neck matching the one covering her hair. It was perfect mission clothes, modest but not threatening to worldly life.

Mikhail had instructed them to set up the 'Pilgrims' Way' stand on a corner, with their backs towards the Catholic church. Rose breathed in. Only a few days ago, she'd been walking along Wardour Street in her short skirt and knee highs and Converse. A couple of days later, she'd been unbuttoning her top while Kye smiled behind his camera. Now, she was a silly bitch.

'I trust you know how to hand out leaflets, Sister Rose,' Gayle said.

Rose blinked hard. It just about stopped the tears.

'Sister Rose?' Gayle was glaring at her. She turned to Mikhail. 'Please remind me, Brother. How many stages of atonement has our Sister completed?'

'Be assured, Sister Gayle. Sister Rose is seeking the knowledge through immersion in a programme of atonement and mission.'

'Really?' Gayle slid a shelf into a bracket. 'It didn't look like that last time we were here.'

Mikhail unzipped the trolley and handed Rose a bundle of leaflets. 'Smile, Sister Rose. The Worldly Wise can't often resist smiling back.'

'You are full of the Lord's love,' Gayle said.

'As are we all, Sister Gayle.' Mikhail passed her leaflets too. 'I'm sure you will be an excellent example to Sister Rose. Your mission work is admirable.'

Gayle's head bobbed. 'Thank you, Brother.' She smiled at Rose. 'Look ahead, but be ready to make eye contact if a worldly makes eye contact with you. It makes you look friendly.'

Getting friendly with the Worldly Wise? That's my speciality, Sister Gayle.

Rose looked over at Gayle. How old was she? Twenty, max. She'd spent every moment of her life with Pilgrims. Outside was a terrifying place, infested by Satan's plans to turn her from the Lord. Gayle held the burden of cleansing worldly souls ready for the Clean Slate tally. She hadn't known anything else. She couldn't be anything else. And perhaps Gayle really was better off staying where she was. The world *was* terrifying. It was full of games with rules made to trip you up and when you fell, the hurt stayed forever.

Midday. Not a single one of Rose's leaflets had left her hand. Her cheeks ached from smiling and her eyes were watering from sunshine and staring. The others weren't doing much better. A homeless guy had taken a 'Pilgrims' Way' leaflet from Mikhail, proclaiming that the African man was God's chosen one. He was ready whenever God was. Gayle had given out two. One was to a lone girl backpacker and the other was a tall guy in a suit. He'd told Gayle that he had grown up as a Jehovah's Witness but had moved over from Australia and lost his faith. He was missing his mediation with God. He'd spent a long time talking to her, standing too close until Mikhail had joined the conversation. Then he'd abruptly walked off. Rose had seen him shove the leaflet between the two scaffolding boards jutting out from a closed-down pub opposite.

Mikhail said, 'Any man who looks at a woman with lust for her has already committed adultery with her in his heart.'

Gayle looked devastated. 'Brother Mikhail, I didn't mean to . . . I was trying to be modest.'

'You are modest. It's his sin, not yours.'

They smiled at each other. This seemed like the perfect time.

'I'm afraid I need to . . .' Rose attempted a slightly shy smile in Gayle's direction. 'I need a moment of privacy.'

Sister Gayle gave an ungodly eye roll. 'Surely you can wait. Sister Lina and Brother Wesley will be here soon to continue mission.'

'I'm afraid I can't. It's . . .' She tried to look embarrassed. 'Women's needs. I don't think I can wait, Sister Gayle. I'm sure you understand. I know this area well. The big stores have bathrooms.'

Gayle and Mikhail had swapped a look when she said she knew the area. Gayle had opened her mouth, but had taken her lead from Mikhail and said nothing.

Mikhail glanced at his watch. 'Go, Sister Rose. Be quick.' He offered some leaflets. 'Do the Lord's bidding on your journey.'

'Thank you, Brother.'

Rose took the leaflets and hurried across the square, Lily-Beth's long skirt tangling round her legs. She glanced back. Mikhail and Gayle were side by side, backs straight, leaflets outstretched.

Rose stopped on the main road and looked up and down. The nearest guaranteed Wi-Fi was the big bookshop on

270

Charing Cross Road. She hurried inside and headed straight for the lift, retrieving the phone from her bra on the way up. As she stepped on to the shop floor, her phone connected to the Wi-Fi like an old friend.

You silly bitch . . .

So what game was she playing for Kye to call her that?

She leaned against the wall next to the lifts and opened Kye's second message. It had been sent a few seconds after the first one. It was buffering, trying to download a picture. Rose watched as the image became crisp. It was a girl. Her face was hidden, but you could see her breasts, her thighs and the thin sliver of the underwear shielding her complete nakedness. The girl wasn't ashamed. Her arms were flung out like she was cheering. Her nails were shiny orange and close up you could see the tiny hairs on the dark skin of her arms. There were leather bangles on her left arm and a small comma-shaped scar on her right wrist. Around the edges of the picture, the dark blue stripy duvet, the same duvet where Kye had first tried to take Rose's picture.

There was writing underneath. It said, 'Next time it's Rose.'

Rose. Next. Next for what? For this? To be passed from phone to phone? Was that it? That picture of Rose, shirt unbuttoned, bra on the bed beside her, was going to pop up on strangers' phones? Was this the game? He thought Rose had shared this picture, so now he was going to destroy her?

Rose ran into the toilet. There was a queue but she almost shoved the woman aside who was coming out of the cubicle. There was a murmur of anger from the people waiting.

'Sorry.' She gasped. 'Sick.'

Each spasm made the picture flash stronger. She flushed and came out. There were a few sympathetic glances, but no one was in a rush to use her cubicle. A woman standing by the sink handed her a paper towel. She glanced at Rose's baggy clothes.

She said, 'It usually gets better. It took until month five for me.'

Rose nodded. It was easier. She splashed water on her face, across her lips and into her mouth. She leant deep into the sink to spit it out and wiped her face. She always cried when she was sick, but this was double tears. She dropped the paper in the bin and left.

Her head hurt, but she had to make herself think. She spotted a spare chair in the cafe, opposite a man engrossed by his laptop screen, and made herself look at the messages again. *Silly bitch*. Her eyes kept getting stuck there, but she had to focus on the other bit. *Is this your revenge?* Rose didn't get it. Why the hell would she even have a picture like that? And why would she put her own damn name on it. What the hell was going on in his mind? Her screensaver blinked Care Bears back at her.

Another message notification popped up. Kye again.

Sickness curled up and she pushed it back down. She took a breath and tapped.

Ok. It wasn't you. Seen Rudder. He didn't mean to share it, but this is still trouble. Deep, deep shit, Rose

Huh? Kye had called her a silly bitch. He'd accused her of looking for revenge. But now it wasn't her. It was Rudder. Rudder had what? *He didn't mean to share it.* Rose's thoughts couldn't unravel themselves. Rudder had . . . her innocent little brother had a picture of a topless girl posing on Kye's bed on his phone? Then he'd shared it? Who the hell with? Rose dropped her phone on to the table and buried her head in her hands. The guy opposite shifted his laptop closer to him. Rudder should be at school. How did Kye get to see him? Unless . . . was this why Dad was out this morning? That's why he'd come back so upset.

What the hell, Rudder? A few days ago, you didn't have any numbers in your contacts except me, Mum and Granny Yellow's landline! Now you've got contacts that you've shared a nude picture with?

Shit. He must have seen the writing underneath. *Next time it's Rose.* He'd still damn well shared it, though. What was going through Rudder's mind? She had to speak to him.

Deep, deep shit, Rose. Yeah, Kye. You don't say.

She tapped out a message.

Rudder, I don't know what the hell . . .

No. She mustn't seem angry. Mustn't scare him, or he'd just retreat inside himself.

Rudder, we need to speak . . .

But what if he didn't have his phone? The school could have taken it by now, or Mum . . . God, poor Mum. She found Mum's number and started a new message.

I know Rudder's in trouble. I'm going to try and call u after supper prayers. Need to speak to him. Hope ur ok. Love u xxx

She slipped the phone into the pocket of Lily-Beth's skirt and walked down the four flights of stairs to the entrance.. The shelves of books swept out from all directions, pages and pages promoting the Pilgrims' definition of evil, from the sinful lies of evolution in the science section to the God-baiting fantasies in the basement. Just a year ago, Mum had brought them here so Rudder could see the shelves of Harry Potter. Now Rudder was sending round a booby picture and that bastard Kye had a picture of her. Not just a picture, a threat.

*

Rudder balanced the Time-Turner pendant on the pile of

sinful stuff on the other bed. It didn't matter that Rose had given it to him. He had to be strong and resist temptation. He rolled his Columba socks into a ball too and balanced them next to the Time-Turner. He'd already added the Columba scarf and tie. All of it had to go.

Mum was on the sofa watching TV, her phone right next to her on the arm. He wasn't allowed to close his bedroom door in case Rose rang. Mum said that Rose wouldn't have much time and every second counted. Rose shouldn't be phoning anyway, because it was prohibited, but when he'd said that to Mum, she'd just shouted again.

Supper prayers should be over by now. He bowed his heart. He used to love that moment, when they would open their hearts to prayer while the food smells from the kitchen reminded him that there was something good to follow.

Mum's phone rang. This must be it. She answered it straight away, paused and smiled. The smile was so sudden and real it made Rudder jump.

Mum said, 'Rose! Oh my darling, I'm so happy to hear from you. How are you?'

Rudder waited while Mum made agreeing sounds.

'Yes,' Mum said, 'I've taken it from him. Though the school's getting the police involved. They'll probably want it for evidence. He deleted the picture, but these things never disappear. I heard –' Mum paused and wiped her eyes – 'the Sex Offenders Register. Worst case, but you never know.'

Mum had said all that earlier, shouting words at him and

crying. He'd curled up in the armchair, and waited for it to be over.

Mum said, 'Okay. I understand. I don't want you to get caught.'

Mum looked through the door at him and held out her phone. 'Hurry up and take it, Rudder. As you've pointed out to me, Rose is breaking Pilgrim law.'

He came and Mum dropped the phone into his hands. Her phone felt much lighter than his. She stood up, went into the bathroom and closed the door. The water pipes started howling.

He said, 'Hello?'

'Take your time, won't you, Rudder.'

He pressed the phone into his ear to hear her better. 'You sound like you're in a cave.'

'Close. I'm under the duvet in my bedroom. I've got the old box room and Lily-Beth's in the bed above me and I bet she's listening out in case I do anything prohibited. I had to stop myself humming one of your damn Simon and Garfunkel songs earlier. Ruds, we need to talk about that picture.'

His shoulder jerked up, pushing the phone further into his ear. It sounded like Rose was right in his head.

He said, 'I didn't mean to.'

'I know that, Rudder, but you did and we need to work out what to do next. I haven't got much time. I need you to tell me exactly what happened.'

'I don't know what to say.'

'Start with when you got the picture.'

He did and then once he started, he couldn't stop. She didn't say anything. She just let him speak. He told her everything, about Ms Leppard and the drama group, about Rash and Dominic (maybe not quite everything about Rash), about how he'd forgotten it wasn't just the three of them on the chat group and how hard he'd prayed afterwards. He even told Rose how he wanted to change places with her right now and that he was scared he'd be left on his own after the Clean Slate was tallied. Then he mentioned Kye. That was the first time she made a noise. He stopped talking. Rose was quiet again.

He said, 'I've finished now.'

'I know. I heard footsteps outside my door. I just wanted to make sure they passed. Kye came to see you today?'

'Yes. He was waiting for me when I got back from school. He said that he could help me make things better.'

'Don't go near him, Rudder. He's not a good person.'

'That's what I kept telling you, but you were ignoring me. You wanted him to help you with your stupid decommissioning list.'

'It wasn't stupid!' Her voice rose, then silence.

'Rose?'

'What did you say to him?' She was whispering again.

'He asked about you. He didn't know you've gone back.'

'There was no reason why he should know. Then what happened?'

277

'I told him to leave me alone and I went into the flat.'

'Good. And you're sure you don't know who sent you the photo?'

'Yes. Well, kind of.'

'Kind of sure or kind of not sure?'

'It was God testing me . . .'

'God doesn't have a smartphone, Ruds.'

Rudder thought he was supposed to laugh, but Rose's jokes about God weren't funny.

'It came when I had music on,' he said, 'and I was . . .'

Dancing.

'What?'

Nothing.'

'If God was testing you, who do you think he was using?'

'Well, I was thinking about what happened in the library. It might be Bella.'

'You mean Kye's sister?' There was a little laugh in Rose's voice. 'Why the hell would she send you a picture of a naked girl? She doesn't even have your number, does she?'

'Yes, she does. Remember?'

'Oh,' Rose said. 'Yes.'

Bella had been the one who'd found out that he'd signed up to the Potter Patter spell forum and told everyone else. Rose had gone mad when she'd seen he'd included his address and number in his profile.

'But even if it was her, why would she send it to you?'

'Because I think she thought you would be next.'

Kye leaving the bedroom, slipping his phone into his pocket . . .
Bella, saying 'Don't let Kye do it' in the library . . .

It was hard to say the words but he had to ask. 'Rose, did you and Kye—'

'It's not me in the picture. That's pretty clear, even though you can't see her face. Right, Rudder?' He felt himself blush. 'This isn't about me. She's the one who matters here.'

'I'm going to make amends.'

'That might be difficult.'

'I have to. I have to atone and that includes making amends.'

His phone crackled as she sighed. 'Look, I can hear it getting busy downstairs. I can't pretend period pains for much longer. I'd better go down and help serve supper.'

The line went dead. Rudder stood up and went over to put the phone on the sofa for when Mum came out. It was weird that Rose wanted to sing Simon and Garfunkel. She was always complaining about Rudder's music. He tried to call up 'The Boxer'. He closed his eyes, spread his arms and spun around and stopped. A child ran across the flat upstairs. The pipes started shouting again. Rudder let his arms drop to his side and went into his room. He lay down on the other bed and wrapped his arms around the pile of sin.

Rudder's Sound of Silence Playlist

1. The Boxer by Simon and Garfunkel

2. The Sound of Silence by Simon and Garfunkel, except the prophet bit. Why's that the only bit that Rose sings loud?

3. America by Simon and Garfunkel, though I don't want to go there because they threw the Pilgrims out

4. Cecilia by Simon and Garfunkel, though I may have to delete it after Rose said it's about forni*****n. I said I was going to ask Mum. Mum agreed with Rose. Sin is EVERYWHERE, even in Simon and Garfunkel.

5. I Feel Pretty by Maria, though I don't think she's as pretty as Anita

6. A Boy Like That by Maria and Anita, because Anita was right. Sometimes people should listen to other people about boys.

7. Put on Your Sunday Clothes from Wall E except the bit about kissing girls. Pilgrims didn't do that on Sundays.

8. I Could Have Danced All Night by Eliza the Flower Girl in My Fair Lady

9. Bridge Over Troubled Water by Simon and Garfunkel, though sometimes it makes me cry.

22

'Rudder?' Mum was standing over him, holding a mug. 'I have to go to work. I was going to say no, but I can't afford to. Just stay here and do your school work.'

Some time in the night, he must have shifted over to his own bed, though his neck hurt, as if he'd been sleeping with his head against the sin pile.

'An answer, please, Rudder.'

He made a noise that sounded like 'yes'. She closed the bedroom door and then he heard the flat door shut, then the street door nine seconds later.

He stretched and reached for his phone. Of course. It wasn't there. Mum had it. That was how it should be. He sat up. Did someone just knock on the flat door? He froze. Those people couldn't be back! Mum had paid the money and the man in the skull top and the woman were happy now. They'd promised to leave Mum alone. Rudder waited. There was definitely someone knocking on their door, but it was gentle, like they didn't want to frighten him.

Rudder got up and went and stood by the door.

'Rudder?' Another knock. 'It's Kye. Please open the door.'

Kye? Rudder ran back into his room. He was going to call the police. No, he couldn't, because Mum still had his phone.

And anyway, the police had no authority.

'Rudder?' Kye was louder now. 'I don't have to be anywhere else. I can stay here all day.'

Rudder crept back towards the door. 'How did you get in?'

'Your mum was coming out. I said I was visiting the people upstairs. She let me in no problem.'

'What do you want?'

'I told you yesterday. We need to talk about that picture. That girl's going to be well stressed if she finds out what you've done. Do you really want me to shout about it from out here?'

'I'm not allowed to let anyone in.'

'For God's sake, Rudder! Okay. You don't have to let me in. I can take you out for some breakfast, right? But I really need your help. I'll be waiting for you across the road.'

Seven, eight, nine steps. The street door banged shut. Rudder crouched on the sofa and looked out the window. Kye crossed the road and went and sat on the hostel wall.

Kye needed Rudder's help? Kye. Needed. Rudder's help. And Kye was going to take him for breakfast. Rudder went into the kitchen. There was bread and chocolate spread and a Weetabix thing in an open box. But proper breakfast with bacon and beans and eggs? He hadn't had that since his last birthday.

He went back to the bedroom and put on his sweatshirt and tracksuit bottoms. He fished the spare keys out of the drawer in the kitchen, laced up his trainers and left. He locked the flat door carefully behind him. He shouldn't disobey Mum, but this was for the greater good. He could make amends to the girl and show Dad how sorry he was.

Kye stood up, watching Rudder come towards him. Rudder had never noticed before – Kye wasn't that much taller than him.

'Thanks for coming out, Rudder.' He stuck out his hand for Rudder to shake. Rudder looked at Kye than at the hand. He took it. Kye smiled and shook Rudder's hand hard then let it drop. 'I know we haven't always got on that well. I suppose it seemed like I was taking your sister away from you. Honest. It wasn't meant to be like that. I just wanted to help her get that church thing out of her head.'

'It wasn't a church. We were Pilgrims.'

'Sorry. Yes. Pilgrims.'

Kye had a funny little smile on his face when he said 'Pilgrims'.

Rudder said, 'Are we going for breakfast?'

'Sorry. Yes. Of course we are. We can get this bus.'

Bus? But it was too late. Kye had stuck his arm out and the bus was slowing.

'I don't have my pass.'

'Just go in through the middle doors.'

'But—'

'Don't worry. You don't have to pay anyway.' Kye nudged Rudder in ahead of him. 'Let's go upstairs.'

The top deck was virtually empty. Rudder slid into the seat behind Kye. That had been an easy rule to learn. Wherever possible, you never sat next to someone, always behind or in front or sometimes across the aisle. Kye's arm was stretched across the back of the seat. Rudder did the same. Kye turned to face him.

'Do you know about Bella?'

'I told Rose that I thought she'd sent me –' Rudder looked around and lowered his voice – 'the picture.'

Kye narrowed his eyes. 'You think my sister sent that photo to you??'

'No.' His ears were heating up. 'Well, yes, sort of, but Rose thought that was stupid.'

'Did she? Right.'

Kye turned away. If Rudder said something else, would Kye hear him? Could he tap Kye on the shoulder? Rudder hadn't seen boys do that on buses. He leaned forward so his mouth was near Kye's ear.

He said, 'How's Bella?

It was the right thing to say. Kye turned back. 'She's all right. She's staying with my aunty, though. Didn't Rose say?'

'No.'

'It's because my dad's a twat.'

A what? Was that good or bad?

'He always thinks he knows best and won't listen to anyone else.'

Not good, then.

'My mum's gutted Bella's gone,' Kye said.

'Will she come back to my school?'

'No. Probably not.'

Rudder should be pleased. Instead, he felt sad.

Kye rang the bell. 'See that place across the road? That's good.'

The café was busy. Rudder sat down by an empty table near the window while Kye went and placed the order. Kye slid back into the booth opposite and placed a tray with two Coke cans and two glasses full of ice between them. He handed Rudder a Coke and a glass.

Kye said, 'It's a bit like being on a date.'

Men with men . . . The Pilgrims said— No, he mustn't think about that now.

Rudder poured his Coke. He was too quick and the ice made it fizz on to the table. Kye snatched away his phone.

'Sorry,' Rudder said.

'That's okay. It was an accident.' His eyes settled on Rudder and didn't move. 'Like sending round that picture was an accident, wasn't it?'

Rudder nodded.

'But accidents have consequences, yeah?'

Kye leaned forward. Rudder jerked back.

'It's okay, Rudder. I need to talk quietly because I'm going to let you into a secret.'

A secret. Rudder looked down. It was going to be worldly business, Rudder knew it. But still, why would Kye tell

Rudder a secret? Nobody ever told Rudder secrets.

Kye said, 'I wanted to talk to you yesterday but you looked like you were going to pass out when you saw me.'

Was Rudder supposed to say something? That couldn't be the secret.

'I took that picture.'

Rudder's mouth fell open. He quickly slurped up some Coke, but tried to breathe at the same time. Kye waited for him to finish coughing and dry his eyes.

'Sorry to shock you, Rudder. But I think it's important that we're honest, don't you?' Kye didn't wait for Rudder to say anything. That was good. Rudder couldn't agree. It was a sin to lie but Rudder didn't want to be honest with Kye.

'She's an old girlfriend of mine,' Kye said. 'Long before I met Rose. It was . . . just something personal.' He took a sip of his Coke. 'Somehow it got sent to you. And then you sent it to your drama group. It went around a few times and you know the way these things are.'

Rudder didn't, but he did now.

'One of the boys in your drama group's got an older brother who's always sending round this stuff. When it ended up back on my phone, I almost had a heart attack. God knows what the girl's parents are going to do. They're really strict.'

'I'm . . . I'm sorry.'

'You keep saying that, but that's not going to help my ex, is it? You're going to have to do something big to get everyone out of this mess. Agree?'

This time Rudder could be honest. He nodded.

'I want you to go to the police, Rudder.'

'The what?' Rudder's heart was bashing about like the Boggart in the wardrobe. 'I can't! I'm not allowed!'

'Who said that? Your mum?'

He shook his head. 'The Pilgrims don't believe in the police.'

Kye levered out an ice cube from his Coke and popped it into his mouth. Rudder watched it bulge from cheek to cheek until Kye's teeth crunched down on it. 'They're the police, Rudder. Not fairies. You don't have to believe in them, because they already exist.'

'Yes, I know . . . but . . . The police don't have Our Lord's authority so we can't recognise them.'

Kye's head was so close Rudder could see a spot on the side of Kye's nose.

'You're not a Pilgrim any more, Rudder. You're in our world. In our world, the police have authority and I need you to go to them.'

Rudder wrapped his finger round his glass. The ice made it heavy to lift and the cubes knocked against his lips, almost making him dribble.

Kye said, 'I'm sorry. I know that sounds a bit harsh. It's just this is really important. I can't go to the police. It's . . .' He scratched his head. 'It's a bit tricky. But I really need you to take that picture to the police.'

Rudder stared at the ice. Kye was watching him. 'Why can't you go?'

'I just can't. I've promised someone I can't. It will cause too much trouble. Please, Rudder, I just can't.'

He said, 'Can I tell the police that you took the photo?'

'No!' Kye's hand flailed out, hitting his glass. His other hand caught it before it tipped. 'Who took it isn't important. The girl's name isn't important, neither.'

'Mr Abdi at school thought it was, especially if no one knew how old she was.'

'She's over eighteen. But you can't tell them that or they'll want to know how you know. Look, go into a police station and tell them that you sent round an indecent picture. Say you found it on a revenge site and you can't remember the name. Something like that. They'll ask you lots of questions but they'll easily work out that it was an accident and you didn't know any better. They'll want to see your phone.'

'I deleted the picture.'

'That's okay. They can recover it if they have to investigate it some more.'

'The school said they referred it to the police anyway. I don't need to go.'

Kye sat back. 'Good. So, you'll have to speak to the police anyway. This way you're in charge. Would you prefer them to come to your house and take you away in a police car? The police are busy, Rudder, so you'll never know when they're coming. That's gonna be stressful for you and your mum. Or do you want to go there on your own terms, when you know exactly what you're going to say?'

'I've never been to the police before. I don't know what I'm supposed to say.'

Kye took another sip of his drink. 'Look, Rudder, there are lots of things at stake here. You sent my ex's picture round to masses of people. It was private and you shared it. It could cause her all sorts of consequences if anyone recognised her. We need to make sure the picture gets taken off the internet.'

'Why's it on the internet? I thought it was on phones.'

'That's what I meant. But the police can check that no one you've sent it to puts it on the internet. Sometimes pictures end up on there without the girl's permission. If that happens, the police can get them taken down. Imagine if that girl was Rose. How would you feel?'

Kye must know how Rudder would feel. Kye knew how Rudder felt when he swore at him but he didn't care. He knew how Rudder felt when he took Rose into the bedroom and slammed the door shut but he didn't care. So why should Rudder care? But what if the next picture that buzzed on to his phone *was* Rose?

He said, 'If you took a picture of my sister, don't send it to anyone.'

'What?'

'Don't send anyone a picture of Rose.'

'Why would I do that?'

'Because you must have sent the other picture to someone who sent it to me.'

'Yeah. Yeah, of course. If . . . if I had a picture of Rose, I wouldn't send it to anyone. Not if you go to the Police. Are you going to do this, Rudder? Even if you don't want to help me, you'll help my ex. If she ever found out what you did, she'll know that you tried to put it right.'

Make amends.

Rudder said, 'I want you to say sorry first.'

'You want what?'

'You laughed at me when I was dancing and you swore.'

A smile flickered across Kye's mouth. 'You laying down the conditions, Rudder?'

'I want you to say sorry, Kye.' The name felt hard in Rudder's mouth. He'd never used it to Kye's face before.

'All right, I'm sorry!' Kye gulped back more Coke. 'Does that mean you'll help me?'

'Yes. But I want one more thing.'

'What else?'

'I want to see Bella.'

Five Trains I Would Like to Go On

1. The Polar Express, though not on the roof because you get knocked off.

2. Hogwarts Express, though not after The Prisoner of Azkaban. The Dementors ruined it. There should have been one place that was safe, where magic was so strong that nothing bad could break through, but the Dementor flew right in and attacked Harry.

3. The train going to Zenibaba's house in Spirited Away. I'd like to be one of the see-through people.

4. The Train of Thought in Inside Out. I want it to be inside Rose's head so I know what she's thinking.

5. A train to the seaside. Mum says she'll take us to Southend next year if she can afford it. She's never been to the seaside, neither.

23

Rose had to go on mission. A proper mission – a street mission, as if Mikhail was making it his own mission to save Rose's soul. It had been almost impossible to get out of bed and put on her clothes. Her stomach still felt like she'd been eating bad yoghurt and her eyes wanted to prickle with tears.

Gayle was furious that Rose was there. Even the bare patch of neck skin between her plait and the collar of her blouse seemed to radiate rage. Rose had to forget this and focus. She had to forget phones took photos. She had to forget photos spread quicker than a zombie virus. She had to forget Rudder. Forget Kye, and how three letters formed the shape of him so quickly. She had to make those words, 'forget Kye', loop round and round her head, and remember one thing: the Pilgrim way is the right way. *The Pilgrim way is the right way.* Pilgrim men were soaked in righteousness, flowing directly from the word of God. As a Pilgrim daughter, she should have absorbed those drips until, letter by letter, the word of God permeated her too. She should feel the scriptures coursing through her veins. She should be powered by the knowledge that when the Clean Slate tallied up the redeemed souls and the End of Days came, only the righteous would be saved. It was Rose's God-given duty to spread the word, to save souls, to help the worldly break free of their sins, and then maybe she would be chosen too.

She had to say those words knowing that if it was true, her own soul would be carried to Hell and she would be taking her little brother's soul with her.

Couldn't Mikhail see how much she was hating this? It was different from standing by Soho Square, forcing a smile and brandishing copies of 'Pilgrims' Way' to tourists. It didn't help that it was close to home. People from her college – her *old* college – might live round here. Imagine it, knocking on a door and when it opened, Mina or Tammy were smirking back at her. The Elders had the whole of London and Essex to play with – it wasn't as if there were armies of Pilgrims fighting over the top spots. Even before Rose left, she'd known that the Woodfords were the last London Sanctuary. All the other families had migrated to the north where it was cheaper to buy detached houses so Pilgrims didn't have to share any amenities with the Worldly Wise.

She tensed her chest then relaxed. In her other clothes, it would have made her boobs jut in and out. She hadn't noticed that until Kye told her. In Pilgrim attire, every move was like fighting liquid concrete. Kye would never— Why was she still thinking about him? Why couldn't her brain *obliviate*? Just swipe out every memory of closeness, mouths, hands, skin.

'Sister Rose? Are you with us?'

'Yes, Brother Mikhail. Just offering our Lord a short prayer before I begin.'

Mikhail nodded. Gayle glowered. *She'd* soaked up so much righteousness she was shiny with it. Rose readjusted her bag over her shoulder and opened the gate in front of her, closing it firmly. She would not look back. She passed a mini-trampoline in the front garden and one of those red and yellow plastic cars children moved with their feet. The Pilgrims loved those. They were low tech and just happened to be the same colours as the *Libros Rojos*.

At least only one family lived here. Rose didn't have the humiliation of ringing a row of buzzers to get someone to let her in. There wasn't a doorbell, though, or a knocker. If she lifted the letterbox flap, it might drop too hard and irritate whoever opened the door. She knocked on the wood between the glass panels. Nothing. Rose could almost feel Gayle's eyes poking into her back. She knocked again, harder. She saw movement behind the glass and the door opened a crack. A woman peered out. Her hair was soaking wet and a towel was draped around the parts of her body that weren't hidden behind the door.

She glanced down at the leaflet in Rose's hand. 'For fuck's sake!'

The door slammed shut.

Rose walked back down the path, opened the gate and closed it again. Across the road, Mikhail had somehow managed to make the person who'd opened the door talk to him. Mikhail offered a leaflet. The person took it and closed the door. It was probably going to go straight into the recycling, but Mikhail still looked pleased with himself as he came back towards them.

He said, 'We'll call on them again.'

Gayle grinned. 'You have God's blessing, Brother Mikhail.'

He nodded and bestowed a smile back. 'We are all blessed, Sister Gayle. Even Sister Rose.'

Rose said, 'Even?'

Mikhail laughed. 'You came back to us, but not everyone agrees that those who return are equally eligible for God's love. You missed our community's big struggles last year.'

That's because we had plenty of our own. 'Struggles, Brother Mikhail?'

Gayle's lips had tightened into a line. 'How can those touched by Satan have clean souls?'

'We must all maintain vigilance,' Mikhail said. 'But our Founders agreed that those who return to us are often the most vigilant of all. They have suffered for their temptations and are never complacent. Excision must be the exception and atonement encouraged in its place. Do you agree, Sister Rose?'

'Of course, Brother. Charity suffereth long, and is kind.'

Gayle spun round. 'We give too much charity. What's the point of our Excision Committee if it doesn't excise anyone? People release themselves to Satan and then after a few days of atonement, they're back in.'

'Are you saying my father is too lenient?' Mikhail said.

'No.' Gayle bobbed her head again. Her voice surprised Rose. Gayle had lost her hushed awe. 'I would never challenge Elder Enoch's authority, especially since, as I understand, your father prayed against leniency.'

Mikhail brushed past her. 'Shall we move along?'

Gayle bobbed her head once more and clamped her hands together. Maybe all Pilgrims did this, not out of piety, but to stop themselves strangling someone.

Knocking on strangers' doors did get easier. Rose imagined tucking her worldly and Pilgrim selves away in separate drawers. If she slid one open, it was full of long skirts and heavy blouses, circled scripture and God's love. Open the other drawer and her brain crackled with pink and yellow and sparkle and questions. Every time a door slammed on her she bounced between the drawers. She felt the pain of another soul condemned to the agony of eternal hell fire. A second later, she was with the Worldly in the next house enjoying a few moments reading or watching TV or listening to music before their Saturday was interrupted by an unwanted door knock.

'Our final mission for the day,' Mikhail said. 'Let this soul be saved. Shall we all focus God's love together?'

Rose stepped towards the house, but Mikhail caught her hand. Rose looked down at his fingers.

'A moment's prayer,' Mikhail said. He was holding Gayle's hand too.

Rose bowed her head. Mikhail's lips moved in the corner of her vision. He said 'Amen'. Rose and Gayle echoed. Gayle's was louder and brighter.

Mikhail released their hands. 'Go forward, Sister Rose.'

Gayle cleared her throat but said nothing.

The house was on the corner, facing two roads at the same time, as if the owners wanted to make extra sure they wouldn't be interrupted by unwelcome visitors coming from either direction. The windows were hung with net curtains, just like those in Pilgrim homes that kept the Worldly at bay. Rose had forgotten how shocked she and Rudder had been that people would turn on the lights in their houses and not care that everyone could see inside. The door was solid, dark blue with a heavy knocker below a spy hole. Rose would place a bet – if gambling wasn't so absolutely prohibited – that the door most certainly wasn't going to open.

She lifted the knocker and tapped.

'Once more, Sister Rose.' Mikhail was so close she could feel his words in her hair. 'I feel this soul calling to me.'

She knocked again, harder. This time she heard the footsteps coming towards her, a pause then a key click on the other side of the door. Rose knew what she should say. She had role-played it with Mikhail. She had muttered the words into her pillow. *Good morning, sir. Good afternoon, madam. Why do you think the world is so unequal? Good . . .*

The door opened. The man was tall and wide, African, maybe. Behind him, a short hallway opened into a bright kitchen.

'Good afternoon, young lady.'

Yes, definitely African. Probably Nigerian.

'Um . . . Good afternoon. Why do you think the world is so unequal? Sir?'

'Because God made it so.' He smiled and nodded at Rose and then over her shoulder at Mikhail and Gayle. 'Don't you agree, my friends?'

'The Lord decrees it,' Gayle said.

Gayle was drawing breath to carry on. *Oh not you don't!* This was the only person to speak to Rose all afternoon and Gayle damn well wasn't going to take this away from her.

Rose fixed her best smile. 'He does indeed. How shall we end this inequality?'

'We must transform this world of sin to the Holy Realm of Jesus our Lord and God.'

Ah. Rose stopped herself nodding. Pilgrims didn't believe that bit. This world had to stay the same until it sinned itself to destruction and the Clean Slate tallied the reformed souls destined for ascension. According to Grandma Yellow, the worldly Christians were worse than the atheists because they already thought they were getting it right.

Rose said, 'Praise God.'

Mikhail was shifting behind her. Suddenly, he was next to her on the doorstep.

298

'Sir, you are a man of God,' he said.

'Pastor Timothy Ndidi. Retired now, but I still spread the Lord's word when I can.'

'I am Brother Mikhail.' *Of the Woodford Pilgrims.* He'd somehow forgotten to add that bit. He held out his hand for the retired-now pastor to take. 'How do we prepare this world's wretched souls for the final reckoning?'

'With humility and grace.'

Was that a twinkle in the pastor's eye?

Mikhail nodded like it was the best advice he had ever received. 'For by grace are ye saved through faith and that not of yourselves. It is the gift of God.'

'I agree, my son. If you declare that Jesus is Lord, and believe that God brought him back to life, you will be saved.'

Rose could almost hear the rustle of the scriptures flicking through Mikhail's head.

'God is good. Whosoever believeth in him should not perish, but have eter—'

'Dad!' A girl appeared by the pastor's side. 'Your tea's getting cold.'

She was in t-shirt and jeans, about Rose's age, or slightly older. In bare feet, she was almost as tall as her father. Her eyes met Rose's and she smiled, definitely a 'I feel your pain' smile. Rose frowned. She'd seen that face before. It was at college. No, it wasn't there. There were only a handful of African girls, mostly Somali, who hung around together. There was one Nigerian girl, but she had a long, wavy weave. This girl had natural hair, twisted down into China bumps.

She handed the pastor his tea. Rose had definitely seen her before. Maybe it wasn't in real life, just— oh, Jesus! Rose shouldn't even think of blaspheming like that, standing between the pastor and the Pilgrims, but this was the girl from Kye's feed. The one where he seemed to be grinning at her boobs.

Don't look at her boobs! Rose glanced down at her own feet.

'Go in peace,' the pastor said. 'May God go with you.'

He started to close the door. No! Not yet! The girl was still smiling at Rose. Rose stretched out her hand. 'I'm Sister Rose.'

The girl looked startled. 'I'm Remi. Nice to meet you.'

The pastor tapped Remi's shoulder. 'Back to work, Moremi.'

Remi let go of Rose's hand and the door closed. Remi. Her name was Remi. She should text Kye. *Guess who I met today?*

'Sister Rose?' How could Gayle be so annoying in just two words?

'Yes, Sister Gayle?'

'Our work here is done.'

Rose glanced back at the door. Remi, the pastor's daughter used to be with Kye. Did her dad know? Pastor Timothy looked like he'd want a whole lot more than Kye for his daughter. It was weird. When Remi smiled at Rose, she wouldn't have been close to realising what they had in common. A girl whose Dad quoted scripture and a girl who'd left the Pilgrims.

What the hell, Kye?

*

Rudder wouldn't ever add this train to his good train list. Though two weeks ago, he could never have imagined getting a train by himself. How could he be on it for so long and still be in London? He'd have to do what he needed to do quickly if he was going to be back before Mum.

He checked the map. There were three more stops. The train had been busy when he'd got on, so busy there hadn't been anywhere to sit. He'd huddled by the door until gradually the train had emptied and he'd found a seat right at the very front next to the door to the driver's cab.

The train announced the next stop. It was getting dark outside. They passed over a bridge, taxi signs glowing yellow below, buses crawling past a parade of shops busy with people. The train slowed and stopped. The door slid open and Rudder got off.

The station was open on both sides. The rush of air from the departing train pushed Rudder back. He sat down on a bench and took out the directions. He could catch the bus by the old people's home opposite the railway arches, or walk. If he didn't get lost, the walk would take twenty minutes. Just to be sure, he'd take the bus.

The directions Kye gave him were perfect. The bus stop was right there across the road next to the Saint Antony

Retirement Home. Only one bus went from there, so he couldn't get on the wrong one. He crossed over and checked the departure board. He only had to wait for two minutes.

The front seat at the top was free. It was starting to rain, making the streets all smudgy. The directions said that it was five stops and then he had to get off, double back and turn off the main road into the estate at the end. She'd be there at six thirty. The clock on the bus said 18:02. He was going to be on time.

The Bible Dad had given him was in his rucksack. He should take it out and read a little bit. Rudder had seen other people do it on buses. He'd even seen people praying and nobody else had been bothered. He loosened the string on his rucksack and pushed his hand in until his fingertips touched the Bible. He didn't need to take it out. Just touching it gave him strength. Three more stops, then two. It was time to get off.

The rain wasn't as heavy as it looked from the bus, but it still coated Rudder's skin. He turned back towards the roadworks and left into Claudia Street. He could see the estate at the end, two tower blocks and some smaller, shorter blocks. Lights were coming on. There were people behind all those windows, all different kinds of people, more than Rudder could ever imagine. Kye had said there was a boxing club, a Costcutter, a post office and a dentist. Just behind that was the football cage. That's where Bella wanted to meet.

The gate to the cage was open. There were no special lights for it, but the street lamps by the shops made it just light enough. A basketball hoop drooped at one end and goal posts waited at the other, like someone had invented a new game. A glove had been jammed in a gap in the net. Should he go in or just wait by the fence? She'd said wait inside. There was only one way in and it was the same way out. If he went in there and someone came and stood by the gate, he'd be trapped. The net was high. His feet could never fit in the gaps, his hands weren't strong enough to pull him up and over. He'd be pushed against the net until it dug shapes in his back and then they'd—

'Rudder?'

He looked around.

'I'm here.'

The voice came from the other side of the court. There was a small blue portacabin, and next to that, a shadow. The shadow waved.

'Bella?'

'Hi! Can you come over here? I still can't really walk properly.'

Rudder skirted round the edge of the court. Every kid who passed by must dump their snack litter here. It was like the plastic bottles, crisp packets and cans were all crowding against the net to get in and play their own games when everyone else was gone. The shadow stayed where it was. As he turned the corner it took shape. A puffa jacket, an arm leaning on a crutch, a leg in a support cast. The face was still hidden in darkness.

'I'm not very good with these things and I'm scared I'll fall over.'

It was Bella's voice, but not the loud, hard voice he'd been used to.

He scrambled up the slope to the portacabin and stopped in front of her. She gave him a little smile. She'd pulled a beanie hat right down to her eyebrows and a strip of plaster bridged her nose. A dark patch across her chin looked like a scar.

She touched it. 'They said it's all going to fade but not completely. There's make-up you can use to cover things up.'

'Sorry.'

'*You* didn't knock me over, did you?'

The feet hammering the pedals. The orc with his hands raised. The quiet scream. The thud.

'When I saw you outside the library, I knew something was wrong, but I didn't know what to do.'

'I don't blame you. Honest, Rudder. I haven't got long, though. Why do you want to see me?'

'I wanted to say sorry.'

'That's it? Still not sure why you want to, but, yeah, all right. I'll take it. Though I should be saying sorry to you for being such a bitch when you started at Pitt. I heard you nearly got chucked out.'

'Yeah. I . . . I . . .'

'I heard what you did, Rudder.'

'The school wanted to know where I got the picture from. I didn't tell them that I thought you'd sent it to me.'

'That's good.' A little edge of hardness was back. 'Because I didn't.'

'You didn't?' He wiped his face with his sleeve. 'But I thought . . . No one else has got my number. I don't understand.'

'I got your number off the internet, remember? It doesn't mean no one else did. Look, I'm getting soaked. Let's get out of this rain. My aunty's gonna throw one if I walk street water through her nice carpets. There's a shelter over by the little kids' playground.'

Bella's face scrunched up every time her foot touched the ground. She stopped and pushed her fist into her chest.

'I'm supposed to be lucky I'm young, right? They reckon my ribs are gonna fix themselves, but man, it feels like some wasteman's bashing them with a hammer.'

'I'm sorry.'

She sighed then grimaced. 'You don't have to keep saying sorry, Rudder. Over here.'

The playground was a flat concrete space with a roundabout and some springy ducks. The bench was covered by a wooden shelter, like a bus stop. They sat down, Bella stretching her leg out in front. Rain dripped from the edge of the roof on to her toe. She didn't seem to mind.

Bella said, 'It used to be a paddling pool, but the council

covered it over. Dad was so mad he was gonna knock on the Mayor's door and cuff him one. They promised to build a really cool playground instead. We're still waiting.'

'Do you live here?'

'My aunty does. My dad got posh and bought a house nearby.'

'Bella?'

'Yeah?'

'Did you mean it? You really didn't send that photo?'

'I wouldn't send that stuff. It's nasty.'

'Who did, then?'

She grunted and grabbed at her chest again. 'For fuck's sake!' She saw Rudder flinch. 'Sorry, Rudder. I forgot you don't swear, but this hurts so much even you would swear.'

'It hurts me more when people say "God" and "Jesus" in vain.'

'One of my other aunties is like that. She threw my dad out her house for too much bad Jesusing. Have you ever had a go at anyone?'

That first day in school, putting up his hand and telling miss that the boy behind him was blaspheming. Didn't Bella remember? She was the one who'd laughed the loudest.

'Oh, God!' She clapped her hand to her mouth. 'Oh, sorry. Seriously. I was just so stupid.'

Not so stupid that she'd shared that picture, like he had.

'Did Rose tell you about that time she came round and I was crying?'

306

Rudder shook his head. He'd thought Rose would definitely tell him something like that. She hadn't liked the way Bella kept digging at him.

'Some family stuff had kicked off and Mum had been shouting at Dad on the phone. I thought Rose was going to blank me because of the way I treated you, but she asked me if I was all right, made me a drink and everything.'

'But you were always horrible to me.'

She wiggled her wet foot and brought it under the shelter. 'I . . . it was like all my friends expected it. It was hard not to, even though I was vexed with myself for doing it.'

Didn't she know how much he hated going to school? How every time he'd seen her, he just wanted to curl up in a corner? Sometimes, though, even if you knew something was wrong, you still kept doing it. He should know that.

He said, 'I really did think you'd sent me the picture.'

'Why?'

'Because of the message underneath about Rose. It was like what you said at the library.'

'I haven't seen the picture, Rudder. There's laws against my brother sending me crap like that. What did it say?'

'Rose is next.'

'Right. And you thought she was going to be next up for the nudie photoshoot.'

He could only nod. Thinking about it made him want to cry. 'I thought maybe you found out something and wanted to make sure I warned Rose.'

She gave him a thoughtful look. 'Do you know who took the picture?'

'Kye.'

Her eyes widened. 'Serious? He told you that?'

Rudder nodded again.

'It's probably one of his old girlfriends.'

'That's what he said.'

'Man! He told you that too? Rudder, I love my brother. We've been through so much crap together, but he's trashy to his girls.' The water dripped off the roof of the shelter. It was louder than her voice. 'He doesn't mean to be, but he is. I hope he wasn't trashy to Rose.'

Kye, slipping his phone into his pocket as he left the bedroom . . .

Rose, shouting at Rudder and not coming out for ages . . .

Sitting here in the cold and the damp, Rudder could still feel the burn of it.

He said, 'I . . . I don't know. So in the library, were you . . .'

'I was trying to warn you. Rose was all right to me and I didn't want her getting too deep into stuff.'

Stuff?

A group of boys came out of the car park behind the shops. One of them chucked a ball to another one. They ran down to the court. Bella was looking at them, not moving.

'Sorry,' she said. 'I'm still a bit para. I suppose Kye told you who those boys were at the library?'

'No. But I saw one of them at the hospital.'

'The hospital?'

'I came to see you after the accident, but he was there.'

'Did you? Oh, man, Rudder!'

Rudder had thought it was just rain, but she was crying. He reached across and rested his hand on hers. He felt like she was going to pull her hand away, but she left it.

She said, 'Sorry. It really stresses me out when I think about that day. The one with the really short hair is my brother.'

'The orc's your brother?'

'Orc?' She laughed loudly. 'Don't ever let him hear you say that. Though knowing Briley, he'd probably be flattered. He's my half-brother, on my dad's side, from before he was with Mum. Or that's what Dad says. There's only eighteen months between him and Kye.'

'Why . . . why were you in the toilet? I thought . . .'

His face glowed. He imagined steam rising off his skin.

'Yes,' she said. 'I know what it looked like. Briley. Man, he's such a . . . I don't wanna use the word I want to call him. Not with you sitting next to me. Even Dad's given up on him. Dad was always giving Briley loads of money. Probably guilt money for dumping his mum for mine. Briley set up a weed business, but that ended pretty quickly when someone snitched on him. Briley's always reckoned it was my mum. Who knows? I wouldn't blame her. Anyway, he was found with so much drugs he ended up in prison for a few months. That's where he met the blond boy, Span.'

'That's a weird name.'

'It's not his real one, but that's what everyone calls him. Briley moved back in with Dad and Span sort of moved in too. He said he didn't have anywhere else to go and Dad's got all that space. And then—'

A boy ran up to the basketball hoop, bouncing, bouncing and then a throw. He missed the hoop and the others yelled at him, laughing.

'Kye and Briley used to get on all right,' Bella said. 'Or as all right as you can when your mums want to kill each other. But Kye did this crap thing. I think it was Briley's idea, but Kye went along with it. Do you know what a bait-out site is?'

He shook his head.

'I'm glad you don't. It's a website. You post pictures on it, usually of someone you don't like. Then people say stuff about them. Last year, some Year Nines started one about the teachers, but they got found out and excluded.' Bella watched the boys bounce the ball down to the other end of the cage. 'Briley and Kye, their site was about girls. Briley got dumped and he wasn't happy about it, so he stuck pictures of his ex online. Proper naked ones. Him and her . . .'

She didn't need to say the sinful words. Rudder understood.

'It was a bastard thing to do, Rudder. The girl's little sister was in my year. She said her sister's gone to uni in Leeds and won't ever come back to London, not for holidays, not nothing, because it stresses her out so much. Her parents don't get it and keep having a go, but who's gonna tell them the reason?'

Rudder thought about the way Dad had looked when he'd heard Rose's name at the school meeting.

'Their site is really nasty,' Bella said. 'They say stuff like "who's the dog?"'

'The dog?'

'Rough. Ugly. You know.'

No, he didn't know. 'How did you find out about it?'

Bella blew out her cheeks. 'A girl came round to Mum's and started yelling at Kye about a picture he'd put on there. I told Dad and he chucked Briley and Span out. He'd been looking for an excuse anyway, I think. I've been avoiding Briley ever since and then he found me in the library. You've seen what he's like. He wanted to make sure I wasn't gonna tell anyone else.'

But she had. 'What happens if you do tell someone? You just told me.'

She gave him a sideways look. 'I trust you. Maybe it's because you've never been part of all this rubbish and . . . I don't know. I looked up some stuff about your religion. They're really big on what's right and wrong, aren't they?'

'I suppose so.' Immodest women were wrong. It definitely said that.

'Maybe whoever sent you the picture knew that you'd get why it wasn't right. Especially if it ended up happening to

311

your sister.'

If.

'Kye wants me to go to the police,' he said. 'Pilgrims don't do that. Why can't you?'

Bella watched the boys passing the ball up and down the cage. 'I just can't, Rudder. Believe me, I can't. That's why Briley and Span came to the library. They wanted to let me know what would happen if I told anyone. So they told *me* something . . .' She rubbed her eyes with both hands and stayed like that, her face hidden. 'They told me something about someone . . . someone in my family . . . and when I didn't believe them, they showed me. It was . . .' She shook her head. 'God, Rudder. It was . . . God. If they ever knew I said anything, they'd . . . You have to understand . . . I just can't. Kye won't really talk to me about it, but I've got a feeling . . . I've got a feeling Briley's running things and Kye doesn't know how to stop it. No, not doesn't know . . . he *can't* stop it, for the same reasons I can't tell nobody.'

Bella grabbed Rudder's shoulder with one hand and pushed down on the bench with the other. She picked up her crutch. 'I've got to go. Dad's coming round to check on me soon.'

Rudder stood up. The Bible made his bag heavy. Hopefully the rain hadn't seeped through and damaged it. He pressed his hand against his bag until he could feel the ridges of the pages.

If Kye couldn't stop it, then would Rose be put up on the

312

website, her immodesty on full display for everyone in the world to talk about?

He said, 'What about my sister? Do you think her picture's been put on there?'

'I don't know, Rudder. Sorry. You'll have to find that one out for yourself.'

Rose and her stupid decommissioning programme. Rose, who kept sneaking around so she could see stupid Kye, even though Rudder had tried to tell her it was wrong.

Rose, who'd put the Time-Turner round his neck so when he woke up from nightmares he could touch it and imagine all the times in the future when he was going to be happy.

Bella limped out of the shelter. Rudder followed. The raindrops were gusting around like the clouds were trying to shake themselves dry.

He said, 'I don't know what to do.'

'If you're worried about Rose, find out if the site's still live and get it taken down. Even if she's not there now, if Kye's got a picture of her, it'll end up on there eventually. You'll be doing my friend's sister a massive favour too. And that girl whose picture you sent round.'

Making amends.

He said, 'How do I find the website?'

'You've already got the info.' She had one hand on her crutch. The other one was in her pocket. 'It's called Hot Dogz. The password's on the bit of paper I threw at you in the library. You still have it, don't you?'

He nodded. 'Do you think I should go to the police?'

She took a step and screwed up her face. 'Man, sitting down just makes it worse. I just think . . .' She stretched out her leg and rested the heel on the wet ground. 'This crap's happening, and like it or not, Rose is all caught up in it. I can't tell no one. Nor can Kye. Maybe whoever sent you that picture hoped that you could.'

24

Rose peered through the gap in the curtain as Grandma Yellow took her seat in the back of Dad's car. She looked like the Queen going on tour. Grandma wouldn't appreciate that comparison. Pilgrims were definitely prohibited from admiring heads of state, royal or otherwise.

When Dad complained about the price of a parking permit earlier, it had been hard not to remind him that Pilgrims didn't vote so he shouldn't really complain about anything. Lily-Beth was in the front of the car. They were off to buy baby gear from some Pilgrims in Chingford. Rose definitely hadn't been welcome. Perfect. She had her own plans.

She moved away from the window and over to her bag, unzipped the inside pocket and fished out the twenty-pound note Mum had made her take. This was more than enough to get her where she needed to be. She slipped off her skirt and pulled on her sleep-joggers. That was another clever idea of Mum's.

'These aren't trousers,' Mum had said, rolling them into a ball. 'Even if they really look like trousers. They're pyjama bottoms.'

On with her grey hoody, her trainers and her coat. She was halfway Rose – not quite Pilgrim, not quite worldly. No

Bible, no make-up. Just her. She ran down the stairs and out the front door. Grandma had been very clear. Rose couldn't come and go as she pleased, so no key. It was just as well one was left under the dustbin for the Pilgrims who shopped and cooked meals for Grandma Yellow.

It was after six and still light, though the world was turning towards twilight. Lights were coming on in the houses along the streets. The two Pilgrim homes had already drawn their curtains, but the Worldly Wise were starring in their own mini-films. A man in a dark jumper stood with his back to the window chopping food in his kitchen. It was even smaller than the one in Rose's old flat. Next door, a cat stretched across the windowsill, its tail dangling into the plants below. The woman on the other side of the window was ironing. She was wearing big headphones and smiling. Lights blazed in the basement underneath. An empty bed and a rack full of coats.

Rose hurried along. The flicker and glare of enormous TV screens, music thumping out of an upstairs room, laughter from a high balcony in the flats across the road.

Rose turned left. Last time she'd walked this way, she and Rudder had been making a dash for the cinema. This was the bus stop that had taken them towards home, but that wasn't the plan now. She looked up at the info board. It was six minutes to the next bus. She checked the bus map. None of the stop names looked familiar. A woman wheeling a trolley stopped and checked the bus times. She sighed and sat down on the thin plastic bench.

Rose sat down next to her. 'Sorry, do you know how I get to Montano Street?'

'It's the stop after the big Tesco. Double back and cross the road. You can't miss it.'

'Thank you.'

Four minutes, three, two, one. The bus pulled into sight.

The sky seemed brighter over Montano Street. The clouds were probably reflecting the shine off Tesco's car park back to earth. That was the house with the trampoline. Rose passed it quickly. Even if the woman in the towel was looking out the window, she probably wouldn't recognise Rose now, or care.

The lights were on in the corner house, two downstairs and one at the top. Someone was in. *Please let it be Remi.* Even better, *please let Remi open the door. Please let Remi be as kind as her smile seemed.* Even better than that, *please let Remi make everything right.* Please.

Rose almost ran to the door. Any slower and her brain would kick in and make her go back to the bus stop. A quick knock on the door and a quick step back. A security light flicked on and Rose was in brightness.

A woman opened the door. She could be Remi's mum. She was the right age.

She said, 'Sorry, we support our own charities.'

Rose shook her head. 'I'm . . . I'm not from a charity. Is it possible to speak to Remi?'

317

'Remi?'

'Yes, please.'

'Are you a friend? I don't think we've met before.'

No, we have a boy in common. He's called Kye and he likes to take photos.

'We met recently. My name's Rose. I came round this morning with my friend, Mikhail. Pastor Timothy and Mikhail were discussing scripture.'

The woman smiled. 'Yes. I can imagine that. And you want to speak to my daughter?'

'Yes, please. It's not about scripture.'

The woman laughed. 'One moment.' She turned back into the house. 'Moremi?'

'Mum?' The reply came from the top of the stairs.

'There's a girl called Rose to see you.'

'Rose?'

Rose heard the thud of footsteps as Remi came halfway down the stairs. Remi bent down, squinting towards the door.

Rose gave a little wave. *Please, Remi. Please!* 'We met earlier. I think we have a friend in common. I just wanted to ask you about them.'

Remi's mum looked from Rose to her daughter. 'Make up your mind quickly, Remi. The heating's going out the door.'

'Sure, Mum.'

Remi came all the way down as her mum retreated into the house. She was definitely taller than Kye. She looked Rose up and down.

'You've changed out of your God clothes.'

Rose nodded.

'I thought it was weird that you shook my hand earlier. It didn't look like your lot's thing.' She clapped her hand to her mouth. 'Sorry. That sounded rude. It's just with a street front property we get loads of door knockers. I didn't put your posse down for spontaneous bodily contact. And I didn't expect to see you back here in normal clothes. What's this about?'

'Can we go somewhere private?'

Remi frowned. 'Do we need to?'

'I'd like to. Please.'

Remi shrugged and shouted back into the house. 'Mum, I'm just popping out with Rose for a second.'

'Have you finished your essay?'

'I'm on the conclusion. It will be done.'

Remi sat down on the bottom stair and slipped on some trainers. She unhooked a jacket from the coat stand and pulled the door shut behind her. She strode away towards the pavement. Her legs must be double the length of Rose's.

They reached the corner opposite the Tesco.

Remi said, 'I needed some fresh air anyway. That essay was driving me nuts. So who do we both know, then? I can't even begin to guess.'

A woman rattled a wire trolley past them towards a row of cars. She didn't seem to have enough shopping to need a trolley.

Rose said, 'Kye.'

'Kye?' Remi whispered the word in the same way Rose had whispered it in her own head.

'Maybe I've got it wrong,' Rose said. 'Maybe you don't know him.'

But Rose knew she was right. There was heaviness in the silence. Remi sat down on the wall skirting the car park.

She said, 'So you know Kye too?'

'We were . . .'

She gave Rose a sideways glance. 'Did you convert him? I don't remember him being the religious sort.' She laughed. 'Far from it.'

'I've just reconverted myself.'

Remi nodded, still smiling. 'I did wonder. You didn't burn as brightly as your mates yesterday. Yes, Kye and me were something but aren't any more. I take it you aren't either.'

'No.'

'Kye's slippery. You can't hold on to him, even if you want to.' She looked away for a second. 'How do you know about me? He's not exactly open about his old girlfriends.'

'I saw a picture of you.'

She frowned. 'What sort of picture?'

'It's on his feed. You're at a festival, or something. You were with some other people and then there was one with you and him.'

'Of course. I remember. It was fun. So how did it happen between you and Kye? I thought maybe you and that boy

320

having the verse-off with my dad . . . Kye, though.'

'Me and Mum and my brother had to leave the Pilgrims. I'd been there all my life. I only came back a few days ago.'

'Hell, that must be tough. Going out and coming back. The Pilgrims are pretty full on, aren't they? No technology and all pretty Old Testament.'

'It depends who's in charge. We once got a decree that told us to get rid of all modern appliances like toasters and washing machines. Then it got retracted. The official line was that God's word had been misinterpreted, but Mum reckoned that the Founder's wife had complained.'

Remi laughed again. 'There are often many, many interpretations. Dad can preach the hellfire stuff, but he's also pretty liberal. Which do you prefer? The outside world or the Pilgrims?'

Cars were queueing either side of the barriers, to come in and go out. How could one shop hold so many things?

She said, 'It was hard to understand the outside world at first. Me and my brother, Rudder, didn't know the rules. Rudder especially. He's thirteen but I think he seems younger.'

'He didn't return with you?'

Rose shook her head.

'So you're not around to help him any more.'

'Rudder's not great at accepting help. He just wants to be a Pilgrim again.'

'Maybe he's just being a kid, Rose. You know, doing the

opposite of what everybody wants. I've got a sister. She did everything she could to wind up my dad. Then she went off to uni to learn how to be a quantity surveyor.'

It wasn't the best time to ask what a quantity surveyor was. Rose took a deep breath. 'He does need my help, but I'm not sure what to do. It looks like both me and him made some really stupid mistakes.'

Remi's voice was so quiet it slipped between the car wheels. 'What's this actually about, Rose?'

'I . . . Kye . . . He took a picture of me.'

Cars in, cars out.

'What type of picture?'

'One he shouldn't have.'

'Is that why you came back to the Pilgrims?'

'Sort of. It's just . . . I really trusted him. I thought I was important.' And thinking about him still squeezed everything inside her.

'He's good at making people feel important,' Remi said. 'Not so good at the trust thing. What do you want from me? I haven't seen him in ages.'

'I don't know. I thought you'd understand. Even when I was doing it, I knew I shouldn't have. My little brother doesn't know. I think it would break him up.'

'I can't imagine you're going to tell him!'

'No, but it's like someone *wants* him to know.' She took out her phone. 'Whoever it is sent him this.'

Remi watched while Rose tried to find the picture.

322

'I'm sorry, Rose. I better go. Mum's probably already storming down the street to find me.'

There it was. Rose tapped on it and held the screen up so Remi could see. 'They sent my little brother this. With my name on.'

Remi turned away. 'Just delete it. Tell your brother to as well.'

'He has.'

Remi nodded. 'Good. Sorry, Rose. I really need to go.'

'But he sent it round to loads of people first.'

Remi stood up. 'He did *what*?'

'He . . . he didn't realise. He thought it was just friends.'

'Your brother sent a nude pic round to his mates? That's just sick. Does he know . . . does he understand how much shit that could cause?'

Rose looked Remi in the eye. 'No, he didn't.'

'But why? Why would he do that?'

'I think he wanted help. I'd gone back to the Pilgrims and he didn't know what to do.'

'So he played pass the nudie instead. Nice work.'

Rose stood up too. Her thighs ached from the cold bricks. 'Then the school found out and excluded him.'

'Good.'

Remi rubbed her eyes with her knuckle. As her arms dropped, her sleeve scrunched down low. Rose saw the birthmark on the inside of Remi's wrist. Small, dark, shaped like a comma. Rose's phone had flicked to standby, but she didn't need to see the picture. It was so obvious. The pastor's daughter. A Pilgrim girl. *Undo those buttons. Lean forward. Pose.*

Rose said, 'Kye dropped me right afterwards. Did . . . did he do the same to you?'

Remi met her eyes. 'I really don't want to talk about him.'

She started walking away. Rose ran after her. 'My brother thinks he's going to prison.'

Remi carried on walking.

'The school are calling in the police. They think the girl in the picture might have been forced into it. Or that she's under eighteen. If they knew the truth . . .'

Remi stopped so suddenly Rose almost slammed into her back. 'The police? How the hell are the police involved? You're joking, right?'

Rose shook her head.

'If you can let the school know that it's you, that—'

'It's not me.'

'But I saw . . .'

'Did you see my face in that picture, Rose?'

'No, but—'

'Then leave me alone.'

'But Rudder . . .'

'I liked Kye, he was fun. But then, he dropped me. Just like that. It was like I'd fallen through a hole into a different universe. It was like I didn't exist any more. Now just when it's stopped hurting, you turn up.' She glanced up the street towards her house. 'Sorry about your brother, but I need to go.'

'Please, Remi.'

'No. There's nothing even to talk about.'

She hurried away without looking back.

Sister Rose Santos
78 Napier Mews
IG11 3TU

Dear Rose,

I hope you are well. I want to text you but Mum still has my phone.

I'm really sorry for all the sin and the hurt I've caused you. I still want to be a Pilgrim, but I need to atone more.

Kye took me for breakfast. Now I know how I can make things better. I went to see Bella and she said that the photos are on a bad website, but I can't look.

Lots and lots of love,

Rudder (your brother)

P.S. The other bit of paper in the envelope is the password for the website called Hot Dogz. I can't read all the letters, but you're clever and can work it out.

P.P.S. If I go to prison, you don't have to visit me.

25

Rose read the letter a second time. She bet Rudder would have called it God's will that she'd been standing by the letterbox when it happened to flop through. She'd managed to poke it in the waistband of her skirt just as Grandma came out of the prayer room. Rose had made herself walk slowly up the stairs back to the box room feeling Grandma's eyes burrowing into her spine.

Now she sat with her back against the door, paper dangling between her fingers. The letter was bad enough, but this? Lined paper torn from a notebook, rough, with random creases where it had been crumpled and flattened out again. She held it up, pulling it tight. The writing was in pencil, smudged letters and numbers that blended into the lines. It was the note that Rudder had shown her the day Bella got knocked down, but now it was looking way worse.

So, the website was called Hot Dogz. Hilarious, Kye. The password was impossible to read. This was why Kye had come to her, smiling on the outside and killing himself laughing underneath, everything all planned out. One, find a lonely girl. Two, smile. Three, offer her chips. Chips, for God's sake. If she'd wanted chips, she could have got them from the kebab shop below the flat. But nope, she'd wiggled her damn boobs because he'd given her chips. She was probably starring on a website called Hot Dogz because the bastard had given her chips.

Jesus!

It was more than that, though. It had been him stroking her arm and her back, wrapping her into him, making her feel real in the new world. Every time he'd touched her, a layer of Pilgrim peeled away. He'd given her the strength to decommission. Except here she was. Back again, one sock off and one sock on, sitting among boxes of 'Pilgrims' Way', waiting to be summoned to save souls. Mikhail would be able to look into Rose's eyes and see it: her soul, if she ever had one, had been burnt to a crisp.

So what was she going to do? Just sit here? Could she really just leave Rudder to it? Of course damn not. He'd sent her the password for a reason. So first, she was going to find out for sure that her picture was on the website. God, imagine it – back arched, shirt hanging off her shoulders, grinning for the demon behind the camera. Next, she had to speak to Rudder. He'd sent that letter yesterday. What state was he in by now?

The doorbell went. Typical. Mikhail and Gayle were early. Rose retrieved her phone from her boot. She'd text Mum and tell her – what? That while Mum was out working all hours, Rose had let her boyfriend take nude photos in the bedroom? A fact that Rose had somehow left out when they were talking about Rudder's photo share? Okay. She needed a different plan. She'd get Dad to drop her round to the flat. She'd tell him it was an emergency and that Rudder was in danger. But Dad would demand to know why, and she couldn't lie to him. Then Dad would what? He'd return straight back to Sanctuary to consult with the Elders. What if they advised him to shun Rudder for good?

She was heading out on mission with Mikhail and Gayle anyway. As soon as they were putting up the stand, she'd make a run for it back to the flat, to talk to Rudder. Yes, that's what she would do. She slid the letter and note with the password back into the envelope. She wrapped the envelope around her phone and rolled a hairband over it. The doorbell rang again. Rose shoved the package into her bag and headed downstairs.

Grandma Yellow was standing by the open door as Mikhail came into the hallway. There was no sign of Gayle. Maybe she was ill. That would be a real blessing. Elder Enoch was there, though, with two more Elders behind him. Where the hell were they going on mission today? St Paul's Cathedral? It had to be somewhere impressive to bring together such big-man righteousness.

They all watched Rose as she came down the stairs. The more they looked, the more she wanted to leap into some mid-air splits, do a hands-free cartwheel and finish up with a forward roll at their feet. Instead, she had to act the good Pilgrim girl and carry on down, one foot after the other, her bag banging her side.

Mikhail nodded. 'Good morning, Sister Rose.'

Grandma Yellow and the Elders trooped into the prayer room. Mikhail headed to the kitchen. She heard him turn on the tap. She sat down on the bottom step, took Lily-Beth's borrowed brogues from the shelf, slipped them on and waited. If Mikhail didn't hurry up, she'd run out the door without him. Had Rudder even tried to get on Hot Dogz? Probably not. Any more guilt and he'd combust. Imagine, just imagine if he'd seen a picture of Rose . . . *Jesus, please God, don't let it be on there.*

She stood up and went into the kitchen. Mikhail was standing over the sink, gulping back water.

She said, 'Are you okay?'

She thought he'd put the glass down in her presence but he took another sip of water and nodded.

She said, 'You and Dad are the only people who will eat and drink in the same room as me.'

He knocked back the last dregs and placed his glass on the side. 'I believe in the power of God's forgiveness, Sister Rose.'

The doorbell rang again. There was a flurry of noise in the hallway and the low hum of a man's voice outside.

Mikhail gave her a tight smile. 'The neighbours won't be happy.'

'Why?'

'All these cars.'

'I don't understand.'

'Sister Rose, haven't you noticed? My father's here and Elder Obadiah and Brother Joel. And that's Elder Namuh just arriving. Doesn't that mean something to you?'

She thought hard. 'A special prayer meeting. Has someone died?'

'No, Rose.'

She frowned. When else was there such a gathering in a home?

He said, 'It's an Excision Committee, Rose.'

'Excision?'

'Surely, even you must remember what that is.'

Even. Again.

'I know what it is, Mikhail. I just thought that it was held at the home of the member being considered.'

'Correct.'

She searched Mikhail's face, but he'd turned away to fill his glass again. He raised it to his lips then put it down without drinking.

She said, 'It's about someone here? It can't be Grandma. Surely not.'

He kept his back to her.

'Me? They'd love it to be me. They wouldn't even organise a committee, but they'd have to wait until I was eighteen anyway. Lily-Beth?' Rose frowned. There were no circumstances in which Rose could imagine Lily-Beth being excised. Which meant—

'Dad? Jesus!'

'Refrain from blasphemy, Sister Rose.'

Refrain from . . . ? 'Dad would do anything for the Pilgrims. He'd even give up his family. Me and Rudder, he let us go just so he could stay here. Why the he—' Rose took a deep breath. 'Why is Dad being brought before the Committee? He's probably a better Pilgrim than all of them.'

Mikhail emptied out the water and plonked the glass into the sink. 'I have to take my place.'

'You? You're on the Committee judging my father?'

'Yes, Rose. Me.'

'I want to be with him.'

'Your turn is later.'

'My . . . my what?'

'An excision hearing requires testimony.'

'Testimony? Mikhail, are you saying you want me to testify against my own father? No!'

'Sister Rose.' He'd lost any hint of a smile. 'You are either a Pilgrim or you are not. You abide by our rules.'

'My little brother fell into a fire, *Brother* Mikhail, because everyone was determined to "abide by our rules".'

'No, it was because of a prohibited book! Who gave it to him? Satan! Satan is everywhere and he infiltrated our community!'

She leaned forward, 'So was it Satan who kissed me in the garden that time?'

'For goodness sake, Rose. We were chil—'

He pressed his lips together.

'Yes, Mikhail. We were children. Like my brother.'

The kitchen door opened. Dad came in and Mikhail sidestepped him and went out.

Rose said, 'Dad? What's this about? Why didn't you tell me?'

'The Committee isn't required to give notice.'

'You mean you didn't know?'

'I was alerted this morning.'

'I don't understand. What have you done?'

Dad touched the Bible in his waistcoat pocket. 'That's for the committee to adjudicate.'

She wanted to launch at him and wrap her arms around him. They stood there, looking at each other across the kitchen.

She said, 'They've asked me to give testimony. I don't want to.'

'You must.'

'I don't agree.'

He scratched his head. 'You asked to return, Rose. It was your choice. You can't pick and choose the parts of our life to agree with.'

'A choice? Really, Dad? Do you have any idea what it's like out there? Maybe you *should* leave the Pilgrims. Maybe every Pilgrim should spend time in the outside world. I grew up convinced that Satan was all around me, a real Satan, Dad, hiding under my bed waiting to carry me to hell for the tiniest reason.'

'You were vigilant. That's how it should be. When you lost sight of Satan, your heart became open to temptation. Both you and Rudder.'

Rose put a hand on the sink. The cold against her wrists was calming. In his own way, Dad was right. She and Rudder had done things that they would never have thought possible in their Pilgrim life.

She said, 'It's hard to fight Satan when you're hungry. If you really cared, you'd have done more.'

'I cared enough to fight for you to return, Rose. Do you know how hard that was? I made promises about your deference to God. I atone daily for your sins and Rudder's. Why am I summoned to the Committee, Rose? Because I gave my word that my children were Pilgrims at heart. I believed it. I believed you wanted to atone. I believed Rudder wanted to return. I swore on God's word this was true.'

The kitchen door was pushed open again. Mikhail had returned. He joined his palms together and bowed. 'Uncle Amos.' Another bow. 'Sister Rose.'

Dad gave him a small nod. 'Brother Mikhail. Am I to attend?'

They both went out. How could anyone doubt Dad? Mum said he even mumbled prayers in his sleep. And Mikhail was on the committee. Had he changed so much? Rose used to know the twitch of his lips and the crinkle around his eyes when he was holding in a smile. They even used to

334

speculate about being matched and how she'd end up living with Mikhail's family out in Chingford. Though that would never really have happened. Mum's family had been tainted. Aunty Hagar and Uncle Enoch would demand the best for their only son. Gayle's betrothal sum had probably already been agreed.

The front door was opening and closing again. More voices. She rinsed out Mikhail's glass and filled it with water.

'Rose, we need more glasses.'

Grandma Yellow had glided in silently. Rose searched her face, but it was blank.

Rose said, 'But Dad . . .'

'Now, please, Rose. They're about to start.'

Rose reached up to the shelf by the side of the sink and retrieved the glasses. 'They want me to testify.'

'Once you've taken the glasses in, there's a chair for you at the back. It's next to mine.'

Rose's elbow knocked a glass. It rolled but didn't break. 'You have to testify too?'

'Please, Rose.' Rose could only just hear her voice. 'Just take in the glasses.'

'Yes. Sorry.'

Rose clustered the glasses on to a tray around a big jug of water. She paused by the open door to the prayer room. The men were there, standing, kneeling, some with heads bowed, others eyes towards heaven. If Rose was a true believer, she'd close her eyes and feel the whisper of the Spirit as it circled the room. She'd believe that a tiny wisp of the Spirit's love would circle each man's heart. She'd also believe that as a woman, the Spirit could never come to her. Mikhail looked up. His eyes met hers and he looked away again. Elder Enoch was kneeling, his Bible open on the floor beside him as his mouth moved.

The sitting room had been transformed into a judgement chamber. The table was lengthened to its full size. Rose counted the chairs. Twelve, including some of the fold-up ones kept under the stairs. It was going to be a tight fit. She distributed the glasses. One for Dad, one for Mikhail, slamming down the others for those righteous men who'd watched Rudder's book shrivel and the words dissolve into ash. She banged down the jug. All of them ready to praise God while finding her father lacking.

'Go to your seat, Rose.' Grandma had come in behind her.

Two folded chairs had been placed by the far window. Rose sat down on one and Grandma on the other, staring straight ahead. Her expression was as flat as the tray.

The men came in and sat down, Mikhail's father leading, the rest following behind. They took their places at the table. Elder Enoch poured water for all of them. Mikhail was facing Rose, but he was doing his best not to notice. Dad had his back to her. None of the Elders acknowledged the women.

Elder Enoch blessed the table and started. 'We are gathered before our Lord to determine the pathway of our brother, Uncle Amos Santos. And if any man obey not

336

our word by this epistle,' he laid his hand on his Bible, 'note that man, and have no company with him, that he may be ashamed.'

Dad bowed his head with all the other men.

'The Lord will guide us to the correct path,' Uncle Enoch continued. 'The Committee has been called to adjudicate upon the activities of the family of Brother Amos Santos.'

The family? Not Dad?

Uncle Enoch continued. 'As you are aware, Amos, the conduct of your children and your excised spouse brought worldly intrusion and distress to our Sanctuary and beyond. We accepted your recompense and atonement and were pleased that Lily-Beth embraced our proposal to join with you. However, we have learnt that sadly, your family has acted on sinful temptation with consequences for our Sanctuary once more. Please address the Committee, Uncle Amos.'

Dad's back straightened. Rose leaned forward.

'Elders and Brothers, you are aware that my family splintered. My son Rudder moved with his sister and their mother away from us.'

He fell into a fire, Dad! He's only just stopped screaming in his sleep!

'They have been absorbed into worldly life, but you graciously interceded to permit my daughter Rose to return.'

Elder Enoch patted Mikhail's shoulder. 'My son pleaded with us to invoke God's forgiveness. Thank you Lord for your mercy. Another soul saved.'

337

Wait. Mikhail argued for her return? He still wouldn't look at her.

Dad continued. 'It pains me to say that my son has been stained by sin.'

A murmur from the Committee members. Even Mikhail's mouth moved like he was agreeing.

'I have tried to help him. I have tried to shield my family from Satan, but I have failed. I plead with the Committee to cloak me and my wife, Lily-Beth, and our child in God's love. Show your forgiveness once more.'

Dad fell silent.

Elder Enoch said, 'Can you share the nature of your son's sin, Amos?'

Dad seemed to slump a little. 'It would be considered a sin of lustful intent.'

Elder Enoch's eyes widened. 'In one so young? Satan's grip is truly strong. Is this true, Amos?'

Dad's head twitched more than nodded. More murmuring.

An Uncle stood up. Rose didn't recognise him. He'd probably travelled down from Cumbria to witness her father's humiliation. He bowed to Elder Enoch. Elder Enoch nodded. 'Speak, Jonathan.'

Jonathan held his arm out towards Dad.

'For this is the will of God, ye should abstain from fornication and so should the family you hold in your authority.'

Rose wished she could laugh. If anyone was abstaining

from fornication, it was Rudder.

Uncle Jonathan wanted to be Elder Jonathan. He was in full preach mode, showing off.

'Every one of you should know how to possess his vessel in sanctification and honour not in the lust of concupiscence.'

A chorus of 'Amens'. Were they really talking about Rudder? He'd blushed when Rose told him what periods were! He'd rather die than possess his vessel. She shared a room with him. She would know. Uncle Jonathan still had the floor. Rose had to press her feet into the carpet and her hands into her thighs to stop herself from yelling at them all.

'That one so young is dishonoured is troubling and, I believe, can only cause discord if tethered to our community.' More agreement. 'He cannot be excised because of his youth. However, we must not enable the germination of sin. Seeds scatter far and wide and soon forge roots. We must remove both seed and root.'

Grandma Yellow made a sound, a tiny puff of air escaping. Her expression still said nothing.

The Uncle sat down.

Dad, say something. Please don't let them condemn your son so easily.

Dad turned to Jonathan. 'Rudder is a child. Without our love and protection he has gone astray. He wished to atone and return to us, but if I am excised, I can no longer guide him. And my new child will also be lost to God.'

'You can guide Rudder from the outside,' Jonathan said. 'It will probably be an improvement.'

'And my wife?' Dad said. 'This isn't her making.'

'Sister Lily-Beth may choose to remain.' This came from one of the men who'd arrived with Mikhail. He'd mentioned Elder Obadiah. Was that him? 'Of course her baby will be baptised as a Pilgrim. Does that satisfy you, Amos?'

'No!' Dad's hand slammed the table. Rose gripped the edges of her chair. 'I've lost one family. I cannot lose another!'

Elder Obadiah was shaking his head. 'You are a Pilgrim, Amos, or you are not a Pilgrim. The Lord has delivered us here for a reason and we need the Lord's strength to follow his word. We cannot be divided. We cannot be tempted. We must stay pure. We believe that you are perpetuating your family's sin.'

The member at the end of the table tapped his Bible. He was old, perhaps in his eighties, and also wore the bright white handkerchief of an Elder.

'Amos, let us consider this. Your son's mother was part of the worldly life before returning to us. I argued against rescinding her family's excision, but I accept that our Lord is a forgiving Lord.'

Amens. Rose couldn't see if Dad joined in.

The Elder carried on. 'But Satan was in your son's mother's heart as it was in her brother's.'

Satan was in Mum? Mum who worked so long and late her

340

feet looked like the bones were in the wrong order. Rose felt her lips move, popping the swear words before they made a noise. Dad said nothing at all. Rose realised she'd tipped so far forward in her chair, she was close to falling off.

The Elder hadn't finished. 'I also argued against the return of your daughter. I believed her worldly ways would disrupt our community and I am right.' He thumped the table. His Bible bounced. 'I understand from Sister Lily-Beth –' Dad's back twitched – 'that you have ignored our teachings to accommodate your daughter's ways. Her atonement was curtailed. You eat with her. Sister Lily-Beth has heard her voice in the atonement room.'

'In prayer?' Uncle Enoch asked.

'No. As if she is having a conversation. On a telephone. I believe Sister Lily-Beth reported her concerns to you, Amos, and you refused to take action.'

Dad?

'These are not the actions of a devout and honest Pilgrim father.'

Mikhail took a sip of water and stood up.

Uncle Enoch frowned. 'Son?'

Mikhail picked up his Bible and held it in front of him. 'Last month I swore on my Bible that I believed that Sister Rose's heart was still Pilgrim and that she would humble herself before our Lord in atonement.'

Grandmother Yellow breathed in heavily but her eyes were on Mikhail.

341

'Sister Rose has accompanied me and Sister Gayle and –' he held the Bible to his heart – 'I am satisfied that her soul has returned to God.'

If Rose hadn't been sitting down, she'd have had to find a chair. *He was satisfied?* He was pushing the Holy Book into his heart and saying that? She'd managed just three missions including one where she'd had to leave early. Was he lying for her? Her face ached as if his words were drawing the sin out. Rose, unbuttoning her blouse, Kye's camera in position. Rose, head turned away, bare.

'Sister Rose has been a worthy acolyte.'

It was just as well that Gayle wasn't allowed in. She would have launched herself across the room and disgraced herself. Grandma Yellow still hadn't moved. Her head was bowed, the hems of her grey skirt pooled at her feet.

Mikhail looked from one man to another. 'I believe that we should honour Uncle Amos for his efforts. We are a small community. Isn't our way to save rather than exclude?'

Rose tried to project her thanks out and across to Mikhail, but he was a Pilgrim – he had a thick wall of scripture protecting his mind from unGodly forces.

'Save through sin?' This was a Brother sitting two seats away from Mikhail. 'Let's just go to the churches and the mosques and say everyone inside is a Pilgrim too.'

Elder Enoch turned to him. 'Brother Joel, please contain yourself. Perhaps we should call the first testificado. Step forward, Sister Rose.'

Grandma Yellow kept her head bowed, her hands clasped tightly in her lap.

Rose stood up. Elder Enoch was holding out a Bible. Elder Obadiah was studying the page of the *Libro Rojo* in front of him.

'You must swear on the Lord's word,' Elder Enoch said. 'If you take it to be true.'

Rose took the Bible. It was warm from the Elder's touch. She was supposed to make the oath, promise the truth no matter how much it hurt. She was standing right behind Dad's shoulder.

She said, 'Dad?'

At last, he turned. 'This is important, Rose. If you swear, you must give us God's truth. If you are uncertain of the truth, leave the room.'

She had a choice. Answer the questions that may lead to her father's excision, or gently place the Bible back on the table and go.

Elder Enoch said, 'Do you wish to continue, Sister Rose?'

Elder Obadiah eased over a page of the *Libro Rojo*. 'Perhaps our Sister doesn't remember the oath.'

Rose held her palm flat, the Bible parallel to her heart. 'I will make this vow before the Lord my God and I shall not slack to pay it. I vow that every word I speak is . . .'

Even if they asked about her worldly life? Even if she had to stand there and watch their faces as she described that last afternoon with Kye?

343

'Every word you speak is the truth,' Elder Obadiah said. 'The truth. Is that the word you're looking for?'

Could she say the words – naked, photo, breasts – to these men? Did she want them to understand that rush of warm energy that filled her body when Kye was close to her, how her skin seemed to pull away from her bones, stretching towards him?

She cradled the Bible in her right hand, the left hand on top. 'I vow that every word I speak is the truth.'

Elder Enoch beckoned her over to stand by him. She placed the Bible on the table, next to the stack of *Libros Rojos*.

'Tell us, Sister Rose,' he said, 'about your brother's sins.'

'Rudder?'

'Our understanding is that his sinful behaviour began while under his father's jurisdiction.'

Which ones, Elder Enoch? Reading about a boy wizard? Sharing the picture of a girl called Remi? Or was it how he brought police and social workers into your Sanctuary?

Mikhail's voice was gentle. 'Sister Rose, the Committee need to know if your brother can be saved.'

She said, 'Being a Pilgrim is all Rudder's ever wanted. He struggled after we left here. He'd had his heart set on being an Elder.'

Elder Obadiah turned a page in the folder. 'No Elder has ever spent time in the outside world.'

Elder Enoch held a finger to his mouth. 'Please continue.'

'We were in a hostel. When we turned the television off,

we could hear the mice running up and down behind the skirting boards. After market days, we'd see rats by the bins under our window. The guy in the room below us used to get really drunk and start shouting and swearing. Rudder would cry all night because his hands hurt so much and when he fell asleep he'd remember what happened.' All eyes were on her. 'Those . . . prohibited . . . books comforted him. Sometimes we'd read them together and I'd tell him that people who frightened him in real life were characters from Harry Potter. The drunk guy in the room was really Hagrid on too much butter beer.'

Twelve unsmiling faces and Grandma Yellow behind her. Of course, they had no idea who anyone in Harry Potter was. She didn't have time to explain.

'Rudder loves Harry Potter books and he loves dancing. He's a brilliant dancer. He's kind and loyal and too innocent to be a worldly. He's the same age as the worldly children but much younger. He made a big mistake but it wasn't his fault. Someone sent an . . . an immodest picture of a girl to his phone. He was scared and didn't know what to do. He knew the photo was wrong but didn't want to share the immodesty with me or our mother or the police.' *Or you, Dad! You just left him alone to deal with it himself.* 'All he did was send it to some friends to ask what to do next.'

Elder Obadiah restacked the *Libros Rojos* and opened a fresh volume. 'Seed and root. I am in accord with Uncle Jonathan.'

345

'We are Pilgrims,' Mikhail said. 'Our tools are atonement and forgiveness.'

Brother Joel tapped the edge of his glass. 'Your family have a habit of breaking our rules, don't they, Uncle Amos? Your son, his mother and . . .' He waved a hand in Rose's direction without looking at her. 'How can you atone for all this vice? Prayers alone cannot cleanse these sins, can they?' He paused, as if he was thinking. 'How about a sacrifice, Uncle Amos? Do you have a lamb or a goat to offer us? No, something bigger. A tiger, perhaps, or an elephant, because your family has stained our Sanctuary with sin. The sacrifice must be a great one to compensate for that.' He nodded to himself. 'A bull rhinoceros. Do you think you can manage that?'

Elder Enoch gave him a warning look.

Rose said, 'If Rudder could return, he'd forget his books and his dancing. He would do whatever you say. If my father is excised, Rudder's soul will be lost.'

Elder Enoch said, 'Remember you have taken oath on God's Bible, Sister Rose. Do you truly believe that Brother Rudder will embrace our Pilgrim life?'

Rose reached past Elder Enoch until her fingertips rested on the Bible.

'I swear with all the truth in my heart that my brother, Rudder, will renounce the world outside and re-embrace the Pilgrim way.'

'Thank you, Sister Rose.' Elder Enoch nodded. His face

seemed gentler. 'You will need to leave now.'

Should she thank them? No! This shouldn't be happening in the first place. She turned towards the door. Grandma Yellow still hadn't moved. Rose opened the door, went through and closed it behind her. She went into the kitchen and opened the cupboard, but there were no glasses left. She took a mug and filled it with water. She knocked it back and filled it again.

'Well spoken.' Mikhail was standing in the doorway.

'Thank you. But why did you . . . why did you vouch for my return? You held the Bible and—'

'I was trying to make amends, Sister Rose.'

He disappeared again. What did Mikhail have to make amends for? Did he sneak into a karaoke bar in Soho after all the leaflets were handed out and sing 'I Feel Pretty'?

Someone was knocking on the front door. Pilgrims used the bell. It was a gentler interruption to prayers. Rose went into the hallway. Mikhail had left the door of the sitting room slightly open and she could hear the voices rising and falling inside. She peered through the front door's spy hole and stepped back. Police officers, two of them, a man and a woman, like Adam and Eve in uniforms.

Rudder?

'Who is it?' Grandma Yellow was just behind her.

'Police,' she whispered.

Grandma Yellow grabbed her arm. As she frowned, a deep wrinkle curved across the top of her nose between her eyes. 'Don't open it! You mustn't let them in.'

'I have to,' Rose said. 'They won't go away.'

The wrinkle deepened and Grandma took a deep breath. She let go of Rose's arm. Rose opened the door. The police officers stared at her and then past her, into the house.

The woman said, 'Is this the home of Mr Amos Santos?'

'You have no authority in this household.' Grandma was just behind Rose. Even so close, her voice sounded tired, as if it had waited too long to say those words again. If the police had even heard her, they didn't show it.

Rose said, 'He's my father.'

'No authority.' A whisper.

'We need to speak to him,' the man said.

'I'll get him'.

Grandma took Rose's place by the door, a barrier between the Worldly Wise and her Sanctuary. Rose could see both the police officers' heads above Grandma's. That was strange. They had both been about the same height as Rose. Was she really taller than Grandma?

The men were spilling out of the sitting room into the hallway. Dad looked from the police to Rose.

'Amos?' Lily-Beth was coming down the stairs. Her grey jumper was struggling to stretch over her belly. 'What's happening?'

The police woman said, 'Are you Amos Santos, the father of Rudder Santos?'

Dad nodded.

'Your son is at the police station. He's asked for you to be there.'

'You've arrested my son?'

Rose glanced at the Committee members. Did they hear the sadness in Dad's voice? They were doing their best not to look at him apart from Mikhail, who seemed to be reflecting back Dad's sadness. Oh, and Jonathan. God, if a bull rhinoceros ever found itself loose in Woodford, Rose so hoped that Uncle Jonathan would be standing right in its path.

'He hasn't been arrested,' the police woman said. 'He came in to speak to us and we feel that it's appropriate to question him. There's a social worker with him in the station . . .'

'More social workers!' Was that loud whisper from Uncle Jonathan? Perhaps the hate radiating off Rose would kill him more painfully than a rhinoceros.

Lily-Beth said, 'You don't have to go, Amos. Their world isn't ours.' She patted her stomach. 'You have us now.'

'Dad?' Rose touched his arm. 'Rudder needs you. If you go, I'll go with you.'

Dad shook his head. He walked out the door behind the police. Grandma Yellow touched his shoulder then closed the door after him. Keeping her back straight, she walked past Rose, but for just a second, her fingers found Rose's, curved round them then let go.

26

The Committee members went back into the prayer room, the swell of their voices creeping beneath the door. Lily-Beth had disappeared upstairs. Grandma Yellow was in the kitchen. Nobody cared if Rose was there or not. They probably preferred that she wasn't there, tainting their Sanctuary. She swung her bag over her shoulder, dug her jacket out from beneath the Elders' coats on the coat hooks, opened the door and went out.

She turned left and started walking. She didn't want to linger outside the house just in case she was called back. Left again. Her feet traced this path automatically. Her first school was just there on the right. Ms Wormwood must be long gone. It was hard to see the school now as it was surrounded by a high wire fence with a gate and buzzer. Rose couldn't remember that. When she was there, she was sure she used to sit by the window in her classroom and count the cars on the road beyond.

She passed the school and turned right. The library was on the corner, just as she had remembered it. The main entrance was now around the side. She walked up the gentle slope and passed through the automatic doors. The Wi-Fi code was written on a white board near the librarian's desk.

She took out the envelope with Rudder's letter and her phone and signed into the Wi-Fi. She found a free chair in a nook between two shelves in the reference section and tipped out the sheet of paper again.

Hot Dogz

She tapped the words into her phone. Her screen filled with dogs dressed as snacks. Some were cartoons. Not all though. It would take a very long time to fully understand the worldly world . . .

She squinted at the paper, holding it closer to her eyes. Both the Os were quite long and thin – could they be zeros instead?

H0t D0gz

The screen went blank and a photo of a dog's head appeared. It was a Chihuahua, or one of those other little dogs. A white collar had been drawn on so it looked like a vicar and cartoon make-up added, heavy red lipstick across its muzzle and long false eyelashes. Its mouth flipped open and a speech bubble came out.

Password!

Rose took a deep breath and studied the scribbled word on the note. Bella had written it quickly. Was that a *B*? No, it

351

was an 8 followed by a lower-case *L* or a capital *I* or even a number 1. The next letters were smeared into each other and unreadable. The last two figures were a 3 and a 5 or an *E* and an *S* or a mixture of both. So what did she have so far?

81 35

Most passwords had letters in them to make people remember them, or the numbers were used because they looked like letters. So, what if they were letters?

BI ES

The dog opened its mouth and silently barked 'Password' again. The dog. Of course – it wasn't a dog. It was wearing make-up. It was female, a *bitch*. How could Rose have missed that? The hilarious Briley would never have passed up an opportunity to run down his girls. And though Rose still couldn't make out anything like a *T*, *C* or *H*, nor had she any idea whether they'd be written as lower case, capitals or both, she was pretty sure that's what the password would be. BITCHES. If Satan was real, if he was literally the embodiment of all evil on earth, if his realm was everlasting agony and suffering, then he needed to come out from Hell.

She tapped the keys slowly. An eight and a one, the three letters, a three, a five.

81TCH35

The dog – the bitch – opened its mouth wider and disappeared.

Rose's hatred was fierce. Every single follicle in her skull was a mini-furnace. The tiny flames licked inside her head and out. The hate bubbled through every pore in her face down through her neck into her lungs. Her breath hurt. Her thoughts hurt. But none of it was going to hurt as much as Kye would when she found him.

She scrolled through images. The bastard must have done some serious research on dogs. It was all there: breeds, nicknames, dogs from bloody films and cartoons. Lassie, Howler, Tramp, Scrappy, Doggo. The girls had their clothes on, faces turned to the camera, so much easier to comment on. *It's sexier to get some shots when you're still dressed.*

Do you think Goofy's nose is too big?
Cujo gets wasted and throws herself at anyone!
What do we think of Lady's arse in that skirt?
Click into the special section and see the real thing!

The special section was password only, but the same stupid password. There was some crap about having to be eighteen to look and that pictures were all by consent. *Yeah, Kye, you might have got consent to take them, but to stick them on your filthy site?* Anyone phoning up those girls and checking if they minded?

The captions under these pictures were different. They were nasty. Her stomach cramped. All that water she'd drank was boiling with her hatred. Bastard. So when was he planning to add Rose's picture? She slapped her forehead. He wouldn't. Not yet. She wasn't eighteen. He and Briley were waiting until worldly law said she was a woman, because they were so moral and considerate.

Once I'm eighteen, then you can happily make your snidey little comments about my thighs being too fat, or my belly too flappy, or my boobs too runaway. Too runaway? What the hell did that mean? Bastard. Was he going to zoom in to where the razor caught Rose's skin just below her belly button and make a joke about it?

Bastard, bastard, bastard.

And there was Remi. *Pastoral Care, click to enlarge.* Poor, poor Remi. The daughter of a pastor. Go for the girls who'd get heaped with extra crap if anyone they knew found out. Girls who'd never tell or make a fuss. Rose scrolled through. How many were there? Him and that tankhead of a brother must have been damn busy to get the clothes off so many girls, girls like Rose who wanted to trust him.

She should feel relieved she wasn't there, but Mum had once tried to explain the rage she'd felt when she was told about Rudder's burns. She'd said it was the first time since she'd been a child that she'd believed that hell's monsters were real. She'd felt it swell beneath her skin, the scorch of its breath inside her. She'd waited, even willed it to burst out of her. She'd known the damage it would cause. It was strength, pure strength.

Now Rose understood.

'BASTARD!'

It had exploded out of her. People looked round, but she didn't care. She needed that hot blast of her anger to face him.

*

Rudder took a sip of his tea. The milk was right, but there wasn't enough sugar. It was still hard to believe that he was actually inside a police station. A real police station. The room they'd brought him to was bigger than a cupboard under the stairs, but smaller than the bedroom in the flat. They arranged a social worker to stay with him. Rudder hadn't been sure about that. Pilgrims thought social workers brought more worldliness than police, but this one seemed okay. He was called Lewis and he told Rudder that his father was born in Lagos and his mum in Cornwall. They'd met studying medicine at university. They'd wanted Lewis to be a doctor like his older sister, but Lewis couldn't imagine himself ever giving someone an injection. He'd started off working in a bank but realised that he still wanted to help people so retrained to become a social worker. He hadn't been doing it long, but he enjoyed it. Rudder nodded. He was pleased that Lewis was happy.

'My parents still want me to be a doctor though,' he said. 'We sometimes can't help disappointing our parents.'

Rudder smiled. It was a pity that Lewis's parents didn't appreciate him. He seemed very caring and didn't mind being called in at short notice to wait with Rudder until Dad came. Actually, Rudder was glad Lewis was there. Pilgrims were always expected to be careful about their behaviour in worldly places to save themselves from harm. Everyone knew about Aunty Deborah. She'd been reciting her scripture on a train going out of London and some drunken men had pulled her Bible out of her hands and tried to touch her legs and hair. Some of the other passengers had helped her, but she'd said that many of the Worldly Wise had just laughed at her.

Dad's behaviour might not be good. He'd be angry, worse than at the school meeting. No Pilgrim ever set foot in a police station. Why should they, when it was only God's authority that mattered? Even when Dad calmed down, would Rudder be able to explain it to him? It had been hard enough to take it all in when Bella had told him. Girls agree to boys taking photos of them without their clothes on. The boys then put these pictures on a website and ask other people to say nasty things about them. The picture Rudder had been sent could be on the site. There was no way Rudder was going to look to find out. That was a good thing, because if Rose . . . Rudder must never, never see that.

He'd thought hard about it. The only way for those pictures to be taken down was for someone to go to the police. No one else would. It had to be Rudder.

He said, 'What's the register for sex offenders?'

Lewis gave him a sideways look. 'It's where the police record the names of people who commit sex crimes – that is, um . . . crimes that have a sexual nature.'

'Like I did.'

'I don't think you have to worry, Rudder. Your circumstances are—'

'What about if a girl said it was okay for someone to take a . . . an immodest picture of her? Would she be on the register?'

Lewis scratched a hairy patch above his ear. 'It's sort of complicated, Rudder, and I'm not a lawyer, but the way I understand it is that if she's under eighteen and takes an immodest picture of herself, she could be committing an offence if she sends it to someone else. If someone takes a picture of her, they are definitely committing an offence. If she's older, taking the picture is not illegal, as long as she knows about it and doesn't mind, but the problem is if the other person, or anyone else really, shares it without her consent.'

'Like I did.'

'Yes, but as I said, try not to worry too much.'

'Kye said that the girl's future could be affected. He said that people could keep the picture and it could be on the internet forever. Even if the site gets taken down, the photos won't really disappear.'

'Kye's right. People can still keep them on their phones,

but most aren't in a hurry to if there's a chance that they'll be arrested. Who's Kye, by the way?'

Rudder bit his lip. He'd almost broken his promise. He must not mention Kye.

'He . . . he was just someone I met.'

'Right.'

The door opened. It was a policewoman and she had Dad with her. Dad looked from Rudder to Lewis. Lewis stood up and held out his hand.

'I'm Lewis. I was asked to act as the appropriate adult in case they couldn't get hold of you.'

Dad looked at Lewis's hand until Lewis let it drop.

Lewis said, 'The police probably filled you in. Rudder walked up to the police desk and asked to be arrested. They saw there was previous social services involvement, so I was called.'

Dad said, 'Come on, Rudder. I'll take you home.'

'I can't go home,' Rudder said.

'Yes, you can.'

'Rudder isn't under arrest,' Lewis said, 'but the . . . the nature of Rudder's disclosures are quite serious and the police would like to ask him a few more questions.'

Dad's eyes were drilling in to Rudder, like he wanted to make holes for Rudder's thoughts to come out.

'Your disclosures, Rudder?'

'I told the police that I sent the picture around. It's against the law, Dad.'

Dad sat down and rested his face in his palms.

Lewis said, 'The police rarely take matters further in these cases, Mr Santos. Rudder is positive that no one has asked him for a picture in return.'

Dad's head shot up. Rudder couldn't read Dad's expression. At first he'd looked angry, but now he looked more frightened. 'Please, God, be merciful to me. Please protect me from all the evil this world holds.'

Rudder touched Dad's shoulder. 'There are other pictures, Dad. Some boys put them on a website. If I tell the police, they'll get taken down.'

Dad shook his head, slowly. 'This isn't our world, Rudder. Those souls . . . those girls . . . you cannot save everyone.'

'I sent the girl's picture round, Dad. I've sinned. I have to understand it, don't I? Then make amends and atone. That's what I'm doing.'

Lewis said, 'Are you okay here, Rudder?'

Rudder nodded.

'Right. If you're sure. I'll go and check with the custody officer if I'm still needed.'

Lewis left them alone.

Rudder held Dad's shoulder tighter. 'I just want to be a Pilgrim again, Dad, but I can't leave this world until I've atoned for my sins here. Please help me.'

Dad's frightened expression faded. He sat up straight, shifting away from Rudder's hand and put his own hands on his knees. 'The Pilgrims are God's messengers on earth,

Rudder. They must be careful who they choose.'

'They chose me once. They could choose me again. Look!'
Rudder took the Bible Dad had given him from his jacket
pocket. 'I brought it so we could pray.'

Dad closed his eyes. 'I wasn't talking about you, Rudder.'

They were called into the interview room shortly
afterwards. Dad sat by Rudder's side as he was asked
questions. The policewoman reminded Rudder of his last
teacher at The Pilgrims' Free School, talking a little bit too
slowly to the children. Her name was Inspector Shin, and
she explained that this was just an informal chat. After
their conversation, she would decide if the matter should
be taken any further. She took out a notebook and pen
and laid it on the desk. She had already written today's
date at the top. Dad sat stiff, looking ahead. He didn't even
react when Inspector Shin talked about nude pictures of
young women.

She said, 'Do you know who sent you the photograph,
Rudder?'

'No, miss.'

'Do you know who took the picture?'

Kye said it was him. Would Rudder be telling a lie if he
said he didn't know? Yes. He couldn't add sin upon sin, but
he had to keep his promise too.

Rudder said, 'Yes, miss. But I promised not to say.'

Inspector Shin looked up from her notes. Her voice was
quiet. 'Was it you, Rudder?'

Rudder heard Dad's teeth clamp down. Dad didn't say anything though.

'No, miss. It definitely wasn't me.'

'Can you explain a bit more then, please?'

'It was the girl's boyfriend, though he's not her boyfriend any more.'

'Do you know who the girl is?'

'No, miss.'

'And her boyfriend?'

'I promised not to say.'

'Is he threatening you?'

Dad made a little coughing sound and his fingers on the desk tensed, then relaxed.

'No,' Rudder said. 'He isn't threatening me. He's . . .' Rudder frowned. 'I think he's worried about getting into trouble.'

'Yes,' Inspector Shin said. 'I imagine he must be. We may need to come back to this. Do you know how old the girl is?'

'No, miss.'

'Is she from your school?'

'No, miss.'

'You're sure?'

'Yes, miss.'

The police woman cocked her head to the side. 'If you don't know who she is, how are you sure she isn't a student at your school? What school do you go to?'

'Pitt Academy, miss.'

'It's a big school. It could be someone from your school. Or someone from your school could have taken the picture and sent it to you?'

'I don't know who sent it to me, miss. I think . . . I think that if she was from my school, someone would have said. The drama group didn't know who she was.'

The drama group. Dominic and Rash and Idil . . . none of them would ever want to be his friend again. That was right though. That was part of the punishment.

Dad pushed himself upright. 'Will you be charging my son with an offence?'

'The law's complicated, Mr Santos. If the victim's under eighteen, Rudder was committing an offence simply by having the photo on his phone. A further offence was committed by distributing it. However, if an adult sent the image to Rudder, then they have committed an offence.'

'My son has set himself up as a scapegoat for other people's bad behaviour.' Dad stood up. 'He wants to save the world. He had no reason to come here. Let's go, Rudder.'

Rudder stayed sitting down. 'It's not just that picture,' he said. 'It's the other ones.'

Inspector Shin cocked her head sideways. 'Other ones?'

'Some boys set up a website. It's called Hot Dogz.' He frowned. 'It's a bait out site.' *She'd said*. He'd nearly added that, but then the Inspector would want to know who 'she' was. 'They put up pictures of girls without the girls knowing and ask people to say things about them.'

Inspector Shin scribbled something on her pad. 'Hot Dogs?'

'Yes, but the "s" is a "z".'

She changed the 's' into lines and corners. 'Have you seen the site?'

He shook his head so hard it made his eyes dizzy.

'So how do you know about it?'

'Someone told me. She was scared to tell.'

'She?'

'Is it a girl that's on the site, Rudder? If she's under eighteen, it's important that we know as she could be in danger.'

'No,' Rudder said. 'She's not on the site. Her friend's sister was. She went away to university and wouldn't come back.'

'Probably over eighteen, then.' Rudder thought Inspector Shin was talking to herself. 'Rudder, is there anything else you can tell us?'

There was, but he couldn't. He'd promised.

'Okay. Thank you for coming in. We will definitely follow this up and do our best to get the content removed if appropriate, but we will need to talk to you again. Do you know if there's a password to the site?'

He nodded.

She nudged her notebook over to him.

He said, 'I don't know it, but I can find out.'

'Good. Thank you.'

She stood up. Rudder was the only one still sitting down, but his knees were too wobbly to hold him.

The police woman was facing Dad. 'Do you have a phone number?'

Rudder said, 'Pilgrims don't believe in mobile phones.'

'No,' Dad said. 'Pilgrims do not.'

Inspector Shin opened the door for them to leave. Rudder and Dad went back into the main waiting room.

Dad said, 'Your mother's here.'

'Mum?' Then Rudder had spotted her, sitting on the last row of chairs by the wall.

She'd seen them too. Rudder looked from Dad to Mum, but they were both looking at each other.

27

Rose waited outside the flats. If she rang the buzzer, Kye would know she was there. He'd feel her rage and wouldn't let her in. This time, there'd be no texts.

A guy with a bag of leaflets came out and she dodged past him into the foyer. What if Kye's brother was there? And his nasty-faced mate? Could she take them on? The fire was still alive, hunkered down and spitting. The bottom of her belly ached with the pain of it, every nerve raw and sparking. Yes, she could.

She moved quickly up the stairs and turned the corner on to the landing outside Kye's flat. Rose fished her phone from her bag and strode towards the door. She knocked harder than she intended to. In the back of her head, Mikhail was giving her a disapproving look. *Be considerate, Sister Rose.* Not now, *Brother* Mikhail. Not bloody now.

A woman's muffled voice behind the door said, 'Hang on! Give me time!'

The door opened. 'Can I help you?'

'I'm . . . I'm Rose.' The fire disappeared, as if the draft from the door had blown it out. 'Rose. I was Kye's . . . You're his mum.'

She gave Rose a curious look. 'Yes, I am. Sorry, he's not here.'

Kye's mum looked tired. Her blonde hair was piled up into a loose bun on the top of her head. The mug in her hand had a faint trace of lipstick on the rim, though she wasn't wearing any now. She had been last time Rose saw her.

Dark pink and glossy lipstick on parted lips, a face frozen on a screen, a naked body exposed on a chair.

'Rose? Are you okay? Do you want a glass of water?'

The sitting room door was open and Rose could see the coffee table where Kye's brother and his friend had tapped play and turned the screen to face Rose. It had been her. It had definitely been Kye's mum.

'Rose?'

'I can't . . . It doesn't matter. I'm sorry to bother you. Sorry. I have to—'

Rose turned and ran back down the steps, through the door and out on to the patchy grass between the block and the pavement, not stopping, running, on and on. A street with shops, a square of grass, more flats. An estate of old red brick blocks and bright, new ones with yellow and green balconies. A children's nursery with pictures of toys stuck on the windows above a dry-cleaner's. Past a small church, United Reformed, Reverend Eliza Rolling, OAP lunch club on Thursdays. She turned another corner and she was by a drive-thru McDonald's.

She sat down on the wall by the drive-thru entrance. She had to give herself head space to think. Kye's mum was in that film. Kye's stepbrother and friend were watching Kye's

366

mum, in front of Kye, in Kye's own home. Even the whole damn universe wouldn't be space enough to understand that. She took her notebook out. If her thoughts couldn't stay stuck in her head, they'd at least stick to the paper.

Rose's list for – what?

<u>Rose's list for understanding why the hell I'm sitting by a McDonald's drive-thru trying not to cry my heart out in the car park</u>

1. Kye took a picture of Remi. She agreed.
2. Someone sent the picture to Rudder. Remi didn't agree to that.
3. Rudder sent it to people. (And now he's gone to the police.)
4. Kye visited Rudder. What did the bastard say?
5. Kye took a picture of me. I think I agreed.
6. Remi's pic's on Hot Dogz. Mine isn't. Yet.
7. Kye's mum was in a porn film and Kye's brother was looking at it in Kye's sitting room.

Even written down, number seven . . . Kye's mum. That film. Briley and his mate in Kye's sitting room. What the hell were the rules in this world? Had Rose really not understood anything?

A taxi pulled into the drive-thru. Rose could just about

hear the driver giving his order. Why couldn't her life be like that, shouting out a list of things she wanted that then arrived without a wait? When she was little, she'd thought prayers were like that. You closed your eyes and put in your request to God. Grandma Yellow had soon told her otherwise. Pilgrim women should be grateful for what God gave them and never ask for more. It was only when Rose was older that she'd noticed that Grandma always glanced at Mum when she came out with this. But now, on the outside, there were so many choices and every one of them was wrong.

But if God was in the booth taking the order and Rose was driving that cab, what would she ask for?

Please God. Help me find a way to understand this . . .

The noise and the fumes were curdling Rose's head. She rubbed her eyes. Kye had her picture. With one flip of a switch, it could up on there too. With one flick of a finger, it could be circling round his mates, radiating out from phone to phone. It didn't need to be on a damn site.

Please, God, help me find a way to make this right . . .

But God wasn't going to reach out and hand her a burger box filled with answers. She had to look for them herself.

The gate to Remi's house was open. Either someone was in, or the last person couldn't be bothered to close it. Pilgrims wouldn't do that. Mikhail had kept repeating the necessity of good manners and empathy. '*The Worldly Wise have their stereotypes,*' he'd said, '*that denigrate us by calling us religious nuts, intense, humourless.*' He'd smiled then, that old smile that Rose remembered from long ago. Gayle had nodded, serious. '*The Lord's word is worth it, Brother Mikhail, and so will be every soul we save.*' Rose had wanted to giggle and tell her about all the times when they were younger and Mikhail had rolled his eyes when the Elders had come up with lines like that.

Rose walked through, up the path and knocked. This had to be worth it too. Even if Remi shouted or swore at Rose, or threatened to call the police, the answers were on the other side of that door. Rose knocked. The door opened. It was Remi. She was wearing shorts and a vest as if she'd been doing her exercises. Her birth mark was covered by a red towelling wrist band.

She said, 'You again.'

'I need to talk to you.'

'There's nothing to talk about.'

'Please, Remi. I really need your help.'

Remi didn't move.

'I don't know what to do.'

'And you think I do?'

'Please.'

Remi pulled the door wider. 'Mum'll be home soon. You'll have to go then.'

'I will. Thank you.'

Rose followed Remi down the hallway and into the kitchen. A bowl of cereal was on the counter, a spoon

369

balanced across the rim. A glass of orange juice stood next to it.

Remi said, 'Do you drink tea?'

Rose nodded.

'I'd heard that the Pilgrims believed caffeine was poison.'

'My grandma likes tea so she's always ignored that instruction.'

Remi flicked on the kettle, her back to Rose, and dropped teabags in two mugs. 'And I take it you must be ignoring Pilgrim instructions if you're drinking tea with me now. I still don't know why you think I can help you, though.'

'I need . . .' It had all muddled up again. Rose took her notebook out of her bag.

'Seriously, Rose. You haven't prepared a sermon, have you?'

For a second, their eyes met. A laugh should have come, but it was stuck somewhere deep.

'I made a list of the things I don't understand.'

'How many things are on your list?'

'Seven.'

'Is that all?'

Did Remi mean that was too many or not enough? She went over to the fridge and took out the milk. Was it fair to say this to Remi's back? The words tumbled out. 'The first thing is about your— the picture.'

'Rose . . .'

'Kye took it and you agreed. I wasn't sure if you really

agreed. I'd thought I wanted to when he asked me, but then I don't think I did.'

Remi glanced out the window. 'Can we just leave this?'

Was it the same for you, Remi? Or had she really trusted him? Rose wondered what was worse.

But Rose went on. She couldn't stop now. 'My brother sent your picture round to people and the school found out.'

Remi plonked the milk down on the kitchen surface. 'Yes, well done, Rose's brother. Have you got any closer to understanding that? Because I haven't.'

It wasn't Rudder's fault. Remi just didn't want to understand it. Rose had to stay calm.

'I want to understand who sent it to him.'

'A pervy little friend?'

'He hasn't got any friends.' Pervy or otherwise. 'He thought it might be Bella.'

'Kye's little sister? Now that would be weird.'

'Not if she wanted to warn me about him.'

'That would be even weirder. One, because Kye said she was a big pain in the arse. And two, because she could just, like, warn you. Without sending a picture to your brother.'

'I don't think I would have listened to her if she'd tried to warn me.' Rose stared at Remi's back. 'Rudder tried to warn me about Kye. I ignored him. The other reason I thought about Bella was because she was one of the few people who had Rudder's number. He'd put it on a Harry Potter forum.'

'Of course. You both missed all the lessons about internet

safety. Though I'm not sure if it always makes a difference. You do have milk, don't you?'

Rose nodded. Remi splashed milk into one of the teas and brought the mugs over. 'That's one thing on your list. Sorry I can't help you cross it off. What are the others? You'll need to be quick. Mum's back in the next quarter of an hour.'

Rose stared down at her notebook. *Remi's pic's on Hot Dogz.*

She said, 'Kye went round to see Rudder and now Rudder's gone to the police.'

Remi stared at her. 'He was so impatient he couldn't wait for the school to call them in?'

'It wasn't easy for him . . .'

'Really?'

'Yes! Really!' Rose was surprised by the loudness of her own voice. 'Pilgrims don't go to the police. We don't believe in the police. But my little brother, Rudder, he's walked into a police station even though he had nothing to do with the picture of you on his phone. I can't talk to any of the other Pilgrims about it, or even my mum. That's why I came to you.'

'I still don't know what you expect me to do.'

'Even . . . even though Kye's put the picture of you on a website.'

'What?'

'A website. It's called Hot Dogz. It's got pictures of girls on it.'

Remi fiddled with the handle of her mug.

'Your picture's on it.'

'Yes, Rose. I heard you the first time. How the hell did you find out about that?'

'Rudder . . . he . . .'

'It always seems to lead back to your bloody brother.' Remi whisked her bowl and glass off the table and dropped them in the sink. 'I'm half-hoping the police do damn well charge him. He didn't need to bloody send it round to everybody. Even he could have worked that out.'

Rose tried to hold herself down, but she was out of her chair, two strides over to Remi, looking up at her.

'Stop it! You have no idea what happened to him.'

The fridge hummed. The radio was on in another part of the house. A motorbike revved in a nearby street.

Remi stepped away from Rose. 'You need to go.'

'Rudder fell into a fire,' Rose said. 'That's why we had to leave the Pilgrims.'

Remi said nothing. It was like running up a seesaw and waiting, knowing that just one tiny step will make it topple. One tiny step.

Rose said, 'It was on the news and everything. Mum said that journalists were even pretending to be Pilgrims so they could get into my grandmother's house.'

Remi rubbed a smudge of cereal off the counter with a tea towel. Her voice was quiet. 'I remember hearing about something like that. A couple of years ago, right?'

'That was us.' Rose took a deep breath. 'Mum was never a proper Pilgrim. I mean, she was proper in some ways. Her grandma had married into them just after the second world war. When Mum was little, her older brother got caught listening to worldly music. Mum's family were excised and had to move away from the Sanctuary. Mum's brother, my uncle, went off and joined the army. My grandparents atoned enough to be allowed back in, but Mum had seen the outside world and she liked it.'

Remi nodded. A tiny shuffle back, the seesaw wobbling.

'Mum did her best to settle in and was set up to marry my dad. My dad's mum wasn't too impressed, but she's a widow. Without a husband to speak for her, there wasn't much she could do. Mum and Dad married when they were eighteen.'

'That's young.'

'Yes. I suppose so. All Pilgrims do. You get married and try and have a family straight away. I thought everybody did that. I hadn't met a mother who wasn't married until we moved into the hostel.'

Remi moved back over to the table and sat down. Rose followed her. Remi raised her mug to her lips, peering at Rose over the rim. She took a sip and rested the mug back down, eyes still on Rose. 'You were in a hostel?'

'Yes.'

The seesaw slammed down on Rose's side.

Rose took a gulp of her own tea. She should have added sugar, but it wouldn't feel right, not now.

'I used to go to a normal primary school, but then the Pilgrims set up their own school and I had to go to that one instead. There are lots of things Pilgrims can't do. We can't go to the cinema or listen to music that isn't cantas or read books that aren't about the Bible, well, the Pilgrim version. Just before I left my first school, my teacher helped me join the library. I took out a load of books for me and Rudder. One of them was the first Harry Potter.'

Remi raised her eyebrows. 'Funny enough, my parents weren't into them neither. They thought it was all a bit dark forces.'

'Pilgrims are seriously not in to them. Anything to do with magic or the supernatural or superpowers – all of it's going against God's way. The only power is God's word and anything else is . . .'

Is what? Since she'd left, she'd been fighting so hard against all that and she still couldn't find her own words to describe it.

'Satan's work?' Remi gave her a small smile.

Rose shrugged. 'I suppose so. And then my grandmother found Rudder's Harry Potter book. And—'

Bang. Grandma and the Elders, their fingernails digging into the book spines, yanking them from the shelves. The atlases and dictionaries and *Beano* annuals and *James and the Giant Peach* and the *Just So Stories*, they could have burnt any of those, but somehow they knew Harry Potter was his favourite book, and that's what they went for.

'I was taken downstairs and Rudder was already outside. He looked so small next to Dad.'

'How old was he?'

'Eleven. Some Year Sevens are enormous, but Rudder's not one of them. Elder Enoch had built a little fire in the garden. They dropped the book on it and lit it all up.'

The smell. Scorched newspaper, melting plastic, the sharp heaviness of firelighters deep in her lungs.

'Everybody else was looking at the fire and praying, like they really could see Jesus in the flames. I was looking at Rudder.'

And Dad. How could he just stand there and let this happen? Couldn't he see how Rudder was shaking and crying and looking at Rose, his eyes pleading for her to do something?

Rose had looked around for something, a shovel or a stick or a broom handle so that she could drag the book out. It would still have been burnt, but Rudder would have known that she cared, that she was on his side.

'He put his hands in the fire to save his book.'

She was looking away when it happened. She'd heard it, Rudder's little gasp and by the time she'd turned back, his hands were in the flames. And there was the other smell, the one that wasn't paper, or plastic, or wood. It was the smell that clung to Rudder for weeks after, or perhaps it was stuck to her, curling its way up to the inside of her head, trapped there.

'All the prayers stopped, but nothing happened. Rudder

didn't even scream. It was like everything in the world had frozen.'

Then the world switched back on again. Rudder was screaming and Rose was diving forward and pulling him away and someone had run into the house to call an ambulance and somebody tried to stop them and Dad was cradling Rudder and running back to the house with him.

'I don't know if anyone actually called an ambulance. Dad wrapped Rudder's arms in damp towels and took him to A&E.'

'Where was your mum?'

'She'd gone to see her brother. He'd had a new baby. She wasn't supposed to because he wasn't a Pilgrim. Nobody told her until she came back. She went mad.'

Those were the first swear words Rose had ever heard in a Pilgrim home, though she'd known straight away what they were. Spit flew from Mum's mouth as she shouted, storming up the stairs to pack their bags. She persuaded their neighbour to drop them off at the hospital, the neighbour whose children Rose had never been allowed to play with. A neighbour whose name Rose still didn't know.

She said, 'We never went back to the Pilgrims. Rudder told the nurse what happened so then social services and the police got involved in case it was deliberate or there was abuse. Pilgrims don't have anything to do with the police. If someone does something bad, we – they – just excise them. The police ended up interviewing everyone who'd been there and it caused a bit of a split. Some people thought burning the book was over the top and that Pilgrims should be going forwards. Others blamed the Elders for taking Mum's family back in the first place, because they always knew she'd be trouble. I only knew all this stuff afterwards.'

Because when they were in the hostel, talking about the Pilgrims made everyone hurt. Rudder had to sleep in the day time because he had too many nightmares when it was dark. Rose had never told Mum about her own nightmares. She was silent and didn't move, so no one knew.

Remi said, 'How is he now?'

'He still has scars.' On his hands and in his dreams.

Remi slid off the stool and went back to the fridge. She came back with a bar of chocolate.

'Dad insists we keep it in the fridge so it doesn't melt.'

She peeled back the foil and slid the bar towards Rose. Rose broke off a row of squares. Her mouth was sour. She needed the sweetness.

Remi said, 'I'm sorry, I really am. I wish I could help, but I really don't know what you want me to do.'

'If you went to the police, told them it's you, that you're over eighteen, that you consented—'

'No, Rose. My parents can never know. They're liberal, but this is pushing it. My dad would go mad. But it's not even that. It would hurt him so much.'

'Yes,' Rose said. 'So you can imagine how my dad felt when he had to go into the school to hear from all these strangers about what his son had done. Imagine if he ever found out about me.'

'So that's it, then,' Remi said. 'We're stuck.'

Rose bit off a corner of chocolate. It made her mouth feel even dryer. 'Did you ever meet Kye's mum?'

Remi broke off a square and popped it into her own mouth. 'A couple of times, but not for very long. She seemed all right.'

'Okay,' Rose said. 'There's something I want to tell you about his mum. Something I found out. I'm pretty sure it's not normal, but I haven't got a lot to judge it against.'

'Ok-ay.' Remi rested her chin on her hand. 'Go on, then.'

Rose stared at the words in her notebook, looked up at Remi, then back down again. She slid the open page across the table. Rose broke off a row of three chocolate squares and managed to fit them all in her mouth at the same time. Remi's eyes flitted across the page then back to the start.

Rose said, 'Kye's brother turned it on when I was there. I didn't know who she was then, but I've just been round to Kye's flat and saw her.'

Remi slammed the notebook shut. 'You're sure, aren't you?'

Rose nodded.

Remi said, 'Imagine, your own mum . . . Your mum! God, everybody knowing. Nasty, nasty, nasty.'

'But why would his mum . . .' *Do that?*

'God knows. It's weird. Our classics class had to go to the British Museum to look at pots and stuff. Some of them –

damn! Those Romans liked to put it out there. I suppose people have always done stuff like that.'

'Europa,' Rose said, quietly.

'Sorry?'

'It's a painting.'

'Yeah,' Remi said. 'Those old artists liked their booby pics.'

They looked at each other. The jokes weren't working.

'It's different, though, isn't it?' Remi said. 'Now anyone can make a film for the whole world to see.'

'Can't we do something?'

Half the chocolate was gone. Remi attacked the next row. 'Want some more?'

'No, thanks.'

'We're still stuck. Briley's got the top card. If Kye doesn't do what he says, Briley's probably threatening to tell everyone about his mum. She'll probably be Star of the Week on Hot Dogz. So Kye keeps on getting girls to flash their boobs for his shitty website and Briley stays happy.'

'We should go to Kye. Together.'

Remi shook her head. 'I tried that already. I even offered to pay him, but he wasn't interested. He can get money from his dad if he needs it.' Remi folded the wrapper over the leftover nub of chocolate. 'You know you asked me if I agreed to the photo?'

'Yes.'

'When Kye first asked me, I had to think hard about it. We'd had this really heavy talk in Year Ten about sending nudie pics. It was the most awkward lesson I've ever sat through, if you don't count the periods one. It was a bit fire and brimstone, and believe me, I know fire and brimstone when I hear it! I bet you know what I'm talking about.'

Fire and brimstone, yes. The periods lesson, no.

'The thing is, I wanted to do it. He was fun and it seemed like another fun thing to do. And – well – Mum and Dad are brilliant, but . . . well, I've always been the good one. It was exciting and – God, I was so into him. So into him, I checked out the law about it because I didn't want him to get a criminal record. In the end, we decided it was worth taking the risk.' She went and put the chocolate back in the fridge. 'That's the long way of saying "yes". I did agree. I thought he cared.' Remi glanced out the window. 'Shit! It's my mum!'

'What if we told her . . .'

'You're mad! You met many African mothers, Rose? I'd rather face down that wasteman Briley than tell Mum about any of this.' She grabbed Rose's mug. Tea slopped over the table. 'Just leave it, Rose. It's me up there, not you, and anyway, my face isn't in the picture. No one probably even bothers with a site like that when they've got the pick of the whole internet.'

But someone did. Rose had seen what they'd written about the other girls. It was like the paintings in the gallery where people stood and pointed out the bits they liked and the bits they didn't.

Rose touched Remi's left wrist, just below the birth mark.

'I knew it was you, straight away.'

The front door clipped shut and Remi's mum came into the kitchen. She was carrying two bulging Tesco bags in each hand. Remi ran over and took them from her.

Her mum flexed her hands. 'It's just as well they don't sell washing machines or I would have bought one of them too. And I only went for some tomatoes.' She smiled at Rose. 'Are you distracting my daughter again?'

'Sorry.' Rose picked up her notebook. Remi's eyes flicked from the notebook to her mum. 'I was just going.'

Remi's mother went ahead of her, opening the front door. 'I honestly don't want to throw you out. You're welcome to stay a bit longer!'

Rose looked back into the kitchen. Remi's back was to her as she organised vegetables in the fridge.

She called back. 'Thank you for the tea and chocolate, Remi!'

Remi nodded, but didn't turn around.

*

Mum was in the front of the cab, Dad in the back next to Rudder. The driver was talking into a mouthpiece on his earphones. Rudder couldn't recognise the language. Mum turned around.

'You need to talk to him, Amos, about this End of Days rubbish.'

Rudder glared at Mum. 'It's not rubbish, is it, Dad?'

'No, it's not.'

Mum turned back. Rudder saw her shoulders lift and fall.

The driver lowered his voice, then stopped his call. Rudder watched the traffic crawl across the flyover ahead. It was weird that most of those people in those cars and lorries didn't know what was heading their way. Maybe some of them would ascend after the Clean Slate, but most of their souls would wander in loneliness or be dragged to hell.

He said, 'I know I've done sinful things, but I tried to make amends. If I can go back to the Pilgrims, I can fully atone and—'

Mum snapped round again. 'You've done enough atoning, Rudder.'

Dad's hands locked together on his lap. Rudder glanced at him. Dad didn't look back. He wouldn't, though, if Mum could see. Dad didn't want Mum to know that he was on Rudder's side. Dad's mouth was moving. Rudder tried to work out the prayer. It could be the *expiación*. That would be it. '*Prepare for the end of days. Prepare for the glory of ascension . . .*' Rudder let his lips move too. Mum faced the front again and didn't say anything else until they pulled up in the side street next to the hostel opposite their flat.

Mum got out. 'You'll have to pay for this, Amos. Come on, Rudder.'

Rudder looked at Dad. Dad pushed himself out of the cab and on to the pavement. Rudder copied. Dad pulled his wallet out of his waistcoat pocket and paid the driver. It was the pocket where Dad always kept his Bible, but it wasn't there now. Maybe he'd been praying when the police came round for him and he'd left it in the prayer room by mistake. Rudder looked up at the flat window. It was so dirty from the inside, but from here it was just like all the other windows. A face was pressed against the window of the flat upstairs. It must be one of the children. She didn't look like a vampire. She just looked small. Rudder waited for Dad to get in the front and drive off in the cab, but he shut the door firmly and waited on the pavement until the cab pulled away. Dad was coming up to their flat?

'Come on,' Mum said.

Rudder wasn't sure if Mum was talking to him or Dad. Dad joined Mum and the three of them waited in a row to cross the road. A red light stopped the traffic further up and Mum darted forward, Dad next to her. Rudder looked backwards and forwards again. No bikes. He ran across and reached the other side first. Mum and Dad were side by side, legs moving together like soldiers.

There was the young homeless man with the dog again. Rudder wondered where the woman in the green hat was. He'd been too busy getting away from Kye to give her the twenty pounds in the end. Rudder hoped she was all right. Dad was stooping down and handing the man a palmful of pound coins. Mum watched him, then carried on unlocking the door. She went ahead up to the flat and held it open for Rudder and Dad. Dad closed the door and looked around. Mum was watching him again.

She said, 'Do you think I was lying, Amos? This is

where your children live. Rudder, show your father your bedroom.'

Rudder moved towards the door. The pile of sin was still on Rose's bed. Would Dad want to look under the cover and see how far Rudder had really wandered away from the Pilgrim path?

Dad wasn't even looking at Rudder any more. Him and Mum were just looking at each other.

Mum said, 'I hear congratulations are in order.'

'Yes,' Rudder said. 'Lily-Beth's having a baby.'

Mum went into the kitchen. 'I'll put the kettle on.' She filled the kettle and clomped it down on the stand.

'Dad?'

'Yes?'

At last, Dad seemed to realise that Rudder was there again. 'I only did it because I want to be a Pilgrim again. I don't want to be alone when the Clean Slate tallies.'

'You won't be alone,' Dad said.

'You'll be ascending ahead of me.'

'No,' Dad said. 'I won't.'

Mum laughed. 'Has the End of Days been cancelled by the Founders this time? Or just put off for another two hundred years?'

Dad would have something to say about that. He'd remind her about the angels in chains and the abominations and the Clean Slate preparing to tally, but Dad didn't say anything at all. Maybe he was leaving it to Rudder. Yes, Dad had told

Rudder to keep reading his Bible and this was a test. Rudder cleared his throat.

'An angel has come down from heaven and . . .'

'I'm being excised, Lois.'

'. . . surveyed the sinful wasteland . . .' Rudder's mouth had carried on running as if it had guessed what Dad was going to say and wanted to stop his own ears from hearing it. Maybe Rudder *had* heard wrong. Maybe Dad *had* said something else, another Pilgrim was being excised, not him. It wouldn't be him. Not Dad.

Dad bent his head into his hands. Some men prayed like that, but Dad wasn't. He was crying. Rudder could hear it through Dad's fingers.

'Amos?' Mum went and stood by Dad's side. 'Rudder, can you give us a moment?'

Rudder went into the bedroom and shut the door. He slumped forward on the bed, pressing his nose against the window. Dad. Excised. How could Dad not be a Pilgrim? He'd be a different dad. What about the new baby? Dad wouldn't be able to see him at all.

Rudder shifted so the whole side of his face was against the glass. The draft around the frame blew into his ear. For once, no one was sitting on the hostel wall, but the roof was covered in pigeons. What if all the people who lived in the hostel *weren't* squibs? Maybe they were magic after all, but had to hide it. Sometimes, though, they couldn't resist perching on the roof and watching the world around them.

386

It could be true. One day people were one thing then suddenly they were something else.

Rudder turned his back to the window and swivelled round on the bed to face the sin pile. Covering it hadn't made it less sinful. How could it when the cover was sinful too? He should have done what was expected of him and rid himself of all temptation. He'd let his head fill with worldly concerns. Dad had been right in the police station. This wasn't Rudder's world. He sat upright. Of course, that's why everything had gone wrong. He'd been weak and let himself become a Worldly Wise. He shouldn't have let Ms Leppard persuade him to join the drama group. He should have understood the moment Kye opened the door and laughed at Rudder dancing – God was sending Rudder a message. STOP YOUR SIN NOW! It was bad enough that Rudder had split up the family, but even after that he'd been weak and had continued in his sinful ways. He'd recognised and named his temptations, then carried on doing them. Now the worst thing ever had happened to Dad.

Rudder could put this right. He had to.

He crawled across the other bed, careful not to touch the sin pile. He levered the lid off the storage box. Rose's yellow jumper was folded on top, next to a purple t-shirt where she'd sown pink lacy stuff round the sleeves. He burrowed beneath, feeling between the layers of cloth. Cardboard. He grabbed it and pulled it out. It was her incense. He dived back in, lifting off the top layer of clothes and then the second. There they were. The matches. He slid open the matchbox. Loads were left.

Rudder took out a match and looked at it. The ones that Elder Enoch had used in Grandma's garden had been thicker and longer, like they were made especially for lighting outside fires. This match was shorter. He struck it against the rough side of the box. It flared up in a little spark of heat that made his fingers glow, the flame moving quickly down the little wooden stick. Rudder could feel the scorch of it on his skin. He quickly blew it out and went and placed it on the windowsill. He pulled the throw off the sin pile. The DVDs tumbled on to the bed. He wouldn't go for the full blaze, because that would be dangerous. This was just a chance to show God that he was serious. He'd save the throw to drop over the fire at the end and put it out.

He placed the lid from the storage box on the floor and started building the fire. He folded the Columba robes in two and placed them at the bottom. Next, his balled-up Columba socks and the blue scarf. He opened *Chamber of Secrets*. If he tore out the pages, he could use them to get the fire going and he would never be tempted to read them again. He tugged at a page. It didn't come out. He closed the book again. He didn't need to go that far. The books would burn easily. He knew that much for sure. He took them all out and propped them up so they all met in the middle. He emptied all the DVDs and CDs out of their cases and poked them through the gaps between the books. They wouldn't all fit, so he had to balance the last three on top of the books. On the very top was *West Side Story*. God needed to see it was there. Then on top of *West Side Story*, the Time-Turner. It wouldn't burn, of course, but Rudder had to show he really meant it.

He struck another match and lit a corner of his robes. They sparked then died. Rudder looked around. His rucksack was by the door. He tipped everything on to the floor and raked through the books and worksheets. There was Mrs Skermidge's homework about voting women. That's what he needed. He tore it in half then in half again. He scrunched each piece into a ball and put them into position, left, right, top, bottom. He was ready to go. He lit one ball of paper, then the other. He needed another match for the other two. It was working, though. The fire was burning.

28

The car park by the big Tesco was emptier than last time, though quite busy for the time of day. Rose sat down on the wall. She was still holding her notebook. She hadn't got a box full of answers, just lots of bits that rolled around and bounced off each other. Now she knew that Remi had agreed to have her picture taken. Even with her strict mum and holy dad, she'd risked it for Kye. Then Kye had dropped her, just like he'd dropped Rose. But unlike Rose, he'd put her picture in his gallery of hate. And Remi had known about it. Just those things rattling around were enough to make her head hurt. Day after day, Remi must have worried that someone would recognise her. Then Rose had walked into her life.

Then there was the film. Remi thought Kye's mum had agreed to that too. Why would she do that? Why would she sit on that chair and stretch her arms out behind her to be tied and show everything? But she had. Kye knew she had too. Rose rubbed her eyes. All the pieces bounced around harder. And right now, Rudder seemed to be trying to get himself arrested.

Rose took out her phone. There was a message from Mum to say she'd gone down to the police station. Nothing else.

'Rose!'

Rose looked up. Remi was running towards her. She'd slipped on tracksuit bottoms and a sweatshirt. She stopped by Rose. She wasn't even puffing.

'I thought I'd missed you,' she said.

Rose shook her head. It felt like that first day back in Grandma Yellow's kitchen, when she'd started crying all over Mikhail. She could feel it pushing through the tightness in her chest.

Remi sat down next to her. 'Mum was chatting away about a cousin she bumped into earlier. Her daughter was sixteen and pregnant or something and my mum had a very strong opinion on it. I couldn't help thinking about you and me how we all do stuff that, I don't know, has consequences, but we do it anyway . . .'

A woman passed them, pushing a toddler in a buggy with one hand and holding the mouthpiece of her phone to her lips with the other. The toddler was clutching a bag of bright orange snacks close to his chest, and his chin and lips were glowing with them. The buggy handles were heavy with shopping bags. The woman was shouting about a bill she'd already paid. Rose realised that both she and Remi were watching her.

Remi said, 'I've got an idea.'

The woman was halfway down the street, but Rose could still hear her so clearly. She was going to take the useless bastards to court, if they didn't sort it out.

'Rose?'

'Sorry.' It was easier to listen to someone else's problems than sort out her own.

'I've got an idea,' Remi said, 'but we have to, I don't know, screw our courage to the sticking place.'

'What sticking place?'

Remi made a face. 'Sorry. It's from *Macbeth*. I don't suppose Pilgrims read Shakespeare.'

'No.'

'Now I feel really pretentious. Sorry.' Remi looked like she meant it. 'I should have just said that we need to be brave.'

'We keep saying sorry to each other,' Rose said. 'My brother's like that. He always thinks he's got something to be sorry for. Pilgrims call it atoning. There is *a lot* of atoning going on.'

'Oh, God.' Remi laughed. 'Now I'm going to say sorry again. I didn't mean to be so harsh on your brother. It was just . . .'

'A bit of shock? I mean, I just turned up on your doorstep and told you he'd . . . he'd shared a picture of you with people. I don't blame you.'

Remi held out her hand. 'No more sorries?'

Rose shook it. 'I'll try.' She let go of Remi's hand. 'So how are we being brave? Are you going to tell your parents?'

'I'm not that brave!' Remi twisted round so her whole body faced Rose. Somehow Remi was managing to balance cross-legged on that thin wall. Rose would have toppled into the car park. 'I just thought about my cousin and all the crap she's getting for having a baby. I bet the damn boy who put it there isn't getting the same shit. And then you and me, scared every day that some moist little goat-face is going to see our tits while Kye and that troll brother of his, well . . . yeah. You know what I mean.'

Yes, Rose did. 'So what's your idea?'

'We take away the thing that gives them their power.' Remi nudged Rose. 'And, I thought – who's really good at turning up unannounced on people's doorsteps . . . ?'

'You mean, go to . . . ?'

Remi nodded. She swung off the wall and offered her hand to Rose.

'You coming?'

Rose smiled and took Remi's hand. 'Of course.'

She was going to screw her courage to wherever it was damn well needed.

Remi pushed the buzzer. It wouldn't be fair to sneak up. At least Kye's mum would know that someone would be at her doorstep any second soon. Rose got ready to announce herself into the intercom, but the door was released without any words. Remi squeezed her hand.

'We can do this.'

Remi went ahead, up the stairs two at a time. She waited for Rose at the corner of the landing. Rose overtook her and walked towards the door. It opened before she had a chance to knock.

'Oh,' Kye's mum said. 'I thought it was Kye. He left his key on the kitchen table.' She frowned at Rose. 'Aren't you the girl who knocked earlier? And . . .' A big smile. 'Remi! It's lovely to see you again. I didn't know you two knew each other! I'm not sure what time Kye's back, I'm afraid.'

It's you we're here to see . . . It was hard to look at her, knowing what she'd come to say. And now Rose wasn't so sure. Kye's mum's face was rounder than in the film. She looked older. It must have been a long time ago. Was it right to throw all this at her now?

Remi said, 'Please can we come in? We'd like to talk to you about something.'

Kye's mum raised her eyebrows. 'You sound like you've joined the Jesus squad!'

Remi and Rose looked at each other. Rose's laugh escaped. Remi just smiled. 'No,' she said. 'It's something a bit . . .'

'It's something we think you should know about,' Rose said. 'It's about you.'

Kye's mum's expression changed. Her eyes flitted from Rose to Remi. 'What do I need to know about?'

Rose felt Remi reach for her, Remi's fingers folded round hers. She took a deep breath. 'It's about a film. You're on a chair and your hands are behind your back and . . .'

If the vampires were real, they'd followed Rose from the flat above the kebab shop. They'd sunk their teeth into Kye's mum. They'd sucked out her blood in one big gasp. She was clinging to the door, as it swayed to and fro. Remi let go of

394

Rose and ran to her. She wrapped her arm around Kye's mum's shoulder and guided her towards the sitting room. Rose stayed outside, staring into the flat.

Be brave. She stepped inside and closed the door behind her.

It didn't feel like bravery. It felt like when you pricked yourself with a needle and then kept on snagging the same wound. It wouldn't be the same for Remi. She hadn't seen the film. She hadn't been in this same room when Briley had turned the screen so Rose could see. She hadn't stood in the hallway and heard the scraping chair and the other noises. That's why Remi could do most of the talking, sitting in the arm chair while Rose and Kye's mum sat side by side on the sofa. Rose had a sudden stupid thought – she and Remi were like Briley and his mate. They'd kept their shoes on too.

Kye's mum didn't say anything at first. Then the anger erupted out from her. It was an ex-lover, the man she'd left Kye's dad for. He'd promised he'd destroyed the film and she'd believed him. And Briley, she'd tried so hard with him, but . . . She used words that made Rose look at the floorboards until she'd finished. She said she was lucky that she had a good lawyer. She scooped up her phone from the coffee table. She was going to phone her straight away. No, she wasn't. She was going to phone Bella. Yes, yes, she was going to phone Bella and say sorry – sorry that Bella had to deal with all this in secret.

And what about Kye? Rose wanted to say. But Remi was standing up and moving towards the door.

'Wait!' Kye's mum was holding her hand over her phone. 'Thank you isn't right, is it? But . . .' Then she shook her head and started whispering into the phone.

They shut the front door quietly behind them. This time Remi followed Rose. They stood on the landing.

Remi said, 'Shit.'

Rose nodded.

'We did the right thing, didn't we?'

Rose nodded again.

'It doesn't feel like it, though.'

'No.'

'I better be heading back. Even with all this other stuff, the thought of Mum going off on one terrifies me.'

'I've got a grandmother in the Pilgrims,' Rose said. 'She was quiet and deadly.'

Was. Somehow it felt like it wasn't only Kye's power over Rose that had been taken away.

They walked down the stairs together. As they reached the ground foyer, the street door clicked and was pulled open. 'What the f—?'

'Hi Kye,' Remi said, brightly.

He was standing half in the block, half out. There was a girl with him. She was Pakistani, maybe Indian, background, slim, in jeans and a thick pink jumper with sleeves that hung so low they covered half her hands. She gave Rose a nervous smile. Kye looked from Rose to Remi.

Rose couldn't speak. Her face was hot and all the stuff inside her brain was spinning around. It felt like her head was stuck inside their flat's crappy microwave. Remi eased past him.

'Hurry up,' Remi said. 'Your mum's expecting you.'

Kye let go of the door and raced upstairs. The girl hesitated then followed him.

Rose said, 'We should have told that girl about him.'

'I think she's going to find out soon enough.'

Suddenly, Remi scooped Rose into a hug. She kissed Rose's cheek. 'We'll stay strong, yeah?'

'Yes,' Rose said. 'We will.'

'And give your brother my love. I mean it.'

'Yes. Thank you.'

Remi opened the door and ran across the road to catch the bus that was just pulling up. Rose walked down to the next stop. Time to go home.

A bus came quickly. Upstairs was virtually empty. Rose went to the very back and sat down, her bag on her lap. She was back to being nothing. Not a proper Pilgrim. Not a proper Worldly. Not even a proper sister or a daughter. Not a proper girlfriend. She hadn't even managed to complete her decommissioning programme. She should have listened to Rudder. It was never going to work, anyway. It must take years to be a proper Worldly Wise and in the meantime you had to do your best with being stuck in this weird in-between.

What now? Well, she'd delete Kye's number for a start. She wondered if the girl in the pink sweatshirt hung around for long. No, Kye's mum would have sent her off straight away. That would have hurt, but it was better than what else could have happened to her.

Rose found her phone. It was stuck in her notebook between the pages where she'd written her list. Did she understand it all now?

1. Kye took a picture of Remi. She agreed. Yes, she did, because she trusted him.
2. Someone sent the picture to Rudder. Remi didn't agree to that. No, Remi didn't agree, but who was the someone? Rose had an idea who it could be. Maybe that was something to talk over with Rudder.
3. Rudder sent it to people. (And now he's gone to the police.)

Why, Rudder? Why keep it, send it, go to the police? Maybe it was just that weird in-between. He was more Pilgrim than the Founders but still ready to plunge his hand in a fire to save his prohibited book. He told her off for blaspheming but kept a nude photo on his phone. He was in more of a tangle than she was.

Mum had sent a text. She was back home and she wanted Rose to know that Dad was there too. Did it take Dad getting brought before the Excise Committee for him to set foot in their flat for the first time? Maybe that was unfair – the reason he'd been thrown out was because of her and Rudder. No, actually, that *wasn't* unfair! Why should she and Rudder be blamed? The reason he was thrown out was because someone somewhere made up a whole load of rules and Dad decided to try and follow them.

Rose got off the bus. The door to the hostel opposite was propped wide open with a bulging laundry bag. Someone was probably moving in or out. The door further down the hallway was closed. It had to stay that way, according to the notice stuck on it, and smoking was not allowed anywhere inside the premises. More rules. They were everywhere.

Delicious Kebabs was open, but the only person in there was the guy behind the grill staring out of the window. The young guy was back begging outside Sainsbury's. Rose felt in her pocket, but there was nothing in there except gritty dust. An older woman was crouched down talking to him. Maybe he'd be okay for now. She looked up at the main room window. No Mum waiting to dash down and grab her by the arm this time. It must be weird for her having Dad in the same room with her after all this time, him still dressed like a Pilgrim while Mum would be in her leggings and jumper, probably. And what was Rudder doing? He'd be saying sorry. The bedroom window was all misted over. He must be saying a lot of sorry.

She crossed over the road and dug her keys out of her bag. Into the hallway, then up the stairs. It smelled like Kye's flat when the toaster stuck. God knew what the vampires upstairs must be up to. She stuck her key into the lock and twisted. Mum and Dad were in the kitchen. They both looked round as she came in.

Mum came towards her. 'Rose, I'm so pleased you're—'

Rose said, 'What's that smell?'

'The fat probably needs changing downstairs,' Mum said. 'Unless it's the vampires having a day-time barbecue.'

She sniffed. 'No. I don't think it is that. It's stronger in here than outside in the hallway. Where's Rudder?'

'In his bed—'

Rose reached the room first. She flung open the door. 'Jesus, Rudder!'

The smoke made her step back. She heard Mum say something, then Dad, and felt someone rush past her into the room.

'Rudder?' Mum called.

'Leave me alone!'

There he was! A heap of material was smouldering in the middle of the floor. Rose could just make him out through the gloom, sitting cross-legged next to the fire with his top stretched over his nose. She grabbed him and pulled him out into the main room. He tried to wriggle free, but she held him tight. Dad raced in with a pan of water and threw it over the fire. Smoke billowed out. Mum gasped and levered open the window.

'It looks worse than it is,' Dad said.

'Worse than trying to burn the place down?' Mum yelled. 'Call the fire brigade!'

Dad used the pan handle to poke the heap. A blanket slipped off. It was the Marauder's Map throw. CDs clattered on to floor. And wasn't that the Time-Turner Rose had bought for him? Cheers, Rudder! And those books, his Harry Potters, all stacked up together like a monument. Dad came back into the main room. He crouched down next to Rudder, took Rudder's hands and pulled him up towards him.

Dad said. 'You wanted to make it better for me.'

'Yes, Dad.' Rudder's voice was croaky from the smoke.

'This wasn't the way.'

'I did everything wrong,' Rudder said. 'I shouldn't have let myself be tempted. If I'd stayed true, we would all still be Pilgrims.'

'God forgives, Rudder.'

Mum grabbed Rudder and wrenched him away from Dad. Her eyes were blazing. 'You're kidding me, Amos! This isn't about God! This is about the stupid bloody Pilgrims and their stupid bloody horror stories. You are a child, Rudder! You aren't responsible for any of this crap! The same way it wasn't your fault that your hands got burned. There was a good reason that they waited until I wasn't there. Right, Amos?'

Dad stood still. In the middle of their flat, he looked like he was in fancy dress. His fingers were black from the fire and his trouser hems were wet from the dripping pan. He bowed his head, but his lips didn't move.

Rose went over to him and took his hand. She kissed him on his cheek. She thought he'd flinch, but his grip tightened on her hand.

'We've all mucked things up, haven't we?' she said. She looked towards Rudder, who scowled back at her from by Mum's side. 'I should have listened to you more, Ruds. You were trying to tell me stuff, but I didn't want to hear it. I just wanted you to be like me. But then, look what happened to me.'

Mum's voice was low. 'What do you mean "what happened to you", Rose?'

Rudder was shaking his head. *I know*, she wanted to say. *You did your best to protect me.*

'It's okay, Ruds. I have to say this.' She thought of Kye's mum, ready to phone Bella. 'You shouldn't have to hold all this by yourself. I don't want to neither.' Dad's fingers went loose in her hand but she wouldn't let go. 'Like I said, we've all mucked up and I want to tell you about a mistake. A big one.'

Rudder squeaked. 'Please don't, Rose.'

'Don't what?' Mum and Dad spoke at the same time. They looked at each other, then away again.

Screw your courage to the sticking place. Maybe one day, Remi would be brave enough to face her parents, but Rose had to do this now. She wasn't Pilgrim Rose or worldly Rose. There were layers of her, one on top of the other, like a tutu.

Most of it was hidden until you spun around quickly and all the colours were on show.

'I trusted someone.' Rose couldn't let go of Dad's hand. Even if he couldn't look at her, she'd still hold on to him. 'I don't know the rules of this world, Ruds, any more than you do. But I can't keep saying sorry, else I'm never going to work out who I am. I'll be scared to do anything in case I get it wrong again. So I'm going to tell you about Kye and Briley and a photo and a website, and then I'd like it if we could all sit down and work out what to do next.'

29

Three months later

Rose sat on the edge of her bed. It still smelt a bit smoky, but that was probably because she knew what had happened in there. Anyone else would probably think it was burnt chips from below. She peeked through the clothes rail. Why was it that when Rudder woke up it looked like his body was trying to shrink itself back into baby size without telling his skin first? Too-little Rudder in too-big skin . . .

She'd miss sharing a room with him. Only a tiny bit, though. Last week, he'd dreamed he was a house elf. That was so typical of Rudder. He could be a murderous, vengeful wizard if he wanted to be. He could swoop through London and destroy the Millennium Bridge, bringing mass slaughter and full-on fear to the city. (Though that would probably be a bit end-of-daysey for Ruds.) But who did Rudder want to be? Dobby.

He rubbed his eyes. 'Where's Mum?'

'Gone to yoga.'

'*Really*?'

'No, Ruds, she's gone to beg some more boxes from the supermarket.'

'I don't want to go. Luton's miles away.'

'It's not that far by train. You can pretend you're on the Hogwarts Express.'

He shook his head. 'I'd rather go by normal train.'

'Fair enough! I thought you'd want to know, I've made pancakes.'

'Pancakes?'

'We haven't got any blueberries, but I can nuke some Galaxy.'

'Chocolate pancakes?'

With his eyes wide like that, Rose could really see the elf similarities. He scrambled out of bed and followed her into the kitchen. His pyjamas were short at the ankles and wrists. When did that happen?

She said, 'As it's my birthday, I thought we could do something together.'

He shook his head. 'I'm going to see Dad's baby. And it was your birthday yesterday.'

'I've missed a whole load of birthdays, Rudder. I can have two in a row if I want. And, anyway –' she winked – 'you can do both my thing and the dad thing, can't you?'

He'd tucked it in well, but she could still see the Time-Turner poking out from his pyjama top. He touched it and gave her a little smile. He leaned back against the kitchen counter and watched as she dropped a spoonful of batter into the sizzling butter. She flipped the pancake over and spread kitchen roll over a plate.

She said, 'Are you sure about seeing the baby? You know Dad has to wait until Lily-Beth's parents go out.'

'She's bringing the baby over to Grandma Yellow's. By the way, I think we should stop calling Grandma that name, Rose. It doesn't feel right now.'

'Agreed. Maybe just 'Grandma'?'

He nodded.

Another dollop of batter. 'They'll let Dad return, Rudder.'

'How do you know?'

'There are probably more wizards in London than there are Pilgrims. They can't afford to lose righteous men like Dad. They just have to be seen to be punishing him.'

'Dad doesn't think so.'

'I know, Rudder. But even when he knew he was going to be excised, he chose us, didn't he? He could have just turned his back on us, but when it really came to it, he chose us.'

Rudder gave her his smug look. 'I always knew he would.'

I didn't.

'Did you know that Uncle Mikhail comes to see him?'

'*Uncle* Mikhail?'

'Yes, he's an Uncle now. And he's going to marry Sister Gayle.'

'There's a surprise.'

'Are you jealous?'

Rose laughed. 'I'd be a lousy Pilgrim wife. But Uncle . . . so soon? And how come he risks seeing Dad if he's just gone up?'

Rudder shrugged. 'Maybe he's just being kind.'

'Yeah. Maybe.'

'Be back in a second.' Rudder dived into their bedroom and came back straight away, draped in his throw. He settled on the sofa and turned on the telly. She broke the squares of chocolate into a bowl and put it in the microwave. She set it for forty-five seconds and flipped the pancake over again. She could hear the theme tune for the show about the dreadlocked mouse coming from the TV. She smiled. Two years ago, he would have denounced Rastamouse as Satan. Though sometimes even Rose had felt like the Pilgrims were right and Satan really did disguise himself in many shapes and sizes – lately, as a boy called Kye and his angry brother.

Should she tell Rudder that she'd checked and Hot Dogz had disappeared? Hot Dogz. Bitches. It still made her brain sizzle louder than the pancakes. The police were going to keep them informed about the other stuff, but Mum wasn't sure how much Rudder wanted to know. The fact that Rose had let Kye take the picture freaked him out enough. And as for the idea that Kye's mum had made a film like that by choice . . . it was going to take a long time for Rudder to get that to settle in his head. The police were dealing with the ex who put it online, as well as with Briley.

Bella was proving a really useful source of information, especially when it came to working out who sent Rudder that photo in the first place

'It definitely wasn't you, then?' Rose had asked.

'No,' Bella had said. 'I did send Rudder that note with the website on it . . . but I left it after that. If Briley had found out I even did that, he was going to . . . well, you know what he was going to do. And you know he threatened the same thing to Kye.'

That doesn't excuse how Kye treated me. But Rose didn't say it. She knew she'd always stick up for Rudder whatever he did, and if anyone tried to badmouth him, she'd be on to them as well.

Rose supposed that, in his own twisted way, Kye had been trying to do the right thing. He'd asked Bella for Rudder's number, and sent Rudder the photo. He'd reckoned the police would take down the site if they got a chance to investigate it, but he wasn't going to risk his mum going online too. Why not get kind, honest Rudder to do his dirty work for him instead? Ping him a picture or two . . . Though he hadn't bargained on Rudder doing a big send out first. Maybe one day, she'd get Rudder to meet Remi. That was one big 'sorry' he needed to say.

Rose stirred the gloopy chocolate and dribbled some over the pancakes. She went over and handed a plate to Rudder. She wondered if *he'd* worked out who sent him the picture. She'd only talk about it if he wanted to.

She said, 'Eat up. I've got a plan.'

He glanced away from the screen. 'I don't like your plans.'

'You'll like this one.'

Rose was taking ages to put her make-up on. Rudder didn't mind the eye stuff and the lipstick, but he hoped her eyebrows would be a normal colour. The bathroom door opened. He relaxed. She was sparkly, but not her eyebrows. She was wearing lipstick and some of her weird clothes, but it was like she had turned her volume down a bit.

She said, 'Are those your school trousers?'

He felt himself flush. 'So what?'

'Don't you want to put on something more comfortable?'

'They are comfortable. And I want to be smart to meet the baby later. You could come, Rose.'

'Okay. Let me just find those silver eyelashes. Lily-Beth'll love those.'

His eyes widened.

'Joke, Rudder. I'll come another time. I promise.' She ruffled his hair, then looked at her fingers. 'Have you been using my edge control gel again?'

His hand flicked up to his hair. 'Just a little bit.'

She put her arm around him. 'You can borrow it any time. But beware, in case you end up looking like me.'

She was wearing a headband with flowers on and a t-shirt covered in unicorns. He definitely wouldn't look like her, ever.

Rose said they had to get the bus to Oxford Street. He'd only been there once before but as soon as they got off the bus, he recognised it.

He said, 'Do you remember when Mum brought us here to see the Christmas lights?'

'Yes.'

They'd stood at the junction of two wide roads with balls of changing colour reaching back along the street. It was like angels juggling dreams. On the bus home, Mum had pulled a small bag of sweets from her bag – white chocolate mice, pink shrimps, paper-thin flying saucers, a giant gobstopper. It was like she'd turned into Willy Wonka himself.

'This way,' Rose said.

She was leading him down a side street through a square. A man was asleep on a bench. He'd lined it with blue plastic bags and covered himself with an open sleeping bag. Two women were sitting opposite him on another bench drinking from takeaway cups. One of them laughed, kissed the other and stood up and left. Rudder wondered if one of them was Dominic's mum. He'd text him later and ask.

'We're in Soho,' Rose said.

'Oh.' It was supposed to mean something. He could tell by the way she said it. They turned into another road lined with cafés and shops. Doors opened on to staircases like the one in their flat. He squinted at the sign pinned to the inside of the door.

He said, 'Do they have trains up there?'

'What do you mean?' Rose looked where he was pointing. 'Oh. No. These are different models. People models.'

'Why are they up the stairs?'

'It doesn't matter.'

He stopped. 'You promised you wouldn't hide things from me, Rose.'

Rose rubbed her hands over her face. Her fingers sparkled from her make-up. 'Okay, Rudder. You're right. They're not models. Well, they might be. Just not like the ones in magazines and stuff. It's a way of saying that women are there and . . . men pay to have sex with them, Rudder.'

'Like Rahab the Prostitute?'

Rose sighed. 'Sort of.'

One, two, three doors – and more across the road. There must be a lot of men who wanted to do that.

He said, 'Why do they do it?'

'The women? Maybe they need money.'

Another hallway, painted pink this time. 'Beautiful models' – next to a shop full of bright dresses with sticky-out skirts. Rudder knew they would spin like wheels when they were dancing.

'I meant the men,' he said. 'If the women need money, why don't the men just give them the money?'

'You're going to be a man. You should know how it works better than me.'

His face heated up. He imagined climbing those stairs with his money in his pocket and then . . . There was nothing in his head. Was there someone behind a desk who took his coins? How much did it cost? Did he choose his model?

411

Or did he go into the room and she was there on the bed, with no clothes on, and . . . He was filling with sin!

Rose had walked on ahead. He ran after her. She stopped by a junction, waiting for a fleet of taxis to ease along the narrow road. The shop opposite was full of plastic-looking underwear and high-heeled boots. Nobody could ever dance in those.

Rose took his hand like he was small again and guided him across the road. He wriggled his hand free.

'I don't think I'll ever know how this world works,' he said. 'I could never be decommissioned like you.'

She laughed. 'The first time Kye and me were kissing, I opened my eyes and thought I saw Grandma Yellow's face instead of his. I almost bit his lip in shock.'

Rudder wiped his mouth. Just the thought of tasting someone else's spit made his throat tighten.

He said, 'Did you think you were going to marry Kye?'

She shook her head. 'No, Rudder. I was never going to marry Kye. Look, we're here.'

Lights were flashing in the window. Steps led down to a basement. A sign told him he couldn't loiter. A rule. He would make sure he didn't break it.

She took his hand again. 'Come on.'

The noise! It was like having two or three TV channels on at the same time with the volume up as far as it could go. It was a room full of game machines. Gambling? Rose had brought him to a gambling den! His heart was louder than the machines. He tried to pull his hand away, but she was holding tight.

'Rose, no.'

'Look, Rudder!' She pulled him in front of her and held his shoulders. 'This!'

A man was moving strangely, holding on to a red rail behind him. He was looking at a screen that was crowded with arrows. Rudder leaned forward. The floor was covered with squares and the man's feet were moving in time with the arrows on the screen. A woman was sitting on a chair nearby, nodding. The music was loud and fast, filtered through the rest of the clatters and beeps.

Rose said, 'Would you like a go?'

The man's face looked like he'd sipped the amortentia love potion. His feet were under a spell too, so quick that Rudder could hardly see them. The game finished and the man dropped into the chair, fanning himself. Another man had taken over. He was younger, wearing a vest and shorts, like he'd come here specially to do this. He must have set it at a higher level because his feet moved even faster. He didn't hold the hand rail; he was using his arms to make the dance belong to him. He spun round and back again, his feet hitting the arrows every time.

Rudder stepped back. Rose had gone. His breath caught, but no, she was there, heading towards the dance game. She took out some money and placed it on the ledge. She beckoned him over.

413

'Want a go?'

'Yes, please.'

'We'll go together, right?'

'You and me?'

'Yes, Rudder. You and me.'

<u>Rose's Ten Point Programme for Being a Bit</u>
<u>Worldly Wise</u>
<u>Also Known As</u>
<u>Learning From Your VERY BIG Mistakes</u>

1. <u>Worship idols.</u> I should have stuck with the Korean boy
bands. It would have been a lot safer. Rudder's found some
of their choreography vids online and he's been practising,
just so he can beat me the next time we head down to
the arcade. In. His. Dreams.

2. <u>Dress immodestly.</u> There's not much fairy kei happening
in Luton, though the woman in the Age UK shop's going to
put stuff aside for me.

3. <u>Act immodestly.</u> Mum's got a new boyfriend. He's stayed
over. I'll leave that to her.

4. <u>Find out how to vote.</u> Got an address so we can
register. Now I'm not a Pilgrim, I can join the police or be
an MP too. I'll consider my options.

5. <u>Get worldly boyfriend/s.</u> Yeah. Well. They're all going to
be worldly, aren't they? In the Pilgrims, you just have
husbands. But, hey, I'm a mixed-race, fairy kei ex-Pilgrim.
That's got to be worth something.

6. <u>Beget immodesty with worldly boyfriend/s.</u> Going to leave
the begetting to others, right now.

7. <u>Send Christmas cards to Grandma Yellow</u>, enormous

ones that play carols loudly when she opens them. NO. I saw her when I went to see Baby Daniel. She's getting enough stress for letting Dad live there. She doesn't need any more.

8. <u>Visit the Natural History Museum and the Science Museum every month</u> until it feels normal. I'm branching out. Took Mum back to the National Gallery. She was overwhelmed by the boobs.

9. <u>Watch the prohibited films and read the prohibited books</u> (or read reviews if they're boring) Seriously, how many Marvel Universe films are there? And Star Wars? I might watch Sailor Moon backwards and with no subtitles. It will be easier.

10. <u>Make sure Rudder is completely absolutely and finally decommissioned too.</u> Decommission my sin-obsessed, hormoney, dance-master, Potter-nerd little brother?

Decommissioning in progress.

Decommissioning in progress.

Acknowledgements

As usual, there is a community of patient, kind and highly knowledgeable wonders that help me build the story scaffolding, source specialist material and inspect the work for quality. So, here goes.

Josephine – top thanks for introducing me to basement Soho dance machines, answering random questions and the invaluable prompts that bounced me out of my plot holes. And the kimchi stew. Thank you for that too. Oh – and to your friends who are always up for answering my random questions as well. And for introducing me to Trixie and fairy kei. Trixie, you are splendid.

Michelle Brackenborough – your cover art is, as always, superlative. Likewise your Pinterest board. Emma Roberts – I'm not sure what I would do without you. And a big thank you to all the other Hachette folk who have my back, making sure my books are the best they can be and working hard to get them into the hands of readers.

Thank you, Caroline Sheldon, my wonderful agent, for your tireless support, food and wine with the added bonus of Felicity, Jade and Georgia.

My Free Lunch writing group Nathalie Abi-Ezzi, Katherine

Davey, Jenny Downham, Anna Owen and Elly Shepherd – utter gratitude for your advice and support. My SCBWI writing friends - a constant buoy, including Kathryn Evans, Sarah Broadley, Tania Tay, Sue Wallman, Teri Terry, Candy Gourlay, Jo Franklin and so many others. Likewise the Sofa-ites, headed by Liz Kessler.

For the folks who let me retreat to their homes to pick fluff from my Post-it Notes and plough on through with the book – Jo, Chris, Tilly, Harvey, Giz, Moi, Cath and Catherine.

For all the kind people who helped me go beyond the browser to help me get my facts right. Laura Janes – thank you so much for sharing your research and the invaluable work of the Howard League for Penal Reform supporting young people in the criminal justice system. Leroy Logan – your information on police station procedure was just what I needed. Faith to Faithless – your brave panellists inspired me.

The friends who've kept me going in tough times – Sheryl, Pauline, Flo, Natalie, Miranda, Pauline, Odina, Fen, Kerry, Catherine J and, of course Lucy (and your mum!). Little brother, Lee, thanks – sort of – for saving my teenage diary. An – um – interesting resource for research. Also thank you for cheering me on. You know how much that means to me. And finally Silvia, you have worked so hard to keep things going. You are awesome.

418

If you need advice about some of the issues in Rose, Interrupted:

Childline – 0800 1111

Howard League Advice Line for young people in the criminal justice system – 0808 801 0308

From Faith to Faithless – www.faithtofaithless.com

Discussion Points

- Why do you think Rose embraces a fairy kei look after leaving the Pilgrims? Do you have any particular ways in which you express who you are?

- Do you think young people are given enough help to deal with the negative side of social media? How do you deal with it yourself? Rose goes to Bicchi Blogger and the Cast Outs forum for help. How can social media be supportive?

- Rose and Rudder's relationship as siblings is central to the story. If you have siblings yourself, do you think it is a realistic portrayal? If you don't have a brother or sister, can you think of a relationship in your life that might be like a sibling relationship? What do you think makes this relationship like that of brothers or sisters?

- What would you do if you were in Rudder's situation? Why do you think he shared the picture? How do you think he could have handled it differently?

- Rose has to leave behind lots of things she has grown to love when she returns to the Pilgrims. What things in your life would you struggle to be parted from if you had to make the same choice as Rose? Why are those things important to you?

- Rudder often loses himself in music and dance. Do you have any favourite songs that make you forget where you are and what you are doing?

- Rose and Rudder are trying to learn the rules of their new world. If someone with completely different life experiences from you moved into your area and joined your school, college or workplace, what are the unspoken rules they would need to know to help them fit in?

PATRICE LAWRENCE

was born in Brighton and brought up in an Italian-Trinidadian household in Mid Sussex. This meant great holidays and even better food. Patrice lives in east London and shares a cat called Stormageddon. She has been writing for as long as she has been reading. She loves crime fiction, sci-fi and trying to grow things. Her ideal mixtape includes drum 'n' bass, Bruce Springsteen and music from Studio Ghibli films. Music can't help creeping into her books.

@LawrencePatrice

 facebook.com/patriceLawrence.author

patricelawrence.wordpress.com

'A TRULY BRILLIANT BOOK'
Malorie Blackman

COSTA BOOK AWARDS
2016

ORANGEBOY
PATRICE LAWRENCE
Winner of the YA Book Prize 2017

Winner of the *Crime Fest Award for Best Crime Novel for Young Adults*

'A TRULY BRILLIANT BOOK'
Malorie Blackman on *Orangeboy*

INDIGO DONUT
PATRICE LAWRENCE
Winner of the YA Book Prize 2017

'A red-hot mystery' *The Times*